For Allan, you had the dream.

Acknowledgements

Thanks go to –

Everyone on the 2008–10 Lancaster University DLMA, in particular my tutors Jo Baker and Michelene Wandor, my group D girls Agata, Steph and Trish and Sue for her continued assistance.

Brian McCabe for his support and encouragement of my writing. Gavin and everyone at Luath Press for their advice and enthusiasm. Jennie Renton for coping with my many fonts. James Anderson for his help and advice.

The Barcelona contingent of 'Team Eilidh' for not complaining when I turned up at the airport with extracts of Trackman for their holiday reading.

My colleagues in the College Office for letting me have time off work to write.

Mum, Dad, Jamie, Iona and Eilidh for their constant love and laughter. The rest of my family and friends, all you Childs, Elders and Irvines, and my grandparents (Connel and Dundee) for nurturing my love of books.

Finally, Allan, for making me always happy and for waking up that morning and telling me about the dream you'd had...

I

Mad About the Boy

Davie dropped the orange juice.

THE SINGING ECHOES around me and bounces off the walls of the underpass like a rubber ball; I flinch as it whizzes past my face. There's a group of lads standing in the centre of the walkway. The lights in the ceiling are red and give a pink tinge to their hair and faces. One of them's got a guitar which he strums away on. Another is banging out the beat on the wall with a couple of drum sticks. He tap, tap, taps against the brickwork. Another three lads are singing, while a tall guy films them all on his mobile; he shouts directions like he's fucking Steven Spielberg or someone.

I duck as I pass by: don't want to ruin the shot.

'Cheers mate,' Spielberg gives me the thumbs up.

I nod, and carry on through the underpass.

A gutter runs along the edge of the wall; it's full of manky water, pish and dog shite. A syringe lies amongst the crisp bags and the empty cans. Graffiti slides down the anti-vandalism varnish, like trying to paint over crayon.

Co
    ck a
       nd ba
          lls

Fuc
    k th
        e h
           ibs

P
  ole
    s go h
        ome

Davie saw his parents at the far end of the corridor; they sat with their backs against the wall. It looked like they were waiting outside the headmaster's office.

I leave the underpass and smell freshly-made pizza as it wafts from the vents of Domino's on the corner. It smells good, but I carry on. I can't stop. Got to keep moving. Keep moving. One finger, one thumb, one arm, one leg. I head along Dalry towards Haymarket station. As I get nearer I can hear the muffled voice of the tannoy, and the sound of the trains as they approach the platforms.

Hello, goodbye.

People leaving Edinburgh, people arriving.

I'm going to Australia, Davie, I don't know for how long.

The streets are busy and it's not even hit peak tourist-time yet. I get stuck behind a couple holding hands who take up the whole pavement. I walk on their shoulders, skulk right behind them, but they don't take any notice. In the end I jump down onto the road, jog past them and hop back up onto the pavement. I'm all nervous energy tonight: got to keep moving, keep moving, keep moving.

One finger, one thumb, one arm, one leg, one nod of the head.

As I near Princes Street, I can hear the piped shortbread music blaring out from the tourist shops. It's almost ten for fuck sake; who needs towels that look like a kilt at this time of the night? Who needs them at all?

The lights are on in the castle and it hangs above everything, like someone was playing pin the castle on the city.

Then it disappeared in the mist.

It looks out of place compared to the shitty, breeze-block shops down here at street level. The shops shrink in embarrassment; faced with the castle in all its glory.

I'm not ready to stand still yet, so I take a detour onto George Street: walk round the block first. I don't know what's wrong with me tonight. Maybe I've absorbed some of Lewis's excitement. Tonight feels like a big deal all of a sudden.

One finger, one thumb, one arm, one leg, one nod of the head.

I pretend I'm Pacman as I follow the block round.

Forward, forward, forward.

Right turn.

Forward, forward, forward, eat annoying tourist.

Right turn.

Forward, forward, forward.

Back onto Princes Street and the queue from Waterstone's is already snaking round the corner and out of sight. There's still two hours to go. Two hours of standing still in a queue. One finger, one thumb.

I better go join it though; don't want to let him down.

I follow the queue round onto the cobbles of Rose Street, past the dingy pubs and the independent shops. The queue stops outside Dirty Dick's and I'm tempted to go in for a pint. I think of my promise to Lewey though and I join the queue. He's the reason I'm here after all.

There's a few folk outside the pub smoking. I can hear the murmur of conversation and the clinking of glasses from inside. A hen party walks past. They're dressed in identical pink t-shirts; a photo of the bride-to-be pulled panoramic across their chests. The cobbled street is causing them some problems and they totter in their heels, swaying from side to side and clutching on to each other for support as they scream and laugh.

I step from one foot to the other. Keep moving, keep moving, keep moving.

One finger, one thumb, one arm, one leg, one nod of the head.

Don't think about why you're here on your own.

Don't think about why you're here on your own.

One finger, one thumb, one arm, one leg, one nod of the head.

The queue grows as I wait. I stand on my tiptoes and strain my neck to peer over the folk behind me, but I can't see where the end is anymore. A lot of people in the queue have really made an effort: turned up in costumes and fancy dress. I feel totally out of place here. On my own. Fidgeting. Lewis would have loved it.

He should be here, not me.

Keep moving, keep moving, keep moving, one finger, one thumb, one arm, one leg, one nod of the head.

In a parallel universe, Lewis is queuing up to get his own book.

There's a couple of women behind me, wearing witch costumes, who keep blowing cigarette smoke into my face. It's making me want a fag even though I quit ages ago. I want to tell them to stop being so fucking ignorant, stop exhaling in my face, but I'm enjoying the second-hand smoke and I breathe it in.

Hold it inside me.

There are breathing exercises you can try, they should help you to relax if you find it's all becoming too much.

Wait.

Wait.

Wait.

Breathe out.

They've got a wee lassie with them who doesn't even look old enough to be able to read. She's all dressed up in a school uniform, complete with bushy wig and magic wand. Another hen party stops when they see her.

'Aaawwww, look at the wee lassie.'

'Oh my God, she's gorgeous.'

'Hey, Annie, she should be your flower girl, imagine, eh?'

The wee girl points the plastic wand at them, makes them all laugh. I can see it in her eyes though: she's cursing them all.

'Hi, I'm Andy from the *Evening News*. Do you mind if I take a few photos for the paper?'

A guy stops in front of 'Hermione' and the chain-smoking witches. He's carrying a fancy looking camera and pulls an identity card out from underneath his jacket. The card hangs on a cord around his neck, tangled up in his camera strap. I glance at the photo on the card, hope it's not an example of his photography skills.

The witches chuck their fags away and push Hermione towards the photographer. One half-finished fag lies between two cobble stones. The end is still lit and smoke curls from the orange glow.

Loosen your clothing, then sit with your back against the wall.

One finger, one thumb, one arm, one leg, one nod of the head.

I'm about to bend down and pick it up, when someone arrives with a big fuck-off owl. Where the hell did they get that from?

Hermione looks terrified as the owl is placed on her shoulder. I watch its talons curl and clamp onto her. It would be so easy for those claws to pierce the skin; pierce the skin and carry her off like a lamb. Those witches need to be more careful. All it takes is one bad decision. Just one mistake and you're left wishing you had a reset button.

'Okay, sweetheart? That's great. Can I get a wee smile now? Brilliant.'

Andy from the *Evening News* starts clicking away. A few of the hen party try to get in the shot, and then folk from outside Dirty Dick's hold up their phones and take photos, beckon inside for their friends to come out and see this.

The owl rises up and flaps its wings; a gust of air blows across me and the feathers brush against my face.

'Jesus.'

The owl turns its head around, like that lassie out of *The Exorcist*. It stares right at me. Huge yellow eyes. Not blinking. Staring me out.

I get the feeling it knows something I don't.

I blink and break eye contact. Can still see its eyes flashing at me when I turn away, like I've been looking directly into a light bulb. The orbs follow me and I shut my eyes. When I open them again the owl and the photographer are gone. Off to find someone else who looks daft enough to make the paper.

I shiver. Someone walking over my grave.

One finger, one thumb, one arm, one leg, one nod of the head, keep moving, keep moving, keep moving.

Someone inside Dirty Dick's drops a glass, and a cheer goes up from the pub.

Are you going for a drink after work?

Aye, you?

Yeah.

I button up my denim jacket. The temperature's dropped since I got here. A group of lassies pass by, wearing hardly any clothes. How do they do it?

My glasses are smudged so I wipe them on my t-shirt.

Everything's a blur without them on. It's all shapes and colours, nothing has a proper outline.

Without my glasses on, I can pretend the shadow next to me is him: Lewis, waiting with me.

You know, in the 'In Bloom' video?

One arm, one leg, one nod of the head.

The folk walking by get drunker and drunker the closer it gets to midnight.

'Harry dies!' some knob-end shouts.

His friends all laugh like he's just come out with a line to rival Billy Connolly. Like he's the first one to have thought of it. His hair looks like someone filled a watering can with bleach and sprinkled it over his head: Derek Riordan, eat your heart out.

Fuck, I need to calm down.

Start by breathing out. Then breathe in.

Maybe I should ask one of the witches for a fag? One finger, one thumb.

The queue seems to be moving, but we're not going forward, just huddling closer together. The witches are taking it in turns to hold a sleeping Hermione while the other one smokes. I could ask them for a fag. Just one. Hermione's wand is lying on the ground so I pick it up and tap it against my chest.

Tap, tap, tap, tap, keep moving, keep moving, keep moving.

It hits off something inside my jacket pocket and I remember the MP3 player I've got shoved in there. I'm not sure why I've got it with me. It's not really mine and I don't know how to work it.

There's something about it though.

The One Dread Guy stopped Davie as he walked home from work.

Hey you, son, come here.

Davie had never heard the Guy speak before: softly spoken for such a grizzly man.

Aye, what is it? Davie replied, and dug about in his pocket for some loose change.

I have to give you something.

Eh?

Davie had never heard a homeless guy offer to give something away before. The One Dread Guy's life existed in six scabby rucksacks, but he wanted to give something away.

Come here, I've to give you him, Archie says I've got to.

Who's Archie?

Archie, my friend Archie.

Don't worry about it, eh?

The One Dread Guy pulled a pair of headphones off his head. They slid down the matted rectangle of hair hanging down his back like a paddle. His hair and shoulders were littered with flakes, a scrunched up bag of cheese and onion crisps.

Here, take it. The One Dread Guy held something in his hand.

His fingers were swollen and grubby, the knuckles all cracked and bruised. There was a rectangular scar on each palm, like he'd been burnt by something and the shape of it had melted onto his skin. He offered the MP3 player to Davie.

I don't want it, you keep it.

No, Archie told me.

The Guy took a step towards Davie. Davie held his breath against the stale, unwashed smell of him.

Yours now, the Guy said and pushed the MP3 player into Davie's chest. The Guy's breath was warm and sticky; it coated Davie's face with a layer of slime.

What is it? Davie asked.

You'll find out, the Guy replied.

Davie watched as the Guy swung rucksack after rucksack onto his back and shuffled away, muttering to himself.

Davie wiped the player on his jeans. It was covered in greasy fingerprints and looked broken. The screen was blank and there was a crack down one side.

Davie was about to leave the MP3 player lying on the pavement when something stopped him. A voice in his head.

You'll regret it if you leave it. You'll only come back for it later.

It felt valuable. Davie couldn't leave it in the same way he couldn't leave his wallet, his keys, his phone.

Not only that, he had a sudden urge to put the headphones on.

I take the player out of my pocket and turn it over and over in my hands. The headphones are jammed inside the player and won't come out. They've got hinges on them so they can fold up. The hinges are stiff and covered in rust. I slide them backwards and forwards. Open. Closed. Open. Closed. Open. Closed.

The player doesn't have any buttons on it: no volume control, no power switch, no Play button. It's weird.

Maybe the One Dread Guy just used it to keep his ears warm out on the street? I've been carrying it around with me ever since he gave me it. I don't know why.

There's just something about it.

I'm still looking at it when the countdown begins. It starts in front of me, but then dominoes back along the rest of the queue.

'10, 9, 8, 7, 6, 5, 4, 3, 2, 1!'

Everyone cheers as midnight strikes, and I hear a few watch and phone alarms going off. I'm an imposter. It shouldn't be me who's here. I don't deserve to be part of this. It's like I'm at a gig and the lead singer has just stopped singing in the middle of a song. He's held his microphone out so the crowd can sing for him, and I'm the only one there who doesn't know the words.

I just stand in silence, while everyone around me joins in the shared moment.

One arm, one leg, one nod of the head, keep moving, keep moving.

The countdown turns out to be a bit of an anti-climax, as the queue remains motionless and it's two in the morning before I finally make it to the till with Lewis's copy of the book. It's way too late to go and see him now. He'll have to wait.

A lassie hands me a helium balloon as I leave Waterstone's.

I head home up Lothian Road, a Jekyll and Hyde part of Edinburgh: office workers by day, sleazy clubbers by night. 'Saunas' and lap-dancing clubs squeeze out from where they've been hiding between the sandwich shops.

We only come out at night.

I'm Mario in a platform game now. I let old-school Gameboy tunes play in my head as I manoeuvre my feet home.

Dodge drunk man.

Leap pile of sick.

Duck seagull carrying chip.

Leap more sick.

Head-butt block and collect mushroom.

'Hey, can I have that balloon?' a drunken lassie grabs my arm as I walk past her.

I ignore her and continue walking.

'I asked you a question.'

She follows me along the pavement, then swats the balloon with her handbag. It hits off the side of my head and makes that deep, echoey noise that only helium balloons can make.

'Get your own.'

Keep moving, keep moving. One finger, one thumb.

'Please, it's my birthday,' she says as she stumbles against a shop window.

I stop and look at her as she slides down the glass.

'Aye, alright.' I give her the balloon and leave her sitting on the pavement with it as I continue on home.

One finger, one thumb, one arm, one leg.

2

I Want You to Want Me

Davie struggled to unlock the front door. He just couldn't manage to line up key with keyhole.
Davie dropped the orange juice.

'PLEASE, PHOTO PLEASE.'

A Japanese couple step out in front of me and block the pavement. The guy holds out a digital camera, offering it to me.

Not more free electronic shit.

'Please, photo please,' he repeats.

The words sink in and I understand what he's asking me. My brain hasn't woken up yet. They're both smiling, already posing, he puts an arm around her. I focus on the buttons on her jacket. Big and red, the size of a two pound coin. I count them to get my brain working. One, two, three, four, five, six, seven. She has seven buttons on her jacket.

It's half six in the fucking morning.

Half six.

I can barely see through my half open eyes; I'm looking out on the world through slits. I hate early shifts.

Princes Street is dead. Deserted. I hold up the camera. It looks pretty expensive. There's loads of buttons and switches and knobs. I can't work out what to press to take the photo.

I shrug my shoulders and the guy steps forward and points out the correct button. I nod.

'Okay then, say cheese.'

They both flash grins at me, he has perfect white teeth while the girl wears braces. She gives me a peace sign. The castle is in the background, a veil of morning haar shimmers around it. It looks superimposed, like they're in front of a blue screen.

I hand the camera back and the couple inspect my handiwork. She smiles and he gives me the thumbs up and nods his head.

'Thank you much, thank you much,' he says.

'Aye, no bother,' I reply and continue on my way.

The inside of my mouth tastes fuzzy and I rummage in my pockets hoping to find some chewing gum. Nothing doing though. I swirl saliva around in my mouth and spit, wipe my tongue across my teeth. I feel like I've been out drinking or something; something more sordid than standing in a book queue.

I stop walking, turn and look at the castle again. It does look pretty fucking impressive. The Japanese couple are now taking individual shots of each other with the castle behind them. I walk past it nearly every day, but I never notice it. The har is slowly rising and hangs just around the top of the battlements.

Lewis's story was pinned on the notice board in the kitchen.

The Day the Castle Disappeared.

He'd drawn a picture to go with it: a castle with grey clouds swirling around the turrets.

The final sentence was always at eye level when you walked past the notice board. It would stick in Davie's head for hours afterwards, an earworm.

Then it disappeared in the mist.

Then it disappeared in the mist.

Then it disappeared in the mist.

I begin walking again and have to dodge some woman reading the new *Harry Potter*. She doesn't even look up at me as I side-step out of her way, just keeps on walking, eyes focused on the page.

Stupid cow.

I'll need to get that book to Lewis. I'm making him fall behind everyone else.

'Alright?' I say to Louise and Derek, who are waiting outside the shop when I get there. I lean against the wall and shut my eyes, then Laura the manager arrives and begins to open up. Her key clicks in the glass doors and the alarm beeps. She holds a door open for us and we all troop inside. The lights take a while to fire up and I'm down the stairs and halfway across the basement floor before they kick in.

His face was illuminated when he opened the door. He took out the carton and unscrewed the lid.

The shop's quite creepy first thing in the morning, when the lights are off and there's no customers around.

Ghosts.

Everyone jokes about the returns room being haunted. Apart from Stewart in the cash room of course, he actually believes it is haunted.

I've felt a presence there, Stewart said to Davie.

Who do you think you are, fucking Darth Vader or something?

Honestly, I'm not kidding. The room went cold and I could sense it behind me. I tried to communicate with it.

How did you do that?

I just held my arms out, told it I was a friend, a believer.

Oh aye?

Davie looked at Stewart's fingernails, they were painted black. He didn't quite have a steady hand though and had smeared polish all around the tips of his fingers. Looked like he hadn't washed his hands in days. Maybe he hadn't? He'd

22

once told Davie he slept in a coffin. Davie wasn't sure if he meant in the house or in the garden.

I dump my bag and jacket in my locker. I'm just turning the key when I realise I've forgotten something. I unlock the locker again and rummage through my stuff. What have I forgotten? Come on brain, concentrate, concentrate. Name badge? Nah, still pinned to my t-shirt. I never take that off, even put it through the washing machine. Pen? No, I'll grab one from the staffroom. What is it?

I pull the MP3 player out of my jacket pocket and the nagging feeling goes away. The tip on the tip of my tongue stops tipping. With the headphones folded up, the whole thing is no bigger than my wallet, so I stick it in the back pocket of my jeans and head along to the staffroom for a mug of tea.

'Morning, David,' Laura says to me as I pass her in the corridor on the way back to the shop floor.

I nod in reply. Why can't she call me Davie like everyone else? David sounds so formal.

I kick open the door for the shop floor. It's heavy and mirrored and it swings back and hits me on the shoulder before I have time to get through. Tea spills all over the floor, which has just been buffed by the cleaners. I swirl the tea around with the sole of my baseball boot, can't be arsed going back to get a paper towel.

Eminem's blaring out of the ceiling speakers. Louise from upstairs in the classical section must have got to the CD player first. That's what I get for stopping to make a brew. It's not that I don't like Eminem, I just don't want to listen to him at full blast first thing in the morning. Louise claims that it wakes her up but it just makes my brain hurt.

What would the customers think if they knew? That nice wee lassie who sells them their Beethoven and their Russell Watson is actually into very loud rap music.

I'd rather settle into the day at a more gentle pace, float my way through to morning break on a wave of Lambchop, gradually climbing through Malcolm Middleton, before building to a Lemonheads crescendo. Nothing louder than Evan Dando's sweet voice.

No rap.

No death metal.

No new metal.

Definitely no dance music.

Derek's into his dance music and I'm thankful that Louise beat him to the CD player. Moby and Air are about as dancey as I go.

That's what dance music should be like. That Frightened Rabbit cover of Set You Free. Have you not heard it? It's amazing. Shows you how good dance music can be if it's slowed right down, played with guitars and no longer resembles dance music.

Man, what a mood I'm in today. That's what four hours sleep does to you and a promise to your wee brother. I'm fucking knackered. I hide out under the staircase leading down from the main floor. Sip my tea. Try to wake myself up. It's a bit darker under here. I can't handle the full glare of the strip-light. Even the red t-shirt I'm forced to wear is too bright for me just now. I pretend I'm sorting through the boxes of DVDs we've got stashed under here. The cardboard trays are tearing at the edges from the weight of being piled on top of one another. I sit on the edge of one but don't allow it to hold my full weight in case there's a DVD avalanche.

Lose yourself.

I decide to get myself organised so I'm next in line for the CD player. Position myself in a prime location. I can't let Derek get there before me with his dance pish. Plus I can kill the next twenty minutes or so looking for something decent to put on while Eminem finishes. I'm supposed to be doing stock counts and replenishing the shelves before we open at nine, but after being here for so long I've perfected the art of looking like I'm working when I'm actually doing fuck all.

I hate this job, but it's all I'm good for really.

We think it would be best if you took some time out, and then came back and repeated the year when you're feeling better.

At nine the shop opens and I'm joined on the shop floor by Martha. She's in her usual flared jeans and tatty Doc Marten boots.

'Hey,' she says to me, 'what's up?'

'Not much,' I reply. 'Fancy finishing this stock count for me? I'm supposed to have twenty-three copies of *The Shawshank Redemption* on DVD, but I can only find five.'

'Sure,' she replies, reaching for the piece of paper I'm holding.

The light catches her hair, shimmers purple.

'Have you dyed your hair?'

'Yeah,' she replies, 'I felt like a change. What do you think? Nobody else has noticed.'

She looks pleased and loops a piece of hair around her pen while she studies the report I've given her.

'What colour do you call that?'

'Deep Midnight Plum,' she laughs. 'Guess what I did though? I'm such a numpty. I was rinsing my hair over the bath and I dropped my phone in.'

'Is it knackered?'

'Yeah,' she shakes her head, 'but I'm hopeful. I used the hairdryer on it last night and I've left it on the radiator. Fingers crossed. I can't afford a new one.'

CAN MARTHA PHONE THE STOCKROOM PLEASE, MARTHA PHONE THE STOCKROOM.

Derek's voice pages Martha through the speaker on the telephone. I watch her as she leans against the counter to phone him back; her feet are turned inwards and her jeans drag on the floor, the fraying hem catching the dust. Her lips glimmer with lip gloss and she plays with her tongue stud, rolling it left and right, left and right, along her bottom lip.

'Honestly,' she says, and her face lights up. I catch a glint from her tongue stud and I feel that little jump in my tummy.

Her leg pressed against his and he knew it was on purpose. He began to stroke her knee and then her hand was next to his and she ran her fingers round and round on the back of his hand.

Ring a ring a roses, a pocket full of posies.

Davie watched her mouth as she sucked the vodka and orange through a straw. He wanted to kiss her so badly. Her mouth was a strange shape, like a heart, like Molly Ringwald's mouth. She tasted of vodka and orange. Atishoo, atishoo, we all fall down.

Davie dropped the orange juice.

'Hey, they've finally got *My So Called Life* in on DVD,' she says to me, putting down the phone. 'I've been waiting ages for it, I'm just away up to get a copy.'

She jogs across the shop floor and takes the steps two at a time.

'Back soon,' she leans her head over the banister, so that her hair falls in front of her upside-down face.

Deep Midnight Plum.

We all fall down.

I wave at her and glance around the almost empty shop. There's a group of lads in school uniform over in the games section so I wander over to see what they're up to.

'Excuse me, are you a virgin?' one of them asks me.

The rest burst out laughing. Wee prick looks about twelve, freckled face with the sort of cheeky expression that Robbie Williams has. The kind you just want to punch. He obviously went to the same school of comedy as the twats from the queue last night. As if I've never heard that one before. Wee shites should be at school.

Your arm's a mess, that wasn't me, was it?

Nah, it's just a Chinese burn.

Who gave you that?

I'm pish at confrontation, even if it is only schoolboys, but these guys have really pissed me off.

'Aye. They don't let you work in Virgin if you've had sex before. It's one of the interview questions.'

They look at me and I try to keep it together, but I hate the way I can't control my body in situations like this. My hands are shaking and my lungs suck inandoutinandoutinandout. Even when I feel brave in my head, my body betrays me. They're just a bunch of fucking schoolkids too, what's wrong with me?

'Go and ask anyone who works here,' I say, 'we're all virgins.'

'Prick,' the Robbie look-alike says, and the lads push and shove each other as they walk away. Robbie runs a hand along one of the shelves, knocking DVDs onto the floor.

I let them go.

I'm Scottish, I'm meant to be a fucking hardman, like Begbie or Braveheart. It's in my blood. Why can't I do it? Why am I always such a fucking pussy? You can't be Scottish and male and sensitive, it's just not on. We show affection through abuse, that's the way things are. Except for me. Me and.

He was so sensitive. Made him an easy target.

Man, I hate this fucking job.

A shop would be an alright place to work if you took away the customers.

The stupid questions:

Have you got that film with the American man in it?

Can I buy that film I saw at the cinema last night?

Where's the castle?

The weird regulars:

Dirty Old Porn Man.

Woman who loves Taggart DVDs.

B.O. Problem Man.

Stopping you with a big list of things to find for them, just as you're about to go for your break.

Picking stuff up and then dumping it in a completely random area of the shop.

Trying to get a refund for some shitty, scratched CD that's been out of stock for the last twelve years.

Keep the customer satisfied.

Usually I just let the crap you get from wee shites like that wash over me. I don't care enough about my job to get involved, but today I let them get to me. I'm still tired and I've got Lewis in my head. They remind me.

The shop's boiling and I can feel sweat running down my back between my shoulder blades and gathering in the waistband of my boxers. I fan myself using my t-shirt and pick up the DVDs from where they're now lying on the floor.

'It's warm down here, isn't it? I don't know how you stand it,' some old boy says to me.

'Aye, the air-conditioning's knackered.'

'It's lost you a customer.'

'No bother, you're lucky you can leave.'

The old boy laughs.

'You're lucky you've stopped growing,' he says as he wanders off. 'It's so subterranean. No daylight.'

I nod at him. Fucking weirdo. He passes Martha on the stairs as he leaves. She's looking at something at the far end of the shop. I follow her gaze, but she's higher up than me. I don't know what she's seeing. Shoplifter?

'Hey, there's that girl you fancy,' she says hitting me on the arm with a DVD of *My So Called Life*.

'What girl?' I glance over to where Martha's looking;

I thought me and that subterranean guy were the only two down here.

'Her.' Martha points towards the magazines.

'I do not,' I reply, grabbing Martha's arm. 'Stop pointing.'

'Come on, it's so obvious. You're always hovering around her.'

'Get lost.'

I can feel my cheeks warm. If I licked my finger and touched my face, steam would hiss off.

'Ha, you're getting a beamer.'

'Go away, you.'

Martha's right, but I'm not going to admit it. How come girls are so bloody smart all the time? I thought I was being quite subtle about it all.

The girl's completely out of my league so it's not like anything's ever going to happen. She comes in every Monday and checks out the new releases. Never usually buys anything, but it's been enough for me to notice her.

She's fucking gorgeous for one thing. Her haircut is scruffy; reminds me of Chrissie Hynde. And if I'm comparing her to pop stars, then her arse is as pert as Kylie's. She's always wearing this brown leather jacket; vintage looking with creases and rips in it. I imagine slipping my hands inside it and pulling her towards me. Close.

I usually do go and hover about next to her, try to build up the courage to say hi, but Martha's got me sussed now. I do the next best thing and hang around the tills where I can get a good view of her.

I watch her as she picks up a magazine and comes towards me. What the fuck? What is she doing? She never buys anything. I look around. Can I leave, run away before she gets here? No, too late now. She's almost here. Shit, I'm going to have to speak to her. I feel my face flush and my chest tighten. She walks towards me holding the magazine and it all goes slightly Wayne's World-esque. That scene with Garth and the girl and Jimi Hendrix playing on the jukebox.

Foxy lady.

She's in slow motion, hair blowing behind her as she struts towards me, lips pouting; I'm Garth, uber-geek, about to be blown backwards by the force of her foxiness.

She hands me the magazine and I scan the barcode.

'That's two pounds twenty please,' I say.

'There you go. I like your watch,' she replies, handing over a pile of coins.

I don't even count them, just drop them in the till.

One finger, one thumb, one finger, one thumb. Stay calm. Stay calm.

My hands are sweaty and I wipe them on my jeans, hiding them underneath the till tray so she won't see.

She smiles at me. There's a gap between her teeth. Fuck, it's sexy. Who'd have thought a dental disfiguration could cause so many dirty thoughts. Up close her eyelids are darkened with kohl and her blue eyes sparkle through the black smudges like stars. I'm smitten.

Her accent is American or Canadian; I can't tell the difference. And she likes my watch. It's taken a few seconds for this fact to register. The inside of my head is a waterfall, thoughts crashing and breaking. Too much white, foamy noise for me to be able to concentrate.

Come on, Davie, stop acting like a tit. One finger, one thumb, one finger, one thumb.

Alfie, can I borrow your watch? Mine's stopped.

He's not getting it back now. He doesn't need a watch anyway. He lives in his own time zone.

'Thanks,' I say.

'No problem,' she smiles again, her voice is a drawl. Prawblem. Man, those teeth.

'Eh… would you like a bag,' I wave a carrier at her.

'Nah, it's cool. Save the planet and all that, huh?' She shrugs.

'Okay, cool, see you then.'

'See you,' she leans in and reads my name badge, 'David.'

Her perfume breezes over me; it combs the inside of my head and fizzes in the wash of muddled thoughts like sherbet.

My name in her accent sounds so cool. Exotic. I picture us going out. Hey, this is my girlfriend. MY girlfriend. MINE. My GIRLFRIEND.

She turns and walks away. I watch her as she disappears up the stairs. Follow her arse as it sways from side to side. Hypnotised by that swinging motion.

'Tongue in, Davie.' Martha's shaking her head at me from the opposite end of the counter. She blows a kiss towards the stairs and puts her hands over her heart.

I flick her the v's.

She holds her hand up to her forehead in an 'L' shape.

Loser!

I retaliate using both hands to form a 'W'.

Whatever!

Woteva!

What if...

We all fall down.

Martha does that thing out of *Friends*, where she bangs her fists together.

Ba Boom.

I'm beaten. She always gets me with that one. Who cares though? She can have today's battle. I spoke to my dream girl. Spoke to her. She likes my watch. Maybe next time I'll find out her name. A gradual progression. How many magazines will I have to sell her before we sleep together? I don't even know what she ended up buying, I was too distracted to take it in. The fantasy of her keeps me occupied, until I become aware of a burning smell.

31

A flame flickers up the cord of the charity box tied to the counter. Some guy in a tracksuit and a baseball hat is standing in front of me holding a lighter.

Fight or Flight? Fight or flight? Fight or flight?

'Did you just set fire to that?' I ask, leaning over the counter and blowing out the flame. A tiny spiral of smoke hangs in the air between us.

'Nut,' he shakes his head and takes a step backwards. He's missing all his front teeth, there's just an empty gap. It makes a whistling noise and spittle flies from his mouth when he speaks.

Fuck, it's sexy.

'Wasnae me, likes.'

He follows my eyes as I glance down at the lighter in his hand. He puts it in his pocket and gives me a look as if to say what lighter? I pick up the phone and dial #21 to page, speak into the receiver. CAN SECURITY PLEASE COME TO THE BASEMENT COUNTER, SECURITY TO THE BASEMENT COUNTER.

The guy grabs the charity box but the cord's not completely burnt through. As he makes a run for it, the cord catches and he's jolted backwards. He lets go of the box and takes off up the stairs. I follow at a distance. Nobody bothers about shoplifters much these days. It's not like *Trainspotting*. No chases along Princes Street.

The guy's out of the shop and away by the time I get to the top of the stairs, so I head back down to the basement. Chris, our overweight security guard, ambles up to the counter eating a bag of crisps.

'I'm on a break. What do you want?' he says to me, spraying salt and vinegar.

I point at the blackened cord and the charity box hanging from the counter.

You don't realise how many crazies there are in the world until you work in a shop.

3

Welcome to Paradise

He squinted over the top of his glasses as the security light flashed on and illuminated the front garden.
Davie dropped the orange juice.

I OPEN MY EYES and just about fall off the edge of the sofa. Alfie's leaning over me, his face right up against mine, our noses almost touching. At first all I can see is his grin in front of me, a disembodied smile floating in mid-air like the Cheshire cat.

As my eyelids unstick, the rest of his face appears. His smile looks carved from ear to ear.

Davie, do you know what a Chelsea smile is?

'Fuck sake, Alfie,' I say and push him out of my face. He stumbles backwards as I pull myself up from where I'm sprawled half-on half-off the sofa. My neck aches from the position I've been lying in and I rub it, my fingers shaking.

I can see Alfie's mouth opening to speak, but I can't hear anything. What the fuck? I've gone deaf. Alfie leans forward and pulls the headphones off my head. The Mute button is cancelled and my ears fill with sound. I can hear everything. The cars outside. Alfie's laughter. The drip from the dodgy tap in the kitchen. The hum of the fridge. The mice scurrying behind the skirting boards.

'Your face, mate. That was magic,' Alfie says to me.

'You just about killed me there.'

My heart is beating like crazy inside my chest.

Thathumpthathumpthathumpthathump.

I picture The Numbskulls from that old comic strip. The wee men inside me are running about in complete panic. It's about to blow, what'll we do? Steam is hissing off boiling hot pipes.

'Sorry, I couldn't help it,' Alfie apologises, 'I shouted you, like, three times, but you didn't wake up. You must have been well out of it.'

'Aye, it's those fucking seven o' clock starts, I'm always knackered when I have to get up so early.'

'Tell me about it. I'm glad I don't have to deal with any of that pish anymore. Do you want a brew?'

'Aye.'

I'm cold. I always wake up cold if I fall asleep on the couch. The hairs on my arms are standing to attention and I put on the jumper lying next to me, pull the hood up over my head and rub my arms.

'What time is it anyway?' I ask.

'It's about half eleven, eh?'

Alfie looks down at his wrist but he's not wearing a watch so he shrugs at me.

Davie waited for Alfie outside the flat. Where was he? They were supposed to meet the letting agent ten minutes ago. Davie was just about to phone Alfie when he saw him turn the corner and come into view. Not hurrying, not even acknowledging the fact that he was late. Did he even realise?

The letting agent buzzed them in and they went up the stairs to the flat.

It's a kitchenette, the letting agent said, showing them around, the bedrooms are separate but the kitchen is joined to the living room.

Ace, said Alfie, means you can make tea without waiting for the adverts.

The smell of whatever had been cooked in the kitchen

clung to the walls, as if they'd been painted with supernoodle and bacon fragranced paint. The rent was decent though and that was what mattered.

Alfie clicks the kettle on, leans his elbows on the counter and picks dirt out from under his fingernails.

The kettle begins to hiss and spit and smoke.

'Better stick some water in that,' I say.

Alfie salutes me, picks up the kettle and turns to fill it at the kitchen sink. The cold water hits the fizzing element inside the kettle and steam gushes out of the top, obscuring Alfie in a cloudy haze. He puts it on to boil again and helps himself to a bag of crisps out of one of the cupboards.

'Chuck us over a bag, will you?' I ask, then duck as a bag of salt and vinegar flies towards me.

The headphones hang around my neck. My ears are still getting used to all the noise. The kettle beginning to boil. The crunch of crisps as we both eat. Alfie's fingers drumming on the counter top, in time to whatever tune is currently playing on the jukebox in his head. The backbeat to my kitchen symphony.

Alfie forgets that our kettle is broken. He's engulfed in another, much more dramatic cloud of steam before he realises and clicks it off. Condensation drips down the kitchen units and the yellow woodchip wallpaper.

Alfie chooses two mugs from the pile of dirty dishes sitting next to the sink. He holds up my mug, the one that has the Hearts football club badge on it.

Davie hardly saw the games he went to after the funeral.

'Okay?' he asks.

'Aye, perfect,' I reply, 'all it's had in it was tea anyhow.'

I know without looking that the inside of my mug is stained brown with the ghosts of brews past, but it's not going to kill me if it's not washed.

Davie, this place is disgusting.

It's not as bad as all that. It's a small flat, it doesn't take much to look cluttered.

I told your mum I'd keep an eye on you.

What does she care?

'Where've you been?' I ask Alfie, who sniffs the milk before he pours it into the mugs.

'Eh... where was I again? Oh aye, at a gig. A mate of a mate of my brother's band was playing. I tried to phone you but you didn't answer.'

I swivel round on the sofa and glance around for my phone. It's lying on the coffee table in front of me, on top of a pile of old newspapers and magazines.

I pick it up: four missed calls, all from Alfie. I wave the phone at him and delete the missed calls.

'Sorry, must have slept right through.'

'Nae bother, you'd have probably freaked out again anyway,' he jokes.

'Aye, very good.'

Davie knew he'd smoked too much before he went out. It made him feel better though.

Alfie's band was on next and Davie stood next to them as they watched the support act. It was some guy wearing a feathered head-dress, playing dance music on a bunch of sampler machines and a keyboard. The guy walked backwards and forwards, pressing buttons and shedding feathers, as strange noises came out of the speakers on either side of the stage. There was a DVD playing on a projector screen behind him, some weird black and white film. It reminded Davie of that Japanese horror movie, Ring; *the video the kids watch right before the creepy, Japanese girl crawls out of the TV and kills them.*

Davie could feel himself getting more and more worked up the longer the guy's set went on. The sequence of images played on repeat, flashing by so quickly that you couldn't work out what one image was before the next one was on. Davie was sure he could see Lewis flashing by on the projector screen. It was Lewis, he was sure of it. The room began to spin around him, but he couldn't keep his eyes off the screen. Lewis, Lewis, Lewis, Lewis.

The last thing he heard was Alfie asking him if he was okay.

Alfie wanders towards me carrying the two mugs of tea. He stares at the mugs as he walks. He's so busy concentrating on them that he misses the bag lying on the floor, gets his foot tangled in the strap and stumbles, spilling tea onto the floor. Instead of stopping to clean it up, he simply takes a step backwards, blots the tea with his sock, then continues on towards me. It's so slick, like a dance move. Alfie just oozes cool, unlike me.

He swirled the tea around with the sole of his baseball boot, couldn't be arsed going back to get a paper towel.

'You finally got yourself an iPod then?' Alfie asks as I remove the headphones and move the MP3 player off the couch to make space for him.

'I don't really know what it is. The One Dread Guy gave me it.'

'That old jakey?'

'Aye.'

'Seriously? How come?'

'Fuck knows, eh? Cheers for that.'

'Nae bother.'

Alfie puts both mugs down on top of the tower of DVDs we have stacked up the wall next to the sofa, most of which have been bought using my staff discount at Virgin. He produces a packet of caramel digestives he's had tucked under his armpit. The kitchenette means you don't have to carry everything you need in one go, but we're both lazy fuckers.

Alfie deposits the contents of his pockets onto the coffee table.

'Fucking skinny jeans, man, I cannae sit down if the pockets are full,' he says.

He's wearing spotty socks. I look down at my own socks: navy, with a hole in the heel and the toe. It's funny how even his socks make me feel so uncool. He hits the tower of DVDs with his elbow as he sits down; the tower wobbles but doesn't topple.

'Close one,' Alfie grins at me.

The sofa is tiny and, even with Alfie's already skinny arse squashed into skinny jeans, there's hardly room for the both of us. I shuffle along until Alfie slips down into the gap I've created.

'I hate this throw,' he says and pulls the oriental looking material out from underneath us, 'it's too shiny, I feel like I'm sliding off all the time.'

'It was your girlfriend that put it there, not me.'

'She's not my girlfriend, we're just good friends.'

I pick up my mug and wrap my hands around it before taking a swig of tea. It hits the spot. I can feel it flowing through me: down my throat, gathering in my tummy. It leaves me glowing like I've just had my Ready Brek.

His mum used to say that's why he was so clever at school: he always had a good breakfast.

There's bits of crisp stuck in my teeth so I take another gulp of tea and swirl it around in my mouth before swallowing.

'What's this?' I ask, picking up a bar mat with a number scribbled on it in purple pen.

'Some lassie gave me it just as I was leaving tonight.'

'Oh aye? Was she nice?'

'She was alright. A bit Amy Winehouse. She was singing in one of the support bands.'

Davie would never have been invited to a gangsters and molls party if it hadn't been for Alfie. Alfie, real name Lee, nicknamed Alfie after the Michael Caine character.

Man, Alfie, you've really made the effort haven't you, said Davie.

Alfie was wearing a three-piece, pin-stripe suit, complete with silver shirt, Mod tie and black and white brogues. He looked cool as fuck. Davie had worn his dad's suit. He hadn't worn it since the funeral, the hems of the trousers were still covered in dirt. Davie could see people looking at Alfie as soon as they arrived at the party.

Davie watched Alfie as he made his move on some lassie in the kitchen. He couldn't believe Alfie's confidence. He went up to the lassie and pulled out a metal cigarette case from his suit pocket. He took out two fags, put both in his mouth, lit them with a Zippo lighter and then handed one to the lassie.

Fuck sake, how do you get away with shit like that? Davie asked Alfie later.

I nicked it from some old Bette Davis movie, the oldies are always the best, Davie boy.

'Fuck, I wish you'd tell me how you do it,' I say.

He grins over his mug at me. I think he's had a couple of smokes tonight. His eyes are glassy, the pupils big and round: two empty fishbowls staring back at me.

'Are you going to phone her?' I ask.

'Aye, I might, like. Her friend was braw too. Reminded me of that lassie from *Romeo and Juliet*. What's her name again?'

'Claire Danes?'

'Aye, that's the fucking one! Well done.'

He slaps my knee, and shakes his head.

'Claire Danes. I've been trying to remember that fucking name all night.'

'No bother,' I say.

'Do you ken she was once in a video for Soul Asylum?' Alfie asks.

'Who? The lassie you met tonight?'

'Nah, you tube. Claire Danes.'

'I was gonna say, like.'

'What ever happened to Soul Asylum? They were great.'

'Who knows?'

'Man, I wish they were still around, eh? Runaway train la la la la la, runaway train la la la la la.'

'Let's have a look at this then,' he stops singing and picks up the MP3 player.

Something jumps inside me and I swallow down the urge to grab the MP3 player back off him with a gulp of tea.

'They don't come out,' I explain as he tugs at the headphones and folds them backwards and forwards on their hinges.

'It's weird, there's no buttons or brand name or anything.'

He holds the player and turns it over and over in his hands. As it spins, colours flash off of it, like a crystal hanging in the window. *Catch the sun.* I'm sure I can hear a tinkling, wind-chime sound too, but my ears still feel weird.

'Anything?' I ask. 'You're much more techno-savvy than me.'

'Anyone who's upgraded to a personal CD player is more techno-savvy than you.'

'I like having a music collection, something I can see and hold.'

'I know, I know. An album's for life not just for downloading.'

'Well, it's true. The kids today don't know what an album is, they're all part of the one-song download generation. They go to gigs just wanting to hear the one big single, it pisses me off.'

'What about this? You get it working, you could join the kids,' Alfie says, holding up the MP3 player.

'An iPod's all very well but what happens when your hard drive crashes, or you lose it, then you're fucked.'

'Aye, whatever, Aunt Mimi.'

'I know you agree with me, your music collection's just as big as mine.'

'Aye, but I'm not too scared to join the twenty-first century either.'

'You should be. A music collection says a lot about you, it's like what you wear, or the art you put on your walls. I'd never have moved in with you if I hadn't seen your music collection first.'

'Oh aye?' Alfie says helping himself to a biscuit, 'how do you work that one out?'

I force myself to look away from his sticky hands as he fingers the MP3 player.

'Anyone who listens to Ben Kweller is alright by me.'

'I just like that he has a pet hedgehog, maybe it's time I confessed to my secret Westlife fetish.'

'Out!' I point towards the door and he laughs.

'You know I agree with you, Davie boy, I just like to wind you up, you're always wound so tight.'

The first night in the new flat, Davie and Alfie ordered pizza and sat comparing CDs and DVDs.

Some people slag off Dylan for his voice, but I love it. You know he means what he's singing about, said Alfie.

Aye, totally. All those boybands and X Factor pish, they all sound the same, like fucking cheese slices, Davie replied, and opened another can of Tennents.

Pish, all of it. Good pop is someone like Lennon. He could sing a love song sweet as a bird, turn his voice to gristle on a rock 'n' roll number, then make shivers run up your back on A Day in the Life. That's what I'm looking for in my pop.

Aye, and you don't need to be a pretty boy either. Look at Thom Yorke or Eric Burdon. More talent than any of your fucking Ronans.

Girls want a scoundrel, not a pretty boy, they just don't

always realise that's what they want.

You mean like Han Solo?

Exactly, Davie boy, exactly. I knew there was a reason I moved in with you.

Alfie put down his slice of pizza, wiped his hands on his jeans and rummaged around in one of the boxes which surrounded them. He pulled out a poster of Han Solo and blu-tacked it above the TV.

A scoundrel.

Alfie waves his hand in front of my face.

'Sorry, I was in a wee dream there.'

'I noticed. I was just saying, I think whatever this is, it's fucked. Bet that's why he gave you it. You didn't buy it did you?'

Alfie drops the MP3 player and it hangs from the headphones he's got slung around his neck. It swings from side to side, side to side, side to side. I want it back. Give me it back. I sit on my hands, use my weight to trap them underneath me.

'Nah, course not. He just gave me it. He was totally out of it though.'

'I'd chuck it, it's a syntax error.'

'Not syntax,' I reply.

'Aye, time to rewind the tape and start again.'

'Or try a new game?'

Davie looked up as someone joined him at the staffroom table. One of the Christmas temps. Bit of a pretty boy too, with his skinny jeans and his Vince Noir haircut. Davie couldn't be bothered making friends with temps anymore, too much hassle, especially when they all left again once January came around.

Alright, I'm Lee, Alfie said, holding out his hand.

Davie.

What you reading?

Eh, it's about retro gaming.

Cool, does it have the Amstrad in it? That's what I had when I was a kid, fucking ace.

Aye, me too.

Davie moved the magazine so that they could both read it.

Fuck, Harrier Attack, I loved that game.

Totally, and Galactic Plague, what a classic.

Man, remember when you were trying to load a game and it would take, like, forever. The kids today don't know how lucky they are.

Aye, and then you'd get so far and there'd be a fucking syntax error.

Man, that was the worst thing, you had to rewind the tape and start all over again.

Alfie hands me the MP3 player and picks up the TV remote. He starts flicking through the channels, then stops on an episode of *Family Guy*. He reaches under the sofa and pulls out an old video box from underneath. What used to contain *The Shawshank Redemption* on VHS, now contains Alfie's hash, skins, lighter and fags. He takes out a couple of Rizla papers and starts to roll up on top of the video box as he watches the TV. I wipe his fingerprints off the MP3 player, wind the headphones around it and tuck it down between the couch and my thigh.

Han Solo looks down at me from above the TV. The poster is peeling away, one of the top corners is hanging down and the wall has a greasy stain from the blu-tac. Even though the woodchip wallpaper has pressed through the paper, giving Han a pock-marked effect, he still looks cool as fuck as he leans forward holding his blaster.

I'm Han Solo. I'm a scoundrel and I don't give a shit.

Not wound up like me.

Alfie passes me the joint and I hesitate. I've been trying to stop doing this, but ever since that queue last night I've been dying for a smoke. Plus, Alfie's right, I need to loosen up.

It's a quick fix, Davie, but it's not the answer.

It makes me feel better.

Yes, but the effects wear off, they don't last, and in the long-term, you're making things harder.

It can't get any harder.

Fuck it. I inhale deeply. Count in my head. One finger. Two thumbs. Three arms. Four legs. Then breathe out again. The smoke curls in front of me and I feel lighter. My brain is floating around inside my skull like a helium balloon and I'm sinking deep into the couch.

My stomach growls and I hand the joint back and help myself to a caramel digestive. I dunk it in what's left of my tea until the chocolate melts. As I bite into it the caramel stretches like elastic and sticks to my teeth and the roof of my mouth. I lay one hand down on top of the MP3 player. It feels like it's buzzing, like there's a magnetic charge flowing through it. If I tried to stick it to the fridge door, it would cling on. I felt this earlier. This energy. It was what made me put the headphones on in the first place. My fingers tap the side of the player, it's pulsing with energy. Alive.

I stare down at it and realise that I can't see the scratch anymore. My eyes are rolling from the weed, but even still, it's gone. Vanished. Rejuvenated.

I can hear Alfie's words in my head. Syntax error. Chuck it out. Syntax. Error.

A flash of anger and the need to protect the MP3 player surges through me. I squeeze it in my hand, then push it down the side of the couch. Away from Alfie. Away from Alfie who wants to hurt it. It's mine. I'm keeping it. It's special.

I've got a strange feeling about this wee box.

I've got a strange feeling.

I'm Luke Skywalker. The chosen one. Destined for higher things. The only one who can restore freedom to the galaxy.

Alfie hands me the joint again and I take another draw on it.

That'd just be my fucking luck actually. I end up playing Luke Skywalker, while Alfie gets to be Han Solo. The scoundrel.

4

Why Does it Always Rain on Me?

Davie felt like he was under interrogation; the spotlight on him.
Where were you tonight, David Watts? His folks would kill him if
they knew what time it was. Saying yes to that drink after work
had been a bad idea.
Davie dropped the orange juice.

I STEP DOWN off the bus and it pulls away. Almost immediately
there's a rumble of thunder, deep and low above me. The sky
becomes dark and then the rain begins to fall.

'Fuck sake.'

I don't even have a jacket with me. It was sunny when
I left the flat less than half an hour ago. Glorious. I'd stood at
the bus stop enjoying the warmth, absorbing the vitamin D.
Fucking Scotland.

Four seasons in one day.

I shove Lewey's book inside my jumper, tuck it into my
waistband so it's safe and snug.

If it wasn't for the book and seeing Lewis, then I'd turn
round and head home. But it's my first day off since I got it
for him and he'll be fed up waiting. Man, I could have
avoided the rain too if I'd just had the stomach to stay on the
bus a bit longer.

Davie knew he shouldn't have smoked that joint with
Alfie. He'd woken up feeling sick and with a burning throat.
The sun shone through the window of the bus and warmed
the side of his face. His whole head felt too heavy for his
body. He held his breath, and breathed in and out through

his nose. There was a guy eating pickled onions sitting across from him, and the smell was making him feel sick. That and the fact the bus driver kept flooring the pedal between stops and then slamming on the brakes.

Davie couldn't stop watching the guy with the pickled onions. It was like he wanted to make himself sick. The vinegar dripping from the guy's fingers, as they dipped in and out of the jar. The crunch as he bit down on each onion. Just watching him made the cuts around Davie's fingernails sting and his mouth fill with sticky bile.

The fresh air and the rain feels good inside my nose. It puts out the fire from those pickled onions. Who eats pickled onions on the bus, for fuck sake? I stand on the pavement and just breathe.

In. Out. In. Out. In. Out. In. Out.

Come on, Davie, you're not helping.

No, this fucking, hippy shite isn't helping.

You're not letting it work, you have to give it a chance. Now, just try and empty your head.

I can't.

Once the contractions in my gut have eased off, I continue walking. There won't be another bus along for at least twenty minutes and I should be at Lewey's by then if I keep walking. I'll ignore the rain. It's just one of those passing showers. It'll soon be over and the sun will be out again, maybe with a nice rainbow overhead. Glorious.

One finger, one thumb, one arm, one leg, keep moving, keep moving.

One finger, one thumb, one arm, one leg, keep moving, keep moving.

It soon becomes obvious that it's not a passing shower. If anything, the rain is getting heavier and heavier. Puddles start to collect on the pavement. What should I do? What should I do?

47

Shelter somewhere till the rain goes off?

Turn back and grab a jacket?

Wait for another bus?

Give up and head home, see Lewey another day?

Buy something to shelter me from the rain and keep going?

Just keep walking, fuck the rain?

The options whirl in my head like a fruit machine. I hit the nudge button. The options slow their spinning and come to a stop.

Buy Something.   Buy Something.   Buy Something.

Cool, that's what I'll do. I don't want to give up, hit Escape and start again. That would disappoint Lewey and I can't do that after my promise to him.

I don't really know the area around here too well: I usually just pass through it on the bus. I continue onwards, walking a bit quicker now, keeping my eyes peeled for anything that looks like a shop. On both sides of me though it's just houses, houses and more houses. Edinburgh is full of those bloody tourist shops selling emergency ponchos by the dozen, how come there are none around when I need one? No sound of bagpipes calling out to me through the rain.

He heard the piped shortbread music blaring out from the tourist shops.

I hug the bottom of my jumper, protecting the book like a pregnant woman holding her tummy. I'm soaked by the time I find somewhere; my hair is stuck to my forehead and my cheeks are flushed and pink. My glasses steam up as I enter the shop and I can't see a fucking thing. I rub the black, plastic specs on the sleeve of my jumper to try and clear the fog.

Those glasses are really sexy.

You think so?

Yeah, they remind me of Kurt Cobain. You know, in the 'In Bloom' video?

Ring a ring a roses.

I just end up smearing the lenses with rain drops and jumper fuzz though, makes it even harder to see.

There doesn't appear to be any logic to the shop's layout, so I wander around aimlessly, trying to find something waterproof. I stand in front of the magazine rack. Maybe I could buy one and hold it over my head, or fold one of the pages up into a paper hat?

Davie, why are you such a fucking tit?

I leave a trail of water behind me as I scour the shop, my squelchy Converse and cords creating a breadcrumb effect for me. I know which aisles I've already been along and which ones I've not tried yet. This shop is like the fucking Tardis. Eventually I discover a box in the corner with umbrellas inside it. They're covered in a layer of dust. I've got the choice of either Barbie or Thomas the Tank Engine.

I go for Thomas, take it up to the counter.

'I didn't even know we had these,' says the guy behind the till, as he struggles to find a barcode or a price for the umbrella. 'Do you know how much it said?' he asks me.

'Sorry,' I shrug at him and he ambles off, carrying the umbrella. I watch his head disappear behind a shelf of bread and pastries.

'I can't find it,' he says when he returns a few minutes later, 'let's just call it four ninety-nine. That alright?'

'Aye, no bother,' I reply.

'I take it you won't be needing a bag,' he grins.

Fuck, I could kick myself. If I'd just asked him for a carrier bag in the first place, I wouldn't have had to spend a fiver on some kids' umbrella.

'Nah, you're alright,' I reply and leave the shop.

Once I get outside I open up the umbrella. The plastic is folded really tight and sticks; I swoosh it open, it smells of paddling pool.

Davie and Lewis set up the plastic chute in the garden, so that they could slide down it and land in the paddling pool at the bottom. Davie went inside and poured his mum's washing-up liquid down the sink, then filled the empty bottle with cold water. Back outside, he and Lewis took turns sliding down the chute into the paddling pool, while the other one squirted them with water using the squeezy bottle as a water pistol.

I start walking and the rain begins to ease off a little. It remains a light drizzle, fizzing off the umbrella. I pull the umbrella down low so that I can't see what's in front of me, look down at my feet and let them take me where I'm going.

One finger, one thumb, one arm, one leg.

Keep moving, keep moving, keep moving.

One finger, one thumb, one arm, one leg, one nod of the head.

Keep moving, keep moving, keep moving.

My feet reach the familiar turn off and I follow them in, off the main road now and onto the long driveway. There's no pavement so I stay in at the side of the road, avoiding the puddles filling up the potholes. The road is lined on either side by oak trees, drops of rain plummet from the branches and bounce off my umbrella. Despite the weather, there are grey squirrels running around underneath the trees and scampering up round the trunks like they're a wall of death. The place is full of wildlife. I can hear the magpies and the crows.

Davie saw something out of the corner of his eye. A flash of colour. He spun round.

Lewis? That you?

Something rusty and orange slunk in and out of the bushes. Davie thought it was a cat at first, until he saw the bushy tail with white tip. Not a cat, it was a fox. Either way, it wasn't Lewis.

The crematorium building is in front of me on the right hand side of the road. It's a strange looking building, more like a modern art gallery than a giant furnace. White walls stand at right angles to one another, like a row of books standing open. It feels like if you stood at one end and pushed, they'd all close in concertina-effect and the building would fold up into one flat rectangle. A solitary standing stone.

There's a big glass triangle sticking up from the middle of the building; I'm not sure if it's a solar panel or a roof or what the fuck it's supposed to be. I think someone just added it on as an afterthought. We've got this bit of glass left over. Any ideas? Aye, just stick it on top. It reminds me a bit of a sail, the whole building ready to float away. Fuck knows how the architect managed to convince anyone that this could be a crematorium.

Are you film fans? The building's been compared to the Emerald City, you know? said the minister.

Davie couldn't work out if the minister was proud of this fact or if he was just trying to make polite conversation, ease the tension. Davie couldn't see the resemblance, it wasn't fucking emerald for a start, but he just nodded.

Even though it's raining I take my usual route, otherwise known as the long way round. It always takes me a wee while to build myself up to seeing Lewey, and the walk helps me. It's a routine I have now, walk round first, then go and see him. A bit OCD I suppose, but I need it. I can already feel my temperature and heart rate rising and that ache I get in the middle of my chest starting to build.

I turn right and follow the cobbled path encircling the crematorium building. Memorial Walk. This is the only bit of the place that reminds me of *The Wizard of Oz*. The cobbles are custard coloured, like the Yellow Brick Road. The pathway's bordered on either side by small sloping stones. They're exactly like Lego roof pieces, but without the bright colours; there's one for everyone who's been cremated here. My hands are shaking now and I force them into fists, gripping the umbrella with both hands.

One finger. One thumb. One finger. One thumb.

Today is a bad day. I take the extra long way round. I follow the path as it passes the small man-made stream and waterfall. The pool is full of copper and silver pennies. I can see them glinting through the ripples. Water vapour hangs in the air, wishes stuck in time.

I swallow, but my mouth is dry. I lean my head back and stick out my tongue, try to catch as much rain water as I can. I swallow again. I want to force down that ache rising upwards inside me.

I run out of cobbles and the path stops abruptly. They add more cobbles and bricks to it every time there's a new cremation. It's already at least a metre or two longer than the last time I was here. I turn round, follow the path back the way I've just come and head out onto the main driveway once more.

There are waiting rooms on my left-hand side as I leave the crematorium building behind me and approach the cemetery. They look a bit like garden sheds or greenhouses.

Davie couldn't help laughing every time someone mentioned it: waiting room. It wasn't even funny, but he couldn't help it. It was one of those nervous laughs that bubbles up inside you and erupts when you're trying to be as quiet as possible.

It was just the thought of it, a waiting room. A waiting room at a funeral. Like they were all waiting for Lewey to be ready before the funeral could start, like he was getting changed or something.

The body will see you now, Mr and Mrs Watts.

Davie held his breath and the laugh snorted out of his nose. If Lewis was there, they'd both be laughing. He'd have someone to share this with, he would look over at Lewis and try to catch his eye, set him off.

But Lewis wasn't here, Davie was on his own.

I walk past the wooden rooms and glance at my reflection in the darkened window.

They were all in there, the whole family squashed inside the waiting room. All of them wearing black. It wasn't like Davie's grandpa's funeral: sad, but still able to smile at the thought of him. This time there were no smiles. No talking. Davie was wearing his dad's suit. It was too big. The trousers slipped down his hips and he pulled his belt tighter. Even that slight movement was too loud though. In here, even his breathing was too loud. His mum was sitting down. People were crowded round her. Cousin Susan. Aunt Chrissie and Uncle Mike. Lewey's headteacher, Mr Hitchen. Moments earlier his mum's knees had buckled underneath her and she hadn't tried to get up. Slumped. His dad stood on his own. He leant against the window frame and stared out at the cemetery.

I shake my head, pretend it's a snow globe, cover the thoughts under white flakes. I head past the waiting rooms into the cemetery. There's trees and hedges and bushes on either side, rabbits sit on the gravestones, not bothered that it's disrespectful.

The gravestones here are all identical, small blocks of marble, raised slightly off the ground at an angle.

Nobody's different, we're all identical in the eyes of the Lord. We also let you plant things in this cemetery, it's a unique place.

People have really gone to town here. I bet all round Edinburgh there are neglected homes. Neglected gardens. Neglected families. People who spend all their time here making the graves look as beautiful as possible, trying to give something they maybe didn't give enough of when their loved ones were still around.

A lot of the graves are cordoned off by tiny picket fences; flowers and plants growing inside them. They're decorated with garden gnomes, windmills and wind-chimes. When the breeze blows, a creepy whistling and jangling noise can be heard in all directions.

You know they used to bury folk alive?

Before medicine became so sophisticated, people were often mistakenly pronounced dead when they were just unconscious or in a coma. Coffins have been found with scratch marks on the inside.

Is this supposed to be making me feel better? Davie thought.

Sometimes they would hang a bell next to the grave with the rope going right down inside the coffin, then if someone did wake up they could ring the bell and hopefully someone would come and dig them out.

I walk over to the far corner of the cemetery, the children's section; I find it slightly disturbing but totally fascinating at the same time. It's always my last stop before I go to Lewey. Once I've walked round here, I'm usually ready to see him. I can feel my heart rate beginning to slow down and my hands have stopped shaking now. The sweat on my back has evaporated and it chills me.

It's scary the amount of kids who are buried here. This is just a small section of Edinburgh too, it's not even the whole city. It's mostly wee babies who didn't live to be more than a few days old. Born Sleeping: that's a favourite line on the headstones. There's a sweet smell around here: rotting flowers and talcum powder. The graves are surrounded by metal fences. They look like rows of cots laid out next to each other. Toys decorate the ground, hundreds of them. Winnie the Pooh leads as the most popular choice. Solar lights are stuck in the ground so there will always be light, the kids don't have to worry about being afraid of the dark.

I walk past one grave which has an entire Subbuteo pitch set out, with the two Edinburgh teams represented by maroon and green Subbuteo figures. The baby was too wee to have even been to a football game. There are fresh flowers in one of the goalmouths and a tealight in the other. Nobody wins here.

In a parallel universe all these kids are growing older somewhere, not lying under toys they'll never get a chance to play with.

It's really sad but strange at the same time. I always feel weird walking through here and I leave it till last as it helps to take my mind off Lewey and why I'm really in the cemetery.

Lewey is over in the opposite corner. It's a nice spot underneath a tree. It's quite simple compared to some of the other graves: just a single rose bush, planted by Susan.

My tummy does its usual final summersaults as I approach him. My heart rate is back to normal and although the ache in my chest has shrunk, I can still feel it. It never completely leaves me. I'm always on a rollercoaster stuck on the edge of a steep drop.

Drop. He dropped the orange juice. Her lips were on his, biting, urgent, her tongue stud tapped against teeth. His or hers? Davie pressed her against the stone wall outside the pub. He took out the orange juice. Dropped.

Davie stood on his own by the grave, while everyone else wandered back to the cars. The hems of his trousers dragged in the fresh earth.

What can I do? What can I do to make it up to you?

Davie thought about his brother, all the things he'd never get to do. Never get to have sex, get drunk, drive a car. Never get to finish those bloody Harry Potter *books he was always reading. Lewey with his* Harry Potter *obsession, but he'd only made it to book five out of seven.*

Davie patted the ground.

I know it's shite compared to what I should have done, but I'll finish those books for you. I'll come out here and read them to you, so you know what happens at the end. I promise you'll get to know what happens. I know it's stupid, but it's all I can think to give you right now.

Next to the grave there's a bin overflowing with dead flowers. I pull out a piece of cellophane and use it to sit on. I shelter under the umbrella and tug out a few weeds from around the rose bush; dirt collects under my fingernails and I gnaw it out with my teeth.

Alfie clicked the kettle on, leant his elbows on the counter and picked dirt out from under his fingernails.

I feel something dig into my arse as I let my whole weight relax onto the cellophane, and I remember the MP3 player is in my back pocket. I pull it out and rest it on my knee, can feel it humming against my skin. Every day it seems to be getting smoother and smoother, like a pebble inside a stone-polishing machine. It's changing colour too, it looks silver just now, flecks of glitter melded into the plastic. It's weird, I should be freaking out that it's changing like this, but it feels natural. Like it's supposed to happen.

Lewey's stone has been soaking up the rain and looks greyer than usual.

LEWIS WATTS

JUNE 5TH 1992

FEBRUARY 26TH 2005

A MUCH LOVED SON

Davie's mum and dad chose the words. Probably the last thing they agreed on.

Simple but meaningful, his dad said.

Davie felt like he should scratch the words 'and brother' on the end. They never thought to include it.

'Hey, Lewey, I've got it.'

I pull the book out from under my jumper and hold it up

so he can see the cover.

'I went and queued up for it. It's pissing down, but I'll try and read as much as I can.'

I breathe in before opening the book, inhale fresh air. The pages of the book are damp and slightly warped. They feel thin and transparent, like greaseproof paper beneath my cold fingers.

The tree above me creaks and groans; a leaf is blown from one of its branches and floats down in front of me as I begin to read aloud.

5

Susan's House

He'd wanted to go though, as soon as he found out she would be there.
Davie dropped the orange juice.

I STOP READING after an hour or so. My hands are wet and numb and I fumble with the pages, hardly able to turn them anymore. I'm not the best reader, especially when I'm reading out loud. I stumble over words and after a while the text becomes scrambled, like ants crawling over blank sheets of paper.

Davie couldn't read in the car: it made him feel sick. Lewis sat next to him in the backseat, reading The Hobbit. *Davie watched his brother as he read, it was much more interesting than anything flashing by outside the car window. Lewey's eyes flickered as he followed the words on the page. His face kept changing, line by line, page by page. He would smile, screw up his nose, leave his mouth hanging open, suck the air in between his teeth. At one point he froze and stopped breathing altogether; Davie had to nudge him with his elbow to bring him back to life. Lewis was completely oblivious to anything outside his book.*

I shut the book and tuck it inside my jumper.

'Sorry, Lewey, I'll need to stop for now.'

I rub my throat as it's sticky with dry phlegm; I need a drink.

'Aye, I know. I'll come back soon. I want to find out what happens too, you know.'

I'm starting to forget what Lewis looked like, what he sounded like. I hate it, but it's getting harder to see him. His face is just that bit more blurry, his voice further away: a bad line. Fuck, I'd give anything to hear that voice just one more time.

The MP3 player is still resting on my lap, so I fold up the headphones, wind them around the player and slide it all in my back pocket. The hinges are starting to loosen up now, not as stiff as they used to be.

My knees crack as I stand, and my legs ache from sitting in the same position for so long. I circle Lewey's headstone to bring my legs back to life. My arse is damp and the cellophane I've been sitting on has sunk into the grass.

I bend over to pick up the cellophane and stay down, hunched over, my head leaning in towards the headstone.

'See you later, heartbreaker.'

Why does mum call me that? Lewis asked.

Call you what? Davie replied.

Heartbreaker. See you later, heartbreaker.

It's after that old song, you know, See You Later, Alligator.

But she calls me heartbreaker.

When you were a baby, everyone kept saying you would grow up to be a heartbreaker. You had really dark eyes and long eyelashes, I thought you looked more like a lassie than a heartbreaker.

I lay my palm flat against the part of the stone with Lewey's name on it.

He never went back in there, but sometimes stood outside with his palms flat against the door.

I pull the umbrella down over my head so it's just me and the headstone underneath it. Shut out everything else. I squeeze my eyes closed and concentrate on hearing Lewey's voice in my head.

I'm a wild crocodile.

I heard that song, Davie. I'm not a heartbreaker, I'm a wild crocodile.

My Converse boots squelch and my cords flap around my ankles as I walk back along the driveway towards the main road. I need somewhere to dump the cellophane, but all the bins in the cemetery are crammed full of dead flowers. The rotting leaves and petals push their way out of the top of the bins and spill out onto the ground. The rain falls as perfume. It's only when I leave the cemetery that I escape the smell and find an empty bin to dump the cellophane.

The rain patters off the roof of the bus shelter. I put my umbrella down. I'm in no hurry to go home. *Happy to hang around.* The thought of going back to the flat brings me down. I'll just sit in my dingy room all night trying to distract myself, keep myself busy. One finger, one thumb.

A bus pulls up heading in the direction of Prestonpans, and on impulse I get on it. The thought of Susan's warm house trumps going back to my flat. I always feel like this after I've been to see Lewey. Flat. Deflated.

I shut my eyes and lean my head against the bus window. My hair smears messy patterns in the condensation. Shapes and lights flash through my closed eyelids, and I focus on where I'm going. I imagine myself sitting in Susan's living room with a cup of tea; I don't think about where I've just been.

I take out the MP3 player and hold it in my hands. It's weird, I just want to touch it all the time. Feel its smoothness, press it between my palms. I'm sure I can hear it chime inside, like Chinese medicine balls.

You're so full of anger; it's not healthy to bottle things up like that.

I'm still playing around with it when we reach Prestonpans. The Pans.

The Pans has that run-down, shabby feel to it that all the old mining towns do. A glamorous movie icon grown old, who now wishes she'd died in her heyday.

Only the good die young.

Don't give me that cliché; that's bullshit.

The bus drives past rows of identical looking council houses: dull brickwork, satellite dishes, net curtains. Most of the gardens have been slabbed over with crazy paving or scattered with orange chuckies. There's nothing green here.

I can see smoke rising in the sky in front, puffing out from the twin chimneys of the power station.

The smoke spewing out is my cue to hit the bell and make my way downstairs to the front of the bus. It stops in the town centre and I get out.

A lawyer's. A Scotmid. A bookie's. The Jade Garden Chinese takeaway.

Kurt Cobain, unplugged, sings in my head, only I amend the words ever so slightly.

In the Pans, in the Pans...

I wander over to the sea wall and lean on it, look out across the Forth towards Fife. The sea comes right up to the wall, the grey water breaks against the rocks below me.

It's not much to write home about really, but it was my home for a while and that makes it alright by me.

After the funeral Davie's mum wouldn't stop talking about Lewis. She became obsessed; she said talking about Lewis helped keep him alive. Davie's dad just stopped talking altogether, as if Lewis had never existed. Communication breakdown, said Dr Richmond. Davie ended up spending more and more time out at his cousin Susan's house. Pammy wasn't very old and Colin was out of the picture, so she needed a bit of support. Looking after a baby helped distract Davie from what was going on at home. He didn't sleep well anyway, and having someone else up and about in the middle of the night meant he wasn't left to his own thoughts. Days turned into weekends turned into weeks turned into months.

I walk the familiar route toward Susan's. She lives about five minutes away, opposite the battle site.

Davie looked at the tiny cairn with 1745 chiselled into it. What's that for? he asked Susan.

You're not being serious are you? It's for the Battle.

What battle?

The Battle of Prestonpans, you must have heard of it.

Sorry. Should I have, like?

Come on, history lesson.

Susan led the way, across the railway line and up the old slag heap covered in artificial grass.

At the top of the man-made hill you could see down onto a park and a football pitch: the battlefield.

There you go. Susan pointed at a couple of old information boards, weather-faded and covered in graffiti.

Pans Youth Team. PYT. Don't fuck with the PYT.

So who actually battled then? Davie asked.

Susan had Pammy on reins like a horse's bridle and pulled on them as Pammy ran towards the edge of the slag heap.

Have you not read it?

Well, I worked out Bonnie Prince Charlie was involved, but that's about it.

That's obvious from the date, Davie. 1745. The Jacobites. Culloden.

Aye, well, obviously I've heard of that.

The Battle of Prestonpans was before that. We actually won this one. The Corries sang about it. You must have heard it, it was one of Grandpa's favourite songs.

Aye, probably. We won?

Not that you'd notice. Typical Scotland for you. Culloden's a tourist attraction and this is a slag heap. You're in the Tartan Army, you know the deal: Scots love to revel in the glory of defeat.

I crunch up the gravel of Susan's driveway. It doesn't look

like anyone's in. I should have texted her to check. She works funny hours teaching fitness classes, I can never keep up with what she's doing.

Halfway towards the front door I see the blinds move and Pammy's face pops up at the living room window. Before I get a chance to wave, she's disappeared out of sight again. I hear her shouting from behind the closed door.

'Mummy, Uncle Davie's here.'

A key rattles and, as I reach the front door, both Susan and Pammy are standing to welcome me.

'God you're soaked, Davie. Come in and I'll get you a towel.'

'You're soaked,' Pammy echoes and stands watching me as I step inside the house. Susan locks the door behind me as I kick off my shoes and dump them alongside the umbrella and the book. I follow Pammy along the hall. My trousers drag along the carpet, so I roll them up like I'm an old man paddling at the seaside. In the living room I lean against the radiator, even though the heating's not switched on. Force of habit. Susan appears with a towel which she wraps around my shoulders.

'Honestly, Davie, I only let you move out because you said you'd look after yourself. Give me those socks and those trousers.'

'I'm not as bad as all that.'

'Come on, you're soaking. Off!'

I peel off my wet socks, then wrap the towel around my waist before I take off my trousers.

'Come on, you weren't so modest when you lived here. Remember that morning I found you lying drunk in the toilet.'

'No, I don't remember that. And anyway, Pammy was just a wee thing back then. It's not good for her if I'm standing here flashing.'

'Stop being such a prude and give me your trousers. We're all family.'

I take the MP3 player out of my pocket and hand the cords to Susan.

'What's that?' Susan nods at the MP3 player as I rest it on the mantelpiece.

'It's Alfie's.'

The lie comes naturally. I don't even have time to ask myself why I'm not telling the truth.

Susan passes me some old tracky bottoms and a pair of socks. The tracksuit bottoms are too small for me and only come down to my shins. My toes are wrinkled and blister-white, like I've been festering in the bath for hours. I rub at them with the towel, then put on the dry socks: black with pink spots.

'What do you think?' I ask Pammy, and do a wee twirl.

'You look silly,' she replies.

My feet tingle with pins and needles as the blood starts to circulate.

'Am I amusing you, teenybash?' I ask Pammy, who's staring at me.

She's sitting in the corner, surrounded by what looks like her entire toy collection.

'Here we go,' says Susan, appearing with a tray of tea and biscuits.

'Cheers,' I say, and join her on the sofa.

The black leather groans beneath me and I slide down into the cushions.

I never noticed till I lived here how anal you are about stuff.

What do you mean?

Your rooms, the way they're all themed by colour. I bought you that nice vase and it's shoved in the cupboard because it doesn't match.

That's not true. I just don't have any flowers.

Okay, so if I buy you flowers you'll use it?

Yes.

I don't believe you. They'd have to be black and white flowers to fit in here with the black sofa, white carpet, black rug, black and white curtains, that random piece of black and white art above the TV. I feel like I'm a piece on a chessboard in here, or riding on the back of a cow.

You're a cheeky sod sometimes.

'Where have you been anyway?' Susan asks me, handing Pammy a glass of milk and a digestive.

'Just seeing Lewey,' I reply, and take a sip of tea.

The word Lewey floats around me like an insect that won't go away. I try not to say his name out loud too often.

'In this weather? Could you not have picked a nicer day?'

'It was sunny when I left the flat this morning.'

'Was it? It's been raining here all day. Hasn't it, Pammy?'

Pammy nods, then takes a glug of milk, leaves a white moustache above her top lip. She wipes her sleeve across her face, and puts her glass down inside one of the rooms of her dollhouse.

'You'll stay for your tea, won't you?' Susan asks, as I help myself to my fifth digestive.

'I wouldn't mind, if that's cool with you.'

I know that whatever Susan and Pammy are having, it'll be a hundred times better than anything I would have at the flat.

'It's just spag bog, eh? Nothing fancy.'

'Sounds great.'

Susan puts down her tea and stretches her arms up in the air. She leans her head forward and rolls it from side to side. I look over at Pammy, who's copying her mum.

'I've got new music for my class, but the warm-up doesn't seem to fit properly,' Susan says.

Davie came in from work to find Susan marching on the spot in the middle of the hallway.

Alright?

Aye, don't mind me, just learning the routine for my ante-natal class.

Susan picks up her tea again. She glances over at Pammy then leans in towards me.

'I've been meaning to phone you actually. Guess who I got a text from the other day?'

'Who?'

Not mum. Not mum. Not mum. Not mum.

'Colin,' she whispers in my ear.

'You're joking. What does that arsehole want?'

'Sshhh. He said he wanted to see Pammy.'

'I hope you told him to get to fuck.'

'Course I did, I'm not an idiot.'

'What did he say to that?'

'Nothing. He didn't reply.'

'He's not getting anywhere near Pammy, or you. How does he even have your number?'

'Don't get all worked up.'

She squeezes my arm, which is shaking.

'Who are you talking about, Uncle Davie?' Pammy asks.

'Nobody.'

Susan wore dark sunglasses at the funeral to hide the black eye. She told everyone she'd been hit in the face by an over-enthusiastic punter at one of her fitness classes.

Davie lay awake in his new room at Susan's house. He thought he heard something outside. The sound of the doorbell made him jump. Then someone was hammering on the downstairs window.

Susan, open up! I want to see my fucking kid, you bitch.

Davie went through to Susan's room. She stood against the bedroom wall and held on to Pammy.

What's going on?

Colin isn't taking the break-up so well.

Susan rubbed her fading black eye.

Davie opened the bedroom window and looked out. Colin was outside, pissed, staggering around.

Who the fuck are you? Colin picked up a pile of stones from the driveway and threw them up at the window.

Davie wanted so much to shout something back. To say something to get rid of Colin. Go down there and take him out with one punch.

Fight or flight? Fight or flight?

Fright.

Get out of here or I'll phone the polis, Davie said, and shut the window.

His words made him sound braver than he felt and his hands shook. Susan had met Colin at the gym. He was a fucking body-builder. Davie had never been a fighter, he knew Colin could kick the shit out of him.

As Davie picked up the phone, he couldn't believe he had to dial 999 again; before he had a chance to hit the number though, he heard the sirens.

The sirens. He was still holding the receiver.

One of Susan's neighbours had beaten him to it. Davie watched as Colin was bundled into the back of the police car and taken away.

I turn to face Susan. Her hair is tied in bunches and she's staring down into her mug of tea. It's only now that I'm actually looking at her that I notice the purple bags under the bloodshot eyes.

His eyes were open and bloodshot.

They remind me of painted boiled eggs at Easter. The shells have been peeled off but the colour has seeped through, leaving the white of the egg streaky. I'm overcome with a need to cuddle her, to look after her after all she's done for me. I don't though. I'm shit at showing emotion.

I want to say something. I want to help, but as usual I stay quiet. You'd think I'd have learnt my lesson by now. Susan deserves better than me, I wish I wasn't so fucking useless. No fight, all fright.

'Have you called the polis?' I ask.

'Aye, I did that. Don't worry. It's all okay. I just thought I should tell you.'

I'm still feeling crap when Susan starts making tea. I try to help her with it in an attempt to feel useful. I just get in the way though. She crushes the garlic with the presser and it might as well be my balls for all the man I am. She heats garlic and oil in a pan, then adds tomato and mushrooms. The windows steam up and it's like we're in a greenhouse. I open the hatch to the living room to let some air in.

'Pammy won't stop watching that *Lady and the Tramp* DVD you got her.' Susan says as she dishes up. 'It's spaghetti a go-go at the moment.'

The meal lasts a lot longer than it should. Pammy insists that we imitate the dogs from the Disney film, and we take it in turns to sook a spaghetti strand with her.

'Do that again,' she shouts over and over.

She presents us with her tomato sauce stained face, a strand of spaghetti hanging down her chin. Not that I'm much cleaner. I make a right mess of myself, splattering red spots of sauce all down my front and over the table. I wipe garlic bread around the edge of my plate and soak up the excess sauce. As I bite into the crusty bread and the garlic butter fills my mouth, I realise how much I miss living here.

My stomach is bulging when Susan takes my plate away and I'm grateful for the elasticated waistband of the tracky bottoms. I've not eaten so much or so well for ages. Susan replaces my empty plate with a bowl of chocolate cheesecake.

'Skooshy cream?' she asks, taking the can out of the fridge.

'Aye, why not.'

'I'll do it,' Pammy insists, as Susan tries to squirt cream onto her cheesecake.

'Okay, but not too much,' Susan replies, handing her the can.

Pammy presses down on it and covers her cheesecake and most of the table in cream. She looks up at Susan, hands back the can as if that was exactly what she'd meant to do. I can't help laughing at her wee face as she tucks into her pudding, scraping the cream and chocolate sauce off and leaving the biscuit.

'Don't laugh, you'll just encourage the wee madam,' Susan says, but I can tell she's trying not to laugh herself.

She scoops up the dollop of cream lying in the middle of the table and spoons it into her own dish, then sticks her tongue out at Pammy.

'Oh, did I tell you I've started yoga?' Susan asks me, in between mouthfuls of cheesecake.

I shake my head.

'Aye, it's a lot more classes for me.'

'Sounds good.'

'Means that I can afford to take teenybash here to Australia soon.'

'Oh aye.'

'Skyping Mum and Dad's just not the same as being in the same room with them, she needs to spend time with her granny and grandad while she still can.'

I avoid eye contact because I know what's coming next.

'I was wondering if you fancied it?'

'Not really.'

'Come on, Davie.'

'I can't afford it.'

'I could help you with some of it.'

'Nah.'

'Someone has to make the first move. You can't go on like this forever.'

I'm going to Australia.

I take a mouthful of cheesecake, let it fill my entire mouth so I don't have to answer. Pammy is watching the conversation like someone at Wimbledon: her wee head moves from side to side. She stares at me, waiting for my response. I stay silent. Advantage Susan. The chocolate icing and cream dissolves in my mouth, leaving only soggy biscuit. I swallow it and take another mouthful. I don't want to get into this. Not now. Not ever. If mum wants to hide out in *Neighbours* land with Aunt Chrissie and Uncle Mike then that's her lookout.

The temperature drops and the warm greenhouse changes into frosty igloo.

'I spoke to your mum on the phone the other night. She was asking for you.'

'Well, she knows where I am,' I reply, and push my plate away.

I've not finished it, but it's getting to that sickly stage where I can't eat any more. Susan looks at me but I stare down at my bowl and play with what's left of the cheesecake.

'Tea?' she asks, scraping the uneaten cheesecake into the bin before dumping the empty bowls in the sink.

'Aye, cheers.'

Susan clicks on the kettle, then moves into a yoga pose as she waits for it to boil.

'This is called Warrior posture, I'm still trying to memorise the sequence. The music is dead relaxing, all ohms and chanting. I really like it.'

Pammy scrambles down from the table.

'Hey, young lady. Did you ask to be excused?'

'Can I be 'scused?'

'Excused what?'

'Please.'

'That's better. Aye, off you go.'

Pammy runs out of the kitchen. Now that we're on our

own I dread what Susan's going to say.

'So how's work?' she asks.

'Same old shite really.'

'When are you going to leave that place? You've been there too long.'

'I know, it's not that easy though.'

'I thought you were going to go back to uni?'

We think it would be best if you took some time out, and then came back and repeated the year when you're feeling better.

'Come on, stop nagging me, will you?'

The kettle clicks off and Susan makes us both a brew.

'Comfy seat?' She nods in the direction of the living room and I follow her as she carries the mugs through.

As we enter the living room, Pammy spins towards the door and freezes. Musical statues. She's holding the MP3 player, and is wearing the headphones. Caught in the act.

Without thinking I step towards her and grab the player out of her hand. The headphones get stuck in her hair and her whole head jerks towards me as I pull. She looks up at me and her bottom lip starts to wobble like Mariah Carey or Whitney Houston belting out a ballad. The wobble spreads across her chin and up the rest of her face, then sinks down into her shoulders. It's like the plug's been pulled out as the tears start. She runs to Susan and grabs onto her legs.

'Careful, Pammy, I've got hot tea here,' Susan says, and shoots me a dirty look.

'Sorry, I don't know why I did that. Sorry.'

It all happened so quickly. The rush of blood as I realised someone else had the MP3 player, the sudden need to get it back. Mine. Mine. Mine.

He sat on his hands, used his weight to trap them underneath him.

'Sweetheart, you know you shouldn't play with stuff that isn't yours,' Susan says, putting down the mugs and giving

71

Pammy a cuddle. The headphones are still caught in her hair and Susan untangles them.

'You know you can't leave stuff lying about.'

Susan hands me back the headphones. A strand of Pammy's hair is still tangled around the metal.

'I know, sorry. I didn't mean to hurt her.'

I don't know what came over me there. I was someone else. For that split second I forgot who Pammy was. I didn't see a wee lassie. I just saw someone who had stolen my MP3 player. Mine. Mine. Mine.

I kneel in front of her.

'Sorry, can we be friends again, please?'

Pammy nods her head but doesn't look all that convinced. She's stopped crying though and seems a lot calmer. I love how kids have that ability to scream the place down in a fit of hysterics and then go back to normal in an instant. A click of the fingers. Everything forgotten. Pammy lets go of Susan and returns to her toy corner. Susan and I sit down next to each other on the sofa.

The room's chilly and I can feel a draught tickling my bare ankles. I pull the socks up and the tracky bottoms down, try to cover my bare skin.

'What is that thing anyway? It's nothing like my iPod.'

'It's Alfie's. I think it's broken.'

The MP3 player buzzes and my hand jerks in response.

'Did you just get a shock off it?'

'No, it's fine. Someone just walked over my grave, that's all.'

I squeeze the MP3 player in my hand and it buzzes again. My hand twitches and I spill tea onto the tracky bottoms. Fuck. What's all that about? The first time it's done something and I'm stuck with an audience.

'You did, that gave you a shock.'

'No, it's fine, just a loose connection I think.'

'That thing's not safe. Pammy could've been hurt.'

'Aye, I'll give it back to Alfie when I get in.'

I put the player down next to me, push it under my thigh out of sight. I really want to play about with it. I can feel it humming underneath me, my leg is singing all the way down to the bone. I need to get out of here. Something's happening.

I gulp my tea down too quickly and burn myself. Bumps and ridges break out on my tongue and the roof of my mouth.

'I'd better head,' I say to Susan.

'You can crash here if you like.'

'Nah, I'm on early in the morning. Got to be up at some stupid time.'

'See what I mean. Always moaning about Virgin, but not doing anything about it. You need to make a bloody effort.'

'Aye, aye.'

'Someone has to keep nagging you.'

'Where are my cords?'

I know if I hang around any longer we'll end up fighting, and I don't like fighting with Susan. We usually get on so well.

They're still your folks, Davie, no matter what's happened. You only get one mum and dad.

'You mean you don't want to go home in those?' Susan says nodding at my get-up.

I give her a look and she leaves the room. She comes back carrying my trousers, patting them all over with her hands.

'They're still a bit damp, but they'll do. Your socks are soaking though, I'll put them in the wash.'

I stand behind the sofa and change into my cords. They're cold and clammy against my skin. I slide the MP3 player into my back pocket and pat it. Soon. Soon.

'I'd offer you a lift home, but I need to give teenybash a bath and get her to bed.'

'Aye, nae bother, eh?'

73

Susan and Pammy follow me to the front door.

'I didn't know you were into *Harry Potter*,' Susan says as I tuck the book inside my jumper.

'Aye.'

I know it's shite compared to what I should have done, but I'll finish those books for you. I'll come out here and read them to you, so you know what happens at the end. I promise you'll get to know what happens. I know it's stupid, but it's all I can think to give you right now.

'Lewis loved those books, didn't he?'

I nod and concentrate on putting my soggy Converse back on. His name clings to me. Susan doesn't know about my promise. Nobody does.

'Oh, before you go, I meant to ask if you'd come to a party with me.'

'Aye, when is it?'

'Not for a couple of weeks.'

'Cool. Whose party?'

'One of Pammy's friends. Jodie, I think.'

'Josie, Mummy!' Pammy corrects her.

'What? I thought you meant a real party.'

'It is a real party.'

'You know what I mean.'

'Come on, I can't face it on my own.'

'You're really selling it to me.'

'Please.'

'Aye, okay, but only as long as I'm not working or at the football or anything.'

'Don't give me any of that, I know the football's finished for the season.'

'Aye, whatever.'

'I'll pick you up and take you home. You just have to show up.'

'The sooner you get yourself a decent bloke the better.

Have I introduced you to Alfie?'

'Aye, very good,' she pushes me towards the door, 'out with you.'

Pammy refuses to give me a kiss goodbye and I toy with the idea of giving her my brolly as a peace offering. It's still pissing down when I open the door though, so I change my mind.

'Thanks for the tea and the socks,' I say, stepping outside and putting up the umbrella.

'No problem,' Susan replies, 'and keep the socks. They suit you.'

I lift up one leg of my cords and flash an ankle at them. Pammy laughs, but Susan isn't paying attention. She's looking over my head, down the driveway towards the street.

'See you later,' I say.

Susan pushes Pammy behind her and shuts the door. I hear it lock behind me as I make my way along the drive. I turn and look to see if anyone's waving, but the blinds remain shut. I stand for a moment at the garden gate, listening to the rain crackle off the umbrella, then I head back towards the bus stop.

6

Stop Whispering

All the messing about that had been going on for weeks: the
flirting, the teasing, the questions. Is something going on with you
and Martha?
Davie dropped the orange juice.

THE MP3 PLAYER buzzes at me all the way home on the bus,
like a bee hitting itself against the window: manic for a few
seconds, then calm.

Zzzzmmmm.

Zzzzmmmm.

Zzzzmmmm.

I leave it in my pocket, I'm conscious that there's too many
people around me on the bus. I want to be alone before I start
playing about with it; it feels like something I have to do
alone. I don't know why I'm getting so worked up about a
few vibrations, it's like it's coming alive though. There's more
to it than just a normal MP3 player, I'm sure there is.

I run up the stairwell, take the steps two at a time. My
Converse boots are wet though and I slip on the vinyl flooring.
I fall forwards, and crash against a bike someone's got tied
up to the banister railing. The pedal catches and rips a hole
in the knee of my cords.

The door to number nine opens and I turn to see a pair of
eyes watching me from behind a security chain. I give my
spectator the thumbs up and the door shuts. The sound of it
slamming echoes around the stairwell and hums in and out

of the railings. Above me. Below me. Up and down. Up and down.

I run my hand up the scratched, dull varnish of the wooden banister as I continue up the stairs. One step at a time. One finger. One thumb. One arm. One leg.

I can tell Alfie's in before I put the key in the front door: there's all sorts of noise coming from inside the flat. I place my palm flat against the door and can feel the wood vibrate against my skin.

He never went back in there, but sometimes stood outside with his palms flat against the door.

I turn the key and push the door open; the noise hits me even harder. Alfie's bedroom door is closed, but the walls on either side pulse like a speaker. If I opened that door the noise would spill out and knock me down.

I head straight to my own room, close the door behind me and try to soundproof the space with a few t-shirts I've left scattered across the floor. I stuff them around my door, sealing off the gaps like I'm in a fire-safety video. I'm surprised my furniture is still standing where I left it this morning, surprised it's not bounced all over the room, dancing to the noise that Alfie's making.

My ears fill up with pressure; the hair inside sways from side to side, like a crowd listening to a ballad at a boyband concert. I put my hands over my ears, stick my fingers inside the canals, anything to try and ease the feeling that my eardrums are about to explode.

Silence.

'Davie? That you?' Alfie's voice shouts from the other side of my bedroom door.

'Aye, it's me.'

I pull the t-shirts out of the way and open the door. One gets jammed and I slide it back with my foot and kick it out into the hallway. It hits Alfie who's standing in front of me;

he picks up the t-shirt and hands it back.

'Cheers,' I say, and chuck it behind me into my room.

Alfie's hair is all over the place and his eyes are wide and staring. He bears an uncanny resemblance to Doc from *Back to the Future*.

'I've discovered my sound,' Alfie says, like he's just won the lottery.

'Eh?'

'I went to see this singer called Thomas Truax, eh? He's a total mentalist but he's fucking amazing. He's got all these mad instruments that he's made himself, and they add this ace sound to his songs.'

'Sounds good.'

'Aye, he's really inspired me. I've realised what's been wrong with my songs all this time. They've been lacking that special sound. I can't believe I never realised it before now. That's why the band never got anywhere, we were always missing something.'

Alfie is wide-eyed and doesn't drop eye contact with me, not even blinking. I'm not really sure how to reply to his announcement so I stay quiet. I want to get rid of him so I can check out the MP3 player, but he's so excited I feel like I should humour him.

'I'm making my own instruments,' he explains. 'It's fucking genius. Already some of the old songs are really starting to come alive. Did you not hear when you came in?'

'Eh... aye, I thought I recognised that one... eh, what was it called again?'

I try to remember the name of one of Alfie's songs. I know he had a couple named after old Amstrad games.

Daley Thompson's Decathlon?

Fantasy World Dizzy?

My mind goes blank. I can barely remember what his band were called, let alone any of the songs. He's so hyped up, the question of what he's been taking trumps the quest for song titles in my head.

'Blue Heart on the Moon?' Alfie asks me.

'Aye, of course. That was it. Sorry, I couldn't think of the name there. Had a total mental block. Aye, it definitely sounds a lot different from when you and the band used to do it, like.'

'I ken. It's so much better, isn't it? I knew you'd notice. That's just a prototype instrument too. I've not had time to get all the equipment I need yet. Imagine how ace it's gonna sound once I get properly sorted.'

'Aye, cool.'

'I just wanted to come and tell you, eh? I'm so wired about it all. I feel like that missing jigsaw piece has just been found down the back of the couch. I need to get back to it though. I've got all these ideas just racing around me, I need to get it all down on paper while it's fresh.'

Alfie waves his arms around his head while he's talking to me. I've seen him on speed before, but this is something else. I'm waiting for him to grab me by the collar and shout, 'Great Scott!'

'Cool, brilliant, eh?' I reply.

I glance inside his bedroom as he turns his back on me. Fuck knows what he's up to in there. Well, apart from the musical instrument project of course. The red light bulb he insists on having doesn't give out much light, and it's like staring into my granny's old electric fire. I can make out shapes and shadows, but nothing concrete. The face of David Bowie stares down at me from one of Alfie's posters, the glam rock make-up looks even stranger behind the crimson glow. Alfie flashes me a manic smile before closing the bedroom door. Doc morphs into Mr Hyde, and I have a sudden vision of Alfie hunched over his desk, stirring a steaming cauldron. I push the image away with a shrug. Alfie doesn't change personality from day to night: he's a constant state of anarchy.

Davie held onto his pint and leant against the wall next to the stage. Alfie's band was playing, and Davie had come along to watch. The pub was a complete dive, a real old man's pub, but that didn't seem to bother Alfie. Despite the fact that only a handful of folk from Virgin and a couple of regulars were watching, Alfie strutted across the stage like he was Mick Jagger and Jim Morrison rolled into one.

Almost immediately the noise kicks in again. I hesitate out in the hall for a few minutes, curious to see if I can actually recognise what it is he's playing.

Nope.

Must be an early album track or an obscure B-side.

I soundproof my bedroom once more, as Alfie's new sound begins to seep through the walls into my room. I kick off my Converse and my damp cords, and sit down on my bed with the MP3 player.

I turn it over and over in my hands.

'Come on then, I'm on my own now. Do your thing.'

I can't concentrate on anything with Alfie's racket next door. My head is tied up in knots. The noise buzzes around me like a bluebottle and the knots are pulled tighter. I'm surprised nobody's been up to complain. The noise must be reverberating all the way through the building.

Let's try some simple breathing exercises first.

Loosen your clothing.

Sit with your back against the wall.

Start by breathing out.

Then breathe in.

Then breathe out.

Then breathe in.

Out.

In.

Out.

In.

Out.

If you can, try and find somewhere quiet and peaceful.

I fold out the headphones from the MP3 player and put them on. The rust has completely gone now and the hinges slide back and forward, back and forward, back and forward. No effort required. The padded covering on the headphones sucks onto my ears, a plunger on either side of my head. It's so tight that I feel my brain will be sucked right out of my skull if I remove them. All external sound vanishes. Peace. Quiet.

It's like being underwater at the swimming pool. Noise and splash echoing off the bricks and the tiles, then bubbles and swoosh.

I pull them away from my ears, then let them fall back down again.

Pull away, fall back down, pull away, fall back down.

Feel the difference between silence and noise.

Underwater, then break the surface.

Underwater, then break the surface.

Underwater, then break the surface.

Underwater.

Break the surface.

Inhale.

Shivery bite.

The MP3 player is sparkling. The glitter rubs off on me, so when I look down at my palms they're sparkling too. The gaps between my fingers are glowing. The player feels alive. A sleeping baby. No movement on the outside, but all kinds of unseen shit going on inside. Under the surface.

Whispering to me.

I put the player down on my bedside table and lean back against the headboard. It was definitely vibrating earlier on, but now it's staying still. I didn't imagine it. All the way home on the bus, zzzzmmmmmm, zzzzmmmmmm, zzzzmmmmmm. Why's it staying still now?

Come on, talk to me. Don't mess me about.

I know there's more to it than just an MP3 player.

Work, you stupid thing, work.

Fuck sake, what am I doing? I'm acting like a crazy person. *Waiting to go in. Waiting to be seen. Waiting to be picked up. Waiting for the pain to just get a tiny bit smaller. Waiting. Everybody seemed to be waiting at hospitals.*

I pick the player up and smack it down onto the bedside table in frustration.

Fucking hell, what's wrong with me? Getting all worked up over a stupid, broken MP3 player.

I pull the headphones off but all I can hear is Alfie's noise. He's got me trapped. I slip the headphones back on, push my bare legs under the duvet and lie my head down on the pillow. Keep Alfie's noise at bay. Close my eyes.

It's oh so quiet.

I sense movement behind my closed eyelids. The MP3 player is moving. I sit up. Pinch myself. I'm definitely awake and it's definitely moving. It shuffles across my bedside table and tumbles off the edge. I lunge towards it and manage to catch it before it hits the floor.

Reflexes sharp. Put Craig Gordon to shame.

As my hands grasp the player, I feel something surge through me.

Zzzzmmmmmmm!

I'm different. Something's happened to me.

I feel like I've been zapped with electricity. The hair all over my body is fizzing, standing to attention. My cock is hard and alert. It's amazing. I'm wide awake.

I have the power.

The LCD screen on the MP3 player lights up: electric blue.

82

Bright. My hands are illuminated. I can see every line, every vein, every flake of skin.

I glance up at the mirror at the opposite end of my room. Do I look different? My face is lit up: blue from the MP3 player.

His face was illuminated when he opened the door. He took out the carton and unscrewed the lid.

Words scroll along the LCD screen. Right to left.

`Welcome Trackman Welcome Trackman Welcome Trackman`

There's a voice coming from the headphones. It starts off a whisper but then builds and builds. Julie Andrews appearing over the mountain. The voice repeats the same phrase.

`Welcome Trackman Welcome Trackman Welcome Trackman`

It must be jammed: stuck on repeat. I've never heard a song like this in my life. Some sort of experimental pish? There seems to be a loose connection somewhere, because if I shift my hand position the voice and the words stop. Blue light goes out.

Off.

Click... off... gone.

I have to keep my hands locked around the player, which is easier said than done seeing as I'm hanging off the bed after jumping forward to catch it.

The voice reminds me of someone. It takes me a few minutes to place it. That old actor: James Mason. The more I listen to it, the more it starts to freak me out. When I think of him all these images merge in my head. Angelic James in *Heaven Can Wait*. Evil James in *North by Northwest*. Alcoholic and suicidal James in *A Star is Born*. Eddie Izzard and Rob Brydon doing James Mason impressions. Undermining his bad guy status. There's so many versions of him. Which one is this? It confuses me. This voice is confusing me.

One finger. One thumb. One finger. One thumb.

The covers of the DVDs I have to file away and alphabetise at work jump out at me.

20,000 Leagues Under the Sea.
Lolita.
The Boys From Brazil.
Salem's Lot.
The Water Babies.
I want to pull the headphones off but the voice stops me.
`Welcome Trackman Welcome Trackman Welcome Trackman`
Okay, I get it, Welcome Trackman.
`Man You are the Trackman You are the Trackman You`
Fuck.
I let go of the player, and it drops to the ground and bounces out of sight under the bed.

That was a coincidence, right? The way it changed like it was answering me.

I stretch my arm under the bed, pull the player out from underneath and blow the dust off it. Everything has stopped again.

I shimmy my legs over the edge of the bed so that I'm sitting up now; my feet, still in the spotty socks, are flat against the wooden floorboards. I clasp my hands around the player and the voice and the words kick in again.
`Trackman You are the Trackman You are the Trackman`
My whole body is charged. Like there's a key in my back and someone's winding me up. There's a tingle spreading through me. It starts in my hands and flows out to the rest of my body.

Davie's grandpa folded a piece of tissue paper over a comb, and began to play a tune on it.

Come on, Davie, I'll teach you my party piece. Just hold it to your mouth and blow. You have to squeeze your lips together.

Davie put two Penguin biscuits down on the table. It was time to pass on some wisdom to his little brother.

Davie took the comb and tried to copy his grandpa. He

couldn't do it though. The paper made his lips tickle and he rubbed at them with the comb, trying to scratch the itchiness away.

My hair is sticking up; I could stick balloons to the wall.

It's a good feeling.

Good feeling.

I play around with my hand placement.

Hands on. Hands off. Hands on. Hands off. Hands on. Hands off.

Karate-kid-esque.

It's fucking weird the way the voice and the words keep stopping and starting. If I let go of the thing to take a closer look, it dies on me. I try fooling it and swap my hands for something else: my feet, the *Harry Potter* book. I'm Indiana Jones in *Raiders*: I have the bag of sand in one hand and I need to switch it smoothly and seamlessly for the golden idol.

It doesn't work though. The platform sinks down and the booby traps are set off. The MP3 player is still and I'm being chased by a giant, stone ball.

I can't sit still. I'm buzzing. I walk round and round my room, keep pace with the words from the headphones.

Track. Man. Track. Man. Track. Man. Track. Man.

The voice becomes friendly. Soothing. I forget the schizophrenia, all the different characters brought to life by James Mason. His voice is a mantra. Hypnotic.

Click... off... gone.

It's like the batteries have just died.

I stop walking. Why has it stopped?

I can't get it to start again.

Nothing.

'Come back. Talk to me.'

I squeeze it as hard as I can. Shake it.

'Hey, come on! Come back!'

I jump as my bedroom door swings open. Alfie's standing in the doorway and he mouths something at me.

I pull off the headphones. The flat's quiet. How long has he been outside my door? How much has he heard?

'Sorry, man, just going for a pish and I thought I heard you shout me.'

'Nah, just singing.'

'You got it working then?' he nods at the MP3 player.

'Eh... aye, kind of.'

'You didn't sound half bad actually. I might use you when it comes to recording stuff.'

'Aye, no bother.'

Alfie shuts the bedroom door and I squeeze my hands. Exert pressure on the MP3 player. I'm not surprised when it burrs into life again, like it didn't want Alfie to see. It's a secret. Our secret.

I throw myself onto the bed. Tap, tap, tap my feet against the headboard. The headphones hang over my thigh and drag on the floor. The voice spills out of them and buzzes against the floorboards like the cicadas you hear in films. I lie awake and concentrate on the voice. Concentrate on it until it's all I can hear.

Trackman Trackman Trackman Trackman Trackman Track

7

Crush with Eyeliner

So when she asked him if he was going for a drink after work, he said yes. He asked her if she was going too. She said yes. She smiled at him. Cool, he replied.
Davie dropped the orange juice.

I'M COMMITTING THE cardinal sin of the shop worker, breaking the most important rule in the book. Slouching. Leaning. Slumped over the counter with my head in my hands, and flicking through PC *Gamer* magazine. I have my story worked out if Laura happens to show up on the shop floor: research. Some customer asked me about this new game and I was just checking the reviews for him... blah, blah, blah. Load of pish, but I can't be arsed today. I can't be arsed most of the time, but today is worse than usual.

Martha's kicking about over by the chart wall dusting the shelves, Ryan's on his break. They don't give a shit either, but at least Martha has the decency to look busy somewhere else. Ryan insists on doing whatever I'm doing. Two people leaning against the counter just looks like two people skiving, whereas if it's just me on my own then I can come up with an excuse.

The in-store radio has been particularly shite today too.

It's recorded in London and is then piped out to all the individual stores.

Someone upstairs on the ground floor must have got pissed off with it and turned the volume down. It was blaring out earlier, but now you can only hear it if you go and stand directly under one of the speakers.

All the records on the radio are shite.

There's hardly any customers either, it's been dead all morning. I'm so fucking bored. Man, I'm never happy. I moan when there are customers and then I moan when we don't have any. We did have a visit from one of our regulars, B.O. Problem Man though. The smell of stale armpits is still clinging in the air like the moist warmth from a rotting bin-bag.

Davie held his breath against the stale, unwashed smell of him.

The excitement of the day so far has been changing the posters in the light boxes, which hang on the wall behind the tills like a noughts and crosses board. They're a fucking nightmare. Half of them are broken, the magnetic power starting to fade, so it's a risky business trying to slot them back onto the wall. There's a knack to it, I just don't seem to have it.

Martha had to help me.

She ran her fingers round and round on the back of his hand.

Ring a ring a roses.

I turn back to my magazine. I can't concentrate on it though, can't stop thinking about the MP3 player.

Trackman Trackman Trackman Trackman Trackman Track

I can't get it out of my head.

I fell asleep holding onto the player last night, letting the words loop over and over. They say you absorb stuff when you're asleep, that information sticks in your brain that way.

I'm going to prescribe some sleeping tablets, just to get you through the first few days.

Trackman Trackman Trackman Trackman Trackman Track

The metal stairs rattle and I hear footsteps coming down from the ground floor. I make myself look busy at the counter.

I chuck the magazine underneath me where all the carrier bags are kept and pull the top of the till open. I pretend to examine the till roll, even though I saw Martha changing it earlier on.

It gets a wee pink line running through it when it's about to run out. To change it, you just go like this.

I glance up and slam the till shut again. No need to feign work. It's not Laura. It's her. My dream girl.

She looks over at me and smiles as we make eye contact. I've been so busy thinking about the MP3 player, I've forgotten she might be in today.

I watch her as she heads towards the magazines. She's wearing a customised Ramones t-shirt and has her leather jacket hung over the strap of her shoulder bag. The neck and the sleeves have been ripped out of the t-shirt. It hangs down over her shoulder and shows her red bra strap. Her skin looks so fucking smooth, like the top of tablet. Like the MP3 player.

I wanna be sedated.

I glance down at myself. I look a right fucking state. I threw on yesterday's clothes when I got up this morning. They looked fine in the dinginess of my room. It was only when I got to work and saw myself under the strip lighting that I realised what a mess I was. I'm surprised Laura didn't send me home to get changed. That rip I tore in my cords falling up the stairs last night is worse than I thought it was.

Going for the grunge look, Davie boy? Ryan said when he started his shift at nine.

Oh well, not much I can do now. I'm not Superman, can't just rush into the bogs and change my outfit. She looks pretty grungy herself today, maybe it's a sign I should go and speak to her. There's a still a wee bit of that magic feeling from last night running through me. I'm not quite Adam yet, there's still a trace of He-Man about me.

I run a hand through my hair. Take a deep breath.

And another one.

For luck.

 I step out from behind the safety of the counter. No time to stop and think. Just walk. One arm, one leg. Don't chicken out.

'Hey.'

 I nod at my girl and she looks up at me. Fuck, has she forgotten our conversation from last week?

Okay, Davie. Just edge away quietly. Then you can hit your head against the wall somewhere out of sight.

Then...

'Hey yourself,' she replies.

'So, how's it going?' I ask, and flick through the copies of *Uncut* magazine as if I'm looking for something. Yeah, just straightening out the magazines here. It's what I do to keep the shop running smoothly. Be cool. Think Fonz. Think Fonz.

Her eyes are darkened with kohl again, a sweep of green glitter above her lashes. She smells nice, sweet: like those candy necklaces you used to get in ten-pence mix-ups. I breathe in the smell and hold my breath. She obliterates all traces of the B.O. Problem Man. I take another breath.

Lilac wine.

'Fine, I guess. How's you?' she says.

'Aye, no bad thanks, you?'

Shit. I already asked that.

'I'm Astrid, by the way.'

She holds out her arm and shakes my hand. Result! Name and touching all in one go. Her fingers are smooth like the cream on the top of a milk bottle. I'm the blue-tit who wants to peck through the foil lid and get a taste. She'd be like strawberry milkshake, or... or Angel Delight.

Fuck sake, Davie, stop getting carried away and

concentrate on the conversation.

My palms are sweaty, and I try to wipe them on the back of my cords without her seeing.

'Cool name,' I say, 'it's unusual. But in a good way, eh?'

'Do you think so?' She screws up her nose. 'It's after that, um, German girl. You know, the one the Beatles met in Hamburg?'

'Eh, not sure.'

She laughs at me and I feel my face go red.

'What's so funny?' I ask.

'Sorry, you just looked so serious there, like you were really concentrating. She was the girl they met in Germany. She helped style them you know, like, cut their hair, took photos of them.'

'Oh yeah, I know who you mean now.'

Fuck, why am I such an idiot? Of course I know who she means. She must be wondering why they hired me when I obviously know nothing about music. It's just having her here. In front of me. She's making my mind go tongue-tied. My stomach is doing backflips.

'Yeah, so what can I say? My parents really love the Beatles.'

She shrugs her shoulders and her t-shirt slips down even further. Her collar bone protrudes against skin and more of her bra strap is on show. I can feel my cock starting to come alive and I look away.

'That's not so bad, my folks named me after a Kinks song. My name's David Watts.'

'No way, honestly?'

'Aye, not that they had any clue. They only discovered it afterwards. When people kept asking them if they were Kinks fans.'

'That's so funny.'

'Aye, and then they listened to the song and expected me

to be like my namesake, but we're opposite ends of the spectrum, eh?'

I prefer the Amstrad, I joke to myself. I don't say it out loud. If Alfie was here he'd get it, but I don't want her to know I'm such a geek.

She smiles at me, revealing that sexy-as-fuck gap between her teeth. I still can't get over how many dirty thoughts that dental disfiguration can cause.

Control yourself, Davie.

We stand in silence.

Trackman Trackman Trackman Trackman Trackman Track

'I prefer Davie to David though.'

'Sorry, I called you David before. I still like your watch though.'

'That's cool, thanks.'

I play with my watch, twisting it around my wrist. My feet rise off the floor and I'm floating. She still likes my watch.

'Cool, so where are you from?' I ask.

Mental note to self: stop saying the word cool. It's not cool.

'New York.'

'Wow, New York. Cool.'

Fuck sake, Davie.

She says the name in such a great way. Yoik. Nu. Yoik. Nu. Yoik.

'Have you been?' she asks.

'No, but I've seen it in, like, films and... eh... *Friends* and that. I'd love to go. It looks co... amazing.'

I'm not so much blue-tit now as just tit. But for some reason she reaches out and touches me on the shoulder.

'Yeah, I like it. It's funny how you don't realise until you leave.'

'So what brings you to Edinburgh?'

I'm slightly thrown off course by the shoulder-squeezing

incident. I can feel her hand still on me, even when she's taken it away. Like a pulse: the shadow of her hand beating.

'I'm at university,' she replies.

'Okay, what are you doing there?'

'Um, History and Philosophy. I'm really loving it. It's just so beautiful here. All the architecture and history, it's amazing.'

'Aye, it's a great city.'

My confidence starts to slip. What on earth possessed me to come out and talk to her like this? She's far too smart for a dumb-fuck like me.

'Anyway, talking of uni, I'd better get going.'

She grabs my wrist and twists the watch round so she can see the time.

'I've got a class in, um, twenty minutes.'

'No bother, shall I get that for you?' I nod at the magazine she's got in her hand. I don't want this to end. Volts are running up and down my arm from her touch. She's touched me three times now.

She looks down at the magazine, as if she's forgotten it was there. Fuck, maybe she was just reading it and now it's like I'm forcing her to buy it.

'Only if you want to buy it, I mean.' I say.

'I do.'

We walk over to the counter and she smiles at me as I run the magazine through the till. She's touched me three times and is now smiling at me. I know I'm a dumb-fuck but that's a good sign, right?

Trackman Trackman Trackman Trackman Trackman Track

I can feel the final traces of the MP3 player's zhhhmmm running through me. It makes me brave, gives me power.

Fuck it.

Deep breath.

Dive in.

'Em... if you ever need anyone to show you around, then feel free,' I say as Astrid turns to leave.

'Feel free to what?' She rolls up the magazine and slips it in her bag.

Shit. That was awful and now she's taking the piss.

'Sorry,' she says, 'I'm teasing you. I don't mean it, it's just a nervous habit I've got.'

Nervous? She's nervous?

'Well, it's just that I know some cool places,' I lie, not really sure what I'm trying to say now.

'That sounds great. I go to the same places all the time. It would be nice to see somewhere new, huh?'

'Aye, cool.'

'So maybe you could, like, give me your cell number?'

My brain goes into overdrive. Words crash about inside my head and I try to grab onto a few: form a sentence.

'So?' She looks up at me from under her eyelids. There are tiny flakes of glitter on the tips of her lashes and it sparkles. Dazzles me. She holds her mobile out. Waiting for me to give her my number. She wants my number. My. Number. Mine.

Realisation dawns on me as I pat my pockets down. I only have the MP3 player on me, not my phone.

'My phone's in my locker, and I don't know the number off by heart. I'll just run and get it.'

'No, well, I'll give you mine.'

'Okay, great.'

I wanna be your boyfriend.

I pull the top of the till open again, tear off the end of the receipt roll and hand it to her with a pen. I watch as she scrawls her number down on the scrap of paper.

'Give me a call then, Davie,' she says, as she hands me back the pen and the paper.

I watch her as she heads up the stairs. I should be pinching myself. That didn't fucking just happen, did it? I must have fallen asleep against the counter earlier and that was all a dream sequence.

CRASH!

I'm hit on the shoulder by something, which ricochets off me and across the floor. I know without looking that it's one of those fucking light boxes. I pick it up; it's held together by packing tape. No wonder the magnetic strip can't grip the wall. I try to slot it back in place without upsetting the remaining boxes. At least I know it wasn't a dream. That bang would have woken me up. As I'm pushing the box in, I glance across the shop floor. Martha's staring at me.

Caught in the act. She must have seen the entire thing with Astrid.

Martha sat next to him in the pub. As the night went on they moved towards each other, closer and closer, until their thighs pressed against each other. Then he had his hand on her leg, and he traced circles on her knee.

Ring a ring a roses, a pocket full of posies.

After a few more drinks things went slightly hazy. He remembered going outside to text Lewey, but then she was outside with him and they were kissing. Martha's tongue stud clicked against teeth, his or hers? Her lips were smooth and she tasted of the orange juice she'd been mixing her vodka with. We all fall down.

Davie dropped the orange juice.

A punch hits the inside of my stomach as guilt changes to hatred. I have the sudden urge to hurt Martha. I hate myself for feeling like this, but I can't help it. I like her but she reminds me.

Of.

It's not her fault but she takes me back there without even realising. I know she's still into me, and I know she'd like to help me and look after me and maybe even love me, and I know we'd probably be great together, but every time

95

I think about kissing her I'm back there, and I want to punish her for it. I wave the piece of paper at her and then tuck it inside my pocket. She sticks her tongue out at me, and the tongue stud glints in the light. I give her the finger and turn away. I'm not playing our stupid games today. I have to stop messing with her head like that. I flirt with her and act like I want to kiss her all the time. Maybe I do want to kiss her, but I can't. As soon as I think about kissing her, I have the urge to hurt her. Teasing and hurting her all in the same instant and I hate myself for it.

Maybe the Astrid thing will help? Help me and Martha both to move on. I still can't believe Astrid gave me her number. I take it out and look at it again and I can't help smiling. I would kiss it if I was on my own, but I'm not so I just fold it in half and put it back in my pocket.

As I do so, I feel something buzz against my arse and I jump. It's the MP3 player.

Trackman Trackman Trackman Trackman Trackman Track

I pat the back pocket of my cords. It's been quiet all morning so why start up now? Why didn't I just leave the thing in my locker with the rest of my crap? I'm getting used to carrying it around with me. It seems to have moulded into shape with my body, it fits me.

Martha's still standing over by the chart wall, but she's stopped cleaning. She's holding her yellow duster and is just staring into space. She bites her nails, not paying attention to anything, lost in her own wee world. I feel like such a fucking shit. Why do I do that to her?

As I look at Martha the MP3 player buzzes again. It's stronger this time, more insistent. It's quite a nice feeling, a wee, tingling sensation in my arse cheek. I look away from Martha and then look at her again.

Buzz.

Look away, look at Martha.

Buzz.

Look away, look at Martha.

Buzz.

Look away, look at Martha.

Buzz.

It's found itself a pattern, a rhythm. I twist on the spot, enjoying the control I have over the MP3 player, but not really understanding it. What's so special about Martha?

In a parallel universe, Martha and I are together: boyfriend and girlfriend. Happy.

'Why are you staring at me like that?' Martha asks me from across the shop floor. The shop feels suddenly strange, as if we're the only ones here. The only ones in the whole city.

He asked her if she was going too. She said yes. She smiled at him. Cool, he replied.

'Dunno, I don't study wild animals.'

My dumbass reply acts like an incantation and the shop comes to life again around us both. They must have turned the radio back up, as Oasis blasts out from the speakers.

'Very funny,' Martha replies and chucks a DVD from the chart wall at me. I don't react until it's too late, and the DVD bounces off my head and goes sliding across the vinyl floor. I fall to my knees in mock collapse, as if the DVD was a bullet. It hurts a bit, but nothing major. Martha rushes over to me. I see her facial expression change as she gets closer, from 'Oh my God, I've hurt him' to 'You little shit, I thought I'd hurt you.' She lifts a Doc-Martened foot and pretends to kick me, but I'm on top of my game now and I grab her foot in mid-swing. I'm laughing at her hopping on the spot in front of me when I hear our names being called out.

'What are you two doing?'

Laura's glaring at us from the back of the shop, where she's emerged from the staff door. She nods at the counter where a queue of pissed-off looking customers has formed.

Customers are like fucking zombies: they sneak up slowly and silently without you noticing and then pounce. Eat out your brains.

'Sorry,' I say and let go of Martha's foot. I follow her over to the tills and we both work our way through the line of customers. Laura looks ready to spit and hasn't moved from the staff door. I avoid any form of eye contact in the hope that she'll go away. For once I'm grateful for the long line of customers and try to drag out each transaction with some chit-chat.

In a parallel universe, I've won the employee of the month award and my grinning face hangs in a photo-frame on the wall outside Laura's office.

I'm just serving the last customer, handing over her DVD of *The Shawshank Redemption*, when there's a crash and I'm hit by a falling light box.

8

An End Has a Start

And he forgot about going home straight after work, about his parents going out for dinner, about the promise he'd made to stay in, keep an eye on Lewis.
Davie dropped the orange juice.

ONE OF THE SHITTEST things about working in a shop is all the crappy shift-work. I always said when I was growing up that I'd hate a nine to five job, but lately I've come to dream of it. I'd give anything to have weekends off; it's the weekend shifts that get me down the most.

We're going out on Saturday night. Can you keep an eye on Lewis?

I'm a season ticket holder at Hearts, and I usually get to wangle my weekend shifts so that I can get to the games. Dodging away to the football gives me something to look forward to and I miss it when the season ends.

I hate weekend shifts. They really get me down.

You should come for a drink after work, it's not often you're around on a Saturday.

I dust DVDs and put them back into alphabetical order. One finger, one thumb.

In a parallel universe, I'm heading along Gorgie Road to meet Lewey for kick off; past the pubs; past the charity shops; past the wee, greasy-spoon cafes; past the inner-city farm with its goats and rabbits; underneath the railway bridge where the pavement is covered in pigeon shit.

The season ended a few weeks ago and at the time I was happy to see it go. It ended with a dull and meaningless one nil win over Motherwell. Just a few weeks later though, and I'm already starting to dream of next season with that optimism and lack of realism that only football supporters have.

We're from the capital, you're from a shitehole. We're from the capital, you're from a shitehole.

Have you heard of the Heart of Midlothian? Have you seen them in maroon? Have you heard of the Heart of Midlothian? They're the greatest team I know.

You are a weegie, a fucking weegie. You're only happy on giro day. Your maw's a stealer, your paw's a dealer, please don't take my hubcaps away.

We love you jam tarts, oh yes we do, we love you jam tarts, we do.

I'm really missing the football today for some reason. I think it's because of the smell I got from the brewery when I went out for lunch earlier. It made me all nostalgic. I stood on the pavement for a few minutes and just inhaled the creamy, yeasty scent of fermenting hops.

Start by breathing out, then breathe in.

They keep knocking the breweries down so the smell is disappearing. One idiot even decided to invent some sort of filter to get rid of the smell from the breweries that are left. Taking the essence of the city away. Taking its soul away. I always breathe the scent in right down to my toes when I catch it these days, just in case it's the last time I ever smell it. I hated the smell as a kid; it used to make me feel sick. I love it now though.

Davie hardly saw the games he went to after the funeral. All he could concentrate on was the seat next to him. The empty seat. After his grandpa had died, Lewis filled the gap. But after Lewis there was nobody. A square of cold plastic.

Sometimes Davie would sit for the whole game with his hand on Lewey's seat.

He never went back in there, but sometimes stood outside with his palms flat against the door.

A few times he had to leave before the game was finished. The empty seat was a visual reminder of what was missing. He didn't need reminded. He could feel the empty seat inside him, everywhere he went. He almost never went back. He almost threw his season ticket away and said, Fuck it. He couldn't though. He'd been watching Hearts since he was a kid. His grandpa used to say, You've caught the Hearts bug. At the end of the season Davie renewed his season ticket, but he moved stand. The thought of Lewey's seat being occupied by a stranger was worse than it lying empty.

Stuck here in the basement of the shop on a Saturday afternoon, I even miss the taste of the tea you get at Tynecastle. It's got its own distinct taste, you just can't recreate it anywhere else. The grey liquid that confronts you when you pull the lid off the plastic cup, then you dunk the tea bag a few times and brown currents radiate out from it, like blowing on paint with a straw. The way it washes down the floury grease of the scotch pies. The fat seeping out from the pores on your face.

Fuck sake, I can't believe I'm getting nostalgic for those manky pies. It must be a bad day.

You'll have good days and you'll have bad days. Eventually you'll have more good than bad.

What I really miss is the routine and the distraction of it. The being able to lose yourself for ninety minutes. The way your emotions are decided for you by somebody else. It's easier that way.

Hearts lose, I feel shite.

Hearts win, I feel great.

When a goal goes in, especially if it's against Hibs or the

Old Firm, it's like being in the mosh pit at a gig: no sense of danger, just wild abandonment. It's all heightened too, as everyone gets that hit at exactly the same time. A rush of synchronised adrenaline. You can't beat it.

It's not widely used anymore, but primal scream therapy is an option.

fucksakerefereeyou'refuckingjokingwhatthefuckgetthatfl agdownyou

offsidegettofuckhandballthatwasneverabookingfreekick

It's like I'm taken over by some alien being or poltergeist as soon as I pass through the turnstiles.

fucksakerefereeyou'refuckingjokingwhatthefuckgetthatfl agdownyou

offsidegettofuckhandballthatwasneverabookingfreekick

Some crazy creature which interferes with the connection between brain, mouth, arms and legs.

One finger, one thumb, one arm, one leg, one nod of the head.

My phone buzzes in my pocket: text from Alfie.

if ur in flat cn u bring me a knife sharp 1 frm kitchen

knife, knife, knife, cut it, cut the cord, knife.

Fuck sake, what's he doing?

sorry @ work

I remember why I brought my phone out onto the shop floor, and fish about in my pocket for the scrap of receipt paper.

Astrid's number.

I type it into my phone.

Save it to both phone and sim.

How long should I wait until I call her? Maybe a text would be better. Easier. Less scary than having to actually speak to her. My bravery comes and goes, and right now it's definitely gone. Worn off.

I scroll down the phone book, past Alfie and Allan and

Andy and Angela, keep going down the list until I hit Astrid.

Astrid.

I stare at her number, trying to compose a cool sounding message in my head. The thought of texting her makes my stomach lurch. I put my phone away. Too soon. Too soon. I need to leave it for a couple of days. I don't want to look fucking desperate.

I manage to drag myself through the rest of the shift, check my watch continuously for the last twenty minutes. Wishing my life away.

Five.

Four.

Three.

Two.

One.

Shift over. Home time.

I grab my stuff from the staffroom and head out of the shop, feeling sorry for the people who are left doing the late shift.

The smell from the brewery is still lingering in the air and I follow it. I walk past Haymarket station, and along Dalry onto Gorgie Road. It seems so quiet in this part of the city when there's no football on. No police horses on the pavement flicking their tails and depositing shite. No police in fluorescent vests. No crowd in maroon moving to and from Tynecastle, surging across the road, causing buses and cars to stop for them. Football fans always have the right of way. It's in the Highway Code.

Now it's just handfuls of shoppers, mothers with buggies; folk who would normally stay away from this area on a Saturday are free to roam again for a couple of months.

I feel movement in my jacket pocket.

I'm scared to look at my mobile. What does Alfie want now? A new finger?

But I'm wrong.

It's not my phone, it's the MP3 player. It thumps against my chest like a second heartbeat. My jacket is glowing blue. I look like fucking ET: my chest all lit up like a light bulb.

I stop and read the message scrolling along the LCD screen.

must listen she must listen she must listen she

I hold the headphones up to the side of my face and can hear the James Mason impersonator telling me the same thing.

What the fuck? She must listen, she who?

box phone box phone box phone box phone box phone

I whirl around in a circle and clock the phone box a few yards down the road. As my eyes lock on it, the MP3 player gives one strong vibration in my hand. Mission sighted, captain, and locked on target. What the fuck? What the fuck? What the fuck? How does the MP3 player know there's a phone box here? Does it have GPS or something?

listen she must listen she must listen she must

I walk towards the phone box. There's a lassie sitting cross-legged inside it.

How is it doing this? Is this a joke? I look around, is someone fucking me about?

The lassie must be about fourteen or fifteen. She looks terrible: black make-up smeared down her cheeks and her eyes are all red. At first I think it's just her look, but as I get closer I realise she's crying. The MP3 player buzzes in my hand again.

What? What am I supposed to do?

must listen she must listen she must listen she

No chance, she'll think I'm a freak. I turn to walk away and the MP3 player gives me an electric shock.

Hey, watch it.

must listen she must listen she must listen she

I pull open the door of the phone box. It's fucking stiff and

104

I have to strain to get it open.

'Fuck off, can't you see I'm in here?' the lassie shouts before I have a chance to say anything to her.

'Aye, eh, sorry.'

Nice language for a wee lassie. The door slides slowly shut, so I push it fully closed and head on my way. The MP3 player buzzes continuously in my hand.

MUST LISTEN SHE MUST LISTEN SHE MUST LISTEN

I don't think she wants to.

It gives me another electric shock.

Stop fucking doing that.

I drop it, so it's dangling from the headphones I've slung around my neck. The fleshy bit under my thumb is all red from where it's shocked me. I still can't believe this is happening. It can't be talking to me. I'm way behind the times if this is what technology can do these days.

YOU MUST TRY YOU MUST TRY YOU MUST TRY YOU MUST TRY

Fuck sake, I pull the box back up towards me, any ideas?

Jesus, I'm talking to it now. Is this what happens when you finally lose it?

I can hear the voice from the headphones shouting at me. 'You must try' on repeat, like a self-help tape gone wrong.

I turn round and pull the door of the phone box open again. This time I speak before she has a chance to.

'Eh, would you like to listen to my MP3 player?'

'No, you fucking perv, did I not tell you to leave me alone.'

'Aye, you did, but you look upset, eh? And I thought it might help if...'

'Hey, mate, what are you playing at? You alright, hen? Want us to take care of him for you?'

A couple of lads have been outside one of the pubs having a fag; I didn't realise they were watching me.

'I was only checking to see if she was okay, that's all.'

I back away from the phone box.

'Aye, well, she told you where to go, didn't she?'

Gorgie Road is still pretty busy, despite the lack of football fans heading to and from Tynecastle. How dodgy must I look? I've not got much of a defence either. Why were you harassing an upset school girl? Well, m'lud, my MP3 player told me to. No way, fuck this for a bag of soldiers. I wind the headphones around the MP3 player and stick the whole lot inside my jacket pocket. I get about ten yards along the road when there's the most almighty pain in my chest.

Fucking hell. I'm having a heart attack. I double over and grab onto my knees for support. The MP3 player slips out of my jacket pocket and bounces off the pavement. It's going fucking mental, vibrating against the concrete; I half expect a crater to start forming underneath it.

The voice from the headphones is so loud I can hear it from where they're lying on the ground, the volume has been turned way, way up.

No. I don't want to get beaten up. This is all in my head. I'm imagining this. It's not real.

MUSTLISTENSHEMUSTLISTENSHEMUSTLISTEN

No, I'm going home.

Trackman You are the Trackman You are the Trackman

I'm the Trackman.

I'm the Trackman.

What does that even mean?

Trackman You are the Trackman You are the Track

Something stops me. I've never been anything in my life before and now I'm being told I'm the Trackman. I don't even know what the fuck that means, but I think I can make a difference today. Me. I can make a difference. I can be the Trackman. Fucking hell, anything's got to be better than being fucking Davie Watts.

Okay. I accept. I pick up the player and head back towards the phone box. As I get closer the voice becomes softer and the vibrating slows. I can't be imagining this. It's real. I'm sure it is.

The guys outside the pub have gone back inside. I don't know why I'm risking it, going back to the phone box like this, but something is telling me it's all good. I can help.

The girl is still sitting inside. She's pulled her knees right up to her chest and is hugging them as she buries her face out of sight. She's wearing cut-off jeans with stripey tights on underneath. Her ankles are super skinny: sparrow legs. She looks up as I open the door for the third time, but doesn't say anything as I squat down in front of her on my haunches.

'Are you okay?'

'Do I look okay? Leave me alone.'

'I'm just trying to help, honestly.'

'You can't help.'

'Go and just listen to this MP3 player for a second, and then I'll go. I promise.'

'How come?'

'To be honest I've no idea, but I think it might be good for you if you do.'

'If you're some dodgy peedo, I swear to God I'll scream the place down.'

'I'm not, honestly, look I'll stand out here, I won't be anywhere near you, eh?'

She nods at me, and I hand her the headphones which she puts on. I stand up and push the door closed, hold the MP3 player in my hands. It doesn't do anything.

What the fuck am I doing?

I'm just about to open the door and apologise for being such a dick, when I feel pins and needles in my hands. I squeeze the MP3 player to try and stop the tingling, and the LCD screen lights up. It's playing her a song.

Green Day Good Riddance (Time of Your Life) by Gre
I watch her face through one of the grubby panes of glass.

Her eyes glance up at me. She thinks I'm a twat; she's going to take the headphones off.

I'm wrong. She closes her eyes and leans her head back, resting against the wall underneath the phone. The handset is hanging down and swings in front of her face.

The player is warm in my hands, as if I'm cradling a mug of tea. There's a glow coming from inside the phone box. It's like one of those glow-worm toys that all the lassies used to have in primary school. You squeezed the worm's tummy and its face would glow fluorescent yellow. You had to charge them up by holding them next to a light bulb. When the teacher went out of the room, all the lassies would be up on top of the desks, holding their glow-worms up towards the strip lights.

Sammy Lucas is having the shittest day ever.
I'd been all over trying to find a phone box. It was your fault that Mum had my phone in the first place. A sixty-quid phone bill, all because your stupid parents had decided to move to England.
The door of the phone box was really fucking heavy too, like someone was inside pulling against me. Inside it smelt of piss and beer but I didn't care. I wanted to speak to you.
Sammy Lucas is sitting inside a phone box, crying.
I put my coins in, but at first they came right through, and I was, like, for fuck sake, the phone's broken. But then I did that trick you taught me on the school vending machines, where you hold the coin at an angle and then sort of flick it into the slot.
Brrr Brrr
Brrr Brrr
Brrr Brrr
Brrr Brrr
The ringtone was so retro, like my gran's ancient telephone that you still have to spin the dial on.
Sammy Lucas thinks Craig Devlin is a complete fuckwit.

I wish you hadn't answered.

I hung up on you and hit the phone off the wall. I didn't want to leave the phone box, so I just sat there.

Sammy Lucas has just been dumped.

Then this random wearing a Virgin Megastore t-shirt opened the door, and at first I was all, like, fuck off, but he was kind of hot in a David-Tennant-Dr-Who kind of way, so I let him in.

Sammy Lucas feels so bad she couldn't care less about some weirdo.

He played me our song. The stuttered guitar at the start, like Billie-Joe is struggling to find the right notes, or just struggling to start the song. At first I didn't think I could bear to listen to it, but then his voice kicked in and I was back at the SECC, back at the Green Day concert. I could feel the crowd around me. Billie-Joe was singing about photographs and memories, and it was like you were right there in the phone box with me.

Sammy Lucas is still buzzing from the Green Day concert.

Your hair was all stuck to your face with sweat, and I could smell the stiff, newness of the t-shirt you'd bought at the merch stand. When Billie-Joe started singing that song, you took my hand, and I told you that you were hotter than Billie-Joe, even though it was a lie, and then somehow we were kissing.

I could feel your piercing against my lips. You were right there with me, kissing me in the phone box, and it was like you were kissing me for the first time and kissing me goodbye all at the same time. The lump inside me started to break and melt, and I knew that whoever the stupid bitch was it didn't matter. This was always going to be our song, and whenever you heard it you'd always be reminded of me. You'd have to think of me when you heard it. You wouldn't be able to help yourself.

Sammy Lucas had the time of her life.

The glow disappears and the MP3 player is still. The lassie pushes the door open with her feet, and hands me back the headphones. Her fingernails are chipped with black nail polish and I can't stop staring at them.

What the fuck just happened? I'm all in a daze. I feel really weird. Like I'm not really here. I can't stop staring at her fingernails. I close my eyes and the chipped, black shapes are still there. Floating in front of me. I step from one foot to the other, stamping down on the pavement to check it's still there.

One finger, one thumb, one arm, one leg, one nod of the head.

Solid ground under my feet.

I'm here. I'm awake. Did that really just happen? Did it just play that lassie a song? Fucking hell, I must be going mad, I'm hallucinating.

I pinch myself. Twice. Then once again for luck.

I feel so   fuck, I can't even describe it. Amazing, but like I'm not really here. I can't feel my legs, it's a standing-up-blowjob kind of a feeling. A knee-trembler. I'm ready to collapse but the warmth that's flowing through me is keeping me upright.

'How did you ken?' the lassie asks.

'What?'

'How did you ken to play Green Day? That's our song.'

I look down at the MP3 player lying motionless in my hands.

'I'm the Trackman.'

9

Song 2

He'd meant to text from the pub to say he'd be late, but he couldn't get a signal. He went outside to text, but she followed, distracted him.
Davie dropped the orange juice.

I'M HIDING OUT at the cemetery. I've spent the last hour or so reading to Lewey but I've read enough for today.

Now I'm just sitting with him. I'm not ready to go home. Not yet.

I can't go to Susan's again after being here. Not twice in a row. She'll get suspicious. Think I'm going under again. Make me phone Dr Richmond. Phone Dr Richmond for me.

Davie, it's nothing to be ashamed of.

It doesn't matter how many times I try to tell her. I'm fine. It just gets me down visiting Lewey. There's nothing wrong with that. And it's not like I'm going to stop coming to see him. Just because I'm not skipping out of this place singing Zipadee Do Da, doesn't mean I'm going under again.

You can't treat these visits like an act of penance.

It's a nice evening so I'm happy enough sitting here on the grass. Well, not happy. That's the wrong word. But I'm okay. Adequate.

I'm just. Just. Too many justs right now.

I've stayed later than I planned to, but there's nowhere I need to be and nobody is expecting me home. Nobody expects me home anymore.

I'll be back after work, aye, I promise.

Even though it's getting on a bit, it's still light and the breeze is warm as it rustles the trees. A collective sigh. I can hear the magpies calling to each other and I feel like I'm in the middle of the country rather than the city.

I want to lie back and close my eyes, let the grass and clover and moss grow up over me, cover me. Become part of the earth. I want to be sucked up.

It would be easy enough to freak yourself out, sitting alone in a graveyard like this. All it takes is one rabbit darting by your line of vision, one strong gust of wind lifting the wind-chimes, a blackbird flying too close, the tree branches creaking.

It's easy to let your imagination dream up all sorts. The spirits of the un-dead. A magic MP3 player.

Fuck sake, Davie. I rein myself back in. Back to the real world. The world where the MP3 player is a normal MP3 player and didn't play a song by itself to some random lassie in a phone box.

I couldn't sleep last night for thinking about it. I played the phone box scene over and over in my head. Every single detail of it.

Alfie had been out, so I had the flat to myself. Just me and my thoughts. The phone box scene playing on a loop.

I'm starting to doubt that anything weird happened at all. I just imagined it.

What you got there?

It's a soldering iron, Davie boy. It's magic, much more efficient than the straighteners I've been using, eh? They just weren't getting the job done, even when I cranked the heat up full blast.

There's only room for one nutjob in the flat.

One of us has to keep a grip on reality so that when the flat catches fire, I'll be alert enough to drag Alfie and his soldering-iron to safety. If I believe in magic MP3 players then I've obviously been living with him for far too long.

Exactly, Davie boy, exactly. I knew there was a reason I moved in with you.

I stare at Lewey's name and run my fingers along the indentations of the lettering on the stone. Trace his name, his date of birth. Much Loved.

'At the time it was like magic, eh? Like the MP3 player came alive and chose a song for the lassie. I was buzzing from it.'

My face goes warm as I tell Lewey what happened and I can't even bring myself to keep eye contact with the stone anymore. I glance away and pull up clumps of grass as I tell him what happened. Saying it out loud makes it sound so ridiculous. I'm such a fucking tit.

Basket case.

'The windows in the telephone box were manky, and I couldn't see what she was up to when the door was shut over. She probably did it all herself. She was the mentalist not me. Your big brother's losing the plot, eh, Lew? Would rather pretend his MP3's magic, than admit he can't work the thing.'

I begin to pull thorns off the rose bush in front of Lewis's headstone. They peel off like stickers, leaving behind a discoloured outline on the stem. I line them up on the back of my hand like dinosaur armour, then ping them away one by one, firing them off onto the path.

The truth inside my head is too scary to admit. Much worse than what I've already said out loud to Lewis. Big brother would rather pretend that his MP3 player is magic, than admit that he's trying to reach out and grab onto something which might distract him from the ache.

Which.

Won't.

Go.

Away.

Davie held a finger up to his mouth, ssshhh, then pressed two buttons down on the cassette player: Record and Play together. He held up his hand and began to count down using his fingers, whispering the numbers.

5, 4, 3…

Before he made it to two, he glanced over at Lewis. Eye contact and everything was blown. They both spluttered and burst out laughing. Davie pressed the Pause button.

Stop looking at me like that, Lew.

Like what?

Making me laugh.

The counting's stupid though.

That's what you're supposed to do on radio shows, like on Wayne's World.

Okay, sorry, take two.

I won't count down, I'll just press Pause, okay?

Davie released the Pause button and the tape started rolling again. Lewis picked up the small microphone they had plugged into the cassette player; it was still wound up and as he untangled it, he tugged the cassette player over.

Lewey!

Pause.

Take three.

Pause release.

Dahdadahdahhhh, Welcome to Radio Watts, I'm Lewis and this is my sidekick…

Lewis held the microphone up and Davie moved in so their heads were touching.

… Davie.

Today is the twenty-sixth of December…

… Boxing Day. Nineteen ninety nine!

Silence.

Why's it called Boxing Day?

I don't know, all the boxes lying around I think.

Oh, okay.

Pause.

Take four.

Pause release.

Today is Boxing Day and today we're going to play you some great songs and tell you what's happening and do some charts and that.

So, Lewey, what was your best Christmas present?

Well, I think it was my Diver Dan and my dinosaur sticker book and... what? What are you whispering?

Pause.

Take five.

Pause release.

What about the tape player?

Oh yeah, my best Christmas present was this tape recorder. What about you, Davie?

Boys, lunch is ready.

Mum!

Mum, we're taping, sshhh, you're wrecking it.

You can do that after lunch. Come down. Granny Watts has come all this way to see you both.

Pause.

'See you later, heartbreaker,' I say as I get up and pat the headstone.

I need to get home, away from here. Put on the TV, or some music, or maybe both. People who visited John Lennon say that he used to have the radio and the TV and music on, all at the same time. Not very good in today's age of global warming, but great for distracting you.

I stand still and concentrate on hearing Lewey's reply.

I'm a wild crocodile.

It's louder than normal, almost as if he's standing right next to me. I turn quickly in the hope of catching him but he's too fast for me. I even look behind the nearest tree in case he's hiding there from me, crouched down, giggling with his hand over his mouth.

Take six.

No Pause release though, Lewis is on permanent Pause now.

Stop.

In a parallel universe, me and Lewey are out enjoying the summer evening, playing football at the park and getting a Luca's ice-cream on the way home.

I wander back towards the headstone to pick up the book and my bag, when I feel something move in my pocket. I pull out the MP3 player. What's going on with this thing? With me? I'm fucking losing the plot.

'This is it, Lewey.'

I hold the player up.

'Want a shot?'

I place the headphones around the headstone and hold the player in my hands.

Come on, then, let's see what you play for him? For my brother.

The player stays still.

Play Lewis a song.

Play him a fucking song.

Come on you fucker! Prove to me that I'm not totally losing it!

A rabbit flinches and takes off across the graveyard and a couple walking hand in hand over in the children's section stop and turn round.

Silence.

Come on. I need to know I'm not going crazy.

'Lewis, help me. This thing is fucking me about. What do I do?'

'Please.'

You're right, I don't deserve help, I didn't help Lewis.

I drop the MP3 player onto the grass.

Fuck you then. Not you, Lewis, this fucking piece of shit MP3 player.

I wind the headphones around the player, shove it deep inside my bag.

A bus passes me as I leave the cemetery but I don't make any attempt to catch it. It sits at the bus stop for ages, willing me to make an effort. Run. Catch me. You know you can if you try. I slow down my pace though. I'm doing what I want to do tonight and I want to walk.

The bus pulls off just before I reach the bus stop and I kick a stone along the pavement as I carry on walking. My bag starts to feel heavy and I run through everything I've got in there. I can only think of the book and the MP3 player.

Fucking MP3 player.

There are no bins around but there's a post box up ahead. I stop and balance my bag on top of the post box and dig out the MP3 player. I pull it out and swing the bag back onto my shoulder. Instantly lighter.

I push the player inside the opening of the post box. I think my hand's stuck. Does that mean my hand belongs to Royal Mail now? Maybe I'll have to phone 999?

Davie ran to the landline in the living room and dialled 999. Later when he thought about it, he couldn't work out why he hadn't just used his mobile. It had been in his pocket the whole time.

I wriggle my hand around until it feels more comfortable and then will myself to open up my fingers.

Let go.

Let go.

Let go.

Just let go of it.

Fucking hell, Davie, drop the thing.

My fingers are locked together, they refuse to open.

Davie went to visit Lewis in the hospital when he broke his arm. The children's ward was full up, so they'd put Lewis in the same ward as all the old men.

The man in the bed next to Lewis had really bad arthritis. Davie couldn't stop staring at his hands. They were gnarled over into a claw. His fingers looked like twigs, knobby and swollen and brown.

His fingers were swollen and grubby, the knuckles all cracked and bruised.

When they brought him a cup of tea and a biscuit he could hardly grip the handle.

Davie and Lewis bent and twisted their own fingers, copying the old man's hands.

Eventually the nurse worked it out and told them off for being so insensitive.

The MP3 player begins to hum very slightly in my hand, the zhhmmm of electricity, or a calm voice trying to talk someone down off a ledge.

My eyes are drawn to some graffiti scrawled on the side of the post box, next to the letter opening. A warning in silver marker pen.

ABANDON HOPE ALL YE WHO ENTER HERE

A glow comes from inside the box and I tug my hand out, bruising my knuckles. The LCD screen has lit up and there's a faint noise coming from the headphones which are still wound round the player.

yet not yet not yet not yet not yet not yet not yet
One more chance.
Why should I?
Why am I talking to it? Like it can speak to me. Fuck, what's wrong with me?
yet not yet not yet not yet not yet not yet not yet

I drop to my knees, lay my head against the letter box. Jesus, what's wrong with me? Why can't I do this?

Why?

Okay, I'll let you away this time, but any more fucking me about and you're gone.

I shove the player inside my pocket and head in the direction of home. It's such a nice evening; I'm wasting it. Princes Street Gardens will be full of people sitting having picnics and drinking carry-outs. I can see Alfie in The Meadows now, strumming one of his new musical instruments, a group of adoring lassies gathered around him, all smoking and drinking, the fucking indie messiah.

I almost text him to see what he's up to, but have a change of heart and delete it mid-text. I'm not really in the mood for making happy chit-chat.

I suppose I could have done something with Astrid if I'd thought about it earlier. No point texting her now, especially the mood I'm in. Up, down, up, down, up, down, up, down. All over the fucking place.

The sun's warm and my back is sticky and moist. Sweat gathers underneath my bag, drips down the small of my back and soaks through my t-shirt.

I stop and take off my jacket and tie it round my waist, then slow my walk down. I'm in no hurry.

As I get nearer to town I pass people in skirts and t-shirts and shorts and vest tops, carrying Frisbees and eating ice-lollies. It doesn't take much to make Scotland bear its peely-wally skin.

The Odeon cinema is ahead of me, the big glass windows covered in film posters.

Davie looked at the cinema tickets as they waited in the queue for popcorn.

What does Odeon mean anyway? It doesn't make sense as a cinema name.

Oscar Deutsch Entertains Our Nation, replied Lewis.

Eh, how did you know that?

Lewis shrugged, just do.

Hey, is that not Paul over there? Davie asked.

Lewis looked to where Davie was pointing.

Aye, I think so.

Do you not want to go and say hi?

Nah.

How not?

I just don't okay. Come on, I don't even want popcorn anymore, let's just go into the film.

As I pass by the doors, I get a whiff of popcorn and something jabs me in the thigh. I look down and notice the MP3 player is hanging out of my jacket pocket, about to fall to the ground, making a bid for freedom.

must listen he must listen he must listen he must

I grab it before it crashes to the pavement and it moves around in my hand like a trapped spider.

Is it happening again?

There's a guy leaning against the wall of the Odeon. The MP3 player shudders in confirmation as I look at the guy. He's swaying ever so slightly and keeps glancing up and down the road, checking his watch, playing with his phone. The MP3 player spins faster and faster, a break-dance frenzy on my palm.

MUSTLISTENHEMUSTLISTENHEMUSTLISTEN

Easy, tiger.

As I head towards the guy, the player calms down a bit.

That's more like it.

I walk straight past the guy. Stop trying to control me. The player speeds up again. Even though it's hurting my hand with friction burns, I keep on going, my back to the guy. We're doing this my way.

When I can't take the pain anymore, I stop and spin on the

spot until I'm facing the guy again. The MP3 player slows. Ha, I'm in control.

Okay, this time.

Nope, fooled you. Hey, you wee fucker, no need to shock me.

Fuck, I really am going mad.

Losing your mind.

'Alright?'

I walk towards the guy. He doesn't answer me, just looks straight past me down the street.

I'm about to ask him if he'd like to listen to the MP3 player when I change my mind. That sounds too weird. I fish around in my brain until a light bulb switches on.

'I'm in the music business.'

Technically I am.

'Eh?' The guy's eyes are glazed over and there's a strong smell of booze coming from him.

'I'm doing some research,' I reply. 'Can you listen to a song for me and then let me know what you think of it?'

'Nah, I don't have time. I'm waiting for someone and the film's about to start.' He looks at his watch and then waves two cinema tickets at me.

'It's really short and I promise to stop it if your friend gets here.'

'Nah, I'm no interested.'

'Please, it would really help me out.'

'Look, I've not got time.'

'Come on, give me a chance, eh?'

He's folding, he's folding.

'Aye, alright, but be quick, okay?'

Yes, got him.

The guy puts the headphones on and takes the player from me. 'IT'S NO WORKING,' he turns it over in his hands, 'HOW DO YOU SWITCH IT ON?'

'Hang on,' I take the player off him and squeeze it, feel it warm up.

'AYE THAT'S IT NOW,' he gives me the thumbs up and I nod back at him.

Dress by The Wedding Present My Favourite Dress by The Wedding Present My Favourite Dress by The Wedding

He turns away from me as the song starts and leans his head against the wall of the cinema, his arms hang loose at his side. There's a blue tinge surrounding him and I can smell Juicy Fruit chewing gum. The colours whisper around him, changing shade like he's inside a bubble.

I feel like my life is one big David Gedge song at the moment. The empty bed. The mug I've not washed because you used it last. The brush with your hair still in it. The t-shirt you wore to sleep in that I keep under my pillow. The empty chewing gum wrappers I've not put in the bin. All that's left of nine years.

You didn't love me that way anymore. Which way? Fucking clichés. A spiel well rehearsed. I love you but I'm not in love with you, get it? No, I don't fucking get it. There's nobody else, I promise. I just don't think I want to be with you anymore. Think or know? Don't make this harder than it already is.

Three months later we were both grown up enough to meet for a film. You were trying. Trying to show me that you appreciated my efforts. And I had gotten better. I'd stopped the phone calls in the middle of the night, the constant texting, the turning up outside your work. It might have worked if I hadn't bumped into you the day before. Literally. Bump.

You. You and some fuckwit in a Levellers t-shirt. His arm around you, thumb rubbing across your back. Your blue dress. The one I bought you when we went to Greece. That time. You were so smitten you didn't even notice it was me who'd bumped into you. Sorry. You didn't even look at me.

You fucking, cheating whore. You lied to me. You promised. Who do you think you are? Stop it, it's not like that. It certainly looks like that. Don't speak to her like that. I'll fucking have you. You, ushered away onto George Street. Both of us in tears. No text to cancel or apologise, so I turned up at the cinema. It crossed my mind you wouldn't show. But after nine years. I bought the tickets.

Everything was a blur around me. I'd had a couple of drinks before I left the flat. It was like those speeded up CCTV videos, the cars were all yellow and white flashes, stuttered fireworks. The people on fast forward. I was the only fixed point. The North Star.

Then this guy appeared. The only one walking at normal speed. A movie star emerging from the smoke of an explosion. A slightly scruffy movie star. He looked familiar, like he should be in a band. His entrance was how I hoped you would arrive. Blue dress ruffled. Fitted denim jacket from Save the Children keeping your shoulders warm.

David Gedge world. Breaking up. Cheating. Sex with strangers. Love. Pain. Jealousy.

I pushed my face into the wall, to be part of something concrete and solid. To block out the flashing lights and the movement and the chaos. You danced in front of me in that dress. Blue. Spinning so that the skirt lifted slightly but not in a sleazy way. In a playful, naive, Seven Year Itch way. I could smell the Juicy Fruit chewing gum. You liked to eat it with milk because you said it made the flavour better. I never asked you if you meant the milk or the gum. Gedge was doing that thing where he plays the guitar so fast his hand becomes a blur. Just go. Don't think. If you think about your hand moving that fast, you'll lose it. Then the guitar stops. Final line. Wail. What's the fucking point? I knew we couldn't be friends. Not after nine years.

I'm so entranced by the colours that it's only when the guy turns and pushes me backwards that I realise the song's finished. The MP3 player has cooled and stopped moving.

He steps towards me, his finger pointing, poking me in the chest. I put my hands up to protect myself, but we're both joined by the umbilical cord of the headphones.

'Did Suzy put you up to this?' he asks, spraying spit into my face. His forehead is pockmarked from where he's been pushing it against the wall.

'Sorry, I don't know Suzy, any Suzies actually.'

'Just leave me alone, okay.'

He tugs the headphones off his head so forcefully that the player is pulled out of my hands. My glasses slip off and he becomes a blur in front of me. He chucks the whole thing onto the pavement then heads off down Morrison Street. I stoop to pick everything up and realise that he's also chucked his cinema tickets at me, for a film that started over an hour ago. They're all scrunched up and sweaty from where he's been squeezing them inside his hand. There's a rectangular indentation on my palms. It disappears when I rub them together. As I put the MP3 player back in my pocket and look at the balled-up cinema tickets, I'm hit by an ache of loss so intense that the breath catches in my throat and I have to lean against the wall to steady myself.

The Trackman strikes again.

10

Three is a Magic Number

*Davie stumbled and fell backwards down the front steps,
dropping his keys.*
Davie dropped the orange juice.

EVEN THOUGH IT's a shite day, I've still decided to spend my
lunch break out in the Gardens. I had to get out of the
staffroom. The noise was doing my head in.

*Ryan and Mark were playing Pro Evo on the old playsta-
tion when Davie went into the staffroom.*

Fancy a game once I finish kicking Mark's ass?

*Nah, not the now, eh? Need to head out and get some
lunch.*

What's up with... fucking YES! You are shite!

*Ryan stood up and pulled his Virgin t-shirt over his head.
Mark threw his controller at the TV, as the screen showed a
replay of Ryan's goal. Davie took that as his cue to leave.*

Even on a cold day like today, the heat inside that staffroom
is suffocating. The air out here is cool and refreshing; I splash
it on my face and it wakes me and helps me think clearer.

I follow the path downwards into the Gardens, down into
the crater that divides shops from castle. I bet last night the
grass was full of people sitting just chilling out. Today, it's
fucking deserted. Folk scurry past wearing big jackets and
hats like it's November not July.

At least I get a rare choice of which bench to park my arse

on. Usually I end up having to perch on the end of one, next to some couple making out or some dodgy old boy. I head towards the nearest one, dedicated to someone called Elizabeth 'Lizzie' Dickson. Rain drips down the brass plaque, the beads of water obscuring the rest of her dedication.

A Much Loved Son.

I wipe down the seat with the cuff of my jumper.

Fuck it. Sit down. A damp arse isn't going to kill me.

I've got a Boots meal deal which I balance on my lap. It hardly seems worth the fighting past people and the queuing for ten minutes, but it'll do. I peel the cellophane off the triangular packaging and take a bite of my cheese ploughman's. I need to use both hands to stop all the filling from spilling out and a bit of lettuce and a slice of tomato can't be saved. The brown bread is full of bits that get stuck in my teeth as I eat. I unscrew the lid of my smoothie and take a drink. I swirl it around inside my mouth.

Ring a ring a roses.

The thick, pink gloop reminds me of Calpol and I wish I'd just gone for Coke instead. I'd had the bottle in my hand but then I put it down.

Why don't we try some changes to your diet? Cut out caffeine, alcohol, that sort of thing.

My head spins with noise, like the smoothie in my mouth. Thoughts and questions whirlpooling. What was that Obi Wan Kenobi said about millions of voices?

I could do with some fucking silence.

One finger, one thumb, one finger, one thumb.

There's millions of voices talk, talk, talking in my head. Is this how it feels when you start to go mad? Or is that when you start listening to the voices?

Or when you start listening to MP3 players?

Trackman Trackman Trackman Trackman Trackman Track

I can't believe that I'm actually starting to think a box can see inside folks' souls. That it can look inside someone and help them with music. How fucked-up does that sound? I must be totally gone.

My poor brain.

How can I not believe what I've seen though? What I've been an eye witness to? It wasn't even like I'd forgotten to stick my specs on or something. I saw it.

I helped people.

The lassie in the phone box was in a bad place and I helped her. I know I did. I could feel it. A meaningless little shite like me made a difference to someone's life.

A big drop of rain falls from one of the trees and drips down my neck. Cold and rolling. I hunch my shoulders up and wait for the shudder to go. Someone walking over my grave.

The castle looms above me, rising out of the craggy hillside. Rock juts out from underneath the castle, like the glass cemented on the tops of walls to keep folk from climbing over. The windows are all in darkness, anyone could be looking down at me from inside. Wondering what the fuck some guy is doing sitting in the Gardens, eating lunch in the rain. Maybe I'm already crazy? Maybe it's already too late?

So okay, I helped the girl. But that guy outside the Odeon? He was really shaken up, shell-shocked. He pretty much told me to fuck right off. I didn't make him happy.

Did I?
Maybe I did?

I let the thought fight its way through. Let it speak its piece. It's telling me I did help that guy. That I woke him up to something he'd been hiding from, something he didn't want to accept.

This is the day.

In a parallel universe, I get the MP3 player and I use it on Lewey.

Trackman Trackman Trackman Trackman Trackman Trackm

I can hear the buses above me on Princes Street. The swoosh as they drive through the puddles spraying folk with water. The footsteps of people hurrying to get out of the rain.

Way back these gardens used to be a loch. How much rain would it take to refill the valley? I could sit here and watch the water rise.

Another voice becomes clear and jostles for attention. I'm reluctant to let this one speak. Been trying to keep him out of the way, but he shouts out the names anyway: Bruce Wayne, Peter Parker, Clark Kent.

Surely now I am going fucking mental? Superheroes are fictional. Not. Real. And even if they did exist, why me?

Easy. Normal every day guy becomes superhero. Your friendly, local, neighbourhood Trackman.

That voice answered far too quickly for my liking.

Trackman Trackman Trackman Trackman Trackman Trackm

What am I if not a normal, everyday guy?

Average joe.

Geek.

Loser.

Waste of fucking space.

The falling rain has trapped the perfume from the flowerbeds around me. It sinks to the ground instead of rising. I'm sitting in a giant bowl of pot pourri. It's making me hallucinate.

My descent into madness.

One finger, one thumb, one finger, one arm, one finger, one finger, one finger.

I shake my head and try to mix up all the thoughts like a magic eight ball. Shake it up and allow one thought to rise to the surface. One thought only. Let's make it a good one.

Don't count on it.

As I'm waiting for it, I finish off my salt and vinegar crisps. I tip the rustling bag to my mouth and let the crumbs fall in.

Reply hazy, try again.

I chuck all my rubbish in the metal bin next to the bench, stand up and brush myself down. As I head towards the exit, a squirrel and a pigeon face off for the crumbs.

Most likely.

Trackman Trackman Trackman Trackman Trackman Trackm

I climb the hill that leads out of the gardens, depressurising my head as I do so. The air is lighter up here on Princes Street. The real world.

Signs point to yes.

I swing the black gate open and am about to step out onto the pavement when the magic eight ball chooses a thought.

As I see it, yes.

Three is a magic number.

What the fuck does that mean?

I stop and lean on the gate. Wait for the voice in my head to elaborate.

Three is a magic number.

If the MP3 player does it one more time, then you can believe it. Once can be ignored. Twice is a coincidence. Three...

Trackman Trackman Trackman Trackman Trackman Trackm

Okay, you heard the man, I pat my jacket pocket.

Three is the magic number.

'David, what have you been doing?'

Laura stops me outside her office as I'm about to head back onto the shop floor.

'Eh, I was on lunch, but I'm not late back.'

I glance at my watch. Okay, I am slightly late back.

'I just mean you're soaking, go and dry your hair off or

something before you show yourself in front of customers.'

I run a hand through my hair and shake my head like a dog. Water runs down my face and sprays onto the walls around me. Drips run down the 'employee of the month' photo and makes Donald from Specialist Music look like he's crying.

'Sorry, I didn't realise I was so wet.'

I head back along the corridor and down the steps to the staff toilets, check myself out in the cracked mirror. My hair is sticking to my face and beads of water drip off the end of my nose. Tree blossom sticks to me like I'm some sort of walking mosaic.

The pink petals stuck to his gym kit and his pencil case and his jotters like confetti.

I wipe my glasses on my jumper and try to dry the wet patches on my clothes with toilet paper. It disintegrates in my hand and leaves white specks of tissue all over my t-shirt. I turn round and glance back over my shoulder into the mirror. There are two wet stripes running across my arse from the bench I was sitting on. I turn the hand dryer on and stick my head underneath it. It's not powerful enough to dry my hands but it burns my scalp all the same. I balance one foot on the urinals and aim my backside at the dryer in an attempt to dry my arse.

'You'll have to do,' I tell my reflection and head out onto the shop floor.

'Go swimming at lunchtime?' Martha asks me as I join her behind the counter. I can tell she's just been standing here waiting for me to come out so she can say that.

'Aye, aye, very good.'

'Sorry, I couldn't help it. You should have said you were heading out, you could have taken my brolly.'

'I'd have looked a right wanker walking around with that giant sunflower thing of yours.'

'Aye, okay, so it's not very manly, but it's not as if you look brilliant now is it?'

'Do I really look that bad?'

I look down at myself and see that a small puddle has collected at my feet.

'Nah, you're fine.'

'I didn't realise how wet I was, it's that sort of rain where you're soaked before you realise how heavy it is.'

'You should have heard Laura, it was so funny.'

'How? What did she say?'

'She came out to tell me you'd be late back from lunch, then was going on about how you looked like a drowned rat and were going to scare away half the customers.'

'Half the customers look like drowned rats themselves. I'm projecting an image of sameness to make them feel more at ease.'

'Cool, I'll tell Laura that the next time she comes past. Anyway you'll dry off in no time with this shite air conditioning.'

'Good thinking, Batman, I'll go and stand under one of the vents for ten minutes.'

I head across the shop floor to where the air conditioning is firing out hot air rather than cold. There's a wet trail leading from the counter to where I'm standing. My jeans are baggy so it's not so much footprints, but a trail like I've dragged myself Quasimodo style. Ryan comes over and stands one of those yellow 'wet floor' signs next to me.

'Aye, very good.'

He heads over to Games and I watch Martha leave the counter and go chat to him.

The hot air buffets against me and my t-shirt fills with air, Michelin Man.

There's lots of customers milling about for a weekday afternoon, but nobody's buying anything.

Shelter from the storm.

It doesn't take long before the PVC flooring is covered in rain and dirt.

In-store radio is blaring out tune after tune. The Kaiser Chiefs followed by R.E.M. followed by Franz Ferdinand followed by Blur. Instead of zoning it out, I let the songs in. Chase away the voices and appear normal.

I'm still damp, but I'd better go do some work. There's a stack of porn DVDs sitting on a shelf under the counter which need filed away. They've been sitting there for a day or two while we all laughed at the shitty titles.

Shaving Ryan's Privates.
Ally McSqueal
Pulp Friction

I sort them into a rough alphabetical order and pile them on my forearms, holding them steady with my chin. The porn shelf is over in the far corner of the shop by the lift. I've never worked out if management stuck it there to hide the porn or to hide the people who buy the porn. There's an old boy, Duncan, who likes a bit of the filthy DVDs. He usually asks a female member of staff to show him where it's kept, even though he knows fine well where it is. The lassies all hide when he comes in, but I'll chat away to him. Old boys still have to get their jollies somehow.

I'm starting to file it away, along with collecting the empty boxes that the disks have been nicked out of, when the lift pings. The doors open and a guy steps out. He's wearing a knee-length leather jacket which comes down to the top of his Doc Marten boots. He has long hair, going slightly grey. It hangs out from under a beanie hat with 'Metallica' embroidered on it. Drops of water have collected on the wool of his hat, like pearls. He walks over to the posters and starts flicking through them.

Clack. Clack. Clack. Clack.

The plastic cases hit off each other, while movies, models and music scroll past.

I turn back to the porn and feel a buzz against my arse. I look down. I'm not getting turned on by *Hot and Heavy, Six* am I? And if I am, what's wrong with me?

My trousers buzz again and I dump the pile of DVD boxes that I'm holding and take the MP3 player out of my pocket. My heart is beating like mad and I'm scared to look at the player. Scared to find out either way. I'm either a superhero or I'm crazy. Which one do I want to be? Which one is the least fucked-up?

Trackman Trackman Trackman Trackman Trackman Trackm

I tap the guy at the posters on the shoulder, and he turns to face me. He's already got earphones stuck in either ear, but he takes them out as I hand him the headphones.

Rain by Guns n' Roses November Rain by Guns n' Roses November Rain by Guns 'n' Roses November Rain b

You're having a fucking laugh. I'm at work, Laura is already pissed off at me, and this guy gets a fucking nine-minute epic.

The player burns my hands and I want to let go, but it's stuck to me. I squeeze it tighter to try and dull the ache.

As the song plays, the beads of water on the guy's hat change colour. They flicker through the spectrum like a rainbow.

Red, pink, purple, blue, green.

He continues to scan through the posters as he listens. The pictures start to swell up and jump out at me like I'm wearing 3D specs. They're grotesque and leering, remind me of that music video Soundgarden did for Black Hole Sun. I can't decide if it's just me who can see it, or if the guy can too. He doesn't act like he does. He's looking beyond the posters to some unseen audience.

Verse 1:   Do you remember when we were kids?
      The first time we heard November Rain.
      And we knew what we wanted to do with our
      lives,
      We ate, slept, lived for the band.
      Out on the road together,
      We shared the same wine, women and drugs.
      Huddled together when our van gave up,
      Shared the same bed just to save a few bucks.

Pre-chorus: And Antelope Carcass was all that we had.
      And all of us said that we'd die for the band.
      That nothing could ever take it away.
      All we needed was to plaaaaaayyyyyyy…

Chorus: Now Antelope Carcass is over.
      Antelope Carcass has lost itself.
      Antelope Carcass dead and decaying.
      Antelope Carcass through.

Verse 2:   Now Eddie's hitched with a couple of kids.
      Scott got promoted, changed his leathers for a
      suit.
      Liam thinks we're getting too old for this shit.
      My writers block got so bad, I said, quit.
      I kicked over the drum kit, in practice one day,
      What's the fucking point? We talk, we don't play.
      Drum kit in pieces, I'm leaving the band.
      Bass and toms abandoned, door slammed.

Pre-chorus: Back when Antelope Carcass was all that we had.
      Remember we said that we'd die for the band.
      What happens when everything's taken away?
      What happened to wanting to plaaaaaayyyyyyy…

Chorus: Antelope Carcass is over.
      Antelope Carcass is lost.

Antelope Carcass dead and decaying.

Antelope Carcass through.

Solo

Bridge: Then something happened that changed me.

A stranger who played me a song.

The song that started us all off,

On that rock 'n' roll road that's so long.

And now Axl says Slash is a cancer.

I don't want us to end up that way.

Who cares if we don't hit the big time.

We'll keep rocking the rest of the day

Pre-chorus: And Antelope Carcass is all that we have

And yeah, we would all still die for the band.

No one can ever take it away.

All we need to do is to plaaaaaayyyyyyy…

Chorus: Antelope Carcass not over.

Antelope Carcass is strong.

Antelope Carcass alive and we're rocking.

Antelope Carcass belongs!

When the song finishes, my legs are wobbly and the images start to fade. The guy lunges at me and at first I think he's going to go mental, like the cinema guy, but he shakes my hand instead. He squeezes it and the pressure eases the pain in my hands. He looks like he's about to say something but instead he turns, his jacket floating out behind him like Dracula and heads back inside the lift.

Three is a magic number.

This one has taken the wind out of me. My legs turn to jelly and I lean against the wall. I feel amazing but knackered. Much better than any porn DVD could make me feel.

I drag myself back to the counter and lean over the silver, metallic surface, use a till to prop myself up.

The voices are shouting over each other.

Now do you believe? Three. Three is. One finger, one thumb. You can't blame me for being sceptical. Trackman Trackman Trackman Trackman. Now do you accept your gift? One finger, one finger, one. Three. Three. Three is. Three is. Why me? Trackman Trackman. Magic number. One arm, one leg. What do I do now? Keep moving, keep moving, keep moving, keep moving. Magic number. Three. I'm not crazy. This is real. I believe. I believe. Magic. Number. Three.

Trackman Trackman Trackman Trackman Trackman Trackm

I rest my forehead on the counter, close my eyes. I think I'm going to pass out. I don't know how long I stand like that for. It feels like I'm awake but asleep at the same time.

'Excuse me? Are you alright?'

I look up and the guy in the leather jacket is back.

'Aye, just a bit wobbly that's all.'

'You've gone a bit white.'

'Have I?'

I rub my hand across my face.

'I just wanted to say thanks, eh?'

The guy hands me a blue carrier bag which has a six-pack of Tennents and a tub of Pringles in it.

'Eh... thanks very much,' I say and take the bag.

'It's not nearly enough, but it's the best I could do on short notice.'

'Cheers.'

'No, thank you.'

The lager is straight from the fridge. I take one of the cans and hold it between my hands. It's sweet and cold. I try to think of something cool to say to the guy and then feel like a total wanker when I come out with:

'The Trackman doesn't need thanks.'

The guy leans forward and I think he's going to bow before me, but he's off again. Up the stairs and out of the shop, his boots rattling the staircase.

My hands sting and I'm a bit dizzy, but I feel fucking great. I could have donated a year's wages to charity and then shagged Jennifer Aniston and I don't think I'd feel this good.

After the last couple of years, I'd take anything. Anything if it makes me feel better.

You know that button on the computer: system restore. It's like time travel. You click a date in bold on your online calendar, and your computer restores everything back to the way it was on that date. I spend all my time wishing I could click that date in bold. Go back and restore everything to the way it was.

Then this fucking box lands in my lap and I'm feeling things I thought had died with Lewis. I thought the nerve endings to joy and pleasure had been cut.

Bullet proof... I wish I was.

That guy thought I was amazing, just because I played him a fucking Guns n' Roses song.

This is an adrenaline buzz. A sex, drugs and rock 'n' roll high. This is like when you hit puberty and you realise what your cock's for.

This is something I want more of.

'You'd better hide those in case Laura catches you on the shop floor with them,' Ryan says as he emerges from the Games department, 'where did you get them anyway?'

'Eh... I helped this guy find a film he's been looking for, he couldn't remember the name of it.'

'Oh aye, what film was it?'

'The Trackman, part three.'

11

I'm a Believer

Fuck it, he said, and rang the doorbell. Nobody answered.
Davie dropped the orange juice.

MY BEDROOM'S IN darkness.

Davie's mum and dad had rented a holiday home in the middle of nowhere. There were no street lights outside the window and when the lights were turned off, it was black inside the room.

Davie woke up in the middle of the night, needing to pee. It was so dark he couldn't move, he was frozen to the sheets.

Fight or flight.

Fright.

His arms and legs wouldn't work. He couldn't move. He could hear Lewis breathing in the other bed, but he couldn't see him. Couldn't even make out a head, a lump under the blankets, nothing.

My bedroom's in darkness but I can still make out shapes. Semi-darkness. As dark as it ever gets in the middle of a city. The streetlights shine in through the thin, cheap curtains, casting shadows and shapes. The rented furniture and the piles of clothes and CDs change form, morph into figures. People watching me. They're not real. Not real. I know they're not real. Blink them away, blink them away.

I glance over at the alarm clock on the bedside table, the

time in red light blinks out from the darkness.

3:41

I've been lying awake for about forty-five minutes now.

Where do the nights of sleep go to when they do not come to me?

When I'd gone to bed a few hours earlier, I'd fallen asleep instantly. Even the racket coming from Alfie's room hadn't kept me up. Then I had one of those dreams. One of those dreams where Lewis is still alive. I have them every now and again. I wake up and have to remind myself that it's just a dream. Just a dream. It's hard to get back to sleep after those dreams.

We were in a house, that I knew was my folks' house, even though it looked nothing like their actual house. Lewis and I were playing the computer, but he kept telling me that he wanted to go into the kitchen. He had to go into the kitchen. The dream me knew that something bad was in there and I kept saying to him no, don't go in there. Stay and play with me. He opened the kitchen door and that was when I woke up. I woke up and my groggy brain and half-closed eyes saw a figure at the end of my bed. I sat up and it merged into a rucksack, hanging off a chair. Sleep and shadows playing their tricks.

I've not been able to get back to sleep. My eyes are tired and heavy and they want to close, but they don't bring sleep.

I know it sounds stupid, but focusing your mind on one thing really does help. It doesn't have to be sheep, it can be anything. The repetitive motion of the counting helps to relax you into sleep.

One finger, one thumb, one arm, one leg, one nod of the head.

Trackman Trackman Trackman Trackman Trackman Trackm

To distract myself from the bad dream, I've been going over what's been happening with the MP3 player; going over it again and again and again and again. The girl in the phone box. The guy at the cinema. The Guns 'n' Roses fan. I can't deny what's happening now. I said to myself in the park: three times. If it happens three times then you have to believe it.

I'm a believer.

I sit up and crawl down to the end of the bed where I can reach my rucksack. I put my hand in to rummage around for the MP3 player, but it's sitting on top of all my crap. The bag is warm around it, like it's been left switched on. I pull it out and lie back down, so I'm the wrong way round in bed. My feet stick out from under the duvet onto the pillows and my head is flat against the mattress. I pull the duvet over my head and rest the MP3 player on my stomach. It goes up and down, up and down, up and down, as I breathe, rising and falling with the movement of my chest.

It's weird and scary and exciting and unbelievable all at the same time. In fact whenever I think of it, adjectives just tumble around in my brain, until a giant FUCK comes out of nowhere and stamps on them all like the foot in *Monty Python*.

It's funny how in the middle of the night your entire point of view changes. Earlier on today all I'd wanted to do was tell people what I'd discovered. I kept going over the conversations in my head. What I would say. How Susan would react. How Alfie would react. I decided that as soon as I got home, I'd tell Alfie what had been happening to me.

Davie heard Alfie's bedroom door open and New Order blared out into the hallway.

Alfie.

Aye? Alfie turned and looked round, as if it could have been anyone shouting on him in his own hallway.

It's me.

Alright, Davie boy, how's it going?

You got a minute? I want to show you something.

For you, anything. Just let me go for a pish first though, eh?

Davie hovered in the hallway. The red bulb in Alfie's room was switched off and the only light was coming from a desk lamp on the floor. It spotlit an ashtray full of half-smoked rollies and Davie could smell weed.

Davie heard the toilet flush and waited for Alfie to emerge.

Davie, what you up to?

You said you'd come and look at something.

So I did, lead the way.

Alfie followed Davie into the living room and put the kettle on while Davie rummaged about for the MP3 player on the sofa. He had definitely left it there; he was sure he had. Davie started to feel a bit funny, uneasy, like it wasn't such a good idea anymore. What if telling someone broke the spell? What if it meant the MP3 player disappeared? Davie didn't want to go back to his nothing, humdrum life. The life where he was no longer the Trackman but just plain old Davie.

Trackman Trackman Trackman Trackman Trackman Trackm

Davie stuck his hand down the back of the couch and rummaged about underneath the cushions. Steam from the kettle was starting to fill the room. Davie pulled out fifty pence and an elastic band before he found the MP3 player.

Hey, I could use that, Alfie said and took the elastic band from Davie. He squeezed it over his hand and wore it around his wrist like a bracelet.

Davie watched Alfie as he leant against the kitchen counter and stirred milk into the mugs of tea. The teaspoon tinged against the side of the mugs and Davie realised that the MP3 player was still. No pulsating energy. No hum of power. Just a plastic box. Dead. Playing dead?

Oh, did you finally get it working? Alfie asked and nodded at the player.

Aye, well sort of. It's a bit strange.

Come on, spit it out.

Davie hesitated. What would Alfie think of him if he told him what was happening?

Well, it's like, almost like it's got a mind of its own. It's kind of hard to explain actually. Just forget about it.

Nah, come on, tell me.

Well it called me the Trackman, and it played this lassie a song. A song that meant something to her.

He knew how daft it sounded when he said it out loud, so he stopped himself, didn't mention the other two people, just the girl. That was enough. He felt sick, like his stomach was empty. Hollow. He shouldn't have tried to tell Alfie, this was wrong. All wrong.

Alfie put down his tea and picked up the player; his hands were covered in oil and dirt and Davie had to grip the sofa to stop from grabbing the player back. Alfie was getting it all dirty. He was covering it in greasy fingerprints.

Alfie put the headphones on and tapped his nails against the player, like a bank robber in an old movie trying to open a safe. The noise grated inside Davie's head. Went right through him. All he could see was the dirt under Alfie's fingernail tap, tap, tapping. Scratching and scraping and tapping.

Davie swallowed down the bile gathering in his throat.

This was wrong. This was wrong. This was wrong.

So you're the Trackman? Alfie said taking off the headphones and putting the MP3 player down on the counter. He picked up his mug of tea, blew on the surface and took a drink. Davie took the opportunity to swipe back the MP3 player. He rubbed it against his t-shirt, wiping away the dirt of someone else's touch.

It sounds pretty fucked-up to me. You're the chosen one or something. Alfie put down his mug and waved his arms up and down in an 'I'm not worthy' salute. Davie smiled back and put the MP3 player in the muffler pocket of his hooded jumper. *Safe now. Safe now. Safe now.*

What are you going to do? Alfie asked.

Davie shrugged his shoulders.

Nothing I suppose. To be honest I was pretty stoned, I probably just imagined it. You know how paranoid I can get.

The room began to spin around him, but he couldn't keep his eyes off the screen.

I could take it into my workshop and mess about with it if you like? Open it up and see what's inside.

Alfie ran a hand through his hair.

Nah, you're alright. I bet it's nothing. Me being an idiot.

Davie felt the MP3 player hiss inside his jumper, warning Alfie off like a cornered snake.

Did you try googling 'Trackman' or anything? Alfie asked.

Aye, nothing. Davie was struck at how easy the lies were coming. Usually he was a shite liar, but this was easy. Natural.

Oh well, worth a shot. I thought maybe, you know, like, in Dr Who, where they find mentions of the Doctor on the internet. It could be part of some world-wide mystery. Bad Wolf!

Davie nodded at him, wondering how he could end this conversation. *Just end it. Now.*

Oh, imagine if it was a time machine, Alfie said.

I think you're getting a bit carried away.

Yeah I know. If it was though, I'd love to go back to the sixties and shag Marianne Faithfull.

I might have known you'd use my powers of good for debased purposes.

Come on, she was gorgeous back then.

Aye I suppose. I don't think it's a time machine though.

I think it's just a fucked-up MP3 player with a fucked-up owner.

Aye, pity.

There was a noise outside and Davie and Alfie both moved towards the window. It was the alkie from next door, locked himself out again. Davie watched as the old boy staggered into the middle of the road and began to shout up at the next along window.

Jean. Jean. Jean! JeAN! JEAN. JEAN!

The MP3 player buzzed inside Davie's jumper, as the old boy's screams began to get more desperate. Davie put his hands across his middle: he didn't want Alfie to see.

Don't reckon Jean's up for his pish tonight, Davie said.

Aye, can't really blame her, although I feel sorry for that old boy.

How's the music coming along?

Oh aye, great, eh? That soldering iron works a treat. I got carried away just melting stuff onto other stuff.

Davie felt a cold sensation against his stomach as Alfie left the room. Freezer burn. The old boy next door had stopped shouting now.

I'm sorry, Davie patted his jumper. I'm sorry, I shouldn't have done that.

Superheroes have a history, a tradition of maintaining their secret identity. I can't break that.

I place my hand on the player as it lies still on my stomach. I'm breathing in stale air under the duvet and I lift it away from my face. The air changes, becomes cool and fresh against my skin.

In. Out. In. Out. In. Out. In. Out.

Why do I have the MP3 player? Why has it chosen me of all people? That's the one thing I am sure of. Alfie was right. It chose me. Chosen. I am chosen.

Maybe it's a chance for me to do a bit of good in the world. Redeem myself for the lives that I've ruined.

A second chance. Second. Chance.

It's kind of ironic that I've been given this chance to help complete strangers, when I couldn't even help my own family.

In a parallel universe, I help Lewey. I help Mum. I help Dad. We're a family.

After the funeral they went back to Susan's house for tea and sandwiches. Davie's mum was still surrounded by friends and relatives. Everywhere she went she leant on someone. His dad was nowhere to be seen, taken off as soon as the cars dropped them at the house. Lewey's school photo was on the mantelpiece; his tie was squint and his hair had been recently cut. His eyes followed Davie wherever he went, like the fucking Mona Lisa. Davie couldn't escape Lewis's eyes. He left the room, went through to the kitchen. Aunt Chrissie was in there, trying to be busy. Can I get you a drink, Davie? A glass of wine or orange juice?

I sit upright. If I can't sleep then I should just get up. Get up and go and do something. I shouldn't lie here, thinking about things I don't want to think about. Going back to places I've tried to shut out.

They talked about him like he wasn't there.

He just needs some time. When you've had a shock like that, the repercussions sometimes take a while to manifest.

Bad dreams, insomnia, flashbacks, panic attacks, depression.

I think we should give him sleeping pills for the first few days. Just to get him through the initial stages.

I push the duvet off me and am hit by the chill of early morning. Keep moving, keep moving, keep moving. No central heating or double glazing in this old flat. The alarm clock tells me it's just after five. I can hear the seagulls outside squawking at each other.

Those fucking seagulls just dive bombed me out there. I'm not trying to steal their fucking babies. What's their problem?

I'm going to phone the council, get someone out here to get rid of the nests. What? Stop laughing at me.

Sorry, it is pretty funny though.

I walk across to the window and pull back the stained beige curtain. My breath steams up the glass before I have a chance to look out properly. I rub the cold pane with my hand; without my specs on, it's just a blur of cars and bins and other people's windows. Something moves out on the street and catches my eye. I grab my specs from where I've left them and look out again. Something's rummaging about down by the bins; someone's left a black bag of rubbish out and I can see it moving. There's the noise of a tin can scraping along the pavement and a fox comes into sight from behind the bin. It walks along the street, front paws prancing like one of those daft, poncey show horses. It's got something in its mouth which I can't make out. It stops. Ears prick. Tail stiffens. Nose sniffs. It looks right at me. The eyes are glassy and flash red, like I'm watching the fox through a night vision camera. Can it see me? The way it's looking at me.

Like it knows something I don't.

Then it's off, running along the pavement and out of sight.

I push the curtain back, grab my damp towel from where it's hanging over my wardrobe door and go for a shower. The flat is silent. As I creep down the hallway, the floorboards creak underneath me. The noise is amplified. Every tiny sound feels so loud. Too loud.

In there even his breathing was too loud.

The toothbrush against my teeth. The flush of the toilet. The hum of the electric shower and the water as it falls off me and hits the marble bathtub I'm standing in.

I turn the dial until the water is really hot.

I hate going in the shower after you, it's like you've got no nerve endings.

I don't anymore.

I wash my hair and myself with some cheapy shampoo and shower gel combo that I got out of Asda. It smells clean and green.

I've got morning cock, so I play with myself as the water rushes over me and the room fills up with steam. I lean against the wall tiles to steady myself. They're cold against my wet skin. I shudder and kick away the mess as I come all over myself and the bottom of the bath. The hair just under my belly is sticky and I use the shower gel again to clean myself.

Once I'm dressed, I make myself some tea and toast. There are no clean knives left so I pick one up from the pile of dirty dishes next to the sink, and wipe it on a dishtowel, before spreading my toast.

Once I'm finished, I sit on the edge of my bed and stare at my feet. What should I do now? I'm not due at work till ten and it's only just before six now. I can hear Alfie snoring through the wall. A deep, nasal inhale followed by a grunty, throaty exhale. I listen to him and count his snores.

One finger. Two thumbs. Three arms. Four legs...

He gets to thirty-four and suddenly stops. I stand up and strain my ears to listen. Has he stopped breathing? Is he dead? I'm just about to go in there and shake him when there's a choking cough and the snoring begins again.

Davie, what are you doing?

My heart is beating fast inside me and the hairs on the back of my neck are standing on end. I grab a shoulder bag, chuck Lewey's book, the MP3 player and a t-shirt for work inside it. My jacket is lying at the front door. I put it on and leave the flat, locking Alfie inside. I can get in a few more chapters for Lewey before work I tell myself, as I jog down the steps, my footsteps echoing around the stairwell.

Keepmovingkeepmovingkeepmovingkeepmoving

I leave the building and jump as a voice behind me speaks.

'Can you spare an old soldier the price of a cup of tea?'

The old boy is slumped in next door's doorway. He's wearing tartan trousers and reeks of piss and stale booze. Jean obviously didn't let him in last night. I rummage in my trouser pocket and find the fifty pence I found in the sofa last night. I bend down and hand it to him.

'God bless you son,' he replies.

I turn and walk towards the bus stop. As I pass the bin, I glance at where the fox had been. All that remains is a shredded bin bag and some scattered rubbish across the pavement. The seagulls are already scavenging and turn their heads at me as I walk past them. Even they don't rate me as a threat.

The streets are deserted and I feel like the last man alive as I stand at the bus stop. The sole survivor of some catastrophe.

It's so quiet. I hear the bus long before it turns the corner and comes into view. It stops in front of me with a steamy hiss and I get on. I glance at the passengers on the bottom deck before I head up the stairs. A guy in a suit is dozing with his head against the bus window, a girl in a tracksuit listens to her iPod.

Davie always sat upstairs on the bus. He liked the way it gave you a different perspective of the city. He'd notice things up on high that he wouldn't normally see, especially in the winter when it was dark out and people left their curtains open and their lights on. Davie liked to look into other people's homes. He liked to see what their rooms looked like, what they were doing, what they were watching on TV. Rooms flashed by like the pictures in a zoetrope, static images becoming film-like. Families merged into one. One perfect family. Not the Watts.

There's an orange glow in the sky and the clouds are purple and pink. The bus turns up a street of old Victorian houses and the jagged rooftops are lit up by sunlight. A row of diamonds against the sky.

We're nearly at the cemetery when the bus stops and I hear the stairs creak as someone comes to join me on the top deck. It's an older guy, looks about my dad's age. He's holding a carrier bag with a plant inside it. Leaves and greenery poke out the top. He makes his way along the bus, using the seats to steady himself and pull him along. He reminds me of a mountaineer scaling some snowy peak: the way he doesn't let go of one seat until he has a firm grip on the next.

My shoulder bag is resting next to my legs and I feel it twitch against my thigh. I open it up and the MP3 player is sitting on top of my red work t-shirt. It's glowing, humming to life as the familiar He Must Listen message scrolls along the LCD screen.

Thank fuck. I could do with helping someone, with getting a pick-me-up.

When I glance up at the man sitting a few seats in front of me, the MP3 player spasms in confirmation. I take it out of the bag and feel its quivering excitement in my hands. I stand up and make my way towards the man. He's staring straight ahead and doesn't notice me as I take the seat immediately behind.

'Excuse me,' I say as I tap him on the shoulder.

He jumps and turns around. His hair and beard are flecked with grey but you only notice it close up because his hair's so fair. He's probably been grey for years but nobody noticed.

'Gosh, I thought I was the only one up here. Didn't even notice you.'

LISTENHEMUSTLISTENHEMUSTLISTENHEMUSTLISTEN

I haven't really thought this far ahead, but on the spur of the moment, I decide to give him my spiel about doing music research. It worked on that guy at the cinema and I can't think of anything else.

'Am I no a bit too long in the tooth for that?'

'Course not, everyone's got an opinion on music. Besides, we need a cross-section to make it a fairer poll.'

'Aye, gies it here then. I'll give it a go.'

He smiles at me and the wrinkles crease up around the edges of his eyes. He's got dirt under his fingernails and soaked into the lines on his hands.

I hand him the headphones. He puts them on and turns away from me to face the front again. His carrier bag lies next to him on the seat. This was easier than I thought it would be. I'm easing into my role as Trackman, as if it's what I was born to do.

I am the Trackman. I. Am. The. Trackman.

I tighten my hands around the player. Make the connection.

Sayer One Man Band by Leo Sayer One Man Band by Leo Sayer One Man Band by Leo Sayer One Man Band by Leo S

The man grips the seat in front of him with both hands. The carrier bag falls to the side and the plant is exposed. I smell toast and fried breakfast and the bus windows begin to steam up.

I'm back in that room we shared when we worked in the Gordon Arms Hotel in Fort William. Ian and Isobel lived in the room opposite us and when your folks came to visit us, we'd have to pull the beds apart and move our stuff around. Make out like it was you and Isobel sharing one room and Ian and me in the other. Your folks didn't believe we should live together before we were married.

You'd be on the breakfast duty and you'd get up so early and put your Leo Sayer records on to wake yourself up. You had that wee record player that I bought you for your birthday. It was a great wee thing, so it was. Paul still uses it now when he's home. The banjo would start up in One Man Band and you'd jump up and down on the beds, singing along, trying to hit all those high notes. If I felt awake I'd get up and jump with you but mostly I'd just lie there and let you bounce me up and down, up and down, on the mattress. The breakfast would be cooking down in the kitchens, I'd smell the coffee and toast and the bacon, but you'd be jumping on the beds like you had all the time in the world to get downstairs. You said it woke you up. You'd never make it through your shift if you didn't wake yourself up first. You in your waitress uniform and me in my jammies. Your ponytail swinging behind you and your cheeks pink. If you jumped high enough you could see over the building opposite the window and get a blue flash of Loch Linnhe. You said it felt like flying. Then the song would end or you'd jump so much that you'd send the needle flying off the record and you'd kiss me and head off to serve the guests their breakfast and I'd lie in bed till you came back up. We lived in that room for almost eight months. Back when we worked in the hotels. Before we got married. Before the boys came along. Before we settled down and got proper jobs. Before you found the lump. Before you got too sick to stand up, let alone jump.

The MP3 player stops and the smell of toast disappears. The man hands me back the headphones and picks up his plant.

'That's an oldie that one,' he says, 'takes me back so it does. You know I've got that record at home somewhere, all scratched from being played too much. That's the first time I've heard that song without jumps in a long time.'

He wipes a circle in the steamed up window and peers out.

'Gosh, that's my stop coming up. I was miles away there.'

He stands up and pushes the bell. As the bus begins to slow down, he makes his way along the deck and down the stairs. I watch him disappear out of sight. The body vanishing from the feet up, until all that's left is the top of his head and the beginnings of a bald spot. Then he's gone.

My hands are hot and sore, but I feel great. I'm buzzing.

Everything's tingling. Every little part of me on fire. I feel like I'm flying.

At the last moment he'd jump, arms outstretched. He could fly.

I love this, this feeling. I love being the Trackman.

12

Boys Don't Cry

He pushed open the letter box and shouted into it.
Lewey. Lewey, let me in.
When nobody answered, he peered through.
Davie dropped the orange juice.

I SIT ON my jacket next to Lewey.

'Sorry, my eyes are hurting, need a wee break.'

I put the book down and look around.

The guy from the bus is in the cemetery too, over in the far corner. I watch him for a few minutes. He's standing next to one of the graves and he's speaking away to it. It's really funny how much chatting goes on in here. I bet some people chat more to their loved ones here than they ever did when they were alive.

It's more sad than funny actually.

The guy straightens up and walks away from the grave. Who's he been visiting? He notices me, and gestures like he's tipping a hat as he follows the path out of the cemetery.

I watch him as he walks past the waiting rooms.

It was just the thought of it, a waiting room. A waiting room at a funeral. Like they were all waiting for Lewey to be ready before the funeral could start, like he was getting changed or something.

The body will see you now, Mr and Mrs Watts.

Davie held his breath and the laugh snorted out of his nose.

I didn't notice on the bus but he walks with a limp, and it takes him a good fifteen minutes or so to disappear out of sight.

I look at my watch: it's almost eight. I take my phone out of my pocket and scroll through the phone book.

Work

I hit call. We're supposed to answer within four rings so as not to keep the customers waiting.

Hanging on the telephone.

Nobody answers for about twenty seconds, and I'm about to hang up when:

'Good morning, Virgin Megastore, Stewart speaking, how can I help?'

'Hey, Stewart, it's Davie here, is Laura about?'

'Alright, Davie. How's it going? Aye, do you want to speak to her?'

'If you don't mind, eh?'

'No bother.'

The phone rings again as Stewart transfers me from the cash room to the manager's office. I hawk up phlegm from the back of my throat, need to sound convincing for Laura.

'Hi, David.'

'Hey, I'm not feeling too great today, been up all night with sickness and diarrhoea.'

I put on my most pathetic sounding voice.

'Okay, have you taken something for it?'

'Eh, aye, I've taken some... Imodium and that. I don't think I'm going to make it in today though.'

I've never pulled such a blatant sickie before. I'm starting to lie like a pro.

'Okay.'

'I can't move for stomach cramps, I think I just need a day in bed.'

'Is everything else okay?'

'Aye, fine, how come?'

'No reason, you just seem distracted these days, I've been a bit concerned.'

'No, I'm fine, eh?'

'Alright, David. I'll hopefully see you tomorrow then.'

'Aye, see you then.'

What the fuck was that about? Distracted? I'm the Trackman. I've got other things to think about, more important things than that place. That guy on the bus for one thing, I'm not going into that shitehole after what happened. I wouldn't be able to work, I can't file DVDs and serve customers after that. I want more. I want more of the Trackman.

Trackman Trackman Trackman Trackman Trackman Trackm

The MP3 player doesn't seem awake, so I pick up the *Potter* book and start reading again. Poor Lewey, if he was reading this himself he would have been finished ages ago. It must be shite for him having to wait for me to get through it.

Distracted? Who the fuck does Laura think she is?

The MP3 player shuffles on my lap. Are you waking up? No, okay, I'll keep reading.

I read until after eleven. Get myself into a wee groove and just go with it. The MP3 player is still quiet. That bus guy must have drained it. It needs a rest. I guess it just depends on how much help the person needs: some must need a bit more power than others. I feel it myself. When a song's playing I can feel the energy flowing out of me, but then I get that hit, that buzz. The tiredness is always cancelled out by the buzz.

I may look like shite and could do with some more sleep, but I feel great. It's like that tired feeling you get in the morning if you've been shagging. You're fucking knackered, but there's a warmth running right the way through you. It's delicious.

I'm almost halfway through the book now. It's pretty

brutal: main characters getting killed all over the place.

Davie walked past Lewey's room on the way to the toilet. The bedroom door was open and Lewey's book lay in the middle of the floor.

The bathroom door was locked so Davie knocked on it.

Lewey, that you?

There was no answer.

Lewey, you taking a dump?

Go away, I'm in here.

Hurry up, I need a pish.

Well, I'm in here.

Well, hurry up.

There was silence.

Davie knocked on the door again.

Lewey, do you want me to pish all over the floor out here?

Davie heard the toilet flush, then the tap was turned on and off. The lock clicked open and Lewis emerged from the bathroom. He pushed past Davie with his head down, not making eye contact.

Davie grabbed him as he went past.

Get off me, Davie.

What's up with you tonight?

Nothing, okay.

Lewey's eyes were red.

What's wrong?

Nothing.

Lewis pulled his arm, but Davie held on.

Tell me.

No.

Why you been crying?

She killed off Sirius, okay. Can I go now?

Eh?

J.K. Rowling killed off my favourite character. Happy now? Lewis pulled his arm away and slammed his bedroom door shut behind him.

He was so sensitive. Made him an easy target.

The MP3 player hums into life, like what I'm thinking about is interesting to him. He wants me to go on: spill my guts about Lewey.

Sorry, I didn't even do that with Dr Richmond, and Christ knows, he tried his best to make me.

I put the headphones on. Maybe he'll speak to me? Come on, Jamesy. Is there something you want to ask me? No need to eavesdrop.

He doesn't respond.

Jamesy has left the building.

How can Jamesy stay so calm after helping that old boy on the bus? I guess he's been there, done that, a million times before. I can't stop thinking about it. Can still feel it running through me. It's addictive. Jamesy, you're addictive.

I shiver, someone walking over my grave.

What do I do with myself now? Wake up, Jamesy, I want to go and play someone a tune.

I could go for a wee wander? See who I meet on the way. He'll have to wake up if I find someone who needs a song.

My phone beeps.

Susan.

ru sure about Oz? Id lk u 2 come wit us x

I'm not even going to reply to that. She knows fine well how I feel about everything.

You promised me, Davie, you looked me in the eye and said you'd come straight home after work.

I can't even look at Mum, so why would I want to go out and visit her in Australia. She sure as hell won't want to see me either.

Jamesy stirs again. You're fucking nosey aren't you? Very interested in my private life.

157

I stand up and pack the book away into my rucksack. That text has ruffled me. I need to move, to be out doing something. I need another hit of Trackman.

One finger, one thumb, one arm, one leg, one nod of the head, keep moving.

I leave the cemetery and just start walking. Only instead of my usual, blinkers-on walk, I pay attention to the folk that pass me. I look at them, try to guess if they're happy or sad. Do you need a song? Do you? I spend my whole life surrounded by other people, but I never take the time out to look at them.

His face kept changing, line by line, page by page.

It's fucking interesting, the facial expressions folk make, even when they're out and about. They talk to themselves, bite their nails, pick their noses, plait their hair. I don't even think they know they're doing it. I never realised how funny we all look. It's like even though we think we're in control of our bodies, it's really our bodies that control us.

There's lots of different things we can try, we'll get you better, don't worry. I've been reading up on music therapy and I think that might work for you.

I don't know if Jamesy could have helped me back then, back when I was seeing Dr Richmond. I think I might have needed a whole album, not just one song. Or one song on repeat, looped over and over and over again. I can't think of any song that would have helped me. I was beyond even the power of music.

What's that, Jamesy? There's nothing as powerful as music. Well, you would say that wouldn't you? I know what you mean though, music is fucking amazing. It can take you places without you having to leave your room. Bring people and places to life in your head.

Five songs which had meant something to Lewis and could never be heard again without stopping Davie in his tracks.

It's so powerful, gets inside you, makes you do all sorts. Not always nice though, it can bring you down, even make you kill.

I think you're right up to a point, Jamesy. I just don't think you could have helped me if you'd met me back then. All that shite about getting it out never worked. I'm better hiding it away in a part of the brain where I never go.

I don't even know what song you would have played to me. I suppose that's the point. You don't choose, you just listen.

Sounds like a fucking catchphrase, doesn't it?

You don't choose, you just listen.

It looks like a Caramac bar.

We should put that on our business cards.

I guess anyone can go and put on a tune that lifts them up. It's the extra boost that you give them, Jamesy, that's what makes it so fucking magic. It's like when you hear a song on the radio which reflects your mood, and it's like the DJ played it just for you. But you do play it just for them, don't you? You know exactly what song to play. It's not even the lyrics that mean something, not all the time. It's the song and what that song means to the person. Where it takes them in their head. How do you do that? It's fucking amazing. You're fucking amazing.

It makes my brain ache to think about it too much. There's, like, what? Twelve notes? But people are still coming up with brand new tunes. And those tunes can make you laugh, make you cry, make you want to kill someone. How the fuck is that possible? I'm telling you, they better make sure they pack a lot of music into those spaceships or those arcs. When the planet goes down the shitter, the folks who are left will need music as much as they need food and water.

Davie unpacked a bag of his clothes. It felt weird moving out of Susan's but he needed his own space. Plus Alfie seemed like a sound guy.

He turned the volume up on the radio. Common People by Pulp.

For the next six or seven minutes, Davie was possessed by Jarvis Cocker. The clothes were thrown aside as he danced like a madman around his new bedroom.

Using a pen as a microphone, he slid around on the floor boards doing that crazy Jarvis style dancing.

He felt amazing, like he was someone else.

It doesn't matter who you are. Everyone has a favourite song. I bet in every single house there's at least one tape, one record, one CD.

Everybody hurts.

I walk past a woman dressed in the full burka. The whole works. Black from head to toe, with just a slit for her eyes, and yet she's still listening to her iPod. I watch the headphone wire as it rises up to her ears from some unseen pocket.

You were the last high.

Everyone is into music.

They let him choose a song for Lewis's funeral. The minister was pretty cool. He told them they could choose anything they wanted. Songs which meant something to Lewis. He said it was different when it was a kid's funeral. Not like when Davie's grandpa died. They wanted to play his favourite hymn, but the organist refused to play it because it was too 'happy' for a funeral. Davie thought that was the biggest load of bullshit he'd ever heard.

It took him ages to decide which song to use. He was hollow; everything that used to hold him up had been eaten away, and it wouldn't take much for it all to collapse inwards. Thinking of a favourite song was hard, because it meant thinking of Lewis. When his cat had died, Davie couldn't look at a photo for ages because it hurt too much. This was his fucking brother and it had only been a couple of days.

He finally built up the courage to go into Lewis's room.

He thought it might help him. Remind him of something. He was scared that he would pick the wrong song, that he wouldn't do Lewis justice. What if in months to come, he heard a song on the radio and was, like, fuck, I should have used that?

In Lewis's bedroom, he walked round and round in a circle. He ran his hand over all the surfaces in the room, trying to feel closer to his brother. Lewis touched this once. His hand touched this. His bookcase, his trainers, his toy koala. Davie ran a hand over the old tape player they used to record themselves on when they were younger. Make up their own radio shows. Radio Watts. He pressed Play to see what Lewis had been listening too, but it wasn't plugged in.

It didn't feel right. The room was different. The police had been in here searching. They'd been respectful, but something had changed. It was a waste of time too, they hadn't found anything. Taken his diaries away though. That was the thing that pissed Davie off the most. Lewis would have hated someone reading his diaries.

I'm not afraid to die.

I'm afraid of staying alive.

Davie only stayed in the room for a few minutes before it started to overwhelm him and he had to leave. It was like one of those Indiana Jones movies where the walls and the ceiling closed in. He never went back in there, but sometimes stood outside with his palms flat against the door.

Between them they managed to choose five songs. Five songs which had meant something to Lewis and could never be heard again without stopping Davie in his tracks.

Man in the Mirror by Michael Jackson.

Everlong by The Foo Fighters.

The Haughs of Cromdale by The Corries.

Run by Snow Patrol.

Everyday by Buddy Holly.

My phone beeps again.

bookin tix 4 oz this wk, let me know x

Leave me alone, Susan. I can't afford to go to Australia. I don't want to go to fucking Australia. Jamesy and I have got stuff to do here, don't we, Jamesy? Let me get through Scotland's lost souls, and then we'll see about heading off somewhere new.

not goin 2 make it

Best cut her off now or she'll keep texting me until she gets an answer.

Oz.

If Mum really wanted me to go out and visit her and Aunty Chrissie and Uncle Mike, how come she's never asked?

Oz.

Davie's dad used to make Oz juice for Davie and Lewey when they were younger. It was a secret recipe, he'd always hide in the utility room where they kept the juice bottles while he made it. He'd emerge a few minutes later with two glasses of Oz juice. It never tasted the same and was always a different colour, but Davie and Lewis loved it. It was only when Davie got older that his dad told him what Oz juice really was: the dregs at the bottom of all the juice bottles mixed together. His dad didn't like things to go to waste.

We're off to see the wizard.

The wizard was a fake. Floated off in his hot-air balloon and left Dorothy behind. Fuck the wizard and fuck Harold Bishop and fuck Australia and fuck Oz.

Sorry, Jamesy. I'm not getting at you. I just get worked up sometimes. I can't help it. Aye, I know. One finger, one thumb, one arm, one. Try what? What other mantra?

Trackman Trackman Trackman Trackman Trackman Trackm

I can't believe what time it is. The day's flown by. Jamesy and I have been wandering. We haven't even stopped for anyone.

We've just been watching people. Watching people, and I've been trying to guess who needs a song and boring Jamesy with my shite. It's easy talking to him about stuff though, he seems to listen. Some things I didn't even have to tell him, it was like he already knew. The day has gone past in a blur.

Maybe this is part of the process. Part of the Trackman training. I've really been paying attention to the folk I've walked by today.

I'm like Luke on Dagobah though. Screw the training, Yoda, I just want to get to the Jedi bit now. I want to feel that buzz again. You're addictive, Jamesy.

It's getting late, so I start to head on home. I've ended up in town, so I wander up The Mound, past the National Library and then down onto Victoria Street.

Nice one, Jamesy. Okay, okay. I'm game if you are.

Which one is it then? Oh aye, I see him.

He doesn't need to spell things out for me anymore. I can feel it.

The lad looks about fifteen. He's sitting on the wall outside the Liquid Rooms, playing with his mobile phone. Above the door of the venue there's a sign up:

TONIGHT – TRAVIS

The lad actually reminds me of the guitarist out of Travis. A bit short, a bit scruffy, a bit out of place. Not the one the lassies would normally go for, but there's something cool about him.

I stop in front of the venue and sit next to him on the wall. There's a mess of torn-up paper at his feet. I catch a glimpse of one of the scraps: **RAVI**.

'Alright?' I say.

He nods at me and edges along the wall.

'How come you're not at the gig?' I ask.

'Those fuckwits wouldn't let me in.' He points at the bouncers.

They're standing at the front of the Liquid Rooms with their backs to us, chatting up whoever is on the box office. One of them's holding a mug of tea.

'How not?'

'They said it's for over eighteens only, and I don't have any ID. Let my pals in though.'

'That's shite.'

'I ken. I've come all the way from Perth for this, and now I'm stuck outside on my own like a right prick. I don't even know where I am, and my pal's dad isn't picking us up till after eleven.'

'That really is shite.'

Poor kid. I'd be pissed off too. Some of the bouncers round here can be total wankers.

Alright, Jamesy, alright. I'm getting there. You keep me hanging on all day and now you're rushing me.

'Do you want to listen to a song, to help cheer you up?' I ask.

'Nah, you're okay, likes.'

The lad edges along the wall a bit more and his eyes dart over to the bouncers. A breeze blows up Victoria Street and picks up the scraps of paper. They swirl around our ankles.

'I'm not being funny or that, just trying to help.'

He's a tricky one. I thought I'd started to get the hang of it, but Jamesy has thrown me a curve ball. Keeping me on my toes.

'It's cool, I'm okay.'

'Come on, I'm in the support band. Let me play you a song?'

'Honestly?'

'Aye, I just came out for some air.'

'What's your band called?'

'Trackman.'

Don't let him know what the actual support band is.
Don't let him know what the actual support band is.
'I've not heard of you.'
'That's why we're the support.'
'Can you not get me into the gig then? That would cheer me up more than a song.'
That's what you think.
'Sorry, my band's not that good.'
The lad looks at me then turns back to his phone. I pass him Jamesy's headphones.
'Come on. If you think it's shite just chuck them back over at me.'
'Aye, alright. It's not like I've got anything else to do.'
'That's the spirit.'
He puts the headphones on, and Jamesy warms up in my hands.
by Travis Happy (recorded live at the Edinburgh Liquid Rooms) by Travis Happy (recorded live at the E
Fucking hell, Jamesy. You're good.
I can smell Lynx deodorant mixed in with sweat and spunk, and there's a purple shimmer around the lad like a heat haze.

Dear Fran,
Remember how for the last few days I've been counting down?
Well, it turned out the countdown was a waste of time. I couldn't believe it. I've been waiting months to finally see you live, and then I get KB'd at the door. They let everyone else in too. That made it even worse, getting KB'd in front of Jools.
Man, it was so shite. Just had to sit outside on the wall while everyone else got to go in. Jools gave me a look, but I just shrugged my shoulders. No point us all missing it.
Ever since I heard my sister listening to you, I've loved you. I'd sit in the hall outside her bedroom door listening, because she

wouldn't let me in her room. If she was out I'd sneak in and listen to you properly; look at the CD cases, at your picture, learn all the words.

I thought you were like me for a while, Franny, and it made me really happy. Then I found out you were married, and I was, like, man; but I didn't stop liking you. I know you get me. When you sing that line in As You Are, I know you understand how I'm feeling. You're the reason I started to write this diary, the reason I'm teaching myself guitar. Nobody knows me better than you, Franny.

Man, I was so upset. I ripped up my ticket and chucked it on the ground, and then I felt even worse because I could have kept it and put it on my wall. Then this guy came along. From far away he looked just like you, all scruffy and skinny. I got a total fright. I thought it was you. Then he got closer and I realised it was just some random, and my heart started to slow down again.

Then in my ear I heard your voice.

'Come on, Edinburgh.'

And the guitars kicked in and you were playing Happy, and I was inside watching you play. I could see you.

I can't hear that song without feeling happy. Sounds dumb, I know. It's like what you said about songs being bookmarks though. That song reminds me of when Jools and I went to Hampden, and Scotland won and at the end they played it. Man, that was such a good night. Jools and I were sat next to this drunk guy who fell over when Scotland scored and couldn't get back up. It was so funny. Then Jools' big brother came and got us in the car afterwards with his girlfriend, and Jools and I sat in the back together all the way home to Perth. I love being with Jools; he makes me feel all funny. Warm and tingly and fuzzy and all sorts. He fancies Chloe and I know I've got no chance with him, but just being around him makes me feel amazing. I'd die if he ever found out; he'd probably never speak to me again. It's just our secret, Fran, okay?

After that guy played me Happy, I got a call from Jools and he was holding his phone up from the gig so I could hear you play. And guess what? It was Happy you were playing. Man, it was so weird. But Jools was thinking of me from the gig and I had the whole car journey home with him to look forward to. He said he'd give me his gig ticket too seeing as I'd ripped mine up, and I almost felt good that I'd been KB'd.

'Cheers, that was great,' the lad says.

As he hands me back the headphones his phone starts to ring and he answers it. I move away and head down the hill into the Grassmarket. Disappear before he talks to his pals and realises what a lot of shite I've been telling him.

The mysterious Trackman.

I like it.

That kid was great. I got a real kick out of helping him. Made me remember what it was like to be a teenager. All that wanking and fancying pretty lassies and being fucked-up and angsty. That kid seemed to have a lot more angst than I ever did though. Wonder what his deal is?

Man, to feel like that all the time again. I know a lot of being a teenager was shite, but the highs were extreme highs. *Teenage kicks.* Back at that age when you believed your dreams would come true. You were going to do something with your life, make a fucking difference. Before reality got a hold of you and ground you down. Fuck, what I wouldn't give to feel like that a bit longer. One Trackman hit isn't enough.

It's gone right to my head.

Man, I'm so wired. I could do anything.

Astrid.

I scroll through the phonebook in my mobile.

hi davie here wonder if u fancy meetin up sumtime

Send.

I start to pick up my walk.

One finger, one thumb, one arm, one leg.

Onefingeronethumbonearmonelegonefingeronethumb

Step.　　　Step.　　Step. Step. Step. Stepstepstep.

I'm running along the cobbles of the Grassmarket like a complete twat. There's groups of folk looking in shop windows, and sitting outside the pubs having a drink and a smoke.

runrunrunrunrunrunrunrunrunrunrunrunrun

They're all a blur as I sprint past. I couldn't give a shit what they think of me. I turn onto King's Stables Road and keep going. I've not run like this for years. I'm out of breath and I've got a stitch but I don't stop. The breeze blows in my face; it makes my eyes water and ruffles my hair. I'm not touching the ground anymore, I'm running on air.

　　　　　　　　　　　　　　　　　　　　sky.

ET on the bikes. Pavement, pavement, pavement,

　　　　runrunrunrunrunrunrunrunrunrunrunrun

　　runrunrunrunrunrunrunrunrunrunrunrunrun

When Davie was in Primary two, he believed he could fly. He would practise all the time when he had the living room to himself. He'd stand on the arm of the sofa, and think really hard about flying. Then he'd go up on his tiptoes and lean forward until he was just about to fall off the sofa. At the last moment he'd jump, arms outstretched. He could fly. Each time he did it, he would make himself stay in the air for a fraction longer than the last time. If he could learn to walk and to ride a bike, he could learn to fly. His goal was to make it to the other side of the room without touching the carpet.

My phone buzzes and I slow down.

runrunrunrunrunrun　　　run　　run　　　　　run

Come.　　　　　　To.　　　　A.　　　　Stop.

I lean forward, hands on my knees and catch my breath.

It's from Astrid.

gd 2 hear frm u, goldfinger on @ movies –
tues @ 8pm, fancy it?

Of course I fancy it.

sounds gd! cu then

13

Goldfinger

The hallway was in darkness and he could hear music playing from upstairs. It sounded like Snow Patrol.
Davie dropped the orange juice.

I'M REALLY NERVOUS despite my new superhero qualities. Did Superman feel like he was going to throw up on his first date with Lois Lane?

Jamesy keeps me company while I wait outside the cinema, although I've already told him he's to keep quiet when Astrid gets here. Okay, none of your funny business tonight, eh? Aye, I know, I know. You insisted on coming along, so it's not my problem if you feel like a gooseberry. I could do with a wee confidence boost actually. Any chance of one before she gets here? Alright, alright, sorry, calm down. I know it's not about giving myself a kick, but I can't help it if that's a side effect, can I?

I'm miles early, so I head up to the box office and buy two tickets. Show Astrid what a gentleman I am. I'm sure it's the kind of trick Alfie would pull. Then I head back to the foyer of the cinema. The double doors slide open three or four times before Jamesy nudges me and I realise that I'm standing too close to the sensor. I head outside and see Astrid heading towards us. She's here. I didn't get stood up.

Fuck, look at her. I never noticed how long her legs were, that skirt she's wearing, Jesus. I'm so nervous I feel like hiding, just ducking out altogether, but those legs... I can't leave those legs.

I look down at myself. Jeans and a t-shirt. One of my best t-shirts, but even so, I still look a bit of a scaff compared to her. I had a shower at least, that's something.

'Hey,' Astrid mouths at me as she waves and heads towards me.

'Alright?' I reply.

'Sorry, am I late? The bus didn't come for ages.'

'Nah, you're fine. We've still got loads of time.'

I look at my watch but don't even take in the time. Try to flash it in her face a bit, tantalise her. Hey, remember that watch you said you liked, I'm wearing it just for you.

Davie, please try not to screw this up. Stop being a tit.

'I hope it's not sold out or anything, it's just a one-off screening.'

'It's cool, I already got us tickets.'

I pull the tickets out of my pocket.

'You shouldn't have,' she hits me on the arm and sort of stamps her foot at the same time.

'Nah, it's fine.'

'Well, I'm getting us snacks then.'

Never buy food at the cinema, Davie boy. I've worked there and I know what goes on. We used to put the tins of cheese sauce through the dishwasher just to save time heating them up.

'After you.'

I follow her through the sliding doors and we head over to the snacks.

'Sweet or salted?' Astrid asks.

'I don't mind.'

'Honestly? Okay, salt then. Back home I always go for butter, but you guys don't seem to do that over here.'

I just don't okay, come on, I don't even want popcorn

anymore, let's just go into the film.

I follow her over to the juice. *Me and my shadow*. She fills a cup with Fanta from the self-serve juice machine.

'Oops, should have put the ice in first, huh?' she says.

She pushes the cup against the lever on the ice machine and juice splashes over the side of the cup as the blocks of ice fall in. She runs her tongue along her fingers, covered in sticky Fanta, and I have to turn away before I get too turned on. I pretend to be interested in the big popcorn machine in the centre of the food court, churning out popcorn. Astrid's scent mixes in with the warm, crunchy smell. I'm hungry and horny.

'Screen number four,' a guy says as he tears the tickets and hands them back to me. I tuck the stubs into my back pocket and we head through to the screen. The adverts have already started but the lights are still on. We climb the stairs and take a seat near the back. Not the actual back row, but nearer the back than the front. Does that mean anything?

She takes her jacket off and puts it on the empty seat next to her.

He imagined slipping his hands inside it and pulling her towards him.

She's wearing a lumberjack shirt and there's a beaded neck-lace round her neck. The beads are like marbles, threaded onto a red ribbon, I follow them from her bare neck as they hang down and rest just above her boobs. I've got a semi and I squirm in my seat trying to hide it and get comfy all at the same time.

Kissin' in the back row of the movies.

'Help yourself, okay?' Astrid says as she puts the juice in her seat cup-holder. I reach over and take a handful of popcorn out of the tub she's holding.

'Cheers.'

'So, how's it going anyway?' she asks.

172

'Not too bad, eh? Just working away. How about you? Up to anything exciting?'

'Well, it was my flatmate's birthday yesterday, so that was fun. Not too much I guess. I had a paper due so I've been in the library most of the week, pretty boring.'

A sliver of popcorn kernel is stuck in my teeth and I try to dislodge it without her noticing. I don't want to smile a big toothy grin at her, with crap stuck between my teeth.

'Oh, I really wanna see this,' Astrid says as a trailer for the new Danny Boyle film comes on.

'Aye, looks good,' I reply.

The cinema is almost half-full and more people come in as the trailers are playing. The smell of nachos wafts along the row towards me, as someone sits across the aisle from me and Astrid. That runny, cheese gloop gives me the boak. Inconsiderate bastard. The smell is so strong, it's drowning out Astrid's scent.

'I love Bond films, huh?' says Astrid.

'Aye, definitely.'

'Especially Sean Connery, he's the best Bond by miles.'

'Totally, he's a bit of a wanker in real life, like, but he's a great James Bond.'

'Aww, what's wrong with him?'

'Ach, I just can't be arsed with all the tax dodging he's up to. Keeps prattling on about the SNP and that but can't be arsed to live in Scotland himself.'

'Ooh, you're getting all political.'

'Aye, that's not a good thing. Let's change the subject, eh?'

'Sure, so who's your favourite Bond girl?'

'Eh, I guess it would have to be Ursula Andress.'

'Obvious, but classic.'

'That's me.'

The chat's coming naturally and I'm starting to relax, have a good time. It feels weird.

You shouldn't feel guilty because you're having fun, because you're laughing. He wouldn't want that.

The lights start to go down and the name of the film flashes up on the screen.

'Good luck,' Astrid whispers in my ear. Her breath coats the side of my face, candy floss clingy and sweet. Fuck, my semi's growing.

Hard on.

I turn my head and try to pick out the bit of popcorn from my teeth. My fingernails are too bitten down though.

Bond appears and shoots the audience, blood runs down the screen and Shirley starts warbling.

'Is this not supposed to be in colour?' Astrid leans across and whispers. I hadn't even noticed. Astrid's hair brushes my ear. I can smell her perfume now and I can hardly process my answer, I'm drowning in candy lipsticks.

'Eh, I'm not sure. Was it maybe originally black and white? I can't think.'

I can't think straight when I'm around her. End up looking like an idiot because I can't get my brain to work. I realise my knee's bouncing up and down. It's a nervous tic, making the seats rock. I lay my jacket over my knees. Stop, Davie, stop.

She made his mind go tongue-tied. His stomach did backflips.

'Um, it was made, when? The sixties, huh?'

'Aye, must be, yeah, it should be in colour then, wonder what's up with it?'

'Maybe it's like *The Wizard of Oz* and it'll suddenly burst into colour.'

'Yeah, with a couple of singing munchkins.'

'You goof!' Astrid hits me on the shoulder.

It's terrifying being this close to her. Great, but terrifying.

We both turn back to look at the screen. Jamesy is trying to get my attention, but I ignore him. Three's a crowd.

The guy in the row in front of us gets up and leaves the cinema. Maybe he's away to complain about the colour? I'm not sure I care all that much, as I'm finding it hard to concentrate on the film. Not with the glorious technicolour sitting next to me. I can still feel where her hair brushed my ear. It's tickly and I want to itch it, but I don't want the feeling to leave me. It's all I can focus on.

'Is that your phone?' Astrid asks.

Jamesy is fucking about in my pocket. He's practically shaking the entire row of seats with his mad vibrations.

'Aye, sorry,' I reply and take Jamesy out of my pocket. I shove him down the side of the chair. Shut it, I'll speak to you later. Watch your namesake for now.

James Bond is fighting someone. We're only ten minutes in and I've lost the plot. Halfway through the fight, the film cuts out and the screen goes blank. A few people look around in confusion.

'Well, that was good, eh?' I say.

'Wonder what's happened?'

'I think that guy in front might have gone to complain about the colour thing.'

'Oh, right.'

We sit in silence for a few minutes before a man in a suit appears and stands at the bottom of the stairs in the centre aisle. He reminds me of Barney Rubble.

'Excuse me, folks, can I have your attention for a second?' he says waving his hand in the air, 'sorry for the interruption, I'm sure you all know that *Goldfinger's* meant to be in colour. It's gold for one thing.'

'Told you,' Astrid slaps my knee, 'man, we're so dumb. The clue's in the title.'

'We're just having a few technical hitches,' the man continues, 'but the guys in the back are working on it. It might take a few minutes, so if anyone wants a refund the folks at the box office will sort you out. I hope you'll stay and enjoy the film though. Thanks, folks.'

'I guess we just wait then, huh?' Astrid says.

'Aye.'

'I think your cell phone's ringing again, I can feel it through the chair.'

'Sorry, it's my MP3 player, I think it's broken.'

I pull Jamesy out of the gap in the seat. He's not impressed at being stuffed down there. Thinks I'm being irresponsible. Helping people is more important than impressing a pretty girl.

I glance around me. It's the guy with the nachos that Jamesy's so interested in. Just go and take his nachos off him, that'll help him more than any song.

Come on, Jamesy, for fuck sake. What am I supposed to say to Astrid? I don't want to freak her out on our first date.

I help myself to some Fanta, sook it up through the straw. The straw Astrid has used. It's almost like we're kissing.

'Man, that's really broken, huh?' Astrid nods at Jamesy.

'Aye, I dropped it the other day, think I knocked something out of place.'

I put Jamesy in my jacket pocket. Give me a break. We had a deal. Okay, I had a deal, but it only works if you play along. I'm not treating you like a game, I'm just asking you to give me a break.

The film doesn't look like coming on anytime soon. Maybe I can give that guy a song and get back to Astrid before it starts again? What could I tell her to get away? You can at least give me an idea, Jamesy, it's you causing all the fucking bother here.

'Oh my God, that's Eddie,' I point at the nachos guy.

As Astrid turns to look at him he drops a blob of fluorescent yellow cheese down his front. He scrapes it off his t-shirt with a nacho and then sticks the whole lot in his mouth.

'The guy with the cheese?'

'Aye, he used to work at Virgin. Not seen him in ages, do you mind if I go and say hello?'

'Sure, no problem.'

I stand but it's against my will. What am I doing? I'm on a date with a gorgeous girl and I'm going to speak to fat Eddie. Jesus. You owe me Jamesy, you fucking owe me.

Astrid stands and I squeeze past her. Just as she sits down again, the film starts up.

'Oh, too late,' Astrid grabs my arm and spins me back round into my seat.

Oh well. No point being pissed off, Jamesy. There's nothing I can do about it. You'll just have to try and be patient.

The film's back at the start again and in colour. Red blood flows down the screen instead of grey.

'Oh, I got a shock off you there, that MP3 player is dangerous.'

'Sorry, it might have been the carpet static.'

'Maybe you've just got an electric touch.'

Fuck. Is she flirting with me? Jamesy's not impressed. He's not really warming to Astrid. I stick him on the empty seat next to me and put my jacket over the top of him. The film's on now, so you'll just have to wait. I'll get him on the way out. I know how Spiderman felt now. With great power.

The film's on for about five minutes when it suddenly switches back into black and white. I peer at the screen over the top of my glasses. It's not just my eyes, is it? People around us are tutting and sighing. The guy in front of us turns and stares at the projection room, giving them the evil eye, as if that's going to help.

'Man, what a joke, huh?' says Astrid.

'I know, I can't believe this.'

Jamesy, will you stop shouting at me. You're ruining

everything. If I go will you shut the fuck up? Okay, okay. I'm going. I'm going.

'Would you mind if I say hello to Eddie now? Sorry, I promise I'll be quick.'

'Oh yeah, cool.'

You owe me big time, Jamesy boy. You're getting it all your own way as usual. I squeeze past her again and her hand brushes my shoulder. Man, she's going to think I'd rather speak to the cheese guy than her. I can feel her eyes watching me as I approach him. I try to hide him from view, so she won't see the blank stare he gives me when I say hello.

'Excuse me,' I say and take the chair next to him. I swivel round so I'm facing him, still trying to block him from Astrid.

'Yeah?'

He clutches his nachos. I can't tell if he's afraid I'm going to steal them or if he's planning on using them as a weapon.

'This is going to sound totally mad, but can you pretend that you know me?'

'Why?'

He pulls the nachos closer towards him. The plastic tray is steamed up with condensation. The smell obliterates all trace of candy lipstick and I really fucking hate this guy. This poor guy. In a bad place and I'm hating him for dragging me away from my date.

'I'm trying to impress that lassie over there.'

I point to Astrid, who's looking over at us. She waves and we both wave back.

'No wonder, she's really hot.'

'Aye, she is, isn't she?'

What the hell am I doing over here with you, when she's sitting there alone? Get on with it, just play the song and go.

'Anyway, so can you put these headphones on and I'll play you a song.'

'Sorry, what? I thought you were pretending to know me?'

'Aye, I am, but this is part of it all. It's all a bit complicated, to be honest. Too long to explain. Basically, it's a new feature of the cinema. If you can name the song, you win a prize.'

'You don't work for the cinema.'

'Aye, well, technically not, but I'm a promoter for this British Film season we're having.'

Jamesy starts to laugh. I never used to be able to lie like this, with such fucking arrogance. I can come up with all sorts of crap these days, right off the top of my head and people buy it. It's all about the delivery.

'But, you just told me you were trying to impress that girl.'

'Aye, I am. We work together. I told her I could get you to win a prize.'

'But, then why did I have to pretend to know you?'

'Look, do you want to try and win a prize or not? If the film starts, it'll be too late.'

'Are you the ones who keep stopping the film, because that's really starting to piss me off.'

Man, you are starting to really piss me off, cheese guy.

'Come on, it's one customer per film.'

'What's the prize?'

'Eh, a goodie bag, with a DVD and that in it, you can collect it at the box office after the film.'

For fuck sake, Jamesy. Seriously? You're interrupting my date with Astrid for this guy?

'Aye, okay. Hand them over.'

Hallefuckinglujah.

I feel a slight tinge of satisfaction, as the guy covers Jamesy's headphones in salty crumbs and salsa. What was that about making sacrifices, Jamesy boy?

Downtown by Petula Clark Downtown by Petula Clark Downtown by Petula Clark Downtown by Petula Clark

'I know this, this one's easy,' the guy says.

His tub of nachos slides off his knee and hits the floor. The cheese sauce splatters across his shoes, but he doesn't even notice. The lights go down and the film starts up, but I'm stuck here until the song finishes. My hands are glued to Jamesy, I don't think I could let go, even if I tried. The guy looks really young as he's sitting there, it's as if his wrinkles have slid down his face and fallen off. It smells like being at the hairdresser's and damp dog all rolled into one.

I know this one. You used to sing it to me when I was a kid. I'd forgotten how you used to do that.

My hands are still dirty from digging the hole. I can see the muck under my fingernails and buried in the lines of my hands like they're an ordnance survey map. I could do with that old nail brush you used to have, you'd scrub it over the Imperial Leather before scraping my hands clean.

Nobody seems to use nail brushes anymore.

The house has been so quiet the last couple of days. I had to get out of there. I kept going back to the kitchen window and looking out at the mound of dirt in the garden.

My last link to you.

His mind's still willing, the vet said, his mind is still willing but his body just can't keep up anymore. I stroked his head and scratched his ears, while the vet did what he had to do. Sam's nose pushed into my hand and he was shaking. Blind and deaf, but somehow he knew something was wrong, that someone else was there. There's still dog hairs all over the sofa, all over the carpet, all over my clothes. I can't bring myself to hoover them up.

You used to sing this to me. Every Saturday before we went up town together on the bus.

I can't believe I'd forgotten that.

I'd wait in the hairdresser's while you got your hair done, then you'd take me to the baker's next door for a custard slice. When I got a bit older, we stopped going. I wanted to be with my friends instead. You'd still sing to me though and even though I'd tell you to shut up, I didn't really mean it. I never got too old for a song from my mum. You must have known that I'd need one today.

'I know it,' he says again as the song finishes, he's not looking at me though.

'Ssshhhh,' the man in front of us turns round.

'Cool,' I say, winding the headphones around Jamesy, 'let them know at the box office after the film, tell them the Trackman sent you.'

I feel like a total shit fooling the guy like that, but I don't think he'll bother going to claim the fake prize. He wasn't even listening to me when I spoke to him. I feel a bit weird, it's not the usual feeling I get from helping someone. It's a bit of an anti-climax, not what I was expecting: like when you go out drinking and instead of having a laugh, you get all maudlin.

'Sorry,' I whisper to Astrid as I join her again.

'Don't worry, we've already seen this bit twice. What were you doing?'

'I'll tell you after, eh?'

I take a drink of Fanta. It's almost empty and the ice rattles in the bottom of the cup. I can hardly keep my eyes open. That guy has taken the wind out of me. I just want to close my eyes.

I wake up just in time to see death by bowler hat. I've missed half the fucking film. Wonder if Astrid noticed I was asleep? Man, she must think I'm such a loser. Fuck sake, I abandon her for the cheese guy and then fall asleep. Some date. I'm blaming you for this, Jamesy.

The film ends and the lights come up. We sit still for a few seconds, that way you do after a film at the cinema.

'Are you not going to say goodbye to your friend?' Astrid asks, as she pulls her jacket on. The cheese guy is kicking nachos off his shoes. I hear them crunching underfoot, as he walks along the row of seats.

'Oh aye, see you Ed,' I shout after him.

He ignores me and heads out of the screen.

'Is he alright?'

'Aye, he's always been a bit funny.'

'Why did you give him your MP3 player?'

'Eh, someone we used to work with is in a band and he wanted to hear them.'

'I thought maybe he'd fixed it.'

'Sorry about that, eh? I've not seen him for ages and he's had a bit of a shite time of it. He got sacked from Virgin.'

Fucking hell, what's wrong with me? I touch my nose to see if it's growing.

'No way, what did he do?'

'He was stealing, he stole some iPods.'

'Wow.'

Change the subject, Davie. Change the fucking subject.

'Yeah, it's a shame really, he had some problems. Anyway, you enjoy the film?'

'Yeah, I mean I've seen it before, but yeah, it was great. Did you?'

'Aye, even in black and white.'

'Man, that was so annoying, huh?'

'I never noticed how dodgy some of that film is before, you'd never get away with it these days.'

'I know, or that fashion. What was that blue, towelling all-in-oner all about?'

'Hey, I've got one of those at home.'

'You're so funny! What about that fight scene at the start?' she squeezes my arm.

'The one we saw three times?'

'Yeah, what was Bond up to there, trying to steal the guy's shoe or something?'

She's laughing and I'm loving it. It's like bubbles popping around my head. Champagne bubbles, making me dizzy and light-headed. She's so cool and so funny and so gorgeous. Fucking hell. And we're taking the piss out of Bond like this. It's the kind of thing Alfie and I do while we're watching DVDs.

'You know, as a modern woman, I shouldn't really like Bond. It's so sexist. I mean, those sisters, what about their poor mother?'

'He probably shagged her too.'

She throws her head back with laughter and I want to kiss her. The way she said modern woman made the blood rush to my cock, and that flash of bare neck when she laughed. Man, I want to kiss her so badly right now.

If only that guy had given me my usual kick up the arse, I'd be doing it. I'd stop her and kiss her, instead of following her like a puppy towards the bus stop. What happened? Why did I not get a buzz? Is this some sort of lesson, Jamesy? Payback or something? I don't appreciate this, you know.

I'm about to ask her if she wants to go for a drink when I yawn instead.

'Oh, you need your bed.'

'It's cool, I'm okay.'

'Come on, I heard you snoring in there. I've got an early class anyway and I've not done the reading for it yet.'

'Aye, no bother.'

My cock starts to droop again. Cold shower.

I wait with her until the bus arrives. Dating is confusing, especially with a girl from a different country. I thought she was flirting with me, but now she's trying to get away. Is she telling the truth about that class or is it an excuse? In *Friends*, they're always dating loads of different people. Maybe I'm just a one-episode date? Destined not to be a recurring character. The one where she dates the weirdo with the MP3 player.

I hear the rumble of the bus and watch it as it comes towards us. Astrid leans in.

She's going to kiss me. We're going to kiss.

She leans in and   hugs me. Her beads press against me, and her smell tickles my nose. I just want to kiss her, press her up against the bus stop and kiss her. Jamesy, where's my super power? That cheese guy should have given me the boost. I should be leaning in, going in for the kill.

'Give me a call, you,' she says and steps onto the bus. I watch as she drops the coins into the tray and then the doors swoosh shut. She's wandering down the bus looking for a seat, as it pulls out and drives away.

Date over.

Man, I feel so shite as I watch the bus disappear round the corner. What's up with me tonight? I'm on such a downer.

You didn't help matters either, Jamesy. You know exactly what I'm talking about. No, get to fuck. I'm done for the night. All I wanted was one night off, well that's me, night off. I'm going home.

Jamesy ignores me as we head back towards the flat. My legs are aching as I climb the stairs and I pull myself up using the banister. Lack of sleep must be catching up with me.

When I reach the flat, our front door is blocked by a massive, paper-maché snake.

Check this out, Davie boy, I made it myself.

What for?

I thought I might apply to art school, they love all that wacky shite.

Fucking Alfie. I lift it up and drag it out of the way, talk about fucking fire hazards. It's covered in glitter which flakes off and sticks to my clothes. I unlock the front door and there's a trail of sparkle leading along the hallway towards Alfie's room.

Follow the glittery road. Follow the glittery road. Follow,

follow, follow, follow, follow the glittery road.

It wasn't fucking emerald for a start.

I follow the trail, but carry on past it towards the bathroom.

Pull the light cord.

Fucking hell.

There's a paddling pool, painted black, hanging over the shower. Another one of Alfie's projects. He must be having a clear out.

I see a paddling pool and I want to paint it black.

Fuck. My heart is beating like mad.

I thought it was a person.

Hanging.

I can hardly hold my cock for a pish, my hands are shaking so much. Man, this night has not turned out how I wanted it to.

I pull at the paddling pool and tear the shower curtain down with it. Fuck. I punch them both over and over and over. One finger, one thumb, one finger, one thumb, one fist, one fist, one fist. Pound them both down into the bath, then lift the lump of plastic and carry it to the front door. I head out onto the landing and chuck the whole lot at the paper-maché snake, before slamming the door shut.

You're not helping, Jamesy. I'm not in the mood, okay. I fling him across my bedroom like a Frisbee, kick my Converse off, and climb into bed fully clothed. Jamesy bounces off the wardrobe and skims along the floorboards. I pull the duvet over my head and press it into my ears so I can't hear him anymore.

14

Mulder and Scully

He shouted to be heard over the music.
Lewey, it's me, LEWEY LEWIS, come on, stop fucking about.
Let me in. I've got something to tell you.
Davie dropped the orange juice.

'YOU LOOK LIKE shite, Davie,' Stewart says as I head into the staffroom.

'Cheers,' I nod and hang my jacket up on one of the pegs.

'Heavy night?'

'Aye.'

Stewart's looking at me like he expects me to go on, tell him all the sordid details. I tap my watch to show him I'm already late, and leave the staffroom. I can't be arsed with this. My date with Astrid gets fucked-up. Jamesy's ignoring me. I'm fucking knackered too, it's like that cheese guy drained all my energy. There's only so much I can take.

'David, can I see you for a second?'

Crap. I knew I should have taken the long way round to the shop floor, instead of thinking that I could sneak past Laura's office without her noticing me. She's half-standing, half-hunched over her desk; must have sprung up from whatever she was doing as soon as she saw me pass. Having a break by the looks of it: there's a half eaten Twix and a mug of coffee sitting in front of her.

She gestures at a chair at the side of her desk as I turn left from the corridor into her office.

'Sorry, Laura, I slept in.'

'It's not just today I want to chat about. Shut the door over, will you.'

Shut the door? That's not a good sign. Laura's always going on about her 'open door' policy of management.

I take the seat next to her desk and wait for her to speak. I'm not really sure what she's going to say. Fair enough, I was late today, but people are allowed to be late once in a while, aren't they? It's not like I do it every week.

'Is everything okay, David?' she asks, sitting back down on her chair.

'Aye.'

'I'm a bit concerned about you. You've been acting out of character the last couple of weeks.'

'How do you mean?'

I start to read the upside down story in the *Metro* lying on Laura's desk. She notices me and folds up the paper, puts it out of sight.

'You must know what I'm talking about?'

'Sorry, I don't.'

'This, David. Your lack of concentration, turning up late for work, phoning in sick. You didn't even bother phoning in on Monday, just didn't turn up.'

'I can't help it if I'm sick, can I? And I didn't get the rota for Monday, I thought I was off.'

'I saw you in town, you didn't look sick to me, and the rota's been up on the wall out there since last Tuesday.'

I don't know what to say to this, so I don't bother replying. Jamesy is awake in my pocket, listening to everything that's going on. One eye open like a sleeping dog. I don't know what she wants me to say. Sorry for missing a couple of shifts at this shithole. Obviously selling DVDs to people is much more important than trying to save someone from sadness. Jamesy sniggers in my pocket. You talking to me again?

The Employee of the Month photo frame is lying in the space where the *Metro* was. Martha's in it now. It's not the best photo of her. Her eyes are half-shut and she's not smiling. I can just imagine her standing out there in the corridor while Laura took the photo, she wouldn't have enjoyed it much. It's a shame she's not smiling, her face always looks so bright when she does that. One of the reasons I find her so attractive.

Ring a ring a roses, a pocket full of posies.

'Is there anything wrong?' Laura asks.

I shake my head.

'I know you've been through a tough time of it the last couple of years.'

What does she know about the last couple of years? She thinks she knows me just because she's read my employee's file. A cv, a couple of old appraisal sheets and a doctor's report; held together with a paperclip and shoved inside a cardboard folder. The lives of everyone in this shop, condensed down to a few sheets of paper and stuck inside that filing cabinet in the corner of her office. All crushed together inside one of the drawers.

'Sorry I'm late, Laura, but I slept in, that's all. I'm fine. I feel great actually. Just didn't get to bed early enough last night.'

She doesn't say anything, just stares at me. I feel like she's Forest Whitaker in *The Last King of Scotland*. Is she about to burst out laughing or is she going to go for me? I hold her stare for as long as I can, but eventually I have to break eye contact. She's trying out some sort of mind trick on me. Trying to bore into my brain for answers.

I wasn't lying when I said I'm alright though. Fair enough, we had a fight last night, but I wouldn't give Jamesy up for anything. I wouldn't give you up, I'm sorry about last night.

This silent treatment is going on for ages. There's a roll of price stickers under Laura's desk. I can see it if I look down at my feet. It must have rolled off and unravelled.

£6.99 £6.99 £6.99 £6.99 £6.99 £6.99
                        £6.99 £6.99 £6.99
                                    £6.99

Jamesy has stopped listening. Bored now. Laura's not happy at me. Cool, I get that. Can we go now?

CAN LAURA PLEASE COME TO THE GROUND FLOOR, LAURA TO THE GROUND FLOOR PLEASE.

Saved by the page.
Laura picks up her phone and calls the ground floor.
'Hi, it's Laura here. What's the matter?'

'Is it that same guy?'

'Huuuuh, okay, give me a minute, I'll be right up.'
She puts the phone down and runs a hand through her hair.
'I'm going to have to go and sort something out, David, so we'll have to cut this short. Just try and sort it out, okay? And come and speak to me if you need to.'
'Aye, no bother.'
'I'm going to have to record this as a verbal warning, okay?'
'Aye, do what you have to do.'
Laura opens her mouth as if she's about to say something, but nothing comes out. We both stand and she opens the door for me. We walk along the corridor in silence until we come to the back staircase. She takes the stairs up to the

ground floor, and I stand at the metal swing door which leads out onto the basement shop floor. That was awkward, but at least Jamesy and I are talking again.

I peer through the porthole window, my palms flat against the cold steel, ready to push the door open.

He never went back in there, but sometimes stood outside with his palms flat against the door.

Martha is serving a customer at the tills, Ryan's talking to someone in the Games department, a couple are browsing the feature films, good old Duncan is over by the porn. My breath steams up the glass window. The shop floor scene disappears. Nobody would notice if I slipped away.

I can't face going out there. My hands refuse to push open the door. I wipe the window and look at them all. It's like a soap. The same shite. Going on. Every. Single. Day.

Groundhog.

I let my breath mist up the window again.

I spin on the spot and head up the back stairs instead. Into the returns room. I'd rather spend some time with the ghost today, than have to go out there. After what I've been doing with Jamesy, selling DVDs seems like such a waste of time. What's the point of it? Jamesy's right. Playing music is much more important, and I need to rest. Make sure I'm up to the job. No half-arsed superhero is going to save the day.

I wander to the back of the returns room and pile up some crates of sale CDs in the far corner. Build myself a wee fort. I squeeze in behind them and continue to build, so I'm walled in; like one of those deformed princes you hear about, who've been bricked up in an old castle: one day they knock down a wall and come face to face with a skeleton.

I curl up on the floor. Shut my eyes.

Something brushes past my ear, and I'm awake. I forget

where I am and kick my legs out. They hit the tower of CD crates. I watch in slow motion as the tower sways to one side.

That was close.

Topples.

Crash!

CD cases splinter and crack as they hit the ground. CDs bounce out of cases, spin and roll in all directions, casting shafts of light and rainbows.

Fuck.

I stand up, dust my self down and wait for someone to come and investigate the noise. What will I say? I tripped?

Nobody appears. In-store radio must be extra loud today to have drowned that out. Either that or we're all going deaf from listening to it every day.

I sort the CDs out as best as I can. Shove them back into the crates and get the hell out of there before anyone sees what a mess I've made. I'll start a rumour it was the ghost. Make sure Stewart gets wind of it.

What time is it anyway? Fuck, I must have been asleep for nearly two hours. Laura'll have me marched out of the shop if she knows that I've been up here sleeping. Written warning here I come.

I jog down the stairs to the shop floor.

'Where have you been? Martha was looking for you.' Ryan says as I join him at the counter.

'Just sorting out the returns room.'

'Should you not be on lunch? I was told to cover the tills.'

'I've not even checked the daily rota,' I reply, and duck under the counter where the rota is lying inside a polypocket. Sure enough, I should have been on lunch ten minutes ago.

'Whoops,' I say, and leave Ryan behind the tills as I head through to the staffroom.

I didn't bring anything to eat with me today, so I rummage around at the back of my locker, where I know there's some emergency change. I buy myself a Twix and a packet of Quavers from the vending machine in the staffroom.

I notice that Janette the cleaner has been baking again. I help myself to a couple of fairy cakes from the tin next to the kettle, and dump my feast at a place at the table.

I turn the kettle on and fill a mug with coffee and milk as I wait for it to boil. The milk smells a bit dodgy, so I add more coffee to drown it out. I stir the coffee and milk with a teaspoon, play with the brown paste in the bottom of my mug until the kettle clicks off. I carry my coffee over to the table and sit down.

There's a pile of magazines, so I pick up a copy of *Uncut*, flick through it as I eat my crisps. They're gone before I even register that I'm eating. Should have gone for something else instead. Quavers are too floaty.

I pick up a pen and start trying to fill in the *Uncut* crossword. Someone's already started it, and has answered all the easy questions. It's only the really obscure ones that are left. The door swings open and I look up as Martha comes into the staffroom with Roy from the ground floor.

'Stewart was right, you do look like shite,' Roy says as he takes the seat next to me.

'Cheers,' I nod at him.

'Two across is GLASS ONION,' he says, leaning across me and looking at the crossword.

'Be my guest,' I reply and slide the magazine across the table towards him. He rips open his sandwich with his teeth and uses his free hand to write the answer.

'I didn't think you were in today,' Martha says as she joins us at the table with a mug of tea.

She empties a Boots meal deal out of a carrier bag and sits down.

'I've been sorting out the returns room.'

'Is that your lunch?' Martha nods at the empty Twix wrapper and cake cases lying in front of me.

'Aye.'

'I've got soup in my locker if you like? It was buy-one-get-one-free.'

'I'm alright, cheers,' I reply, although as soon as the words are out of my mouth, I can imagine hot soup running down my throat. Violet Beauregarde eating Wonka's magic chewing gum.

'Sure? It's tomato.'

'Eh, well as long as you don't mind.'

'Nah, it's cool,' Martha gets up and leaves the room.

I get up and find a clean-looking bowl. Martha hands me the tin of soup, and I open it and fill the bowl, then put it in the microwave. Bollocks, I've chucked the tin in the bin without reading the instructions. Fuck it. I turn the timer on the microwave, and just let the soup spin. I take it out when Martha and Roy start to look up at the exploding noises. It's bubbling on top.

'Cheers,' I say to Martha, as I take a mouthful of soup. It burns my throat, and I feel it slide down to my tummy. I'm glowing.

Ready Brek was always Lewey's favourite. He'd have it every morning before school, even in the summer. He used to add syrup to it and stir it in, until the Ready Brek went a dirty yellow colour. His mum used to say that's why he was so clever at school: he always had a good breakfast. Davie was always changing his mind about what cereal was his favourite. Sometimes halfway through a box he'd go off a cereal, and just stop eating it.

His mum would never let him get a new box until he'd finished the old one though, so some days he didn't bother with breakfast, would just throw a bowl of it in the bin, so it would look to his mum like he was eating it.

'If you eat your soup in the rain, you'll never go hungry again,' says Martha.

'That's pretty good, did you make that up?' Roy asks.

'Nah, I've been listening to a lot of Regina Spektor recently, and someone had posted that on her website. I thought it was cool.'

'I bet you've had that soup waiting in your locker for ages, just so you could use that line on someone.'

'You got me, it was all a set-up.'

'Poor Davie, and he thought you were being nice to him.'

Martha's mobile phone flickers on the table.

'What's up with your phone?' Roy asks.

'Oh, I dropped it in the bath. It's working, but it's gone a bit odd. I kind of like it though. Almost like it's alive.'

I eat the soup and zone out on Martha and Roy as they banter with each other. I pull PC *Gamer* towards me and read the games reviews. Someone has spilt tea over it and half the pages are stuck together.

The soup makes me thirsty and I fill my empty coffee mug with tap water. The water swirls cloudy in my mug, and the cold liquid so soon after the hot soup makes my teeth ache.

'Come on you, time to go back,' Martha says as she tidies her rubbish away.

'Is it that time already?' I ask, looking at my watch.

I stop for a pish on the way back to the shop floor and look at myself in the mirror. I don't look as bad as everyone's making out. Could do with a shave and my eyes are a bit bloodshot, but I'm fine.

I stand behind the till.

Time   seems   to   slow   down.

Serve a couple of customers.
File away some DVDs.

Tea break.

Take twenty-five minutes instead of fifteen. It's not as if anyone is going to miss me out there. I slept away half the morning and nobody noticed. Manage to get a couple more crossword answers.

Talk   to   Ryan about computer games.

Serve a customer.

Lean against the counter.

Nothing ever happens.

THE STORE WILL BE CLOSING IN FIFTEEN MINUTES. COULD CUSTOMERS PLEASE ENSURE THAT THEY TAKE ALL PURCHASES TO THE TILL. THE STORE WILL BE CLOSING IN FIFTEEN MINUTES.

Thank fuck for that. There aren't even any customers down here.

THE STORE WILL BE CLOSING IN FIVE MINUTES. COULD CUSTOMERS PLEASE ENSURE THAT THEY TAKE ALL PURCHASES TO THE TILL. THE STORE WILL BE CLOSING IN FIVE MINUTES.

THE STORE IS NOW CLOSED. COULD ALL CUSTOMERS PLEASE MAKE THEIR WAY TO THE EXIT. THANK YOU FOR SHOPPING AT VIRGIN MEGASTORE AND HAVE A SAFE JOURNEY HOME. THE STORE IS NOW CLOSED.

'So, what's going on with you?' Martha asks me as we cash up the tills.

'Not much.'

'Really? I'm kind of worried about you.'

What's wrong with everyone today?

'How come?'

I slide coins into a cash bag, but my hand slips and I end up dropping half of them on the floor. They bounce and roll around my feet. Martha stops what she's doing and bends down to help me pick them up.

'Cheers,' I say to her.

'You don't have to tell me what's wrong if you don't want to,' Martha says, as we both kneel on the floor, 'but I'm the one covering up for you.'

'Nothing's wrong. I'm fine, honestly. You don't have to cover for me.'

We both stand up and she hands me a pile of coins she's picked up. Her fingers brush against my hands as I take the coins from her.

Then he had his hand on her leg. Martha laid her hand on top of his and her fingers brushed along his skin. It felt like electricity. Like she was charging him up.

Ring a ring a roses, a pocket full of posies.

Maybe I should tell her what's been going on?

'It's nothing to worry about but it's kind of complicated,' I say, 'I doubt you'd believe me.'

'Try me,' she says.

Out of all my mates, she's probably the one who would take me seriously. But it felt so wrong when I tried to tell Alfie.

Hey, I was thinking, can I have that MP3 player if it's broken?

How come?

I wanted to take it apart, use it in one of my instruments.

I've got a hybrid thing, made out of a bike and the toaster, but it's missing something.

Sorry, I chucked it. Syntax error.

What do you think, Jamesy? Should I tell her? I've been selling her *The X Files* on staff discount every payday. She believes in weird shite.

Mulder and Scully.

Why not? Give me one good reason? Just between you and me, eh? Okay, that's a good reason but come on. I pat my pocket. All good heroes need to have someone to bounce off. Superman and Lois. Spiderman and Mary-Jane. The Dr and Rose.

It's lonely.

He doesn't answer me. So what are you saying? Is that a maybe? Aye, not all of it, just some of it. Let me share some of it.

'Okay, do you want to go for a drink once we get out of here?' I ask Martha.

'Are you sure? I thought you...'

'Aye, it's cool.'

I hear the sound of the shop doors lock behind me as we head along Princes Street. Free at last. I know Stewart will be starting rumours tomorrow about Martha and me going out together after work, but I couldn't give a shit.

We head onto Castle Street and down the stairs into the Hogshead. There's an overhead heater above the door and warm air blasts my head as we enter the pub.

'What do you fancy?' I ask Martha.

'Eh... pint of Strongbow, please.'

I head over to the bar, while Martha spots a free table and goes to grab it. We're in luck. She's got one of the sofa tables in the corner. There's a TV above the bar and I glance up at it as the lassie gets my drinks. I carry them back to Martha and chuck my jacket down on the arm of the leather sofa, before sitting down next to her.

'Cheers,' Martha says and takes a drink of her cider. 'I needed that after today.'

'Aye, pretty shite day, wasn't it.'

'It wasn't even like anything bad happened, it was just so long and boring.'

'I know, I wasn't even there for a whole shift and it took forever.'

'How come you were late? Were you out with that girl?'

'Astrid?'

'I don't know what her name is.'

'Nah, just slept in.'

I don't want to get into my love life with Martha. It's too awkward. I always feel like there's a hidden subtext to her questions, but I can never work out what the fuck it is. She looks happier now I've said it wasn't a date, so that's cool. No point upsetting her again if I don't have to.

I take a drink from my pint. I haven't been out drinking after work since.

I promised myself I wouldn't drink again. Then I started drinking. Then I promised myself I wouldn't go out drinking after work. People got the hint, stopped asking me along to things. Now look at me. It's funny how promises you make to yourself weaken through time. Like not telling anyone else about Jamesy. What's the fucking point of promising myself things that don't matter now anyway? The one night I should have gone straight home, was the night I went out drinking. It doesn't matter how much I've abstained since then. That was the night that mattered.

I take a big drink, down half my pint in one go. Think I might need another before I start telling Martha about

Jamesy. She's waiting for me to start. Not asking any questions in case she says the wrong thing and I change my mind.

We sit in silence and watch the flatscreen TV, even though it's on mute. The Man United game is on and I watch the preamble, trying to lip-read what Alan Hanson is saying in the studio.

My pint slips down far too easily, and it seems like no time has passed before Martha is up getting another round. I watch her as she leans against the bar; one foot up on the metal step running underneath the bar stools. She pays for the drinks and puts her wallet into her back pocket, before picking up both pints and coming towards me. She walks slowly, but still manages to spill. She wipes her hands on her jeans after she dumps the drinks on the table.

She ran her tongue along her fingers, covered in sticky Fanta.

The first pint must have loosened her up, as she seems a lot more chatty than she did ten minutes ago.

'So, Davie, what's this story I won't believe?'

'Well, I've got this MP3 player and it helps people by playing them songs.'

'What do you mean it helps people?'

'I'm not sure really. I can just feel that it's making people happy. It's like I take on a bit of their joy. That's how I know.'

'And it's the music that helps them?'

'Yeah, you know how, like, different songs take you back places or remind you of certain people? Well, it's like Jame... the MP3 player knows what song to play, to make them have a happy memory of something. I don't really know for sure. This is just what I think's happening.'

'So do you just pick people who look sad?'

'No, the MP3 picks them; it can just tell they're in need... they're everywhere.'

Jamesy's right. There are so many people out there who

are unhappy. We have to start going out more, just so we can try and help more of them. As many as we can.

'You're like some kind of superhero.'

'I wouldn't go that far, but.'

Trackman Trackman Trackman Trackman Trackman Trackm

'Same again?'

'Is it not my round?'

'No, you bought the last one.'

I should get some food. These pints are going straight to my head. Martha's moved onto vodka and orange.

Davie watched her mouth as she sucked the vodka and orange through a straw.

Orange.

Davie dropped the

My cheeks are numb, I've turned into such a lightweight since I cut down on my drinking. I can see Martha's phone flashing through her bag.

Need a pish. Splash water on my face in the toilets.

'You need to get a new phone.'

'Nah, it still works and I like it this way. It's different.'

dropped the
                    orange juice

'You need to be careful though, Davie, it's starting to affect your life.'

'What is?'

'The MP3 player.'

Why do people keep focusing on the fucking petty things, like missing a bit of work, not shaving? Are they so fucking stupid that they can't see what I'm doing is great?

'Oh, maybe it's one of those government things. I know,
the One Dread Guy was a spy and instead of killing him, the
government have just tried to discredit him by frying his
brain with the MP3 player.'
'You think?'
'Yeah, it made him go crazy, the government do things
like that all the time that we never know about, especially in
America.'
Sticky Fanta.
'You watch too much *X Files*.'

She's not taking it seriously. I should have known. You
were right, Jamesy. As usual, you were right.

Martha bites her nails as she stands at the bar. How many
have we had? I should order food.

Burger? I can't read the writing on the menu, it's too small.

'You should find that One Dread Guy, see what he can tell
you.'
'Okay, Scully.'

One Dread Guy.
There was a rectangular scar, rucksack after rucksack.

Pish. I miss the urinal, it splashes onto the tiled floor.

Tennents. Vodka and orange.
Orange juice.
Half time. One nil. Giggs.
'Can I see the MP3 player?'

I take Jamesy out of my pocket and hand him to her. She turns him over and over in her hands; he leaves a blurred trail behind him as he turns, like the tail of a comet. It doesn't go away, it ribbons around Martha, wrapping her up in spirals of colour. He's not impressed at being stared at like he's some sort of freak. I expect him to zap Martha, but he stays still. I take him off her and put him back in my pocket. Sorry, Jamesy. You're not some pet hamster that I can pass around for all my friends to hold.

'Can you make it work?'

'No, he decides himself.'

'He?'

'It, you know what I mean.'

Tennents. Vodka and orange. Jack Daniels and Coke. Jack and Coke.

'What did you say there? James?'

'No, don't think so.'

'I thought you called it James. Giving it a name, now that is crazy.'

'Same again?'

Goal. Rooney.

Empty glasses clink as the table is cleared.

He asked her if she was going too. She said yes. She smiled at him. Cool, he replied.

Martha's leg is pressed against mine, *ring a ring* and she's slipping down into the sofa. Déjà vu. She shows me a video on her phone and leans her shoulder against mine. I can't make out what the video is of, the cameraman has a shaky hand. She's laughing so I laugh too.

Two nil. Finished. Already? What time is it?

Then he had his hand on her leg.

Kiss her?
'This is nice, I've missed you, Davie.'
'I've not been anywhere.'
'I know, but... you know.'

Her leg presses against my thigh. Table moves. Drink spills. Drip, drip, drips off the table. Count the coins in my hand, enough for another round.

Ring a ring a ring a ring a ring a ring a ring a

Vodka and orange. Jack and Coke.
Martha's tongue stud pings against the rim of the glass. The orange juice is reflected in it.
Sickly sweet.
    Sticky Fanta.

    Orange juice.
'I used to watch *The X Files* all the time, reminds me of school.'
'Do you want to borrow them?'

Vodka
    Orange
        Jack
            Coke
'Let's go get some food or something.'
'Chips and cheese.'

Hard to get out of this sofa, take Martha's hand, pull her up.

Jacket.

Door.
We all fall down.

15

Last Night a DJ Saved My Life

He remembered the story that Irish guy at the bar had told him.
Lewey would love it, would make him feel better.
Davie dropped the orange juice.

EYES WIDE OPEN. Where am I? I have no idea where I am. I'm awake. In my room. I can hear music. Where's it coming from? Why can I hear music?

I'm lying on top of my bed, still fully clothed from last night. I've even got my shoes on, although, give me some credit, the laces are untied. The music stops and I close my eyes. It hurts to have them open. I need to lie here and wait for the spinning to stop.

The music starts playing again.

'Fuck off,' I say and pull the duvet over my head. My brain has woken up enough to realise it's my ringtone that's playing. Who's phoning me at this time of the day? What time is it anyway?

The ringing stops. Then starts again. Stops. Then starts again. Stops. Starts. Fuck sake. I throw the duvet off and stand up, hold onto the bed for support. My legs are unsteady and my head throb, throb, throbs. Where's my fucking phone anyway? I follow the sound of music.

Julie Andrews appearing over the mountain.

My jacket's lying in the middle of the floor, and I rummage around in the pockets until I find my phone.

Susan.

I cut the call. I'm not in the mood for a chat. I'm on my way back to bed when it starts ringing again. I'm about to switch off my phone when I stop myself. What if something's wrong? What if Colin's been round hassling them? I sit on the edge of my bed, take the call.

'Alright, Susan?'

'No, I'm bloody not. Where are you? I'm double-parked out here.'

'What? Double-parked where?'

'Outside your flat.'

I've no fucking idea what she's talking about, but she's obviously not in any bother so I wish I hadn't answered now. I wander over to the bedroom window and stumble over Jamesy's headphones on the way there. I pull the curtains open. It's too bright, squint against the daylight. Right enough, there she is. Double-parked, blocking the whole road.

'Oh aye, I can see you now. What do you want?'

'It's twenty to twelve, we said we'd meet at quarter past. I've been sitting out here for over half an hour.'

She sounds like she wants to swear at me, but is holding the words in. Pammy must be in the car with her.

Pammy.

Quarter past eleven.

The drain unclogs and everything floods into my brain, a big mess of realisation.

'Fuck, the party. Crap. I'm sorry, Susan, I totally forgot.'

'How long are you going to be? Are you even up yet?'

'Aye, aye, I'm dressed and that. Just give me two minutes and I'll be right down.'

As I hang up on Susan, I notice there's a text from Astrid. I must have slept right through it, along with Susan's twenty-four missed calls. Fuck, I was well out of it.

hey u, 2 much 2 drink? lol! I do famby a 2 date –

name the place & I'll b there x

What the fuck? I scroll through my sent messages.

hi goledhngdr ws fun famby a 2 date? x

Sent at 1.57am.

I'm such a prick. I don't even remember sending that. I didn't think I was that pished. I scroll through the rest of the sent messages.

Thank fuck, that's the only one to Astrid. I can't believe she actually wants to go out again. It wasn't exactly a great first date, not with Jamesy arsing around and then the film breaking down, I didn't think she actually meant it when she said call me.

Susan toots her horn outside. Come on Davie boy, you can deal with these later. I pull off my work t-shirt and chuck on the cleanest one within stretching distance, then spray myself with deodorant and grab my jacket. I stop by the bathroom on the way out; cock in one hand for a pish, toothbrush in the other. Then I'm out the flat and down the stairs.

Pammy waves at me from the back seat and Susan starts the engine as I step out the main door of the building.

I get in the passenger side, and don't even have time to do up my seatbelt before Susan's pulled away. The car beeps a warning at me. Seatbelt! Seatbelt! SEATBELT!

'You look terrible, did you sleep in those clothes?' Susan says.

'Nah, course not. I was up when you phoned, I'd just forgotten about the party.'

'Davie, I've been phoning you for half an hour, I've buzzed the flat about ten times and you stink of booze. Do you think I'm an idiot?'

She reaches over and rummages about in the space in front of the gear stick, then throws a half-eaten packet of Polos at me. I take three and put them all in my mouth at once. The mint burns against my tongue and I gag.

'Sorry, Susan. I was working late and I ended up going for a drink after, eh?'

'I couldn't care less what you were up to, you promised me you'd come to this party.'

'I still am, I'm here aren't I?'

'That's not the point. And since when did you go out drinking after work?'

Fuck sake, Susan, chill out. I can't be arsed with this. My head hurts and Susan's driving is making me feel sick. I stay quiet and open the passenger window. I lean towards it and sniff the air like a dog.

'Mummy, what's wrong with Uncle Davie?'

'Nothing, sweetheart, he's just being very silly.'

I turn round in the seat and smile at Pammy, but the hangover is starting to kick in, and it's too much movement. I wish I was still in bed.

Susan tugs at the steering wheel and my stomach lurches.

'You look funny, Uncle Davie.'

'Do I? How come?'

'Your hair's all funny.'

I pull down the sun guard and look in the mirror. My hair's a fucking state: sticking up all over the place, and there's dry toothpaste stuck to my chin. I spit on my hands, clean my chin and then try to flatten my hair down.

'Pass the hairbrush out of my bag, Pammy.' Susan says.

Pammy wriggles about, kicking her feet against the back of my chair. I slide forward and take deep breaths.

She taps me on the shoulder with the brush, and I pull it through my hair a few times. It still looks a fucking mess but it's a bit of an improvement.

Susan looks round at me and then starts laughing.

'I'm going to be the talking point today, turning up with you.'

'I'm not that bad, am I?'

She doesn't answer, just laughs at me and then Pammy joins in.

'I'm more than happy to go back to bed if I'm not good enough for you,' I say.

'No chance,' Susan pats me on the knee, 'I need company and this party can be your punishment for keeping me waiting.'

'Aye, no doubt.'

Susan pulls into the driveway of some massive house in Colinton. There's already five cars parked there, and room for about six more. There are balloons up all over the front of the house, and a banner across the front door:

HAPPY 6TH BIRTHDAY JOSIE.

'Fucking hell,' I whisper to Susan as we follow Pammy round the side of the house to the back garden.

'I know,' Susan replies, 'imagine when it's Josie's eighteenth, they'll have to hire a castle.'

We turn the corner of the house and Pammy almost falls over with excitement at the sight of the garden.

There's a bouncy castle set up on the lawn, and a swing set to rival most council play parks.

'See you later, I'm off to play in that,' I say to Susan.

Someone shouts Pammy's name and she runs towards the bouncy castle. A woman approaches us.

'Susan,' says the woman, 'so glad you could make it.'

'Hi Lorna,' Susan replies and hands over a birthday present. 'This is my cousin, David.'

David? What the fuck?

'Nice to meet you, David. I'm Lorna, Josie's mum.'

We shake hands and she leads us into the conservatory.

'David?' I whisper at Susan.

'Sorry,' she shrugs, 'these people make me nervous.'

A group of women are sitting in the conservatory. I'm introduced and shake hands with them all, but I don't even bother listening to any of the names. I've no chance of remembering them.

'The men are all in the green room watching the rugby, David, if you want to join them.'

Susan just about pulls my arm from its socket, but she's got nothing to worry about. I fucking hate rugby.

'Nah, you're alright.'

'Are you sure?'

'Aye, I'm not really into egg-chasing.'

'Sorry?'

'He means rugby, Lorna; you know, the ball's shaped like an egg,' Susan explains.

'Oh, I see. Well, can I get you both a drink? You're into that I assume?'

'Aye, that would be great, cheers.'

I feel like I've wandered back into the fucking Victorian times or something. The lassies in one room, the blokes in another. I bet they're in there smoking cigars and drinking brandy.

Davie took the bin out for his mum. It was heavy and he dragged it along the garden path. As he pulled it through the gate, the bin caught on a loose bit of pavement and Davie lost his grip.

Fuck sake, he said as the contents of the bin spilled out from where it had fallen. As he lifted it upright, something in the bin caught his eye.

It was Lewey's rugby shirt, the one he wore to PE. He said he'd lost it at school. The front of it was ripped and there was blood on the collar.

Lorna hands me lager in a glass, while Susan gets an apple Schloer.

'Have a seat,' Lorna gestures to the sofa, and a couple of mums scooch up so we can fit on the end. I'm a bit freaked out by the whole thing. The mums look like they've walked right out of Stepford. Maybe I'm still drunk, but it's all a bit surreal. I didn't think people like this actually existed.

I can see Pammy out the window on the bouncy castle and I wish I was out there with her. I don't think I'm making a very good impression for Susan. A football supporter who works in a shop. Full-time? Yes. Oh, I thought you might be a student or something.

Davie sat behind the desk, two men in suits sat opposite him. He didn't make eye contact but looked behind them to the Niceday year planner hanging on the wall. There was a yellow star stuck on the day that Lewis had died. Someone had marked it off as being important. A day to remember. An important meeting? A holiday?

We know you've been through a tough time, but you've missed too much work to be able to catch up now.

Davie nodded. He hadn't been to any lectures since before the funeral.

We think it would be best if you took some time out, and then came back and repeated the year when you're feeling better.

Davie knew he wouldn't be back. He would never feel better.

The first few mouthfuls of the pint are hard going, but I force it down and soon it begins to slide down easily. My fuzziness starts to clear. Hair of the dog.

'You were thirsty, David. Can I get you another?' Lorna asks as she notices my empty glass.

'Aye, cheers,' I reply. My social standing drops another notch.

Susan joins in the conversation and is soon telling everyone about her fitness classes. The mums all sound impressed. It sounds like they're all members of gyms in Edinburgh but use them for coffee mornings, rather than breaking into a sweat.

I know it's not very polite, but I find my mind wandering.

I take my phone out and check that message I sent to Astrid again.

hi goledhngdr ws fun famby a 2 date? x

Man, what a tit.

The conversation has moved onto the fucking *X Factor*, so I decide to delete old text messages in my inbox. The mums all seem to think Simon Cowell's hilarious, so probably wouldn't appreciate my input anyway.

He's fucking awful. Everything about that show goes against what music should be about. It's not about money and being famous, it's about being creative and writing songs and playing your own music. The man's an arsehole.

Delete. Delete. Delete. Delete.

ur such a fuckin prick davie leave me alone ok, wanker

From Martha. Sent last night. What happened last night?

I remember being in the pub; I told Martha about Jamesy, she went on about *The X Files*. How did I get from Mulder and Scully to being a fucking prick? Think Davie, think. Blow some of that fog away.

Davie could feel Martha's leg pressing against his and knew, if he wanted to, he could kiss her and she'd kiss him back. He liked her, thought she was sexy as fuck, but she reminded him. Being here in the pub was too much like that night.

Let's get out of here, eh?

Cool, where to? Martha replied.

I don't know, let's go get some food or something.

Yeah, good idea, chips and cheese.

Davie stood up and pulled Martha up out of the sofa, then they put their jackets on and left the pub. Davie didn't realise how drunk he was until the fresh air hit him and he began to sway. As they walked towards the chippy, he took Martha's hand and they walked close, leaning in on each other, bumping shoulders.

They sat on a wall eating their chips, and then Davie kissed Martha. He closed his eyes and felt her hand on his thigh. Ring a ring a roses. Her tongue stud on his teeth. That tongue stud. It was imprinted on his lips. It left a dent that night that had never gone away.

Davie pulled back.

Sorry, Martha, I can't do this.

Why not? What's wrong?

I just, I can't. I don't like you that way. I'd just be using you. I've met Astrid now and I really like her, and I can't, tonight, I'm drunk, I've drunk too much.

Martha didn't say anything, but he could see tears. She turned her face away and jumped down from the wall.

You dick. I fucking hate you. Why do I always... I'm such an idiot.

Martha threw the remains of her chips at Davie and took off along the pavement.

I look down at my jeans, and can see the greasy stain from the chips and cheese which landed in my lap. I dig deeper, but there's nothing else. Nothing until I woke up this morning.

'David,' Susan nudges me, 'Hilary asked you a question.'

'Sorry, I was in a wee dream there.'

'I just wondered if you can get the rugby score on your phone.' Hilary smiles at me.

'Eh, no, not that fancy I'm afraid, sorry,' I reply.

I can't think straight. I really just want to go home. My head's buzzing. This whole thing with Martha has thrown me off course. Should I text her? Apologise? I help myself to some crisps from a bowl on the table in front of me and try to push everything out. I can't think with all this talking going on. I'm halfway through a text to her, but I don't know what I want to say. I delete it, have to think about this later. Think about everything later.

You can't just shut everything up and hope it'll go away.

'Mummy, can we have the disco now?'

This must be Josie. She has a 'Birthday Girl' badge pinned to the front of her dress. Man, just call me fucking Rebus with detective skills like this.

'Okay, dear, give me a few minutes, I'll need to ask Daddy to help sort it out.'

Lorna leaves the conservatory followed by Josie, and a few minutes later we hear raised voices and the sound of a crying child. The mums all smile at each other and pretend to chat, although you can tell they're all straining their ears to hear what's going on.

Lorna reappears in the conservatory, with a tearful Josie clinging to her leg.

'Peter has gone and left his laptop at work, it has all the music on it.'

An iPod's all very well but what happens when your hard drive crashes, or you lose it, then you're fucked.

What did I tell you?

'Oh no,' the mums chorus.

'Can we go and get it? I could drive?' asks Hilary.

'No, apparently the office is locked and Peter doesn't know the code for the alarm.'

'What about a CD instead?'

'We stored them all in the loft once we'd burned them on the laptop, trying to get rid of some of the clutter.'

Idiots. Idiots.

'We have a PC, so I was wondering if anyone has an iPod with them they could plug in?'

The mums all shake their heads, although a few pretend to search in their bags and jackets.

'I could murder Peter, honestly. I said to him yesterday morning, whatever you do, don't forget the laptop.'

I shake my head along with everyone else. That Peter. I feel my jacket move. As Josie's crying increases, so does the movement from my jacket.

You've got to be kidding me, Jamesy. I can't play the lassie a song in front of all the mums. Jamesy, stop it. You've gone too far this time. This can't work. I shuffle on my seat. Jamesy, will you just sit at peace. I try to act as if nothing's happening, but it makes me look more guilty.

'Are you okay there, David?' Lorna asks.

'Eh, aye. Where's the bathroom, please?'

'Just along the hall, third door on the right.'

I lock myself in the bog and take Jamesy out of my pocket. He's going fucking mental.

What? I can't let you play her a song. Everyone would see. What are you talking about? No. No fucking way.

INPLUGMEINPLUGMEINPLUGMEINPLUGME

Plug you in where? Stop fucking about.

Slow down, I don't know what you're talking about. Look where? Your headphones?

There's a wire with a USB connector hanging from the side of Jamesy, where the headphones used to be.

How the fuck did you do that?

INPLUGMEINPLUGMEINPLUGMEINPLUGME

Jesus, Jamesy. How did you do that? Tell me. Nah, tell me. You always keep me in the fucking dark. I look at the USB connector again, push the tip of my finger inside it. I can't believe it. I must be out of it. It's the drink, that's it, I'm still drunk.   Come on, I'm not leaving here until you tell me how you did that. Ah, you wee fucker. You can't keep shocking me every time you disagree with me.

Okay, okay, I'm going, I'm going. Just when I think I've got you sussed.

I flush the toilet and wander back to the conservatory, where the disco debate is still going on.

'Lorna, I've got an MP3 player if that helps. It's got, eh, a USB connector.'

Susan looks up at me, and I can tell she's wondering what the fuck I'm blethering on about.

'Is the music appropriate, no swear words or anything?' Lorna asks. Josie has stopped crying and is staring up at me.

'Aye, it's fine. I can stay by the computer and play DJ if you like? Make sure nothing dodgy comes on.'

I'm totally winging it. I've no idea if this is going to work or not, and Jamesy plays what he wants to play. He plays what needs to be played.

'David, you're a lifesaver. The computer is just through here.'

I follow Lorna through to what looks like the dining room. A table covered with plates of food has been pushed up against the wall, and a PC is set up on a desk in the corner. The wooden floor is a perfect dance floor for Josie's disco.

Jamesy fits flawlessly into the side of the computer. Like I had any doubt. He's so smug. Look what I can do, Davie. I'm fucking brilliant.

Plug in baby.

I sit next to the PC and squeeze my hands around him.

Music begins to play from the speakers.

`Nelly Furtado Maneater by Nelly Furtado Maneater by Nelly Furtado Maneater by Nelly Furtado Maneater b`

Is this appropriate? The kids all seem to love it. They come in screaming from the garden, and start to sing along. The disco starts with a vengeance. I don't know what I'm going to do when this song ends. Sorry, kids, it's a short disco. One song only.

What a shite song too. How can they like this? But they do, they know all the words. They're dancing away to it like it's the fucking height of disco.

It's coming to an end. What now? Jamesy, help me, give me a heads up. What do I say? You got me into this. Aye, you fucking did. I'm going to end up sitting here looking like a tit.

What will I say? The battery's gone, or it's broken?

I don't have to worry though. Nelly Furtado flows seamlessly into Take That's Shine. Jamesy, you don't provide ear plugs for the DJ do you? I fucking hate Take That.

What next then? Something decent, please. No, not that. Your playlist should be re-named 'Now That's What I Call A Load Of Pish Volume Three'. Aye, I know it's not meant to be for me, but I still have to hear it. They'll think I listen to this music. That I actually like it. What was that I said before about superheroes and sacrifices?

He knew how Spiderman felt now. With great power.

I hope they get bored of the disco soon. Before my ears start bleeding. The buffet is teasing me, I could do with some food now that the hangover is starting to go. Playing DJ seems to be curing me better than any drugs or coffee could. The hangover is lifting, leaving me behind.

Those marshmallow cakes with Smarties chocced on top look good, I could eat the Smarties off the top and stuff the marshmallows in my ears to drown out the shite music. I can't let go of Jamesy though. I'm stuck here as long as the disco is on.

I wink at Pammy, who's right in the thick of things. Dancing away with her wee pals. They run. Slide on their knees. Spin. Jump. Sing. Wotsits are crunched under patent leather shoes, juice spilt from flailing arms holding plastic cups. The music is perfect for them, even if I hate it myself. Okay, okay, I admit it. You know your stuff, Jamesy. We make a great team, you and I.

Every so often, one of the mums sticks her head around the door and smiles or gives me the thumbs up. I'm pretty sure they all think I'm gay. A non-rugby fan who has Girls Aloud, High School Musical and Scissor Sisters on his MP3 player. Ach well, at least they like me now. I've saved the party.

Trackman Trackman Trackman Trackman Trackman Trackm

The fight with Martha flashes through my head, but I push it away. I can't do anything about that now. I'll sort it out later. I'm enjoying myself far too much to worry about that.

Sugababes Push The Button by Sugababes Push the Button by Sugababes Push The Button by Sugababes Pus

I really need to get to Asda this afternoon, how long before I can leave?

Save A Life by The Fray How To Save A Life by The Fray How To

Davie's acting really weird. It's like he was after Lewis died.

Crazy by Gnarls Barkley Crazy by Gnarls Barkley Crazy by Gnar

Mum promised she wouldn't fight with dad on my birthday.

Avril Lavigne Girlfriend by Avril Lavigne Girlfriend by Avril

Does Lorna know about me and Pete? That's why she wouldn't let me drive him to get the laptop?

Stop Me Now by Mcfly Don't Stop Me Now by Mcfly Don't Stop Me

If Hilary hadn't sucked me off in the office last night, I would have remembered to bring that fucking laptop home.

by Justin Timberlake SexyBack by Justin Timberlake SexyBack

Why won't Mummy tell me who phoned her last night? I'm not allowed to tell Uncle Davie she was crying.

Grace Kelly by Mika Grace Kelly by Mika Grace Kelly by Mika

I don't know what's wrong but we just keep fighting at the moment, even Josie's noticing it.

Soldiers by Eminem Like Toy Soldiers by Eminem Like Toy

We need to stop but I can't get enough of him.

View Same Jeans by The View Same Jeans by The View Same Jeans

I'm going to end it, before Lorna finds out.

You Look Good On The Dancefloor by The Arctic Monkeys I Bet

I wanted to tell him about Colin phoning me in the middle of the night, but I don't know if he can handle my problems as well as his at the moment.

The Pussycat Dolls Don't Cha by The Pussycat Dolls Don't Cha

I'm scared he's going to leave me.

Out Of My Head by Kylie Minogue Can't Get You Out Of My Head

Uncle Davie's watching me dance, cartwheel, handstand, did he see that? Yeah, he's still watching me.

I Fall To Pieces by Razorlight Before I Fall To Pieces by Raz

This party's not as bad as I thought it was going to be. Is Susan's cousin single?

The Automatic Monster by The Automatic Monster by The Automat

I'll book that B&B in Pitlochry, take Lorna away on her own for the weekend, try and sort things out.

Love You Less and Less by The Kaiser Chiefs Everyday I Love

I need to stop losing my temper at him, no wonder he spends all his time at the office.

Told Me by The Killers Somebody Told Me by The Killers Someb

Lorna's my friend for fuck sake, what am I doing?

(Is This The Way To) Amarillo by Tony Christie (Is This The

Mummy says I get to have cake soon and blow out all the candles.

Smile by Lily Allen Smile by Lily Allen Smile by Lily Allen

Not long to go until Pammy and I visit Mum and Dad, I can't wait to get away from here for a while, I just hope Davie's okay on his own, I still haven't told him we're going so soon.

Mamma Mia by Abba Mamma Mia by Abba Mamma Mia by Abba Mamma

If I could just get him to come with me, it would do him good to get out of Edinburgh.

Baby One More Time by Britney Spears Baby One More Time by Br

Pete hasn't kissed me like that in a long time, I almost dropped the cake.

Happy Birthday Song Happy Birthday Song Happy Birthday Song

cake   cake   cake time   looks good   want to kiss him   sort this small piece   Davie Susan's cousin   Uncle Davie   one go big   piece David over.

Josie by Donovan Josie by Donovan Josie by Donovan Josie by

My hands are killing me. They usually hurt after one song, but this extended mix is burning right down to the marrow.

Against my better judgement my foot taps in time to the tunes, and I almost feel like getting up and having a wee boogie myself.

I'm not even worried when I see Susan approaching me with a beer, and she doesn't look happy.

'What are you up to?' she asks. 'Here, Lorna said I'd to bring you a beer.'

'Stick it down, will you? The player's got a loose connection and if I let go the music'll stop.'

'Is that Alfie's player you got in such a fuss about a couple of weeks ago?'

She puts the beer down next to me. It looks so cool and refreshing. *Ice Cold in Alex*. I could plunge my hands right into the glass.

'I thought you said you were giving it back to Alfie? Is it even safe with that loose connection? What if you electrocute someone?'

'It's fine, Susan, and look at Pammy, she's loving it.'

Pammy is using a breadstick as a microphone and is singing along to That's Not My Name by The Ting Tings.

'Besides,' I say, 'they all love me now, I'm working wonders for you, girl.'

Is it the buzz from Jamesy, or am I just topping up the alcohol levels from last night? Whatever it is, I feel totally alive. I'm up for chatting away to people, dancing. I'm the life and soul of the fucking party.

The Proclaimers I'm Gonna Be (500 miles) by The Proclaimers I'm Gonna Be (500 miles) by The Proclaim

Susan raises one eyebrow at me.

'Aren't you going to skip that one?' she asks.

I wish I could. As a Hearts supporter, it pains me to listen to that Hibee twosome singing their pish, but I can't do anything. I'll be having words with Jamesy later about his song choice.

I shrug my shoulders at Susan.

'I can't change it, it's stuck on some playlist.'

'There's something not right about that thing.'

'What can I say? It's Alfie's.'

Susan gives me a look and grabs a sausage roll before leaving the room.

She passes Lorna on the way out, who heads towards me, leans over and whispers in my ear.

'I'm going to bring the cake in.'

'No bother,' I reply. Hear that, Jamesy? Cake time.

The adults start to gather in the dining room, and the lights are dimmed. Jamesy stops playing but I know he's not finished yet. I can feel him in my hands. Waiting. Waiting.

Lorna enters the room carrying the cake, six candles on top. Jamesy begins his encore.

Birthday Song Happy Birthday Song Happy Birthday S

Everyone joins in and Josie blows out the candles. The lights are switched on, and Lorna nods at Jamesy.

'It was my pal's birthday the other week there, not had a chance to delete it yet,' I lie, avoiding eye contact with Susan.

Happy Birthday is followed by For She's a Jolly Good Fellow and then Josie by Donovan. The kids all troop off at this one. Old. Boring. Don't know the words. Then Jamesy is off stage. He shuts down in my hands and I slump back in the chair. I'm fucking knackered, my hands sting but I'm buzzing like I've been to an all night rave. Afterglow.

I'm centre of attention for the rest of the party. They love me. I'm chatty, funny, even attractive apparently, some woman gropes me on my way back from the toilet.

'You're welcome back anytime,' Lorna says to me, and leans in to kiss me on the cheek as we're leaving. I hold my jacket over my hands so that nobody can see the mess of them. They're red and aching.

'Thanks, no bother, eh?' I reply as I get into the car with Susan and Pammy.

Pammy blethers non-stop all the way home about the party. Susan doesn't say anything. I can't decide if she's listening to Pammy or thinking about something.

I sit on my hands in the car; the pressure helps with the pain.

'Cheers, Susan,' I say as she pulls up outside the flat.

She turns to face me and I can guess what's coming. I know that face.

'Sorry for having a go at you earlier. Are you sure you're okay?'

'Aye, I'm fine, still a bit hung-over but that's all.'

'No, I don't mean that. I just mean, I'm worried about you. You're acting a bit strange.'

'I think I'm a bit drunk.'

'No, it's not that. It's, well, the MP3 player. And going out drinking after work. It's not like you.'

'I just want to start being a normal guy again, eh? Go out for a drink after work and not freak out.'

'I know, I think that's great. I just, well you know I worry.'

'Seriously, Susan, it's cool. I'm okay. It's under control.'

16

At the Zoo

The Irish guy said he'd been at school with Gary Lightbody out of Snow Patrol. Said Gary got bullied for being too sensitive and writing poetry. And now look at him. Who's laughing now? You just need to stick in, Lewey, let it wash over you.
Davie dropped the orange juice.

I DON'T EXPECT Alfie to be anywhere except his room when I get in, but he's sitting on the sofa smoking a joint and watching what looks like *Come Dine With Me*. Must be giving himself a break from his inventing.

The air around the sofa is shrouded in smoke. Alfie has dragged a chair through from his bedroom, still has some of his clothes draped over the back of it, and he's using it as a footstool.

I'm really happy to see him. We've not sat and had a laugh for ages. I'm still hyped up from what happened at the party, and I feel like sitting up all night and talking shite like we used to when we first moved in.

Exactly, Davie boy, exactly. I knew there was a reason I moved in with you.

My hands are still aching a bit, but I hardly feel it against the high that's still washing through me. I could do anything right now.

'Hey,' I say.

'Hey, how's it going?' he replies.

'Not bad, eh?'

'Where have you been? Working?'

'Nah, I had to go to this kid's party with Susan, keep her company, eh?'

Alfie scooches up on the couch, and I squeeze my arse in next to his.

'This posh lassie is making beef stroganoff for dinner, but the rest of the guests all fucking hate her. It's so funny.'

It takes me a few seconds to work out that's he talking about *Come Dine With Me*. He sits next to me giggling away as the voice-over guy makes sarcastic comments about the lassie's cooking. Alfie's not wrong about her being posh. I watch it for just a few minutes and she's already starting to piss me off, with her chat about her fifteen horses and her many kitchen gadgets bought for her by her rich boyfriend.

'I'm hoping there's going to be a huge barney at the dinner table,' Alfie says and hands me the joint and the ashtray, 'I want someone to tip that pavlova over her head.'

I hold the joint in front of me, just looking at the wisps of smoke rising from the tip of the cigarette. Should I?

He'd woken up feeling sick and with a burning throat.

I hold it to my mouth and inhale, relax into heaviness and sink into the couch. I take another draw, a bigger one this time and hold it in for longer before I exhale. I remember why I used to be so addicted to this. Everything goes a little fuzzy around the edges: a drawing with the black outlines rubbed out. The calm hash feeling nuzzles against the buzz from Jamesy. Bliss. I take another couple of drags before handing the joint back to Alfie.

'What have you done to yourself?' Alfie asks nodding at my hands.

'I think I fell last night, can't remember to be honest.'

There's a stray fleck of tobacco stuck to my tongue and I try to grab it with my fingertips.

'Aye, where were you last night? I heard you come in.'

'I just went for a few drinks with Martha after work.'

'Oh aye, something going on there? I always thought she fancied you.'

Martha. I'd forgotten about her what with all the DJ action. Fuck it. I don't even care about the fight anymore, I'm sure it's cool. Next time I see her we'll apologise and laugh about it. No big deal.

How much does Alfie know about what did actually happen between Martha and me? About what happened to Lewis? He started working at Virgin after the fallout had cleared and he wasn't there for all that long. Just a few months. Neither of us have ever mentioned it. Shop gossip though, he's bound to have heard something.

'Nah, nah,' I say, 'it's not like that. I'm actually seeing some lassie called Astrid.'

I don't know if it's the hash or the high of what happened with Jamesy earlier, but there's a confidence surging through me that I've never felt before. I really do feel like I could do anything. I've been on one, pretty disastrous date with Astrid, and here I am bragging about her to Alfie.

'Astrid, eh? You're a dark horse, how long's that been going on for?'

'Well, not all that long really, I need to text her and arrange to meet up but I can't think of where to go. I want it to be somewhere cool.'

I can't believe I'm coming out with this shite. Fair enough, she did tell me to call her after our one and only date, and she did text me back last night, but up until now I didn't think I was ever going to do it. Tonight I'm feeling totally different though. I'm ready to phone her right now and get a second date organised.

'I'm going to see Ballboy play at Cab Vol on Thursday night, why don't you both come to that? Saint Jude's are supporting.'

He passes me the joint again.

'No offence, Alfie,' I say inhaling and then blowing the smoke between us, 'I'm keeping her as far away from you as possible.'

He grins at me and reaches under the sofa for his video box, then starts to roll up.

'Come on, I'm a decent guy, I wouldn't hit on her.'

'It's not that I'm worried about. You wouldn't need to hit on her. Lassies just gravitate towards you like you're some sort of walking cock.'

He laughs and drops the half-rolled joint. The tips of his fingers are stained from where he's been burning the block of hash and crumbling it like biscuit onto the tobacco.

'Come on, give that here,' I say, 'you're too stoned to make a decent joint.'

I take the box off him and finish what he's started. I roll up the joint and lick the shiny edge of the skin to get it to stick. Then I rip a piece of card off the Rizla packet and make it into a roach. I light the joint and suck on it a few times to make sure it's working, then hand it over to Alfie. Something burns my belly, and I look down and notice a hot rock has burned a hole right through my t-shirt.

'The zoo!' Alfie shouts. I look at him and we both start laughing.

'What the fuck?' I say.

'Take that Alice chick to the zoo. I did that once and all the shagging animals were a real turn-on, almost like watching a porno.'

'You are fucking disgusting, and it's Astrid not Alice.'

'Whatever. Either way, I'm telling you, the zoo is a great place to pick up girls.'

'I don't need to pick up girls, I just need to take a girl on a date somewhere.'

'Yeah, yeah, trust me, Davie boy, the zoo, the zoo.'

Alfie pats his nose with his index finger, like he's sharing a great secret with me. We sit in silence, passing the joint back and forth. The zoo idea buzzes at the front of my head. I start to think that Alfie might be onto something. Fantasies build: walking hand-in-hand with Astrid, eating ice-cream, laughing at the hilarious animal japes that we see. Hmmm, the zoo could actually work. I take my phone out of my jeans and scroll to Astrid in the phone book.

Hey u free 2moro? Fancy goin 2 the zoo wit me? D x

Send.

I read the message over in my sent items box. It feels like someone else wrote it. It's *Freaky Friday* and Alfie and I have switched bodies. I have never signed my name 'D' before in a text message. And I put a kiss. What the fuck was I thinking? I've just asked her straight out to come to the zoo with me. Tomorrow. No pussy-footing around the subject.

No 'I know you're probably busy but…'

No 'don't worry if you can't make it but…'

No 'I was wondering if maybe you'd…'

I put my phone down on the coffee table and there's a reply. Instant. The phone rattles against the table and I jump.

'Fuck, that was quick,' I say.

'You just about shat yourself there, Davie boy.'

Cool, sounds like fun, meet u there @ 12? X

Fucking hell. I really do have superpowers.

Gr8 cu then x

'Cheers Alfie, I now have a date at the zoo tomorrow.'

'Who with, the gorilla?'

Poor guy, he looks sad, said Lewis.

Davie hadn't noticed before, but now he looked at the gorilla more closely. He did look sad.

'Aye, very good.'

'Sorry, what did I tell you though? The zoo is the place to go on a date.'

He blows a smoke ring into the air and tries to hoopla it

onto his big toe. The ring disintegrates around his bare feet and he kicks the smoke away.

This is the first time in ages that I've felt almost content. Getting stoned, having a laugh with my mate, got a date with a hot girl, helping people with Jamesy. Things are starting to move in a different direction, and I'm liking it.

I'll come out here and read them to you, so you know what happens at the end. I promise you'll get to know what happens. I know it's stupid, but it's all I can think to give you right now.

'Davie's got a date at the zoo tomorrow,' Alfie sings along to the tune of that old kid's song.

'Shut it, Alfie.'

'He hopes he'll get his end away.'

'Jesus, how can you make a children's song so fucking dirty?'

'Just a gift, I guess.'

I'm standing outside the zoo waiting for Astrid, and I can't get Alfie's fucking singing out of my head.

Davie's got a date at the zoo tomorrow.

It's really putting me off. Where's the confidence I had last night? There's still a faint tinge left, but I could do with a recharge. Jamesy won't be happy if I suggest that though.

Alright, alright, sorry, calm down. I know it's not about giving myself a kick, but I can't help it if that's a side effect, can I?

Alfie's dirty singing and the thought of having to spend a whole afternoon, just me and Astrid, is making me panic.

Davie's got a date at the zoo tomorrow.

One finger, one thumb, one arm, one leg, one nod of the head.

He hopes he'll get his end away.

I try to sing the original song instead, get Alfie's filthy

version out of my head.

Daddy.

Who's the daddy?

His dad was nowhere to be seen, taken off as soon as the cars dropped them at the house.

Fuck, what am I doing?

The number twelve bus is approaching and I try to act cool in case she's on it. I pretend that I'm looking the other way and haven't even noticed the bus arrive. As it pulls away I look round, but there's just a woman with a couple of kids.

I can hear the sound of something screeching from behind me in the zoo. I can't tell if it's a bird or an animal, or whether it's happy or angry.

Fuck, maybe I dreamt the entire date. Hallucinated it on Alfie's special cigarettes. Why else would she reply so quickly and so positively? My mouth feels manky and my throat hurts after all that smoking last night. I hope I don't stink of fags. I should have bought some chewing gum on the way here.

It's just gone twelve. I'll wait till quarter past, no, half past. I'll wait till half past and then I'm leaving.

I've not been here for years.

Do you fancy a trip to the zoo, boys?

The number forty-six approaches and, as it gets closer, I notice someone get up and walk towards the front of the bus. I'm sure it's her. Is it her? Don't stare. Don't stare. Look away. Look away.

I turn my head, and hear the bus pull up alongside me. The doors hiss open, and I allow myself to glance over. Astrid steps down off the bus.

She spots me and waves, flashing that smile as she walks towards me. I'm almost floored by the gap in her teeth. Dentists should fucking offer that as cosmetic surgery.

'Hey you,' she touches my arm as she stops next to me, 'I'm so glad you said the zoo. I've been wanting to come here for ages, but my flatmate doesn't agree with animals in cages. I mean, neither do I, but Edinburgh Zoo is really famous, huh? And it's into conservation and that, so I'm sure it's okay.'

'Yeah, I guess so, I thought it would be cool to visit.'

There's no chance in hell Alfie's getting any credit for this. My watch. My zoo date.

I'm feeling cheered, lifted by the fact that she's shown. She's a walking S.A.D. lamp.

We climb the steps up to the main entrance, and I pull my wallet out to pay for the tickets.

'Don't you dare, you paid for the cinema.'

'Aye, but still, that was cheaper, and you bought the pop-corn.'

'I don't care, I'm getting this.'

I fucking hate these kinds of arguments. I never know when to fight my corner and when to back down. I'd be more than happy if she paid for my ticket, Alfie never told me that the zoo was so fucking expensive, but it's not really cool to let the lassie pay.

'Look,' she says, 'I'll get this and then you can buy us a pizza or something after, okay?'

'Eh, yeah, okay.'

I'm too shocked to argue. She's already telling me we're going out for food afterwards and we've not even had the date. What if it's a fucking disaster? I haven't thought as far ahead as the polar bear yet, never mind dinner.

We head out of the foyer into the zoo and both stop at the giant stone elephant. The last time I was here, I just followed my folks around; it all seems a bit of a maze to me. Astrid is opening out the map she was given when she paid for the tickets.

'So, where first?' she asks, holding the map out in front of her.

'You choose. I'm easy.'

'Are you now? Okay, this way.'

She folds up the map and points the way ahead. As we start walking she tucks the map into her back pocket and I take the chance to look at her arse.

It's very distracting. I can't catch a thought.

We stop at the sea lions first, lean against the rocky wall of the enclosure. One fat sea lion is lolling about at the edge of the pool, the other swims round in circles. A whiskered nose occasionally pops out of the water with a splash, sniffs the air, before the animal dives back under.

This enclosure is exactly the same as I remember it.

Lewis was leaning over the wall, standing on his tiptoes, watching the sea lion swim round and round. Davie walked over to him and, grabbing onto Lewis's waist, hoisted him up so he could see better.

'They're so graceful in the water compared to what they're like on land, huh?' says Astrid.

'Aye, they're a couple of fatties, aren't they?'

We head up the hill past enclosures containing plants, trees and stagnant pools of water. I'm too conscious of the fact that I'm here with Astrid to take much notice of the animals. I think she might be flirting with me. Is she? What do you think, Jamesy? I was worried about awkward silences, but the conversation comes pretty easily. It's maybe just the American thing, but she chats away and I start to relax.

Halfway up the hill we come to the big cats. This bit has definitely changed since I was last here. The cages are much, much bigger, and you can't actually see any of the lions and tigers for the trees and plants. The zoo's giving them a chance to hide, give us gawping idiots a big 'fuck you.'

Poor guy, he looks sad, said Lewis.

'It's all a bit *Jurassic Park* isn't it?' I say.

'What, like they've all escaped and they're going to eat us?'

'No, I mean, like, at the start, when they don't see any dinosaurs.'

'Oh yeah, you're right. Those little birds are so fearless.'

We watch a couple of sparrows flit around a piece of meat, looks like it's been lying there for a few hours. The sparrows peck away at the ground around it, as flies buzz on top of the meat.

'When I was a kid, I remember being totally confused as to how the birds got in there.' I say.

'You mean, like, how they flew in over the top of the fence?'

'Okay, maybe not here, but some of the cages have roofs, eh? I couldn't get my head round that they fitted through the gaps in the wire.'

'Yeah, I know, I'm just teasing you. They should put sparrows on the signs outside all the cages, it looks like that's all we're gonna see today, huh?'

We wander back down the hill.

'I really wanna see the crazy ape,' Astrid says, turning to face me and walking backwards along the path. She's just about to fall over a bin, so I grab her arms and swivel her around so we're side by side again.

'You've already seen the crazy ape,' I say and give her a little bow.

'Nah, you're just screwy,' she hits me with the map, 'I mean the really crazy ape. A friend of mine is doing a PhD, right, and she comes out here, like, every few weeks, to do research. She says there's this really old ape who's been here for years, like, back when people didn't care about the animals and would bang on the glass and chuck food into the cages and stuff. It sent him mad.'

'That's really sad.'

'I know, but don't you wanna see him?'

'Totally. So, is her PhD on crazy apes?'

'Nah, it's something really dull, like parasites or something. Someone just told her about the ape.'

'Shall we go see the gorilla first? Save the crazy ape till last.'

'Yeah, sounds good.'

There's no sign of the gorilla in the outside enclosure, so we go inside. He looks bored as shit. Probably came inside to get some peace and is pissed off that we can all just troop on in after him. He sits on the straw, scratching his engorged belly, his eyes glancing up at us now and again.

'Look at that,' Astrid rubs her finger across an imperfection on the glass, 'it's on the inside.'

It looks like a bullet hole. Or a fist mark.

'He must have done that, huh?' Astrid says, 'Poor guy.'

Poor guy, he looks sad, said Lewis.

Davie hadn't noticed before, but now he looked at the gorilla more closely. He did look sad.

The gorilla sat in the corner of the cage, picking at the straw on the ground around him. Davie stood next to Lewis, his mum and dad behind them. A family with a pushchair came in. The man knelt down so he was at the same height as the baby, and pointed towards the gorilla.

His head looks like a peanut, said Lewis, and rubbed the top of his own head, it's all pointy at the top.

Davie put his hand on Lewis's head and they stood watching the gorilla. They both took a step backwards and laughed at each other's nervousness, as the gorilla suddenly lumbered to its feet. It hunched forward and then swung a long arm behind its back.

What's it doing? Lewis asked, turning to his parents.

I'm not sure, sweetheart.

As if he could hear them, the gorilla held out his hand to them. Lying on his palm was a fresh, steaming shite.

It's done a jobby, Davie said and he and Lewis burst out laughing.

Ssshhh, said their dad, although Davie could tell he was trying not to laugh himself and was just saying it because of the other people next to them.

Lewis stood on his tiptoes and whispered in Davie's ear.

It looks like a Caramac bar.

After that, 'it looks like a Caramac bar' became their secret catchphrase for weeks.

'Earth to Davie,' Astrid waves a hand in front of my face.

'Sorry, I was in a wee dream there.'

'Right, the crazy ape. I guess he must be there,' she points at the map. Her fingernails are painted pink.

The chipped, black shapes were still there.

'Okay, lead the way.'

I take one last look at the gorilla before we leave, and feel a stuttered movement inside my pocket. I don't think you can help this guy, Jamesy.

'It's warm in here, huh?' Astrid says, as we enter the enclosure. She takes off her jacket and ties it round her waist. She's wearing a sleeveless top underneath and her freckled shoulders call out to me: kiss me, lick me, bite me.

'Wow they're amazing, huh?' she says.

A chimp stares at me from a black, metal nest filled with straw.

'Yeah, they look so, I don't know, their eyes are so human. I feel like I'm looking at a person.' I reply.

'Look at the little one, cute, huh?'

'Aye, although I feel like he's taking us in as much as we are him.'

'They're smart, really strong too, could rip your arm right off.' Astrid shrugs her naked shoulders.

I look at the older chimp and it yawns, Nosferatu teeth. I can see the intelligence behind its brown eyes. It unnerves me. It knows something I don't.

We head out through the flaps of plastic to the outside enclosure. There's a chimp on top of the climbing frame. His fur is going grey and he's pushing a crate backwards and forwards; he hisses at the other chimps.

I nudge Astrid.

'Do you think that's Crazy Charlie?'

We watch him push the crate backwards and forwards, backwards and forwards, backwards and forwards. The other chimps seem to know not to go near him.

'It's not so funny, is it?' Astrid says summing up what I'm thinking. 'Poor guy, what sort of a life is that?'

Poor guy, he looks sad, said Lewis.

She takes my hand and I'm frozen to the spot. We stand and look at the chimp and I don't want to move or speak in case she lets go.

'What happened to your hand?' she asks, rubbing the rectangle burn.

'Oh, I fell.'

'Poor thing,' she strokes the palm of my hand with her thumb.

'Come on, I'll buy you an ice-cream,' I say.

'Cool,' she replies, and smiles at me.

We walk away and she doesn't let go of my hand. We're holding hands. We. Are. Holding. Hands. I don't want to let go. Even when I'm buying the ice-creams, I try not to let go.

We sit facing each other at a picnic table, eating our Soleros and waiting for the penguin parade to start. I try not to stare at her mouth as she sucks on the ice-lolly.

Davie watched her mouth as she sucked the vodka and orange through a straw.

I look behind her instead.

Davie, look the pie... jimm... ie hip... pos, the piejimmy hippos, said Lewis pointing at a sign over one of the enclosures.

It's not piejimmy you idiot, it's pronounced pigmee.

A crowd gathers for the penguins and Astrid pulls me up onto the picnic table, so we're above everyone.

THE PENGUIN PARADE IS ABOUT TO BEGIN. CAN WE REMIND

ALL SPECTATORS TO STAND BACK, AND NOT TO FEED OR
TOUCH THE PENGUINS.

The zookeeper opens the door of the penguin house and a handful of them waddle out onto the pathway, a wall of people on either side.

I turn to look at Astrid and the next thing I know we're kissing. I don't know how it happened or who started it, but fuck the penguins and their fucking parade; all that matters now is that we're kissing and maybe we might get thrown out of the zoo for kissing on top of a picnic table during the penguin parade.

'Mmmm, you taste of Solero,' she says and kisses me again.

I run my tongue over her teeth feeling for the gap, and my cock stiffens.

'You're as crazy as Charlie,' I say.

'I just find you very attractive,' she shrugs, and my cock pushes against the inside of my jeans.

'You do?'

'Don't look so surprised. I only bought those magazines so I could speak to you. For a while I thought you were having a thing with that girl you work with, you were always with her when I came in.'

Ring a ring a roses.

'Nah, we're just mates.'

'I'm glad.'

Perfect day.

'So, do you fancy getting that pizza?' I ask as we head out of the zoo through the gift shop.

'Sure,' she says, rubbing her hand down the neck of a cuddly giraffe.

'Where to then?' I ask.

'How about back to mine and we can order in?'

'Yeah, sounds good to me.'

Sounds fucking amazing to me.

I sit on Astrid's double bed as she phones Pizza Hut. There are piles of books lying next to me, most of which I guess are for uni: a biography of Gandhi, *The Philosophy of Religion*, the *Oxford History of the British Empire*; lying on top is *The Complete Peanuts Volume 4* with a picture of Snoopy on the cover.

Astrid wanders around the room as she places the order, the wire from the phone tangles around pieces of furniture and her legs as she moves. I think about tying her up and have to stop myself from getting too carried away, too dirty. She stops by her desk and plays with her iPod. Only in Dreams by Weezer starts playing. Fuck, you're not kidding, Rivers.

'It'll be about twenty-five minutes,' she says as she hangs up and untangles herself.

There's a poster above her bed of John and Yoko. Yoko is lying on the ground wearing a black jumper and jeans, her black hair lying out behind her. John is completely naked and is lying next to her, one leg curled over her stomach, kissing her cheek.

'It was the cover of *Rolling Stone*,' Astrid says following my eyeline, 'it was taken, like, I don't know, just a few hours before he died. I love it, but it makes me sad too. He looks so vulnerable and in just a few hours she's gonna have to watch her husband get shot right in front of her.'

I don't really know what to say to that, so I just nod and she sits next to me on the bed.

'So, Davie, what can we do in twenty-five minutes?'

She's smiling that gap-toothed smile at me and I lean in to kiss her.

'What can we do twice in twenty-five minutes?' I say.

'Oh, I just got a shock off you,' she says pulling back, 'have you still got that broken iPod thing of yours?'

'Sorry,' I reply and take Jamesy out of my pocket. I slide him across the wooden floorboards with my feet, and he comes to a stop at the oriental style rug in the centre of the room. I kiss Astrid and push her backwards onto the bed.

17

American English

Lewis loved Snow Patrol. That could be you some day, Lewey,
Davie imagined saying to his wee brother, that could be you.
Lewey had a real talent for art and writing, was just too shy to do
anything with it.
Davie dropped the orange juice.

'MORNING, YOU,' ASTRID is lying on her front and kisses me
on the shoulder. Her lips are sticky and cling to my skin.

'Hey, morning, yourself,' I kiss her back.

She tastes musky and stale, and like milky coffee going
slightly sour, but all in a wonderful way. Even though I'm
tired, I let her slide herself on top of me.

We both doze off again, and when I wake up she's lying with
one arm across my chest. Her hair is sticking to her forehead
and her skin is warm against mine. The sheets are damp and
moist, like sleeping inside a tent.

It's fucking ace. I can't believe I'm here.

'I think I heard your phone,' Astrid says opening her eyes
and stretching her arms.

I glance over at her alarm clock. It's after eleven.

'Probably work,' I reply, 'I think I'm meant to be in today.'

'You rebel. Won't they be mad?'

The rebel on his own tonight.

'Probably. I'd rather be here though.'

'You want a coffee?' Astrid asks, 'I need one badly.'

'I'd rather have tea if you've got any?'

'Ha, you're so British.'

'Scottish, actually.'

She pulls the pillow out from behind my head and hits me with it. I fall back onto the mattress, and watch her as she pads naked around her room. She has a butterfly tattoo on her right hip. I follow it as it flutters around the bedroom, before it's swatted by the waistband of a pair of shorts she slips on. Astrid pulls a Blondie t-shirt over her head, ties her hair back in a clip and blows me a kiss.

'How do you take your tea, gorgeous?'

'Just milk, cheers.'

'No problem.' She leaves me alone in her bedroom.

In her bed.

Astrid's bed.

I prop myself up on my elbow and look around me as I wait for her to come back. Her black bra is lying on the floor; I hadn't noticed the pink polka-dots on it last night. It matches those socks Susan gave me. Man, last night was like some kind of crazy fantasy. It's been ages since I hooked up with someone, especially someone I really like. If I pinch myself I'll probably wake up in my own bed.

Alone and with a stiffy.

Don't pinch yourself.

I can smell toast coming from somewhere and my stomach grumbles. We never quite managed the pizza last night.

My eyelid starts to twitch and I rub at it.

His eyelid started to twitch, the only part of him that could move.

The door is kicked open. Astrid is carrying two mugs and balanced on top is a plate of toasted bagels. I can smell the cinnamon from them as she comes towards me.

'Sorry, I took so long,' she says, 'my flatmate was, like, totally giving me the third degree, huh? Budge up.'

I take the plate from her and slide across the bed to make

room. She puts the mugs on the bedside table and gets in next to me. She wriggles her toes up next to mine. Her feet are freezing from wandering around the flat barefoot.

The ring disintegrated around his bare feet and he kicked the smoke away.

'Thanks,' I take a drink of tea as she passes me a mug.

'No problem.'

I bite into one of the bagels and feel melted butter dribble down my chin.

'This is nice, huh?' Astrid says sipping on her coffee.

'Yeah, totally. Just kick me out though, if you've got stuff to do or that.'

'Trying to escape?'

'Nah, totally not. It's just, you know.'

'I know, I'm sorry, I'm so bad for teasing, it's a nervous habit.'

I'd be happy to stay here all day. It's just the awkward morning after thing. What if in her head she's, like, get out, go home and I'm hanging about her bed like a lost sock. A lost spotty sock.

'Do you fancy watching a movie or something? I feel, like, being totally lazy today, huh?' She licks her finger and runs it across the empty bagel plate, collecting the crumbs.

'Aye, sounds good,' I reply, watching as she sucks the crumbs off her fingertip.

Two days later, it's time to make a move. It's like I've been on holiday: away from reality, from responsibility.

I know Jamesy is pissed off at me for ignoring him, but two days off isn't going to hurt him; without my legs he's going nowhere.

I don't want to leave, but I know I have to. Astrid's got uni work to do and I really need to get in touch with work, seeing as I've dingied them for the last few days. The battery in my phone's run out and I'm starting to stink a bit; I could do with a change of clothes and some fresh air. The room smells of sweat and spunk and coffee and toast: eau de Pulp record.

'I'll see you soon, huh?' Astrid says as I stand at her front door.

'Yeah, totally,' I lean forward on the balls of my feet and kiss her.

'Stop that or I'll never let you leave.'

'I don't think I'd mind that somehow.'

'My flatmate thinks I've been abducted by aliens or something and you're gonna be in so much trouble at work.'

'I don't care, it was worth it,' I shrug.

She rises up on her tiptoes and runs her fingers across my whiskered cheeks.

'Okay, right, I'd better head then,' I say, 'I'll see you soon, eh?'

'You betcha,' she kisses me on the end of my nose, and then waves from the door as I finally tear myself away.

I hear the door click behind me as I reach the first landing. The sound of it echoes around the stairwell, and I want to run back up there and force her to let me in.

My heart starts pounding really fast. I have to lean against the wall to catch a breath.

inoutinoutinoutinoutinoutinoutinoutinoutinoutinout

One finger, one thumb, one arm, one leg, one finger, one thumb, one arm, one leg.

I try to visualise myself being back here in a few days, but I can't do it. What if this is it? That I'll never make it back here. The scariness of that thought and the loneliness of the empty stairwell overwhelms me. My eyelid starts to twitch and I push my palms into my eyes.

The only moving body part.

He never went back in there, but sometimes stood outside with his palms flat against the door.

242

The rectangular scar on my hands flashes in front of me.
This is a low.

'Are you alright?'

There's a lassie standing in front of me. Fuck, she must think I'm a right weirdo. Leaning against the wall, blocking the way for her.

'Aye, sorry, I'm fine.'

I run down the rest of the stairs, pull the main door open and breathe in the air outside.

Inoutinoutinout in out in out. In. Out. In. Out. In. Out.

The sunlight hurts my eyes after being inside for so long, and I can hardly see where I'm going. Is Astrid looking out her window? I don't want her to see me staggering about like a fool. I look down and follow a line of tar running along the centre of the pavement.

Jamesy buzzes at me as I unlock my front door.

There you are; I thought I'd left you behind. I know, I'm sorry. I was just having a good time is all. Did you find your own way home? Should I start calling you Lassie? Okay, okay, sorry, I didn't mean to take the piss. Come on, stop being so jealous.

I know I've neglected you for a couple of days, but I'm back now and I'm focused. Yeah, maybe not the now though, eh? I'm fucking knackered.

Alfie pops his head out of his room, as I push the front door shut behind me.

'Your scary cousin's been round here looking for you.'

'Susan?'

'Aye, I think that's her.'

'Shit.'

'Aye, she was pretty worried, was trying your mobile and that, but she said it was dead.'

'Aye, the battery ran out.'

'Where were you anyway?'

'With that lassie I told you about.'

'No way, you sly dog you. What did I say about the zoo?'

'I know, I owe you one, Alfie.'

'Anytime, Davie boy, anytime.'

He leans against his doorframe and crosses his arms.

'I suppose I'd better go phone Susan, tell her I'm okay.'

'Aye, I was half expecting the polis to show up.'

'She didn't call them, did she?'

'Nah, I don't think so. Eh, she might have. I can't remember what she said, I was trying to teach her wee girl how to play my new guitar. I kind of switched off a bit to be honest. She can go on, eh?'

'Aye, that's Susan. Right,' I hold up my phone and Alfie nods and leaves me to it.

I chuck all my crap down on the bed and search out my phone charger. I plug it in and let it sit for a few minutes before switching the phone on.

I'm bombarded by beeps: sixteen missed calls.

I put my mobile on speaker phone, lie back on my bed and listen to all the voicemails.

David? It's Laura here, it's... half ten and you were supposed to be here at nine. Just wondering where you are.

Hey, Davie, do you fancy coming round for tea tonight with me and Pammy? Let me know, okay?

David, it's now twelve-thirty and still no sign of you. Can you phone me, please.

Davie, I'm technically not speaking to you, but Laura is really pissed off. Where are you? Stop being a dick and phone in.

Okay, so you've missed a day's work now. I expect to see you tomorrow with a good excuse.

Why haven't you got back to me? I take it you won't be round tonight now? I need to speak to you about something, can you come over tomorrow?

Davie, where are you? I'm starting to get worried now.

Okay, it's now Thursday and still no word from you. Please phone me, David.

David, I've had your cousin in here looking for you. She seems worried. If you won't phone me, can you at least speak to her?

Davie, where are you? I'm so sorry I shouted at you the other night, just be okay, okay. I couldn't bear it if something had happened to you and we'd been fighting.

It's not even ringing now, just going straight to answer machine. I'm really worried. Please phone me.

Pammy's in tears wondering what's happened to you. I've been round to your work and your flat and nobody's seen you. Where are you?

Alright, Davie boy. Your scary cousin was round today, she's freaking out. Thinks you're dead or something. Can you phone her, pal? Unless of course you are dead, because that would just freak her out more, or maybe it would be comforting, I think it'd be ace to have a final conversation with a ghost. If you're dead you can phone me, alright. Man, if you really are dead, I'm going to feel like a right shit for this message, so phone your crazy cousin. Go do it. Now. Okay. Go.

I'm starting to get pissed off now, Davie. Where the fuck are you? I don't know what to do? I'm this close to phoning the police, or your mum. For fuck sake, get in touch.

I'm really sorry for getting angry, I'm just really worried now and Colin's been hassling me, I'm a bit on edge and I just really want to see you. Pammy and I are meant to be going to Australia next week; I wanted to tell you that we'd got the tickets. We can't go if you're missing though, please, just let me know if you're okay.

Davie, please can you…

Susan starts crying and the final message cuts off.
Fucking hell, I didn't realise what a situation I'd created. It's only been two days.
Is it hereditary? Every time I see that packet of valium in the bathroom, well, I just worry.
The messages don't help with the rising dread I have at not seeing Astrid again.
I text her to calm my nerves. Something soppy.
Hey u missin u already cant wait 2 cu again x
My phone beeps almost immediately. Good sign.
me2 u sexy boy my bed will b cold + empty without u x
I smile, but her text makes me feel worse. It reminds me that I have to spend the night alone in my dingy flat.
My empty room.
My empty bed.
No warm body huddled next to me, fingernails twirling my chest hair. I think I might be sick.
One finger, one thumb. One finger, one thumb.

Breathe, breathe.

Right, better phone Susan now, get this over with.

The phone barely has time to ring before she answers it.

'Davie, that you?'

'Aye, look I'm… '

'Wherehaveyoubeen?'

'I'm really sorry, I was at a friend's, and my battery ran out and I didn't have a charger… '

'What friend?'

'Eh, nobody you know, a girl.'

Susan hangs up on me.

Fuck, I'd better phone her back. I hit redial.

'Hello.'

'That you, Pammy?'

'Yes, Uncle Davie. Where have you been?'

'Just visiting a friend, sweetheart, can I speak to your mum?'

'She says she doesn't want to speak to you, Uncle Davie… she's crying.'

Fuck.

'Pammy, honey, look tell her I'm really sorry. I'll come round, okay. Tell mum I'm coming round just now, right?'

'Okay, Uncle Davie.'

I chuck on a clean t-shirt and spray myself with deodorant. I've been using Astrid's perfume for the last couple of days, and all I can smell is eau de Sarah Jessica Parker. It reminds me of Astrid. Makes me want to be back there with her.

Alfie's in the living room watching *Flight of the Conchords* on DVD. I can hear him laughing from my room. I wish

I could sit down next to him, but I'd better go make it up to Susan.

'Just in case anyone thinks I'm dead, I'm away to Susan's, okay? She may kill me though.'

'No bother, man. Good luck.'

I head out to the bus stop. I really can't be arsed with this. Talk about fucking overreaction. I guess it's my fault though, I'd better make the effort. Plus, I didn't like what she said about that arsehole Colin, what's he up to?

Not now, Jamesy. I can't. I need to go and see Susan. I don't have time for you at the moment. I know, I know. Looks like I fucking owe everyone at the moment. Man, I'm such a fuck-up. Every time I try to have a good time, I manage to wreck everything.

Alright, Jamesy. For fuck sake. If I come with you, will you shut the fuck up? Aye, okay. One person. Count it. One. Then I'm going round to Susan's.

Jamesy leads me off Morningside Road, along by the Dominion Cinema. It's such a cool building. I don't know anything about architecture, but I guess it's like Art Deco or whatever? I always imagine couples in the forties meeting for dates here. My granny and grandpa, holding hands and dodging bombs.

Fucking hell, Jamesy. Pardon me for breathing. I'm not even allowed to look at the fucking scenery now, am I? I know, I've said sorry. My mind's not been focused the last couple of days. Give me a break though. You're overreacting. Man, calm down, you're boiling. I'm going in the right direction now, cool it.

Jamesy is overheating in my pocket. I'm frightened he's

248

going to melt or blow a circuit or something. The sun is setting and the sky is fuzzy peach. I walk past a railing and the sun flashes through the bars like a strobe light.

There's a weird house up ahead of me. The garden looks a total mess at first glance, but it's meant to be like that. A messy elegance. There's a rockery with plants and flowers out of control. Ivy creeps up the walls of the house, and sunflowers arch around the door. My eyes follow the ivy and I notice this weird, fake window painted on the side of the house.

It's a wooden arch hollowed into the wall. There's a painting of a princess inside it. She's dressed in blue, peering out from behind a curtain. She's got blonde hair, puffball sleeves on her dress and one of those triangle hats with a ribbon trailing from its peak, like she's wearing a fancy police cone on her head.

I might have known it would be this house. This better not be another cheese guy.

The garden gate squeaks as I push it open, and black paint flakes off onto my hand.

He swung the black gate open and was about to step out onto the pavement when the magic eight ball chose a thought.

I ring the doorbell, but nobody answers.

I can't just wander into someone's house. That's going a bit too far. I might get arrested.

You sure about that?

I glance around me. There's nobody about, and I'm in a hurry to get to Susan's, so what the fuck. Jamesy won't let up until I do this.

I push down on the door handle and the door swings open. The house is totally back to front. I expect to find myself in someone's hallway, but I'm in a kitchen instead. Some woman's kitchen.

She's sitting at a long, wooden dining table, like something out of Henry the Eighth's banqueting hall. The floor is stone and I can feel the cold through my flimsy Converse. She looks old and young at the same time. Her face is wrinkled, but she's got really long hair. It's almost down to her waist, and it's not grey, but silver. It's sparkling.

I expect her to scream or stand up and throw something at me, but she looks like she's been expecting me. Waiting for me.

She pats the bench running the length of the table and I sit down next to her.

The kitchen smells of baking. There's a plate of biscuits in the middle of the table, next to a jug of iced pink lemonade.

The ice tinkles in the jug as she pours me a drink. She offers the plate to me, and I take a biscuit and bite into it. It's still warm and the centre is gooey: just out of the oven, not had time to crisp up yet. She takes the headphones off me from where they've been hanging around my neck, puts them on and waits for me to activate Jamesy.

Faithfull As Tears Go By by Marianne Faithfull As Tears Go By by Marianne Faithfull As Tears Go By by M

I can smell paint mixed in with the biscuits, and I wonder if she's been decorating. Her hair shimmers and twists in the air, like Medusa's snakes. As she listens, she sways from side to side and strokes her belly.

I lost you twice. The first time was when they made me give you up. It wasn't right for a sixteen-year-old girl to bring up a baby, especially when she wouldn't tell anyone who the daddy was.
The second time was when I was older and I tried to find you.
When I was old enough to realise what a mistake I'd made.
I wrote you a letter but it got returned. At first I thought you didn't want to see me. It was only when I tried to phone that I found out you'd had leukaemia.
I don't know what's worse. Having to watch you get sicker and sicker and not being able to do anything, or not being around to hold your hand and finding out after it's too late.

You'd have been forty-seven today. Almost fifty. I can't imagine that little baby at fifty. I never knew your eye colour, your hair colour, what you smelt like, what your laugh sounded like. I never even got to hold you, they just took you away. They didn't realise that forty-seven years later, I'd still remember your birthday. But you know all this, don't you? I'm sorry I repeat myself. Change the record, Mum, I imagine you saying, but I don't know what your voice sounded like so it's just words in my head. No voice, just words.

I wonder what your other Mum is feeling like today. I wonder if she gets the same ache inside as I do. That same emptiness. The emptiness that I pass on every year. She didn't carry you, she didn't lose you twice, she couldn't possibly feel the same way that I do.

I know your other parents didn't make it happen. They couldn't help it that you got sick. I can't help but wonder though: would you still be here if they'd let me keep you?

She hands me back the headphones and smiles, but she doesn't look happy. I take a drink of juice and press my hands against the cup, allow the drips of condensation to cool the palms down.

This is like the cheese guy. It doesn't feel right. Where's the zzzhhmmmm? Where's my boost?

A bumble bee is crawling across the table, I hadn't noticed it before. She sees me looking at it and holds up a saucer of strawberry jam. There's a cotton bud sitting in the saucer; the cotton-wool part has been pulled off one end and replaced with a blob of jam.

'You can bring a dying bee back to life by feeding it jam,' she says, 'I found him lying on the path out there.'

The bee is buzzing as it wanders around the table. It's hypnotic and fills the room. It makes my lips itch.

Davie took the comb and tried to copy his grandpa. He

couldn't do it though. The paper made his lips tickle and he rubbed at them with the comb, trying to scratch the itchiness away. Davie put two Penguin biscuits down on the table. It was time to pass on some wisdom to his little brother.

The bee looks drunk and zig-zags across the plate of biscuits, like a wino trying to cross the road.

'It takes them a while to get their strength back,' she says and strokes the bee's furry body with her pinkie.

'Burra, burra,' she says, and the bee buzzes like a contented cat.

I finish my juice and biscuit, and put Jamesy away. I'm woozy and I have to hold on to the table for support. Everything's shimmering round the edges.

Dream sequence.

This isn't real. It doesn't feel solid.

What's in those biscuits? I've been drugged.

'You're so young this time,' she looks at me, 'you're the youngest one I've met.'

'Youngest what?'

'What caused so much pain so young?'

I feel like I'm sinking. Low and aching at the loss of something I never had to begin with. I'm missing something. Something is missing.

I need to get out of here.

I climb over the bench and stumble towards the door. She grabs my hands as I go past, and rubs the rectangular scar with her fingers.

'Not long to go now, Trackman.'

'What did you call me?'

She whispers something at the bee; its wings vibrate and it takes off from the table.

Bzzzzzz.

Where's my buzz, Jamesy? This is all wrong, something is missing.

The bee flies towards me and I duck, instinctively closing my eyes. It dodges past my head and drones in my ear. It knows something I don't. I follow it out into the garden, out into the fresh air.

18

Downer

Lewis was always writing poems and stories. After they both got too old for the radio show, Lewis moved onto a home-made newspaper. It was pretty good stuff, even if the subject matter was always kind of depressing.
Davie dropped the orange juice.

FUCKING HELL, JAMESY, what was all that about? She acted like she knew me, like she'd met me before. It was weird, made me feel all funny, and not in a good way. I mean, I get the importance of making sure that bees don't die out, but feeding them jam? Yeah, I know it worked, that's not the point. She scared me. Is that some sort of payback for being with Astrid? Like the cheese guy, I get punished for wanting to spend time with her? For being happy.

I don't deserve to be happy when he can't.

You might have warned me about those fucking cookies too, I think there was something in them. I feel really weird, kind of sick but kind of sleepy at the same time. It's not good, not good at all.

Time stood still in there, I'm sure it did. We were only in there for twenty minutes, but it felt like hours. I don't even remember what we were doing before we went in there. That kitchen was like the wardrobe to Narnia.

What am I doing again?

Oh aye, Susan.

Fuck, I'd forgotten about that, she's going to kill me.

I speed-walk to the bus stop and catch the next one heading her way. I can't shake this weird feeling, it's been hanging over me since I left Astrid, but it's worse since we helped that woman.

Where's the buzz, Jamesy? I know I keep asking you that, but you never explain. What's happening to me? I'm the Trackman, why don't I feel great right now? What's up with this whole downer feeling? This splashdown. This crash. It's like, almost like I sucked the bad feelings right out of that woman. Why do you never explain? Tell me what's going on.

I want to lie along the back row of the bus and go to sleep. I'm drained, what a come down. I don't know if I can face Susan right now, not if she's going to shout at me. I want to sleep.

I hope she's okay. She sounded pretty upset on the phone. Plus that weird message about Colin. If he's done anything to her or Pammy. He's a fucking bully, and I hate bullies.

I'm just going up to Paul's house.

You know, I sort of feel sorry for him, in a warped kind of way. It's not all his fault, Susan said, drinking from her glass of wine.

How do you work that one out?

He didn't have a good time growing up, his dad used to hit him and slap his mum around. If he cried, his dad told him he was pathetic, a wimp, not a real man.

You're breaking my heart, Susan, you really are.

I'm just saying, it's no wonder he turned out the way he has.

If anything he should know better, he knows what it's like to be on the receiving end. Bullies are dangerous, you know what they can do.

I know, he can be so good sometimes though. He could be so good. I always think of that nursery rhyme, you know,

*when she was good, she was very, very good, when she was
bad, she was horrid.*

Ring a ring a roses.

*Susan, you're too nice for your own good, the guy's a
dick, he's no good.*

*I know, you're right, I just, I think about Pammy growing
up without a daddy, you know.*

*Better no daddy, than a daddy who treats her mum like
shite.*

*They'd both spent the day in court. Colin got two and a
half years for domestic abuse, possessing a class A drug and
some other petty offences.*

Colin's sister spat at Susan as they left the court.

*I always knew you were a wee hoor, I telt Colin what a
lying bitch you were, got pregnant on purpose.*

*Susan held onto Davie's arm as they walked away, I feel
like I'm in an episode of fucking* Jeremy Kyle, *how did I end
up like this?*

*Pammy spent the night at a friend's house so Davie and
Susan got a bottle of wine and a Chinese.*

*I just want to get this day off me, Susan said pouring
herself another glass of wine.*

*Davie wasn't meant to be drinking on the pills he was
taking, but he had a glass of wine anyway.*

You sure? Susan asked.

Aye, fuck it. One's not going to hurt.

*Susan fell asleep on the couch, and Davie just left her
there. He took the duvet off her bed and covered her with it.
Her lips and teeth were stained from the red wine, it looked
like her gums were bleeding.*

In a parallel universe, Lewis is still alive, Colin is a loving
dad and husband, and I'm still in bed with Astrid.

The curtains are all shut when I head up Susan's driveway. She hasn't phoned me to say piss off, so I assume she'll let me in. Deep down, I think everyone's fucking overreacting. I'm a grown man and a couple of nights of passion have been turned into some melodramatic mountain out of a molehill. Deep down, I also know the reasons for the over-reaction.

Davie, let me in. Unlock the door. I need a pee. What are you doing in there? You've been ages. Davie? Davie, *let me in! Open this door.*

I just want a simple life.

Fuck knows, all I've ever wanted was a simple life.

I stand in front of the door, my head's really not in the right place for this. My finger hovers over the doorbell. One finger, one finger, one finger, one finger. I push it and hear it ring inside the house. The door opens and Pammy looks out from behind the security chain.

'It's you, Uncle Davie,' she says.

She disappears and I hear her dragging something towards the door. She undoes the chain, and is standing on a chair facing me when the door opens.

'Hey, Pammy.'

'Why have you got a beard now?'

'It's not a beard,' I smooth the hair down on her head, 'I've just not shaved for a couple of days.'

'Mummy's in a bad mood with you.'

'I know, I'm here to say sorry.'

'Mummy says you should never go to bed angry.'

'She's right.'

Pammy takes my hand and leads me along the hall towards the living room. Susan is sitting on the sofa reading a magazine and doesn't look up at me. I linger in the doorway.

'Susan, I'm sorry, I stuffed up, okay.'

Susan shuts her magazine and puts it down next to her. She gets up and walks to the front door, where she puts the chain back on and locks the door, then she walks back into the living room.

'Pammy, sweetheart, can you go up to your room for a wee while, so Mummy can speak to Uncle Davie?'

'But I want to stay too.'

'Pammy.'

Susan uses that voice she has, the one that should be obeyed, and I feel like turning round and following Pammy out of there too.

'Do you have any idea what I've been through the last couple of days?'

'If I'd known you were going to be so worried, I would have phoned. It's not like we haven't gone a few days without talking before. I've said sorry, okay. How many times do you want me to say it?'

'At least act as if you mean it, Davie.'

'I do fucking mean it.'

'And don't fucking swear at me in my own house.'

I sit on the chair facing her. Something digs into my arse, and I pull one of Pammy's dolls out from under the cushion.

'I don't feel like I know you right now.'

I shrug my shoulders.

'You don't care about anyone but yourself.'

'Come on, that's not fair.'

The last couple of days is the only time I've thought about myself recently. Fuck this. I don't need this.

'Stop playing with that bloody doll and look at me.'

I put the doll down and look up. Susan bursts out crying. She pulls a tissue out from where it's tucked up her sleeve and blows her nose. The tissue is falling to bits and white specs snow down on to her cardigan.

'I'm sorry, Davie. Ever since Lewis, I've always been scared that you'd do something silly. And when you didn't get in touch with me…'

'Don't be daft, I'm not going to do anything silly,' I move across and join her on the sofa, 'I'm sorry I worried you.'

'I was this close to phoning the police, and your mum.'

'Aye, like she gives a fuck.'

Susan rolls up her magazine and hits me across the head with it.

'What was that for?'

'Just because, because you're here and you're solid, and I want to hear the sound my magazine makes as it hits off your solid head.'

Susan makes us both a cup of tea. She shouts something to me through the kitchen hatch. I don't hear what she says over the noise of the kettle boiling, so I just shout 'yes'.

She appears a few minutes later carrying two mugs of tea and a packet of Penguin biscuits.

Fuck the penguins and their fucking parade; all that mattered was the kissing.

Chocolate biscuits. I know that we're cool again.

'I booked our tickets to see Mum and Dad,' she says.

'Yeah, I heard your voicemail. Sounds good. When do you leave?'

'Not long, a week and a half, we got it cheaper if we went on a certain date so I just went for it.'

'Cool.'

'Aye, Mum and Dad helped me out a bit, it's more expensive going in the summer, but Pammy starts school next month, and I just thought, fuck it.'

'How long you away for?'

'Three weeks.'

Her answer's a football in the chest. I feel like I'm being abandoned and I hate myself for being such a selfish arse. Three weeks without Susan and Pammy around. I moan when she doesn't leave me be, then I moan when she leaves

259

me on my own.

'You can still come,' Susan says, 'just need your flights.'

'Nah, I've told you I can't afford it, plus I can't get all that time off work.'

'I'm surprised you still have a job.'

'Aye, well, even more reason not to go gallivanting off to Australia.'

'I can't persuade you.'

'Nah.'

Susan unwraps a Penguin and bites the end off the biscuit.

Davie put two Penguin biscuits down on the table. It was time to pass on some wisdom to his little brother.

The proper way to eat a Penguin, Davie said, first take off the wrapper and bite off one of the top corners.

Davie and Lewis both unwrapped their biscuits and bit into them.

Next, bite off the bottom, opposite corner.

Davie and Lewis both ate the second corner.

Okay, now you need to put the bottom corner into your mug and sook tea up through the top corner. Wait, not yet. As soon as you feel tea in your mouth, then stop sooking and put the whole biscuit in your mouth, okay?

Lewis nodded.

Right, here goes.

Davie began to suck, nothing happened at first, but then the tea started to move up through the biscuit. When he felt it on his tongue, he crammed the entire biscuit into his mouth, biting down on it. The biscuit dissolved into delicious, chocolatey goo.

What do you think? Davie asked, spitting lumps of mushy biscuit across the table.

Lewis was still chewing, but gave him the thumbs up. A brown streak of saliva trickled down his chin, and his t-shirt was spotted with soggy biscuit. He choked and a bit of biscuit

flew out of his mouth and landed in his mug of tea. Davie
and Lewis watched it float before it sunk, then they both
burst out laughing.

Right, let's try that again.

'Davie, do you have to?' Susan asks, watching me as I bite
off the corner of my Penguin.

'Aye, it's the best way to eat one.'

'It makes such a mess of my mugs. And if Pammy sees you,
she'll want to do it and she's enough of a midden as it is.'

'You mean you haven't showed her how to do this yet?'

'Don't bother, Davie, I'm still trying to get past the peanut
butter and scrunched up crisp sandwiches you showed her
the last time.'

I never taught Lewis anything except how to use a biscuit
as a straw. That was the only thing I passed onto him. What
does that say about me as a big brother? I should have had
more time with him. Time to teach him about decent music,
about films, about how to cope with being a Hearts supporter,
about how not to get a girlfriend.

'You guys packed yet?'

'Nah, Pammy's stuff is all in the suitcase but I've still to
sort out my stuff.'

I'm really sorry for getting angry, I'm just really worried now
and Colin's been hassling me, I'm a bit on edge and I just really want to see you.

'So, what's that arsehole Colin want?'

Susan looks confused, like she's trying to work out how
I know about that.

'Voicemail,' I say.

'Oh aye, I forgot I said that. Ach, it's nothing. I was just
worried about you and overreacting. He wasn't happy about
me phoning the police the other week there.'

'Well he shouldn't be anywhere near you, or is he too fucking stupid to know what "restraining order" means?'

'Language, Davie. And, aye, he knows that. It's fine. We're going away soon, so it's cool. We won't have to worry about him.'

'He'll still be here when you get back.'

'Nah, he's supposedly got a job in Newcastle. Who was it told me that again? Oh aye, Joan in Scotmid. She heard it from his sister, he'll be away by the time we get back.'

'Good riddance. Do you really believe it though?'

'Aye, I don't think he'd try anything. He's just got out, remember.'

'They should have left him in there. You sure that's all there is?'

'Aye, honestly, I wouldn't lie about it. I know I was a total idiot at times over him, but I'm different now. I've got Pammy to think about and she's the most important thing.'

I hate myself for the flash of jealousy I get when she says that. Jealous of a wee lassie. Fucking hell, Davie.

He wanted her to cuddle him, even though he was all grown up he wanted a cuddle from his mum, but she didn't look at him.

I gulp down the final dregs of tea, and choke on a soggy lump of biscuit which goes down the wrong way. Susan was right. The bottom of the mug is covered in mush and there's a chocolate tidemark.

I run my finger around the inside of the mug, scoop up the lump and eat it, lick my fingers clean.

Astrid licked her finger and ran it across the empty bagel plate, collecting the crumbs   she sucked the crumbs off her fingertip.

I feel my cock move and I move my legs to hide it.

I swear Susan's got a fucking sixth sense or something.

'Who was this lassie then?'

'Nobody, someone I met at work.'

'Not Martha?'

'No.'

Talking of which, I should really text Martha. I've not spoken to her since that drunken mess, I should make an effort. Jamesy's right. I don't have time to be the Trackman and to have a normal life. I'm so preoccupied.

'How's work anyway?'

'Not so good really.'

I don't think I'm going to go back.

'That manager, Laura is it? Yeah, she was very nice to me when I went in. Did she give you a hard time?'

'Not really.'

'Have you even spoken to her?'

'Davie, I can't go off to Australia with you out of a job. Phone her, phone her now. Use the landline.'

I glance at my watch. Fuck, the shop's still open.

There you go. I like your watch.

I still like your watch though.

'Davie, are you listening to me? Go, phone them now, for me, make me feel better.'

I knew she would do this, guilt me into phoning work.

This day started off so well, but it's descending into some sort of horrible mess. I can't even think of the word for it. It feels like ages ago that I lay in bed with Astrid, but it was only this morning.

I scroll through my mobile for the number for work. Susan picks up the mugs and the rest of the biscuits. She peers into my mug and sighs, before she heads off into the kitchen.

Could I pretend to phone work? Susan's shadow flits past the kitchen hatch. No, she's eavesdropping on me. I'm going to have to do it. I dial the number.

'Hello, Virgin Megastore, Ryan speaking, how can I help?'

'Could I speak to Laura please?'

'Aye, sure, who's calling?'

'Eh, Paul Green, she'll know what it's about.'

I don't know why I'm lying to Ryan.

To give Susan something to eavesdrop on?

So I don't have to explain myself to Ryan?

To give Jamesy a giggle and get back in his good books?

Because it's become such a habit lately?

He'll probably recognise my voice anyway.

'Cool, just hold the line a minute.'

The phone beeps at me as I'm put on hold, then rings as I'm connected to wherever Laura is.

'Hello, Laura speaking.'

'Hey, it's Davie.'

'I wasn't sure if I'd hear from you.'

'I'm really sorry, I've not been well and my phone battery...'

'I don't want to hear this just now, okay.'

'Okay, but I'd like to explain.'

'It's gone past that now, I'm afraid. We need to do this formally. I have to arrange a disciplinary meeting with you. Can you make... two weeks on Tuesday... eh... at eleven?'

'Aye, I suppose.'

'I have to suspend you until the meeting.'

'Then what?'

'I'm really sorry, David, that all depends on what happens at the meeting, it's kind of out of my hands now. Do you want a union rep with you? I can ask Stewart.'

'Aye, I guess so.'

'Okay, I'll ask him. See you then. Sorry it's had to come to this.'

'Aye, see you.'

I hang up the phone. I'm a helium balloon that used to be on the ceiling but now flops around on the floor. This day started off so good. I was up there, but now.

I know, Jamesy, it's a shite job. Why should I care? I don't even know if I'll go to this meeting.

'You in trouble?'

'Nah, not really. Got to go and have a chat with her about it, but nothing a bit of grovelling won't fix.'

'You'll be fine, they won't kick you out for one mistake.'

I nod at her, thinking about the verbal and the written warning I already have and haven't told Susan about.

'So, who's this girl? Is it serious?'

'I don't know, I hope so. I don't want to speak about it in case I jinx it.'

'At least give me her name.'

'Astrid.'

'Astrid, that's unusual, isn't it.'

'Come on, I don't want to talk about it.'

'Okay, okay.'

Susan puts the TV on.

'Oh you'll never guess what I caught Pammy doing the other day?'

I shake my head.

'She was filming herself on my camera, she had it set up on top of the bed and was acting out a wee play with her dolls.'

'Aww, that's funny.'

'It reminded me of you though, remember you and Lewis used to tape yourselves and make up radio shows? You'd make us listen to them in the car when we went on holiday.'

Davie held a finger up to his mouth, ssshhh, then pressed two buttons down on the cassette player: Record and Play together.

'Aye.'

'I wonder what happened to all those tapes?'

'Who knows, Mum probably chucked them out with all

the other memories.'

'It was hard for her, everything reminded her.'

'Yeah, well, she wasn't the only one it was hard for.'

You promised. You promised. You promised. You promised.

I stare at the TV and Susan doesn't say anything else. Pammy comes back in and I'm grateful for the distraction. She puts on her *Finding Nemo* DVD, and even though I'm enjoying it, I feel my eyes closing.

I wake up sprawled across the sofa, with a blanket lying over me.

He took the duvet off her bed and covered her with it.

I get up and switch the TV on, then get back under the blanket. I've no idea what time it is, but it must be late. The rest of the house is silent, apart from the walls creaking. I find the remote control down on the floor next to the sofa, and turn the volume down. I'm illuminated by the flashing colours from the TV screen.

His face was illuminated when he opened the door and he took out the carton and unscrewed the lid.

I'm not sure what's on, some film with Clint Eastwood in it by the looks of it.

What's up, Jamesy? I know, I'm sorry. I konked out there. Tomorrow, I promise, tomorrow we'll get back down to business. I'm surprised you didn't want to play Susan a song earlier, when she started greeting like that. What song would you have given her? You can't do it to people I know, can you? It was bad enough at the party trying to explain away what we were up to, it has to be strangers doesn't it? A shared moment with a stranger.

Yeah, I just need a good night's sleep and I'll be back on the case. No work to go to, no Susan to answer to, I'm all yours, Jamesy.

I feel around in my pocket and send Astrid a soppy goodnight text, even though she's probably been asleep for hours. I lie watching Clint do his thing, not really sure what's going on.

19

Bizarre Love Triangle

Davie flicked the letterbox a few times and rang the doorbell again.
Come on, Lewey, where are you?
He bent down to look for his keys.
Davie dropped the orange juice.

MY ALARM GOES off and I can barely open my eyes to see it. I throw my arm out and switch the alarm off, then lie still for a few seconds. I'm fucking knackered. Jamesy and I were out really late last night. I don't even know what time we got in at. Alfie was still up, although that counts for nothing. I think he had a girl in there with him.

Davie noticed the strip of red light coming from the gap under Alfie's door. It shone across the hall floor like a laser beam.

Davie fell into bed. As he lay there his ears tuned into the darkness. There was someone in there with Alfie. He could hear muffled voices. Muffled voices which gradually faded into moans and the sound of Alfie's bed creaking.

Davie put Jamesy's headphones on, pulled the duvet over his head and tried to drown it out. He didn't want to hear that. It was over two weeks since he'd heard from Astrid, and hearing Alfie just reminded him of what he was missing. He'd texted her a few times and tried to call her, but her phone was always switched off, or it just rang out. He couldn't understand what had happened, why she was ignoring him. What had he done to put her off? He wanted to believe that her phone was broken, or she'd had to fly home to America in an emergency and couldn't contact him, but deep down he knew it was something worse. She didn't want to see him again and he didn't know why. He thought she liked him, she acted like she did. Was it just about the sex? Another Scottish conquest to add to her list before she went home. He'd even thought about going round to her flat, but Jamesy had persuaded him not to. He didn't want to look like some desperate stalker.

Jamesy's headphones have slipped off my head during the night and are now round my neck. His wire has curled round me like I'm a fly in a spider's web. Jamesy lies cradled under my arm.

I push off the covers and unwind him, put him on the bedside table.

Now, now, people will talk.

I force myself to get up before I fall asleep again. I grab a damp towel off the floor, better have a shower. I've got that fucking meeting with Laura today. I know, I know. I said I wasn't going to go, but the more I think about it, the more I realise I need to keep my job.

Davie pressed for £20.

You do not have sufficient funds available.

He pressed for £10.

You do not have sufficient funds available.

The ATM spat his card back at him.

We talked about this, Jamesy. I'll go part-time or cut my hours down, but I can't leave altogether. I know, I said that last week, but I'm starting to realise... I am committed. Come on, give me a break. Look, how's this for commitment. I hold my palms up towards him. My hands are aching this morning. I've got a permanent mark now, a rectangle imprint on both palms. I feel like that bad guy from *Raiders of the Lost Ark*.

There was a rectangular scar on each palm, like he'd been

burnt by something and the shape of it had melted onto his skin.

The scabs never get a chance to heal and have turned into raised welts, the scars of a self-harmer: the knife has gone in the same cut more than once. Sometimes I can feel a pulse, my hands beating.

Like a pulse: the shadow of her hand beating.

Davie and Lewis sat in the living room. Davie was watching some comedy sketch show on the TV. *Lewis usually went to the Scouts on a Tuesday, but he hadn't wanted to go tonight, so he was sitting on a bean bag in the corner of the room, reading.*

A sketch came on set in a chippy. One of the characters mistook the other one's hand for a fish. He took the hand, dipped it in the white batter then dunked the whole thing in the hot fat. The hand sizzled and crackled as it cooked in the fat, the sound of canned laughter playing in the background.

What if I cooked your hands like a fish supper? Davie asked. How would you be able to read then?

Lewis didn't look up from his book.

Eh, Lewey, what if I cooked your hands?

Davie crawled across the carpet and grabbed Lewis by the wrists.

Let go, you're hurting me, Davie.

Lewis's book fell to the floor at his feet.

I'm going to fry your hands, little brother.

Please, you're hurting me.

Lewey's wrist was all red and blotchy with broken veins purple beneath the skin.

What happened? Davie pulled up Lewis's sleeve.

Nothing, Lewis pulled his arm away.

Your arm's a mess, that wasn't me, was it? I'm sorry, I was just mucking about.

Nah, it's just a Chinese burn.

Who gave you that?

Nobody, people were just doing it at school today. Loads of people got one.

Lewis pulled his sleeve down, picked up his book and started reading again.

As I pass Alfie's room I hear Common People, the William Shatner version, coming from inside.

The clothes were thrown aside as he danced like a madman around his new bedroom.

I also get a whiff of bacon coming from the kitchen. The bathroom door is shut and I can hear the shower going, so I head towards the kitchen instead. I'll try and scrounge a bacon butty off Alfie, before he and his mystery woman scoff them all.

It's not Alfie in the kitchen after all, but some girl bent over the grill. She's wearing Alfie's retro Scotland football top: the yellow one.

As she bends over it rises up.

Her arse cheeks peek out from under her pants.

A tattoo on the side of her hip.

Butterfly.

A butterfly tattoo.

He followed it as it fluttered around the bedroom, before it was swatted by the waistband of a pair of shorts.

I recognise that butterfly.

She stands and turns to face me.

We both stare at each other without saying a word. The bacon sizzles under the grill and I can hear the fat spitting. Sparks ping off the grill element. The smoke from the bacon makes my eyes sting and they start to water. I don't want to wipe them in case she thinks I'm crying.

In case Astrid thinks I'm crying.

Fucking hell.

Beep. Beep. Beep. Beep. Beep. Beep. Beep.

We both spring into life, as the smoke alarm goes off.

'Jesus, Davie, I didn't know, I swear I didn't know.'

I ignore her and waft my towel across the smoke alarm until it stops. She pulls the Scotland top down and I realise I'm only wearing my boxers. Why are we embarrassed? We've seen each other naked.

Lay with one arm across his chest   *she slid herself on top*   *she sucked the crumbs off her fingertip.*

In a parallel universe, Astrid is making me breakfast. We sit on the sofa eating bacon sandwiches in our underwear and she has just spent the night with me. Me. Not Alfie.

She turns round and pulls the tray of bacon out from under the grill. I feel a strange mixture of concern and satisfaction as fat spits out onto her bare arm and she flinches. She puts the tray down on the counter and turns back to me but I'm already on my way out.

'Davie, wait.'

'Why? You didn't? It's been, what? Two weeks?'

'I know this looks really bad.'

'I texted you, I phoned you.'

'I know, but, please don't shout.'

She grabs my arm and pulls me back into the room, then shuts the door.

'Don't want lover boy to hear, eh?' I say.

'Don't be like this.'

'Like what?'

'I never meant for this to happen.'

'Well, you shouldn't have shagged my best mate then.'

'I didn't know Lee was your best mate.'

'Who the fuck's Lee?'

Nicknamed Alfie after the Michael Caine character.

'Don't get all fucking judgemental on me. I really liked you, I was upset, my friends took me out to get drunk and

I did something stupid, that's all.'

'A stupid mistake. You're fucking cooking him breakfast.'

'He's in the shower, I only came through to check on it because he's taking so long and I thought the flat would burn down.'

The kettle is boiling, but hasn't switched itself off. The kitchen fills with steam, and my glasses cloud over.

We stand in silence and she reaches out to touch my arm, but I pull it away. It still feels like electricity when she touches me and I can't bear it. I feel like crying. I really do.

Davie stood against the wall drinking spiked Coke, while Mike slow danced with Lucy. Davie watched as Mike's hands moved down to Lucy's arse and Mr Henderson the Chemistry teacher came over and told him to behave himself. Davie went home before the lights came up. He couldn't bear having to walk home with Mike and Lucy, not when he'd hoped at the start of the school disco he'd be the one walking her home.

'I can't believe this.' I say, 'I was right then, it was all about the sex to you.'

'Don't you dare, Davie, you're as much to blame as I am. You lied to me.'

'What? I never did.'

'You said there was nothing going on with you and that girl from your work.'

'There isn't.'

'Well, how come my flatmate saw you fucking making out with her outside some fast food place.'

He looked down at his jeans, and could see the greasy stain from the chips and cheese which had landed in his lap.

'That wasn't, we're not together. I don't even know your flatmate.'

'She passed you on the stair that day you left mine, recognised you, she'd been telling us all about this couple she'd seen in the street, started off making out then ended up having a huge fight. We all had a big laugh about it.'

'But that was before.'

'Before you lied to me, told me you were just good friends.'

'So you just believed your flatmate? She doesn't even know me.'

'She was worried about me, said you were acting all weird in the stairwell.'

Leaning against the wall, blocking the way for her.

Fuck, fuck, fuck, fuck, fuck, fuck.

'There's nothing between me and Martha. I really like you.'

'I really liked you too, but I don't want to get involved in something so messy.'

'You slept with Alfie, how fucking messy is that?'

I can't stand to look at her anymore. I head to my bedroom and throw on some clothes, stick Jamesy in my pocket and head back out into the hallway. The stinging in my eyes is turning into real tears now.

'Hey, Davie boy,' Alfie says, as he emerges from a steam filled bathroom with a towel wrapped round his waist.

'Fuck you,' I say and slam the front door behind me as I leave the flat.

I run down the stairs, holding my breath like the air is infected, and burst out onto the street. My heart is thumping inside my chest and I can't get it to slow down. I can hear it inside my ears, behind my eyes, in my mouth.

THUMPTHUMPTHUMPTHUMPTHUMPTHUMP

I look up towards the kitchen window, are Astrid or Alfie looking out at me? I can't work out what window it should be, so I scan along the building.

Someone's hanging.

There's a body hanging in one of the windows.

My heart stops thumping altogether.

Everything inside me stops.

Then.

I realise.

It's only a suit.

Someone's suit for work, hanging up for the day. Flat and pin-striped. No body filling it out. No head. No arms. No feet.

My heart starts going again and I feel it in my stomach this time. My gut contracts in time with each beat, getting faster and stronger and faster and stronger until.

I fall forward and throw up in the road. Retch until nothing's left and my throat and my nose sting with vinegar.

The crunch as he bit down on each onion.

The bones in my legs dissolve and I sink down onto the kerb. I sit there, lean my head between my knees and shut my eyes.

Fucking hell.

I can't believe what just happened.

I need to catch a breath, get myself together. I can't believe that just happened. Jesus. Breathe properly, come on, breathe properly.

Onefingeronethumbonearmonelegonefinger onethumbone armoneleg one finger, one thumb, one arm, one leg, one finger, one thumb, one finger, one thumb.

I try to replay the conversation in my head. Even though I just spoke to her, I can hardly remember what we said. Why did her flatmate have to go interfering?

And fucking hell, Martha. Why is it always her?

We all fall down.

I open my eyes and pick up a twig lying at my feet, trace shapes in the dirt with it.

What's that, Jamesy? Yeah, you're right. She didn't wait very long before she jumped into bed with someone else. She just assumed I was an asshole, didn't even bother to check to see if it was true or not.

Stupid slut. Even if I wasn't completely honest about me and Martha, she still went out and slept with Alfie. She should have spoken to me. I could have explained.

I never even thought of that. You're right. I'm sure I told Alfie what her name was. I did.

Astrid, eh? You're a dark horse.

I definitely did. He should have known. How many Americans called Astrid are there in Edinburgh, for fuck sake? Did he know it was the same girl and took her home anyway?

Anger rises up inside me and I push away the reasoning side of my brain. Push away the voice that says, you know Alfie's memory, he probably didn't remember. Or you know Alfie. He sleeps with girls and doesn't even find out what their names are.

Instead I let the anger and the hurt take over. Jamesy tells me I've been betrayed and I believe him.

Do you know what makes it worse? They actually make a really good couple. They look like they should be together.

I was an idiot to think she'd go out with me anyway. You're right, I'm better off without either of them.

Just you and me, Jamesy.

You and me versus the world.

No, I'm not going to that fucking meeting. Course I'm not going.

I can smell her. I can smell Astrid. I sniff under my armpits. Her perfume's still on my t-shirt from when I stayed with her, clinging to me. I breathe it in, hold it inside me.

The thought of them in there, eating bacon rolls, kissing each other. Tomato sauce on her fingers.

Sticky Fanta.

I grind the twig into the dirt, push it into the ground until it splits and breaks.

In a parallel universe, it's me in there with Astrid, not him. Me.

I need to get out of here. I just need to get away.

Jamesy stays quiet while we walk. Man, I need help. Something to keep me upright. I could do with one of those earlier hits, one of the ones that gave me a buzz. Something to lift me up and keep me up.

I'm a wavelength.

Up.   Up.   Up.   Up.
     Down.   Down.   Down.   Down.

One minute I'm pumped full of rage. The next minute I'm so sad I could cry. Every so often I'll get a waft of her perfume, and it's a punch to the gut.

I want to punch Alfie. Even though he's my best friend, I want to hit him.

Fight or flight?

Fright.

Davie's dad kept telling Lewis to hit them back, that bullies were all wimps at heart. As if Lewis was ever going to do that.

Davie hadn't realised it was so bad. He heard Lewis complaining about being unwell some mornings, faking illness so he didn't have to go to school, but Davie thought it was to do with schoolwork, teachers. Not his gang of friends suddenly turning against him.

By the time Davie found out what was going on, it had been going on too long, had already gone too far.

He came home to find Lewis at the kitchen table. His school shirt was ripped and his top lip was bleeding and swollen. He held a bag of frozen peas to his face, while his mum and dad sat at the other end of the table.

What happened?

I tripped over the strap of my schoolbag.

It didn't sound like Lewis speaking, his swollen mouth had changed his voice into somebody else's.

Dahdadahdahhhh, Welcome to Radio Watts, I'm Lewis and this is my sidekick...

And your shirt?

Lewis didn't answer, just looked down at the table and shut his eyes. Later his mum managed to get the story out of him. Lewis had tripped, but only because he was being chased. He'd been so scared he'd left his schoolbag lying in the street. When Davie and his dad went to look for it, they found Lewis's stuff hanging in some blossom trees. The pink petals stuck to his gym kit and his pencil case and his jotters like confetti.

Tree blossom stuck to him like he was some sort of walking mosaic.

Their mum went to the school and spoke to the guidance teacher, despite Lewis pleading with her not to.

They thought it was all sorted after that.

I don't even know what time it is when Jamesy finally calls me into action. I've lost track of the day. We've just been walking. Like that day back when I first became the Trackman. Since I met Jamesy, I don't think I've walked so much in my life.

Aye, what is it?

We've ended up outside some bar. I've been in here once before, I think, but it was a total dive, a real old man's pub. It looks like it's been done up since then.

The pub door is on the corner of the building and there's a gargoyle thing carved into the wall above it. It's got red lights inserted into its eyes, they flash at me as I enter the pub.

I look around, there's a few groups of people sitting around tables. A couple of guys standing at the bar. Then I clock her.

A lassie sitting on her own, in one of the raised booths facing the bar. She's working her way through a bottle of red wine. I'm desperate to forget about what's happened today. Desperate to lose myself in the Trackman, so I head straight towards her. No messing about. Give me the hit now.

'Mind if I join you?' I ask her.

'Sure.' She shuffles along the seat. Her lips and teeth are stained with red wine.

It looked like her gums were bleeding.

She's pretty pished. There's no need to make up some story for her. This should be easy. It feels like I'm taking advantage.

'Davie,' I say and hold out my hand.

'Kate,' she replies, shaking it.

'Do you want to hear a song?' I ask.

No messing about, Jamesy. You're always on at me for dithering about. This time, no messing. I'm the Trackman. Don't regret choosing me. I can do this, be this.

Trackman Trackman Trackman Trackman Trackman Track

'What song?' She leans across the seat so her face is almost touching mine.

She's got lumps of mascara in the corners of her eyes and her perfume is really strong. It catches in the back of my throat and tickles my nose. It's not soft like Astrid's. I turn away from her.

'Bless you,' she says as I sneeze.

I hand her the headphones.

'Is it The Killers? I love them, I saw them at T in the Park, they were amazing.'

She squints at me when she speaks. It's like I'm one of those old magic eye pictures and she has to screw up her eyes the right way to make me out.

'Just wait and see,' I say.

She picks up her glass of wine and downs the final dregs, before filling it up again from the bottle. There are lipstick marks on the rim of her glass.

'Right, ready now,' she says and puts the headphones on.

'Oh wait, can I choose? Mr Briiiigghtsiide!' She tries to grab Jamesy out of my hands.

Trackman Trackman Trackman Trackman Trackman Trackman Tr

I'm the Trackman. I'm in charge here. I'm not Davie, I'm the Trackman.

I push her away and give her the wine glass to try and distract her.

Alanis Morissette You Oughta Know by Alanis Morissette You Oughta Know by Alanis Morissette You

Everything about Kate seems to intensify. The smell of perfume gets stronger, the stained lips get darker. Her eyes glow red like a badly taken photo, or that stupid gargoyle thing at the door of the pub. The wine shimmers and swirls in her glass like a whirlpool.

What did I do wrong? What could she give you that I couldn't?
I know I wasn't always there all the time, I'd work late, go out with my friends when I could have been with you. I should have been more attentive.
Sometimes I'd push you off when you wanted to have sex. I wasn't in the mood all the time. I couldn't be late for work. I was cold in bed. Frigid. No good.
I was no good. I didn't do enough.
But you didn't do enough either. The first sign of trouble and you shag somebody else. We weren't even in trouble, all those reasons you quoted at me, the ones you'd obviously rehearsed in your

head for the day you got caught. They were all bullshit. You just needed an excuse. An excuse to make yourself feel better because you couldn't keep your dick in your pants.

I'm such an idiot. Why am I sitting here blaming myself? So what if I didn't want to have sex at the exact time that you did. So what if I wanted to go out with my friends instead of you. This is the fucking 21st century. I'm not here to please you all the time. And I work late because I have to, because I love my job. And I'm not cold or frigid. You're just a cock. I can't believe I'm getting drunk over you, shedding tears over you. You're just an arsehole, and she's a slut. I'm better off without you. I'm glad you did this, I'm glad I found out. Now I don't have to waste anymore time on you.

'Jesus, that was great,' says Kate.

I fold up the headphones and stick Jamesy in my pocket, where she can't get at him. My hands tingle like a cold sore.

I was hoping to get a buzz from her, but instead the rage from before has returned. Astrid and Alfie writhe naked and sweaty in my head.

None of them had realised how bad it had got after that. They thought that day in the kitchen had been the summit, but really they had all still been at the bottom of the hill.

Davie wanted to fucking kill them.

The ambulance driver didn't even bother with the lights or the sirens as it pulled away. Davie watched from the front garden as it reached the end of the road then he was out the front gate and on his way to Paul Johnstone's house.

Paul's house.

I'm just going up to Paul's house.

When Davie got there, he kept his finger pushed down on the doorbell so it rang continuously. He was running on adrenaline. This wasn't Davie at all, this was someone else ringing the doorbell. Not him, someone else.

A man wearing pyjamas appeared at the door.

What the hell are you up to?
Where's Paul?
He's in bed, what do you want?
I want to see him.
Get out of here or I'll phone the police.
They should be here, they have to speak to Paul.
What?
Your son's a murderer.
He's been in all night, I don't know what you're going on about but I think you've got the wrong house.
He killed my wee brother.
Saying the words out loud floored Davie and all the rage was sucked out of him. He fell forwards onto the steps where he lay crying until the police came.

He fell forward and threw up in the road.

Kate finishes her glass of wine and tries to refill it, but the bottle's empty. She waves over at the bar.

'Can I get another one,' she holds up the bottle, 'and a drink for... what did you say your name was?'

'Davi... the Trackman.'

'And a drink for Davie, the trackstar.'

The barman looks at me as if to say, you sure about this, son?

I nod back.

'Pint of Tennents, please.'

Maybe I should do an Astrid. Kate's not bad looking, older than me, but what does that matter? I'm happy to flirt back with her. Fuck you, Astrid, two can play at this game. The barman brings our drinks over and takes away the empty bottle.

'So, what's your deal, trackstar?' Kate asks as she fills her glass, spilling wine on the table.

'What do you mean?'

'What's that song shit all about?'

'Just something I do, eh?'

'But it's brilliant, how come you knew to play me that?'

Good question, Kate. Good fucking question. One I don't have an answer to. Jamesy never goes into much detail. This is the first time I've actually spoken to someone after a song was played. A Trackee. I should be making the most of this. I'm wandering the streets playing songs to people and I never find out why.

'You tell me, it's your song?'

'It made me feel fucking, you know, all fired up.'

'Fired up about what?'

'My boss found me crying in the toilets at work and sent me home, fuck sake, eh? Like that loser deserves my tears.'

'Your boss?'

'No, not my boss, trackstar. Adam, the prick.'

'Who's Adam the prick?'

'My boyfri... ex boyfriend. I found out he's been shagging someone else. I had my suspicions. Secret texts, weird phone calls, work trips away. Jesus, it's all such a fucking cliché. I should be laughing, not crying. You know how I found out for sure? You'll love this.'

'How?'

'I found a video on his computer of the two of them going at it on my sofa. That sofa cost me over a grand and now it's fucking ruined.'

'Ruined by fucking.'

'Exactly, you and me are on the same wavelength, track-star,' she waves her hand back and forth between us and sloshes wine onto my jeans.

'Careful,' she says and tries to wipe me clean with the cuff of her blouse.

Jamesy, what have you done? Primed her for a fight rather

than calming her down. She rolls her sleeves up and I notice a tattoo winding around her wrist.

'What's that?' I ask.

'Oh, it says "while my guitar gently weeps",' she twists her wrist to show me the spiral of words and ends up spilling more wine.

'Careful,' she says.

'Cool tattoo, Beatles, eh?'

Do you think so? She screwed up her nose. It's after that, um, German girl. You know, the one the Beatles met in Hamburg?

Stupid, cheating, lying bitch.

'Yeah, I got it done when I was, what, seventeen or something, thought I was being dead deep and meaningful. I used to be in a band when I was at school, thought I was fucking Courtney Love, or something.'

'I like it, it's different.'

'It's my bracelet of words. Sometimes I wish I could change it depending on how I was feeling, kind of like a Facebook status or something.'

'What would you have today?'

'Fuck Adam the prick, and fuck the bint he's sleeping with.'

Kate holds her wine glass above her head, as if she's making a toast. People stare at her and laugh and the barman looks ready to chuck her out. I bet they never heard language like this even when it was an old man's pub. With every sip of wine she's becoming more and more like Billy Connolly.

Like he was the first one to think of it.

'Sounds like you're better off out of it,' I say.

'You're right, I still want to kill the both of them though. I've been sitting here feeling sorry for myself, fucking blaming myself. Asking myself what I'd done wrong. Was I bad in bed? That sort of shit. Jesus, what an idiot. I am brilliant in bed and I did nothing wrong. It was him who couldn't keep his dick in his pants.'

'Aye.'

I finish my pint and order another. Was I shite in bed? Is that what it was? Compared to Alfie, what must Astrid be thinking? I heard her moaning through the wall. Did she do that with me? I don't think I made her moan like that. Did I even make her moan at all? Her and Alfie are probably in bed now, laughing at me. Laughing at how small my cock is.

I think I'm going to be sick again.

'What's wrong, trackstar, why the serious face?'

'Nothing, I got cheated on today too. This girl I was seeing slept with my mate.'

'No way, some friend.'

'I know, it's pretty shite.'

'Play yourself a song, put Alanis back on. Her songs always remind me of her name, there's all these long words and syllabubs.'

'Syllabubs?'

'You know what I mean,' she grabs my thigh, 'come on, let's plot revenge together. Show those fuckers they can't mess with us.'

'Aye, why not.'

She waves her hand at the bar.

'Another pint for the trackstar.'

'Let's go,' says Kate.

She scrambles out of the booth and trips over the strap of her handbag.

'Careful, trackstar,' she says, grabbing my arm for support.

I've had about five or six pints now, but I don't feel very drunk. Just miserable, really. I'm glad I left my phone at home. This is about the time I'd start bombarding Astrid with drunken texts.

hi goledhngdr ws fun famby a 2 date? X

'Which way you going?' I ask.

'Your way,' she replies.

'I think I'm just gonna head home, sorry, don't feel in the mood for going anywhere else.'

'I'll come with you then.'

The thought of revenge sex doesn't appeal anymore. I don't feel anything. I just want to go home and sleep and forget everything. I can smell Astrid on me, I want to keep it there for a while. I don't want Kate to wipe that smell away. Not yet.

You need to let him go.

I'm not ready.

'I'm not sure.'

'I need to, I've missed my last bus.'

'What about the night bus?'

'Nah, I live in Roslin, the buses are shite, finish dead early.'

I'm totally confused. I seem to have dulled my brain activity without getting any of the usual drunk feelings. I can't even think which direction Roslin is in at the moment, let alone what bus goes there.

'Aye, alright.' I agree.

We head out of the pub and wander a few feet along the pavement.

'Hang on, I need a pish,' I say, and head down into the alleyway next to the pub, where I go behind some bins.

As I come out doing up my fly, Kate pounces. She pushes me up against the wall of the pub while her tongue forces its way inside my mouth.

Her lips were on his, biting, urgent, her tongue stud tapped against teeth. His or hers? Ring a ring a roses.

He ran his tongue over her teeth, feeling for the gap.

I didn't realise how tall she was inside the pub. Out here, in her heels, she towers over me. She tastes of wine and perfume and salt and vinegar crisps. It's a heady concoction which, along with the fresh air, seems to act as a catalyst to all the alcohol. The alleyway starts to speed away from me, a tunnel getting further and further away and I have to close my eyes or I'm going to fall.

I don't have the strength or the willpower to fight her off. It feels wrong, like I'm cheating on Astrid or something and I have to remind myself who cheated on who. She started it. I pull Kate towards me and lose myself in the blur of the kiss.

I don't remember how we got home. The next thing I know, I wake up in my own bed. Alone. Naked and alone.

She wriggled her toes up next to his.

My head cracks every time I open my eyes, like ice being dropped into cold, fizzy juice.

My mouth is dry and I can't face moving to get a drink.

I skim my arm around the bed, feeling to make sure I am alone. Did I imagine Kate?

My hand lands on something on the pillow next to me.

A piece of paper.

I pull it towards me and open one eye.

A note.

Hey,

I have to go. Tried to wake you but you were totally out of it. I'll always be eternally grateful to you trackstar for looking after me in my hour of need. Don't stress about last night – we both drank <u>way too much!</u> I couldn't manage much either.

Anyway, maybe see you around sometime.

Kate xx

I scrunch the letter up and throw it away.

What the fuck? Why did she have to write that? As if I wasn't already feeling totally shite, without her going on about my lack of performance. Talk about kicking someone when they're down.

Man, I wouldn't even have remembered any of that anyway. Now it's all I can think of.

I close my eyes and reach down for my cock. It's shrivelled and tiny.

Maybe if I lie here, the rest of me will shrivel up too. Shrivel up until I'm just a flake of skin on the sheet, ready to be eaten by a bedbug.

Jobless.

Girless.

Cockless.

My t-shirt is lying next to me. I put it over my face. It smells of Kate now. Her strong perfume has pushed Astrid out. I can't smell Astrid anymore, she's gone.

I can hear The Shins playing through the wall from Alfie's room.

Fuck, you're not kidding, Rivers.

New Slang.

Is Astrid still in there with him? Moaning.

The tune is beautiful and haunting. It tugs at me so deeply I can't catch a breath.

He had to lean against the wall to catch a breath.

He ran down the stairs, holding his breath like the air was infected.

I pull the duvet over my head, curl up into a ball and cry myself back to sleep.

20

Twenty

*Davie finally managed to get the front door unlocked and
stumbled into the house.*
Lewey, he shouted up the stairs, Lewey, it's me, sorry I'm so late.
Davie dropped the orange juice.

WHAT IS IT? Can you hear something? Jamesy is on guard
dog duty and wakes me with a growl. He warns me of
something on the other side of the bedroom door.

I lay a hand on him, ssshhh.

I'm lying fully clothed on top of my bed, must have just
conked out when I got in last night. I'm losing myself in the
Trackman at the moment. It's easier that way. To become
him. To forget about Davie Watts and his shit life.

Trackman Trackman Trackman Trackman Trackman Trackm

I sit up and listen. Concentrate on listening. What is it?
I can't hear anything.

I wander over to my bedroom door and open it slightly,
peer out into the hall. I can hear voices coming from the
living room.

It's a kitchenette, the letting agent said.

Alfie and a girl.

A butterfly tattoo. He recognised that butterfly.

My insides start to squirm and contract. I listen. Listen
carefully.

My gut slows down again, it's not her, not Astrid.

Who is it?

I curl my head round the door, push my hair behind my ear and listen.

I turn my ear towards the voices. Who is it? I recognise the voice but can't quite... wait. It's her.

Martha.

It's Martha.

Ring a ring a roses, a pocket full of posies. Atishoo, atishoo, we all fall down.

What's she doing here? Is he working his way through all my ex-girlfriends?

Martha my dear.

I grab Jamesy, put him in the back pocket of my jeans and creep into the hallway. The floorboards creak underneath me and I wish I'd thought to take my shoes off first. Too late now. Why's she here? What are they talking about? Sshhh, I'm trying to hear what they're saying. I thought I heard my name.

I step forward. One. Foot. At. A. Time. One finger. One thumb. Slowly, slowly.

Creak.

Stop.

Musical statues.

I listen to the voices. Have they changed? Did they hear us? No, I don't think so. They're still talking.

I stand outside the living room door, next to the crack between door and wall. What's going on? Why did you warn me? The radio's playing in the background. I try to shut out the music, just tune in on the voices. Only the voices.

What was that Obi Wan Kenobi said?

I Only Have Eyes For You by The Flamingos.

ALFIE   I didn't realise he's not been at work.

MARTHA   Yeah, I don't think he has a job anymore. Laura was kind of worried to start off with, but then she just started getting more and more pissed off at him when he stopped turning up.

ALFIE He gets up and goes out though, I hear him doing it. Where's he going do you think? Maybe staying with that psycho cousin?

MARTHA Yeah, maybe. Could you text her and find out?

ALFIE I don't have her number. I don't think we should get her into all this though, she flipped out when he went awol for a couple of days.

MARTHA What? He went awol?

ALFIE Oh aye, it was fine though. He was with this lassie, eh? He's probably with her actually, I never thought of it until now.

MARTHA Is it serious? Are they, like, going out?

ALFIE Eh, maybe. They went on a few dates and that, I think.

Jealous Guy by John Lennon.

MARTHA I'm still worried about him. Just because he's seeing some girl doesn't mean he can just forget about work and that. Besides this has been going on for ages, I don't think it's just to do with her. I just wish he'd reply to my texts, you know. We had a bit of a fight, it was kind of bad, he's been ignoring me ever since.

ALFIE He'll be cool, don't worry about it. Davie's not the kind of guy to hold a grudge anyway.

MARTHA When was the last time you saw him?

ALFIE Eh, not for a while actually. I think he's trying to grow a beard but he can't carry it off. Looks like Paul McCartney, you know during the Beatles' beard phase. All the others looked cool as fuck, but Paul just looked like a tit.

A Life Less Ordinary by Ash.

MARTHA So, you spoke to him about his beard?

ALFIE No, eh, let me think. I had to go and open the

window in his room the other day, thought someone had died in there, it was stinking. He was definitely out then. Nah, don't worry, he's not dead. I told you he was out, no body. I've been checking on him, and I left him a packet of biscuits the other day.

MARTHA   Alfie, that doesn't sound good. Is he not eating?

ALFIE   Don't worry, that sounds worse than I meant it to. Aye, he's eating, I'm sure he is. It's hard to tell, he's such a skinny fucker anyway. He's not daft though.

MARTHA   Is he in just now?

ALFIE   I don't know. I fell asleep around three, and he wasn't in, but he might have come in after that. Want to go and check?

Run by Snow Patrol.

He could hear music playing upstairs. Davie dropped the orange juice.

MARTHA   Nah, maybe later, I don't even know if we should, he might get mad if we try and talk to him? I don't think he's speaking to me just now. When did you say was the last time you spoke to him?

ALFIE   Oh aye, I was trying to remember. I'm sure I passed him in the hall the other night? No, when was it now? He told me to fuck off, that was it.

MARTHA   He told you to fuck off?

ALFIE   Aye, I don't know why, it was really weird. I just came out of the shower, eh, and he came storming out of the kitchen and told me to fuck off. I asked Astrid if she'd said...

MARTHA   Astrid? She was there?

ALFIE   Aye, how? Do you know her?

MARTHA   From the shop, her and Davie.

ALFIE   Does she know Davie? She didn't say.

MARTHA   Wait, I'm confused. Astrid was with Davie, right?

ALFIE   No, she was with me.

Stop My Head by Evan Dando.

MARTHA   I thought the girl Davie asked out was called Astrid, American girl, pretty, looks like Natalie Portman.

ALFIE   Fucking hell, you're joking, eh? No it can't be the same lassie, the girl he took to the zoo?

MARTHA   The zoo? What?

ALFIE   Jesus, no wonder he told me to fuck off.

MARTHA   But why was she with you if she was going out with Davie?

ALFIE   I don't know. She never… wait, she said some thing about being cheated on. Aye that was it, she was really upset and her friends had taken her out to get drunk.

MARTHA   He cheated on her? Who with?

ALFIE   I don't know, I can't remember. I was drunk too, it was loud in the club, I didn't really hear what she said. Man, this is fucking messy, eh?

Davie stood outside the kitchen listening to his parents argue.

You pushed me into it, you're so,   I'm not even allowed to touch you these days, can't even sleep in my own bed.

My son has died and all you can think about is sex.

Our son, and that's not true and you know it, you're pushing me away.

Well go then, she's obviously giving you something I can't.

Was Astrid still in there with him? Moaning?

I don't know   I feel like our marriage

it's all going to hell and you're not doing anything. You've got to try. We have to fight for it.

Was shagging that tart fighting for our marriage? Don't give me your moral bullshit.

Davie heard something bang on the table then his dad stormed past, grabbed his car keys and slammed the front door as he left the house.

You okay, Mum? Davie asked from the doorway.

She was sitting at the table, spinning her wedding ring on top of a chopping board.

Davie, why didn't you just come home after work?

MARTHA He's never been the same since his brother died.

ALFIE He never talks about him, I didn't even realise he had a brother until Ryan from Virgin mentioned it to me.

Car Crash by The Candyskins.

MARTHA He was pretty messed up for a while, but you can't really blame him. Your brother commits suicide, I can't even think about how horrible that would be.

The phone rang and rang and rang and rang. Davie knew his mum and dad were both in, but nobody went to answer it.

There's only so many times you can hear someone tell you they're sorry.

Hello, Davie said as he answered the phone.

Davie? That you?

Aye.

It's Martha.

Davie, I'm really sorry, I heard about what happened. I tried your mobile but it was switched off. I just wanted to say, well, you know.

Can I do anything?

Davie? You alright?

Martha, I   I can't speak okay, I have to go.
Davie hung up. He couldn't bear to speak to her. To hear
her voice. Didn't think he'd be able to look at her again.
She was a constant reminder. If he hadn't been out kissing
the lips that spoke to him on the phone, he would have
been home. He should have been home.

ALFIE Jesus, Martha, I knew his brother had died but
       I just assumed it was cancer or a car accident or
       something. Man, he must think I'm such an
       insensitive bastard.

MARTHA It's not your fault, he never talks about it. It scares me
though. Is that sort of thing not meant to be hereditary?
Is it hereditary? Every time I see that packet of valium in
the bathroom, well, I just worry.
What Have I Done To Deserve This? by The Pet Shop Boys.

ALFIE Nah, I doubt it.

MARTHA You sure?

ALFIE Aye, like I said, he's no daft. He wouldn't do
       anything silly.

MARTHA But, sometimes he can be so, I mean, like, with
       that MP3 player.

ALFIE What about it?

MARTHA Well, he told me things, I can't remember exactly
       what he said, but it was like he was using it to make
       himself feel better, more worthwhile or something.

Celebrity Skin by Hole.

ALFIE He said he chucked it. I don't get it.

MARTHA Neither do I, it was like he thought it had a mind
       of its own. I think he blames himself for his brother.
       I can't explain.

ALFIE The MP3 player has a mind of its own?

MARTHA Yeah, I know how weird that sounds. At the time,
       I was just, like, whatever, but I keep looking back
       and thinking how wrong it all was. The way he was

	letting it control him.
ALFIE	Gollum and his precious.
MARTHA	Don't joke about it, that's exactly what it reminded me of.
ALFIE	Sorry, he did mention something to me about it but he said he was stoned, just imagined it. I didn't think much of it. He sometimes comes out with weird stuff, he can be so serious, eh? I keep telling him to lighten up. Jesus, if I'd only known about his brother. Maybe that's the problem? Smoking some crazy shit.
MARTHA	That doesn't make me feel any better, you know?
ALFIE	You really think that MP3 player's part of it? It just doesn't make sense. It was a piece of shit, didn't even work.
MARTHA	I went to look for that One Dread Guy.
ALFIE	The old jakey?
MARTHA	Yeah, he said that's who gave him it.
ALFIE	Oh aye, shit, my memory is just fucking awful.
MARTHA	I couldn't find him, I even went and asked at that shelter, you know, down at the Pleasance? They haven't seen him for ages. It freaked me out.

People Are Strange by The Doors.

ALFIE	Honestly, I wouldn't stress about that, look, let's just go and speak to him. It'll make you feel better.
MARTHA	Aye, if we just say we're worried, that's all. If we go together.
ALFIE	Cool, let's see if he's… Did you hear something? Davie? That you?

Shit, shit, shit. What do I do? I don't want to speak to them, I need to get out of here, before they realise I've been listening to them. I hear someone coming towards me. Think. Think. Think. What do I do? One finger, one thumb, one finger, one thumb.

I hesitate on the spot. Fight or flight? Fight or flight?

It's always fright. Why is it always fucking fright?

Come on, get out of here. Keep moving, keep moving, keep moving.

I lunge for the front door. Thank fuck I slept in my clothes last night, makes for a quick getaway.

Jamesy and I are out of the flat and halfway down the stairs, when I hear someone shout my name. I look up. Alfie and Martha are on the top landing, looking down over the banister at me.

Deep Midnight Plum.

We all fall down.

'Davie, wait.'

'Davie, please.'

We ignore them, head out onto the street and just run.

21

Smokers Outside the Hospital Doors

*He could still hear music, it was coming from upstairs, definitely
Snow Patrol.*
*Lewey, come here, I've got a great story for you, Davie shouted
and headed towards the kitchen.*
Davie dropped the orange juice.

WE'VE BEEN AVOIDING Alfie ever since we heard him talking
to Martha. I just don't want to have to deal with it and Jamesy
agrees. Their conversation keeps running through my head.
Sometimes it makes me so angry, I think I hate them, but
other times I feel guilty about it, and, sad I guess. I have to
leave them behind if I'm the Trackman. It's taking over and I
like it that way. It's a new focus for me. I'm leaving Davie
Watts the loser behind and letting the Trackman take over.
Trackman Trackman Trackman Trackman Trackman Trackm
They just wouldn't get it. Jamesy was right all along about
telling people, it's not going to work. They'd think I was
crazy, they wouldn't get it. Who do they think they are
anyway? Discussing me like that, like I'm some sort of invalid.
It's not even like they need to worry. Jamesy and I have our
ups and downs but he's the best thing that's ever happened to
me. You're the best thing that's ever happened to me. He's
given me an escape, a release. I feel like I'm worth something,
like I deserve my place here.

We've been staying out later and going out earlier, avoiding
the flat. Sometimes we don't go home at all. It just seems
easier that way. Alfie's sent me a couple of texts and Martha's

tried to phone me but I don't answer. I feel like a shit for ignoring them, but it's what I have to do.

Davie wot u up 2?

Hey sorry if Astrad was the same Astrd. I didn't no.
I wouldn't do that

Hey, where r u, I'm worried + rents due
Davie sorry. I honestly didn't no.

Even if I wanted to reply I couldn't. The not working thing has made a dent in my funds, well, more like a fucking hole in them, and I can't afford to put credit in my phone.

Davie pressed for £20.
You do not have sufficient funds available.
He pressed for £10.
You do not have sufficient funds available.
The ATM spat back his card at him.
Davie took the Mars Bar and slipped it up the sleeve of his jacket. His hands were shaking as he walked towards the shop door.

I spent my last twelve pence on a text to Susan, just to stop her freaking out like before. If she thinks anything's up, she won't go to Australia. She wouldn't understand what we're doing.

I know, Jamesy, I know. I'm not saying what we're doing is wrong. I just know that's how she'll interpret it all. You don't want her on our case do you?

Aye, I know that would make things easier but it would never work. Where would I sleep? How would I eat? What if the weather was shite? I don't want to be homeless, Jamesy.

Davie watched as the guy swung rucksack after rucksack onto his back.

I know, I can't pay rent right now and it would be easier if we were out on our own, but it just wouldn't work. I was thinking, maybe, I could move back in with Susan? I know, it doesn't make sense after what I just said about keeping it a secret from her, but   it's too confusing. Just stop going on okay, Jamesy. Let me have a think about it. Nothing makes sense anymore, nothing except you.

My phone starts to ring.

'Alright, Susan,' I answer.

'Hi, Davie, you didn't let me know how that meeting at work went. Is everything okay? I was worried.'

'Oh, sorry, eh, it's all cool. I got a bit of a bollocking for missing work, but I did like you said, aye, just took it and apologised, promised not to do it again, eh? All that shite.'

'That's great, Davie. I knew it would be okay.'

'Aye, sorry for not letting you know. I've actually been doing a few extra shifts and that, just to try and get back in the good books. So I've been a bit busy.'

'That's okay. Will we get to see you before we leave tomorrow?'

'Shit, is that tomorrow? Man, time is just whizzing by right now.'

Aye, you're right. It's not a good idea, I agree with you. As much as I'd like to see Susan and Pammy before they go, she's good at that intuition shit, she'd work it out. It's best if I just let her go and deal with it all when she gets back. Use the next few weeks to sort out a story, work out what we're going to do long term.

'Yeah, the flight's at eleven.'

'Shit, I don't think I'll be able to, I could phone work and try and change shifts around?' I bluff.

'No, don't be daft, I don't want you getting into more bother because of me. I'll see you when we get back.'

'Aye, I'm really sorry, will you be alright for getting to the airport and that?'

'Yeah, it's all sorted.'

I feel like shit, and fumble around for something worthwhile to say.

'I can keep an eye on the house for you, if you like?'

'If you can be bothered, Mary from next door offered but she knows who you are if you want to pop through.'

'Aye, no bother.'

'Okay, right, I'd better love you and leave you then, Davie.'

'No bother, just you and Pammy have a great holiday, okay?'

Even though neither of us says it, we're both thinking of Mum. I know Susan doesn't want to get into a fight when she's going away and I just don't want to speak about it.

Mummy says you should never go to bed angry.

We leave it unsaid but I can feel it there, both of us thinking the same thing.

'Yeah, take care. I'll have my phone with me, so if you need me for anything.'

'Cool.'

'You'll be okay won't you? You've got that, what's her name again? Angel, to look after you.'

'It's Astrid, aye, I'm seeing her later hopefully.'

He could hear muffled voices. Muffled voices which gradually faded into moans and the sound of Alfie's bed creaking.

'That's great, I'm really happy for you. Right, better go, you take care okay, see you in a few weeks.'

'Aye, see you soon, have a good time, eh?'

The light on my phone goes out and it feels like a goodbye forever. It's not a goodbye forever. I know it's not, but it's like that day I left Astrid's.

The sound of it echoed around the stairwell.

I can't shake the feeling. I want to phone her back and say

301

something else. *Something, anything.* If I never see her and Pammy again, is that it? The last conversation I'll ever have with her? I don't even remember much of it now. A last conversation should mean something, shouldn't it?

Davie couldn't remember what his last words to Lewis were. It was like the brain cell that held that memory had just died with him. He heard someone talking about the brain once. They had this theory, about when random memories pop up, things you hadn't thought about in years. Their theory was that when this happened, it was the brain cell that held that memory dying. It was like the brain cell just threw it at you quickly before it went. Quick remember this, I'm dying and this memory is going with me, so remember it while you can.

Davie couldn't remember his last moment with Lewis. Why was it so hard to remember? He'd traced himself, moved backwards through time, put himself on rewind, but the scene was missing. A deleted scene hidden as a DVD easter egg? Maybe if he pushed the right combination of buttons he'd find it?

He hoped that he'd said something nice. That they hadn't argued or disagreed about something dumb. It must have been something mundane, not important enough for his brain to bother recording. His brain didn't realise until it was too late that it should have pressed record.

Davie held a finger up to his mouth, ssshhh, then pressed two buttons down on the cassette player: Record and Play together.

It was too late now. Gone. He even got sent to a hypnotist, but he couldn't relax, couldn't go under. He was scared. When it came down to it, maybe remembering was worse that not knowing? It didn't matter anyway. Even if he'd known it was his last moment with Lewis, and he'd said everything in his head he'd wanted to, it still wouldn't be enough. It still wouldn't stop his brain, every so often, going, man, Lewis would love that, I need to tell Lewis that, or Lewis would know, ask Lewis, he'll know. Sometimes he forgot that he was gone.

Come on, Jamesy, let's do what we're supposed to do, eh? All these decisions you're asking me to make, it's too much. It's doing my head in. I don't work that way, you know, to a plan. I just   I just need to go. Keep going in a straight line and deal with what happens to me as it happens. I have a track history of bad decisions. It's better if I don't make choices. Keep moving forward. Keep moving, keep moving.

One finger, one thumb, one arm, one leg. Let's leave the head out of it for now. The head needs a rest.

Aye, about time. We should be playing the music, Jamesy. Not wasting our time thinking about stuff that makes my brain hurt.

I follow Jamesy's directions. Off Morningside and into the hospital grounds. Follow the road, over the speed bumps. Ten miles per hour.

This is the mental hospital, Jamesy, the fucking loony bin.

Davie sat on one of the tree trunks that lined the road into the hospital. It seemed he was always waiting there these days. Waiting to go in. Waiting to be seen. Waiting to be picked up. Waiting for the pain to get a bit smaller. Waiting. Everyone waited at hospitals.

Davie saw his parents at the far end of the corridor; they sat with their backs against the wall. It looked like they were waiting outside the headmaster's office.

A girl walked past him. Her legs were so skinny, there was nothing to them, just bone. Even her baggy jeans couldn't hide it. Made it look worse. The way the excess fabric hung off her, clung to the bones jutting out. She bounced rather than walked, her legs didn't look like they worked properly anymore.

She had a scarf pulled up over her chin and a hat low over her forehead, trying to hide the death mask.

It was like those shitey waxworks at Madame Tussauds.

Her sunken cheeks, her face top heavy, trying to hold up blank eyes. She had a disease they could stamp a name on.

Davie was moved from one specialist to the next. Depression. Bereavement. Post-traumatic Stress Disorder. Where was his stamp? Why was it so hard to help him?

Why did you bring me here? I used to come here a lot. Did you know that?

In a parallel universe, Jamesy finds Davie Watts sitting on a tree trunk outside the loony bin and helps him feel better.

My ghost is sitting there, can you see him? See me?

It's like, you know when you get into a routine, every day you do the same thing at exactly the same time. Then one day, you sleep in or something and you end up passing your self somewhere during the day. The ghost of yourself stuck in the routine and the real you running along behind.

A part of me will always be here. Like a part of Lewis is always here, always with me. I can't go anywhere without him being with me. Like the zoo, even though I was having fun with Astrid, I kept thinking of the time I was at the zoo with Lewey.

It looks like a Caramac bar, he ran his tongue over her teeth, mmmm you taste of Solero, poor guy, he looks sad.

And now the next time I go to the zoo, I'll be thinking of Lewis and Astrid. The good memories weigh me down.

I don't even want to go to the zoo again now, because I know I won't have fun, I'll just feel sad. I can't have a good time anymore without thinking of how in the future the memory of the good time will make me sad.

Fucking hell, if they heard me right now, I'd be re-admitted. Let's get out of here, eh? It's bringing too much stuff back.

I need to calm down. One finger, one thumb, one finger, one thumb.

Davie saw his parents at the far end of the corridor; they sat with their backs against the wall. It looked like they were waiting outside the headmaster's office. His mum was crying and his dad was just staring at the floor. Davie could hear his feet tapping against the lino as he walked towards them, it was so loud, it filled the corridor. But his folks didn't move, didn't flinch. Didn't look at him, even when he stopped right in front of them. Then he realised, it wasn't just one son they'd lost.

It feels too weird being back. I need to get away from here.

I notice the guy before Jamesy tells me. An old boy, sitting on a bench outside the main entrance to the hospital. He's staring out across the car park, smoking a cigarette.

I sit next to him and he nods at me. He's dressed really smartly, makes me feel like a right tink.

He looked cool as fuck. Davie had worn his dad's suit. He hadn't worn it since the funeral, the hems of the trousers were still covered in dirt.

A v-neck jumper with a shirt and tie on underneath.

Why does grandpa call trousers slacks?

He takes a draw on his fag and I can hear the lungs straining inside him, sticky and clasping like cling film. When he exhales it's sandpaper over metal. His breathing is so loud, it drowns out the birds and the breeze and the traffic. It's all I can hear.

In. Out.   In. Out.In.Out.In.   Out.Out.Out.Out.

'Sound awful, don't I?' the old boy says like he can read my mind. 'I've got lung cancer, eh? I know, I know, I shouldn't be smoking, but it's the only pleasure I've got and it's too late now anyway. No point stopping.'

'Sorry to hear that.'

'Don't be, I've smoked for over sixty years, I've earned it.' He coughs and spits into his hankie.

'I'm on oxygen,' he says, 'but I can't stand it. It dries my nose and mouth out, I'm thirsty all the time and my throat feels like it's on fire. Having a smoke helps me feel better, can't do it on the oxygen mind, I'd really be on fire then. Whoosh – up in flames.'

He laughs but it makes him start coughing again. He sounds hollow. I can hear the cough banging around in his chest. The Tin Man.

'Aye, I keep asking them to let me do it, blow myself up I mean. Exploding in a big ball of flames would be quick and anything has to be better than this cancer. I don't want it slow and drawn out. Besides, I'm probably heading down to the big fire anyway.'

He lifts his arm and dives his hand down, a smoky trail flowing from the fag hanging between his fingers. He coughs again, rattling tin-foil.

'I didn't know they did cancer treatment here,' I say.

'Oh, they don't. My wife's in here. I'm waiting on my son to bring her out. She's got dementia. We make a right pair, don't we? I have to leave my hospital to come here to see her and vice versa. She doesn't really know who I am these days, it's worse than the cancer. She'll probably come out and walk right past me. My son and his wife are taking us out for lunch, more fool them. Poor buggers, saddled with us two.'

This time he doesn't laugh, just takes another suck on his cigarette.

Jamesy's on at me to play him a song but I don't know how to say the words. I don't want to lie to him and asking him to listen to a song just sounds so pathetic after all he's told me. I'm stuck. I'm not sure we can help him.

'The scary thing is,' the old boy says, 'I'm going to die and she won't even notice.' He tries to click his fingers, but they flop against each other without so much as a cl.

'She forgot about me a while ago now, I'm the disappearing husband. I tried to kiss her cheek the other day and she screamed, actually screamed in my face. Jesus, and they want me to give up smoking.'

I can't find the right moment to ask him to listen. What do you say to someone who's telling you all this? Sorry, Jamesy, I'm sinking here. Words aren't enough.

How can a song help him? We can't cure cancer, Jamesy, or dementia. We're not Gods. What am I forgetting? That I'm the Trackman?

Trackman Trackman Trackman Trackman Trackman Trackm

Yeah, but this guy is dying, Jamesy, he's dying. So what are you saying? It'll still help him? Not a cure but a comfort. I really do want to help him, I really do.

Okay, Jamesy, okay, I don't think I can take much more of this anyway. It's bringing too much stuff back to the surface, just being here in this car park is bringing too much stuff back.

'Have you got time to listen to a song?' I ask.

'Time is something I don't have much left of, I'm afraid.'

He tips his head back, opens his mouth wide and sucks, like he's trying to swallow as much air as he can.

'Sorry, bad choice of words.'

'No, it's alright. I'm starting to cherish the moments I have left, I'll listen to a song.'

He lifts his arm to put the headphones on but it's such an effort and he's struggling. I take them from him and sort them in place on his head for him.

'I've never used one of these things before, if my son comes out and see's me he'll think I'm the one with the head problems.'

Time In The World by Louis Armstrong We Have All The Time In The World by Louis Armstrong We Have All

Jamesy, are you taking the piss? The old boy looks at me and I'm scared he thinks I'm being a dick to him, but then he closes his eyes. His face trembles and tears run down his cheeks. His skin's so dry, the tears are absorbed before they have a chance to reach his chin. Can he even hear the music over the noise of his breathing?

My dearest Nancy,

It came to me today, what I have to do as my final gift to you.

A young lad helped me with the idea.

Do you remember your favourite song? You must do. Just in case you've forgotten, I've put a CD in with this letter. John helped me with it, I'm sure he'll help you play it too. All you need to do is listen to it and then I'm sure it'll jog your memory. I've put a photo of us in here too. It's from when we stayed in the caravan at North Berwick, and we discovered you were pregnant with John.

Remember we used the payphone to call our folks and tell them? I thought you could listen to the song, read this letter, look at the photo and it'll help you. Help you remember how happy we were together.

All the things that we got up to. When we both sheltered under the bridge during the air-raid, that was how we met. Then John came along and we got our first house, it was next to a baker's and the house was full of mice. I carried you from room to room because you were so scared of them. Then when you turned thirty we drove to Gullane and had fish and chips on the beach at dusk. Fish and chips have never tasted as good as they did that day.

If I wrote down everything, this letter would never end. There's too many good memories of our life together, Nancy, love. Try and hold onto a few, please try. I'm not going to be here to remind you soon. I'm sorry, I've tried my best, but I'm not going to manage the whole way. You'll have to manage the last wee bit without me.

I wish we'd known back then, under that bridge, just how quickly time flies by. That song of yours, it means something different now than it did when we first heard it.

I'm sorry for being a sentimental old fool. I just want you to remember there was someone who loved you, when I'm not here to keep reminding you. Our time together was too precious to forget. I'll love you always, sweetheart, and I'll be waiting for you.

Forever yours,

Iain.

It's dark around the man. He's covered in shadow.

I can hardly make him out anymore. Is that fish and chips I can smell?

I take the headphones off his head and he lights another cigarette.

'That's my wife's favourite song,' he says.

I wind the headphones around Jamesy and put him in my pocket. The old boy sucks on the cigarette, like he's trying to suck juice out of a glass bottle. His cheeks sink into valleys with the strain of it, and his hand shakes as he holds the cigarette up to his purple lips.

His lips were blue, like he'd been out playing in the snow.

I need to get out of here, but I feel like I should say something before I go. I don't want to just leave this guy, it's wrong. I feel a weird connection to him.

He always imagined couples in the forties, meeting for dates there.

Look at him? I can see my life running away from me, and it scares the shit out of me. What have I got to show for myself? When I get to his age, I want to look back and know that I've done something. That I've had a good life. Is that even possible anymore, after all that's happened?

'You take care, okay?' I'm about to squeeze his shoulder but I stop myself. Why do I always manage to fuck up moments of intimacy? He jumps, like he's forgotten I was there. His lips are moving. I can't tell if he's whispering to himself or if they're just trembling with the rest of his face.

'Thanks, son.'

'No bother.'

'You blink and it's gone, you know, when you're young you don't realise.'

I nod and walk away. Turning my back on him feels like a snub, but I can't bear to be here anymore. This place sucks you dry.

That old boy did something to me, Jamesy. You were right all along. It just took someone like him to make me realise you were right. I've been given a second chance, a chance to do something with my life, not waste it being Davie fucking Watts. I'm the Trackman. I'm not Davie, I'm the Trackman.

Trackman Trackman Trackman Trackman Trackman Trackm

I have to start taking it seriously. It's not a game, something I can just fit in when I've got a spare minute. I have to give myself up to it.

Trackman Trackman Trackman Trackman Trackman Trackm

Let's leave the flat, take the show on the road. I just need to get a couple of things out of the way first.

I know it's shite compared to what I should have done, but I'll finish those books for you.

Aye, finish that fucking book for Lewey for one thing. A few loose ends to tie up and then I'm all yours.

22

End of the Line

Davie didn't want to be hung-over in the morning. He'd drunk a lot and could feel the start of the hangover in his stomach. That feeling which tells you to stop drinking, that feeling you usually ignore.
Davie dropped the orange juice.

I KNOW, I KNOW, just post it through her door. The note doesn't say what I want it to say though.

I don't even know if I need to leave it. I can still commit to being the Trackman without the disappearing act. How do I explain it to Susan in a few scribbled lines? It's not fair, after all she's done for me. I can't just fuck off without an explanation. *The police had been in there searching. They'd been respectful, but something had changed. It was a waste of time too, they hadn't found anything.*
I have to leave something for her and Pammy.
Davie left the note for Alfie on the counter next to the kettle. He was bound to come in for a brew at some point.

Alfie, I'm going away for a bit, a kind of road trip thing, but without a car. Sorry for being a dick. Maybe see you again sometime. No hard feelings. Davie.

He didn't have much time to write it, if he'd had more time he would have put more thought into it. He'd been tempted to put in some shitty comment about Astrid, but then he felt guilty. Davie didn't want some sarky comment to be the last thing he ever said to Alfie, just in case he never saw him again.

Mummy says you should never go to bed angry.

Jamesy and Davie waited outside the flat until they saw Alfie leave. They had to make sure they were in and out before he came back. Davie threw a few things into a bag then wrote the note. If he'd had more time, he would have written something better.

That's what he kept telling himself. Deep down he knew that if he'd had hours and hours, he'd still have come out with something shite. He'd never been good at saying what he felt. He blamed it on being Scottish. Scottish men didn't do emotions or feelings very well.

Davie had planned to post the flat keys back through the letterbox but he was halfway down the street before he remembered. In the end he posted them through a post box instead. It was only after he'd let go that he noticed the faded graffiti. A warning in silver marker pen.

ABANDON HOPE ALL YE WHO ENTER HERE

Hey, Jamesy, this is where I nearly got rid of you. Aye, I know. What a dumb thing to do. I can't believe I nearly dumped you. Man, where would I be now?

Davie stroked Jamesy with his thumb and Jamesy purred back at him.

I can't think of this as a goodbye anyway, if I do I might chicken out. Not go through with it. We're just going on tour for a while, taking the show on the road.

I'm scared. I'm fucking terrified.

Right, better get this over with. I open Susan's gate and crunch my way up the driveway. I open the letterbox and post the letter through.

Can you hear something? I put my ear down towards the letterbox. I think there's someone in there?

'Hello?' I shout into the letterbox.

The hallway was in darkness, and nobody answered him. Lewey, it's me, LEWEY   LEWEY, come on, stop fucking about. Let me in.

Did you hear that? There's someone in there. I'm sure there is. I walk round the side of the house but the curtains are closed. I turn the corner to the back of the house when something hits me on the shoulder and I fall forwards onto the gravel.

I flip myself over, but with my rucksack on I'm like an upturned turtle, limbs flailing. I can't get myself up.

Colin is standing over me. His face is red and his hair is all stuck to his forehead with sweat.

'What are you doing here?' I ask.

'Saying goodbye, not that it's any of your fucking business.'

'Get away from here.' The saliva dries in my mouth and I can hear my words clicking as I speak.

'Are you going to make me?'

'Aye,' I scramble to my feet. My hands and knees are stinging.

'Come on then,' he pushes me in the chest and I slide in the gravel. Now that I'm standing up, I realise just how much bigger than me he is. Fuck sake. The veins in his neck and upper arms are bulging.

Susan had met Colin at the gym. He was a fucking body-builder.

Fight or flight. Fight or flight. Fight or flight.

Fright.

Help me, Jamesy, what do I do?

Do I keep my thumb in or out when I punch?

One finger, one thumb, one finger, one thumb.

'Come on you wee fucker,' Colin pushes me backwards, 'you're nothing, nothing.'

I lunge at him but he grabs me and gives me a push so I go flying past him towards the front gate. My Converse slide and the weight of the rucksack topples me over into the side of the house. The house is pebble-dashed and as I scrape down the wall, white stones chip off and scatter around my feet. Before I have a chance to even close my eyes, his fist connects with my face and a warm pain soaks through me. It's like someone's emptied a bucket of hot water over my head. My glasses hang off one ear. It's all a blur and the driveway is spinning, spinning, spinning, but through one side of my glasses I see him coming at me again. I duck as his fist swings towards me.

'I'll fucking kill you, you wee prick,' he shouts.

I know he means it. Something inside forces me into action. I need to get the fuck away from here. Flight, you idiot, flight. Now. I stumble towards the garden gate. I need to get away.

Sweat and tears sting my eyes. Is that blood? Am I bleeding? I don't know, I don't have time to check. I swing open the gate and run. He's still shouting at me as I take off along the pavement. I don't turn round. Just run.

sky.

ET on the bikes. Pavement, Pavement, pavement,
onearmonelegonearmonelegonearmonelegonearmoneleg

He doesn't follow. Thank fuck, he doesn't follow. I keep running though, just keep running.

Davie watched from the front garden as it reached the end of the road, then he was out the front gate and on his way to Paul Johnstone's house.

My teeth hurt. It feels like the blood has drained right out of my gums. Are they falling out?

He ran his tongue over her teeth, feeling for the gap.

Her tongue stud tapped against teeth. His or hers?

Fuck, I need to stop. I can't breathe. I'm at the beach, I've run all the way to the fucking beach.

I hold my front teeth between my fingers and shake them, test them for wobbles. I slip my arms out of my rucksack and head down to the edge of the water. Now that I've stopped running, I can't stop shaking. All my muscles are in spasm.

I step into the sea. The water's freezing and soaks through my Converse. The cold is good, extreme. It takes my attention away from my face. I'm cut all over. My hands and knees are throbbing. I kneel down and splash water over my face, swirl my glasses around and put them on properly. The water is foamy and doesn't look very clean but it's salty and it stings, so it must be doing some good. I can taste salt but I don't know if it's the water or my sweat. It nips my eyes.

My teeth still hurt, so I pick up a stone from under the water and bite down on it. Is that my teeth or my jawbone cracking? Did he break my face?

His head cracked every time he opened his eyes, like ice being dropped into cold, fizzy juice.

I gag as the stone hits the back of my throat and I spit it out. My mouth is full of dirt and grit, so I spit again. I cup my hands and fill them with seawater then swirl the water around in my mouth. It tastes disgusting and I spit it out.

He felt like he'd been out drinking or something; something more sordid than standing in a book queue.

What adrenaline I had has left me and I'm starting to collapse. Fuck. Fucking hell. That Colin is fucking mental.

In a parallel universe, I take him out with one punch.

I spit again. This time it's a Han Solo kind of a spit. My hidden scoundrel emerges but it's too late. It's the kind of cool arrogance I could have done with against Colin, but which of course deserted me.

Just be his fucking luck to end up playing Luke Skywalker.

I try to whistle but it hurts too much and no sound comes out.

They say if you whistle at the sea, you're mocking the devil. Can you believe some coastal town up north banned Roger Whittaker?

What do you think, Jamesy? I think we just met the fucking devil back at Susan's house.

He didn't have a good time growing up, his dad used to hit him and slap his mum around.

Sand and grit sticks to the bottom of my jeans as I head back up the beach towards my bag. I drag it alongside me. I'm drained. I don't even have the power to lift it onto my back.

Are you ignoring me, Jamesy? Embarrassed by what a pussy I am? I bet you're sorry you chose me. I wouldn't blame you if you took off. Maybe you can catch up with Colin?

There's a car park up ahead of me. A row of bushes blocks it from view. A path leads through the bushes further down the beach, but I can't be bothered walking down there, so I just plough on through.

I'm cold now. My feet are numb and I can feel it spreading upwards, all the way through me.

There's nobody about, so I walk towards the nearest car and try the door handle. Locked. I try the next one. Locked. The next one. Locked. I try them all, one by one. One finger, one thumb.

He tried the front door but it was locked. He kept walking until he found another. It was locked too. So was the next one. And the next. Locked. Locked. Locked. Locked. Locked. Locked.

Until, amazingly, I find one that's not been locked. What fool doesn't lock their car? Someone like Colin? Oh, no doubt, Jamesy, no doubt.

I leave my bag lying outside the car and get in the passenger side. I play with the seat. Slide it backwards and forwards.

Backwards and forwards. Backwards and forwards. Recline it up and down. Up and down. Up and down.

I wish I knew how to hotwire the car, just so I could turn on the heating, but I've not got a fucking clue.

I swivel round and notice an apple and a bottle of water on the back seat. The apple is really shiny, polished like lip gloss.

Her lips glimmered with lip gloss and she played with her tongue stud, rolling it left and right, left and right, along her bottom lip.

The sort of shine I thought was only possible in Snow White. The car smells of dog and there are wiry, grey hairs all over the upholstery.

I open the glove compartment and a bag of sherbet lemons falls out. The sweets spill across my lap and floor, shedding their flimsy wrappers as they fall. I pick one up and pop it in my mouth, suck on it. I roll it against the roof of my mouth, wear down the criss-cross pattern on the sweet until it's smooth all over. Like a pebble being worn away by the sea.

Up in the mountains, whole pools are formed by one pebble. The pebble gets caught in the tumbling eddy of a waterfall, swirls around in a vortex and erodes the rock into a hollow pool. If you dive down to the bottom of the pool, you'll find one smoothed out pebble.

Aye, see I'm not such a dumb-fuck as you think I am. I know some stuff. That's how I feel a lot of the time. Like I'm swirling around in a whirlpool. Stuck in this never-ending cycle that I can't get out of, because I'm not smooth yet. I'm all sharp edges and angles, knees and shoulder blades and elbows.

I move the sweet around with my tongue, don't swallow any saliva, so it's all frothy and wet inside my mouth.

His or hers?

There's a sharp edge to the sweet and it cuts the roof of my mouth. I crunch down on it, let the sherbet explode inside me. The fizz bursts and bubbles.

I'm tired and cold. I close my eyes. I could just sleep here. It's comfy. It's warmer than being outside. Jamesy nudges me, tickles me. Okay, okay, I'll get up, I'll get up.

I reach into the back seat and take the apple and the water, then I leave the car. I carry the rucksack along next to me, and head out of the car-park.

Davie took the Mars Bar and slipped it up the sleeve of his jacket. His hands were shaking as he walked towards the shop door.

You're turning me into a criminal as well as a superhero, Jamesy.

What do you think Colin was doing there? He was inside the house. Fuck, I just ran away and he was inside the house. We need to go back. In case he's done something. He could have done anything. What if Susan and Pammy are in there? What if he got to them before they left for Australia? I swing my rucksack on my back and start to jog back towards Susan's.

Onefingeronethumbonearmonelegonefingeronethumbone armonelegkeepmovingkeepmovingkeepmoving

Is he still there? Are you sure? He's definitely gone?

The front gate is still hanging open. Jamesy and I go in and circle the house. The gravel on the driveway's scrambled at the place where I fell over, I kick it back, spread it out more evenly again. Cover up my beating.

The blinds are drawn in the kitchen window at the back of the house, but the window looks weird. It's all steamed up.

Fuck, look at that, Jamesy. The back door's been kicked in. How come nobody heard, nobody noticed? Why hasn't the alarm gone off? Fuck sake, I thought Susan's neighbours were meant to be looking after her house while she's away. Good fucking job, Mary. Christ, I hope she really is away.

What if she's in there? What if I go in and. I can't. Not again.

Davie dropped the orange juice.

I don't think I can. What if?

You sure?   Okay.

I'm the Trackman. I'm the Trackman. I'm the Trackman. I'm the Trackman.

Trackman Trackman Trackman Trackman Trackman Trackm

'Susan? Pammy?' I push open the back door and step inside the house. I'm shaking again. Nobody answers me. I can hear the sound of water running. I follow it to the kitchen. When I push open the door, I'm hit by a wall of steam. My glasses cloud over and it feels warm against my battered face. I pull my glasses off and fight through it to the kitchen sink. My feet are still wet from the sea, but I can feel warm water ooze between my toes. That fucker. I turn off the hot tap and plunge my hand into the sink to pull the plug out. Fuck, the water's hot and it burns me. It's spilling out over the top of the sink. The floor is sailing with it. I open the kitchen window to let some air in, try to get rid of the steam so I can see what I'm fucking doing. That cunt. I can't believe he would do this. Actually I can, because he's a cunt. He must know they're away. Thought he'd trash the house and leave Susan with a nice, hefty gas bill when she came back.

Saying goodbye, not that it's any of your fucking business.

Fucking prick.

I try to unravel the kitchen roll but it's soggy and falls apart in my hands. I pull open drawers until I find one with dishtowels in it. I spread them all over the surfaces and floor, soak up the water.

It was so slick, like a dance move.

Man, I want to kill that fucking dick.

Condensation drips down the walls nearest the sink and

falls from the ceiling. I climb up on the counter and wipe it all off. There are boxes of cereal on the windowsill, but when I touch them the cardboard boxes disintegrate in my hand. The tap can only have been on for a couple of hours and already the room's pretty fucked. It takes me a while to clean everything up, but I can't get rid of the damp smell. It clings in the air even when the steam has evaporated.

What if I hadn't been here? What if it had been left the whole time Susan was away? Good job I was here, that I thought to come back. I helped, Jamesy. I helped, and it didn't even involve being the Trackman.

I head through to the living room and crash out on the sofa. Fuck, what a day. A beating and a triumph.

It's dark when I wake up and the streetlights cast shadows on the wall. The drawstring from the blinds hangs down one side of the window.

The looped string.

It looks like a noose.

The shadow swayed on the wall.

Fuck. I sit up suddenly and fall off the edge of the sofa. What time is it? Where am I? I need to get out of here. Why didn't you wake me?

Come on, Jamesy, we're going. One finger. One thumb. One arm. One leg. I grab my bag and head for the back door. Fuck, I can't leave it like this. The fucking door's been kicked in, that's why. Think, think, think, think, what should I do? But, what if they think it was me? They'll want to speak to me about it? Anonymous is just going to make them think I'm involved. It's suspicious. Maybe I should go next door and explain? Aye, aye, you're right. They weren't much fucking good when he was breaking in, were they? Do you think calling the police is the right thing though? Will they not wonder why I'm phoning from Susan's house? It doesn't make sense. Aye, okay, you're right, we need to get going. What is the number for the police anyway? I can't phone 999, it's not an emergency.

Ambulance. My brother.

They're not going to see it that way. Okay, okay. 999 it is.

'Police, please. I think there's been a break-in at 43 Hunter Street, Prestonpans. The lady who lives there is on holiday but I'm pretty sure I saw her ex hanging about.'

I don't know what else to say so I hang up. Come on, let's get the hell out of here before the polis show up. It's going to look fucking suspicious. We shouldn't be here when they turn up. I've seen enough sirens and blue flashing lights.

The ambulance driver didn't even bother with the lights or the sirens as it pulled away.

Right, one more thing to do and I'm all yours, Jamesy boy.

23

Long Time Dead

He needed to get some water, or better some juice, vitamin C and all that shite, that should help. He didn't bother with the kitchen light, just went straight to the fridge. His face was illuminated when he opened the door and he took out the carton and unscrewed the lid.
Davie dropped the orange juice.

'HEY, LEWEY,' I SAY, as I sit down next to him, 'can you remember what page we got to?'

I flick through the pages of the *Harry Potter* book, trying to work out what I've already read. Shut up, Jamesy, I'm trying to think. No, we hadn't got that far yet, I think it was around here, aye, this looks right.

The book rubs against the rectangular scars on my palms, but they don't hurt anymore. I think I've killed all the nerves.

There was a rectangular scar on each palm, like he'd been burnt by something and the shape of it had melted onto his skin.

Not like my face, still aching from where Colin hit me. Jesus, I don't think I've ever been hit properly like that before. Does it make me more of a man? Being punched is some sort of rite of passage?

Come on, Davie. You're here for a reason. To finish that fucking book. I start reading. The final push. I will finish this book, finish this series for Lewis. Make good on my promise.

Davie stood on his own by the grave, while everyone else wandered back to the cars. The hems of his trousers dragged in the fresh earth.

What can I do? What can I do to make it up to you?

I know it's shite compared to what I should have done, but I'll finish those books for you. I'll come out here and read them to you, so you know what happens at the end. I promise you'll get to know what happens. I know it's stupid, but it's all I can think to give you right now.

It's hard to concentrate but I'm determined to do it. So much has happened to me since I made that promise. The world keeps on turning even though he's gone. It's hard for me to keep up. I want to stay with him, so I'm always running behind everyone else. The birds are singing and my face is aching and in the back of my head I'm thinking about what comes next? What comes next? What comes next? It's all a distraction. I try to shut it out, focus on the words on the page. Why can't I shut out those birds, the way I can shut out the in-store radio at work?

A nightingale knows over three hundred love songs, that's more than Frank Sinatra and Edith Piaf put together. I love that I don't understand what Edith Piaf is singing about. It would spoil it if you translated the words into English, huh? The beauty's in the mystery, in the way the words sound.

I think that fucker broke my tooth, I can't stop playing with it. Pushing my tongue into the crack and wobbling it from side to side, side to side, side to side.

He ran his tongue over her teeth feeling for the gap, and his cock stiffened.

Focus, Davie, focus. One finger, one thumb, one finger, one thumb. Jamesy vibrates against me, like he's breathing. In. Out. In. Out. In. Out. In. Out. It's comforting. He comforts me.

Davie woke in the night with a start. It was one of those dreams where you're falling, and then suddenly you wake up on your bed feeling like you've just fallen from a height. His eyes opened at the same time as he sucked in a mouthful of air. He had to sit up and suck, suck, suck, just to keep his lungs working. He needed to get out of the house. Had to do something. He'd got so desperate recently he'd tried all sorts of things. Things to comfort and forget. Alcohol, drugs, counselling, casual sex. What was left? Religion?

Davie hadn't prayed since he'd been in Primary School and they made them say The Lord's Prayer in assembly. Our Father, who art in heaven, hallowed be thy name, he still knew it word for word. Davie didn't know if he believed in God, if he believed in anything, but he had to do something. He was willing to try anything to find some comfort.

Keep the faith.

He got dressed and left the house, walked to where he knew the nearest church was. He didn't even know if it was the right church for him, what religion was he? Did it matter? They didn't discriminate, or they shouldn't anyway. A church was a church. He tried the front door but it was locked. He kept walking until he found another. It was locked too. So was the next one. And the next. Locked. Locked. Locked. Locked. Locked. Locked.

For fuck sake, he thought churches were always open, he banged his fist on the church door, is this how bad it had got? Broken, fucking Britain.

Davie kept walking, tried three more churches before he found one that was open.

Thank God, he said as he pulled open the door. It was only when he stepped inside that he noticed the panel of buzzers, names taped underneath each one, assigned to a number. This church wasn't a church anymore, but a block of flats. He slammed the door behind him as he left.

Religious songs.

I keep reading. Read, read read, read, read. I don't take any of it in, I'm reading aloud but I've no idea what's happening in the story anymore. I don't know who any of the characters are, or who's dead and who's alive. I just need to do this for him. Finish it.

I don't know what time it is. Early, I think. It's light. The birds are still singing. Maybe it's the dawn chorus? Do you get that in a city?

Read, read, read, read, read, read, read, read.

There's mist in the air, the har from the sea. Dew sparkles on the spider webs linking the trees and the bushes and the headstones together. I never even noticed any spiders, and yet look at all the fucking webs. When did they do that? All that hard work, every night spent spinning webs, only for them all to be destroyed in the morning.

Did Mum and Dad think that? All that hard work they put into Lewey. The son who had the most chance of being somebody, gone. All gone.

It's just such a waste.

'Lewey, why did you do it? You were the nice one, the clever one, the good one. Much better than me.'

I place my hand on his headstone and trace his name with my finger.

Jamesy is waiting for me to finish. Waiting for me to get to the end of the book. *It's the end of the world as we know it (And I feel fine).*

It's dumb but I'm scared to finish this fucking book. For months and months this promise has been keeping Lewey alive for me. As I finish each paragraph, turn each page, I feel like he's slipping away from me. It's not just the end of the book, but the end of Lewey too. Promise fulfilled. Obligation over. I slow down my reading. I'm not taking anything in. It's just words. One word followed by another word followed by another word followed by another. They don't join up for me. I'm just getting through them, one at a time.

You've got to take each day as it comes, don't think too far ahead. You'll have good days and you'll have bad days.

Eventually you'll have more good than bad.

The traffic is getting louder. It must be getting close to rush hour. How long have I been here? It feels like days, but it also feels like no time at all. I'm on the final chapter now. Word after word after word after word, pages turn and turn and turn and turn, and then I'm there. The end.

I'm finished. I close the book.

'The end, Lewey, it's finished. Was it worth the wait? I hope so.'

Davie, you have to read this book I got from the library. It's brilliant.

What's it about?

It's about this boy, right? And he has a really horrible life, and then one day he discovers he's a wizard and everything gets better.

It would have got better, Lewey. If you'd only fucking held on, it would have got better. I place the book on the ground in front of Lewey's headstone. He'd like that better than flowers, and it's not going to wither and die, end up as mulch at the bottom of some bin.

It's all a bit of an anticlimax. I thought there'd be some kind of sign. I hoped there'd be a sign. Deep, deep down, I hoped I'd see Lewis. Or maybe just hear his voice. Some kind of final contact. A breath on the back of my neck, a voice just behind me, a glimpse out of the corner of my eye. Something to let me know he heard me and he forgives me now.

Nothing. Even the birds are quiet. All I can hear is the hum of traffic and the branches of the trees creaking. That's it. Nothing else. I can't even pretend to feel something else.

'See you later, heartbreaker,' I pat Lewey's headstone.

When you were a baby, everyone kept saying you would grow up to be a heartbreaker.

Nothing.

Nothing.

Nothing.

'I might not be back to see you for a while. I'm going to go and be the Trackman, see if I can do a bit of good, eh? You'd like Jamesy, you'd understand what we're doing. We can help more people if we're out and about. There's so many people out there, Lewey, people who are sad inside. Like you were.

'All Jamesy and I do is stop and concentrate on them for the length of a song. That's all they need, someone to spend a few minutes with. Be on the end of an unselfish act. There's so much shite going on, I can feel it. When bad stuff happens in the news, like soldiers getting killed in Afghanistan, I can feel it around me. This sinking feeling, more people in need of us. In need of the Trackman. Jamesy and I are trying to fight that sinking feeling. It's hard because there's so much bad stuff going on, but the more we do it, the more we can try to fight back. Fight back the misery. I'm not explaining myself very well, you were always better at the words, eh?'

I'm not afraid to die, I'm afraid of staying alive.

'I've been looking for something for so long, some kind of comfort, and I've got that with Jamesy. Someone to follow, someone to lead me through. Anyway, I'll get going. I miss you, Lewey, see you later, heartbreaker.'

I pick up my bag and head out of the cemetery. I turn quickly at the gate, spin round so I'm facing his headstone again. Hopeful that I might catch a glimpse of him watching me as I leave.

Davie used to believe his toys came alive when he left his bedroom. He'd try to catch them at it. I'm going downstairs, or to the garden, he'd say in a loud voice, trying to fool them. Then he'd stamp along the corridor and down the stairs, before sneaking back on his tiptoes. He'd hold his breath and listen at the door, before flinging it wide open. He never caught the toys.

Lewis isn't there. I can't see him, can't hear him. He'll never grow up, he'll always be stuck as that twelve-year-old kid.

Only the good die young. Don't give me that cliché; that's bullshit.

All I can see is the book lying there. A flash of colour against the grey headstone.

Right, where to, Jamesy? I'm all yours now.

Someone has drawn chalk arrows on the pavement below my feet. Some kid, or someone organising a treasure hunt?

They seem as good a way as any, eh?

Fuck, I can't be arsed carrying this bag. I don't even need it anyway. Aye, I'm just going to leave it.

I put my bag down, then follow the chalk arrows. Head down. Go in the direction they're pointing.

24

The End

It was only when he shut the fridge door that he noticed:
something different about that corner of the kitchen.
Davie dropped the orange juice.

I FOLLOW THE CHALK arrows until they disappear. I don't
know where it was they ran out. Maybe I took a wrong turn?
I just keep walking. Eyes ahead.

One foot after the other.

One foot after the other.

Left, right, left, right, left, right, left, right, left, right.

One finger, one thumb, one arm, one leg.

I didn't realise how small Edinburgh was. My whole life,
I've hardly been out of the city, always lived near the centre
of it. Busy streets. Folk everywhere. Buildings and cars and
people.

But it only takes a couple of hours of walking and we're
out of the city. Me and Jamesy, the long straight of Queensferry
Road, past Cramond, then the footpath along the side of the
A90.

I can't believe how small the city is, eh? I didn't realise
I could just get up and walk right out of it.

Where to, Jamesy? Keep going until we find someone to
play to?

One foot after the other.

One foot after the other.

One arm, one leg.

The Forth Road Bridge looms up in the distance, like a dinosaur.

We're not going to find anyone out here, Jamesy.

I've no idea what time it is, my watch has stopped, but I can tell by the sky that it's getting on. People come out here to stroll during the day, not when it's getting late. Should we head down into South Queensferry? No, okay then, keep going forward.

Grey pavement turns into the green footpath of the bridge. I can hardly hear what Jamesy is saying, the noise of the traffic is so loud out here. There's never a break; it's a constant flow of cars and vans and lorries and motorbikes going in both directions.

I've never noticed it in the car before, but out here walking you can tell it's a suspension bridge. The ground below me starts to vibrate and I know I've left solid pavement behind.

There's an up and down, up and down bounce to the bridge. It's worse when the big lorries go past.

One finger, one thumb, one arm, one leg, one nod of the head.

I run my hand along the railing as I walk, a banister for support.

A metal sign for The Samaritans hums against the railing where it's attached with plastic clips.

How many people come out here to jump?

Does the sign stop them? Saved by the knowledge that someone is out here saying, wait, you're not alone, we can help.

Is this why you brought me out here?

Do you want me to put up a sign?

Remember our catchphrase?

It looks like a Caramac bar.

You don't choose, you just listen.

Don't jump! Call Jamesy and the Trackman on...

Bit hard seeing as we don't have a phone anymore. We could spend our days patrolling backwards and forwards across the bridge, some kind of borderline guard.

I don't know if this is going to work, Jamesy, the sway of the bridge is already making me queasy. I don't think I've got the stomach for it.

Back.

Forth.

Back.

Forth.

Firth of Forth.

I stop walking and look down. The water is dark and mottled on top like the inside of a steel drum. It makes me dizzy and my glasses slip; I just manage to grab them before they slide off the end of my nose.

I can hardly see anything below the waterline, just the occasional black lump of seaweed or a floating jellyfish.

I feel the bridge more, now that I've stopped walking. Up and down, up and down, up and down. Jamesy dares me to jump.

You're joking. Oh right, on the spot you mean, not off the bridge.

Jump, jump, jump: get the bounces going.

No chance, don't you realise how sick this is making me feel? If I was a kid on a wobbly-bridge in a play-park then maybe, but I'm not. I press my hand into my belly, need to stop the bouncing.

Davie didn't want to be hung-over in the morning. He'd drunk a lot and could feel the start of the hangover in his stomach. That feeling which tells you to stop drinking, that feeling you usually ignore. He needed to get some water, or better some juice, vitamin C and all that shite, that should help. He didn't bother with the kitchen light, just went straight to the fridge. His face was illuminated when he opened the door and he took out the carton and unscrewed the lid.

Davie dropped the orange juice.

There's something about being out here. Being out of the city. Can you feel it too?

I see the light from a plane overhead, flashing orange through the clouds. Descending into the airport. In the distance a train crosses the rail bridge.

People leaving Edinburgh, people arriving.

It looks so small from over here, like a caterpillar I could pick up and hold between finger and thumb.

One finger, one thumb.

It's so loud, eh? I can't even hear the train from here, the traffic drowns everything out. I want to say I can hardly hear myself think, but that's a load of shite. Out here my thoughts are becoming clearer. Things are coming out of hiding.

Want to hear a story? Alfie told me that when they built the rail bridge, one of the workies fell down the centre of one of those big support legs. Aye, they're hollow. He fell all the way down; looks like nothing from here, but it's a long, fucking way. A vertical flume with no splash pool at the bottom; he probably hit off the sides as he fell. They couldn't get him out, and they knew he'd never have survived so they just left him down there.

Urban myth? How the fuck do you know, eh? I know, Alfie likes his stories, but do you not think it's a bit creepy? It gives me a weird feeling thinking that there's some skeleton down there at the bottom. Must have been a long way down.

But the step off a kitchen chair can be a long way down too.

All around us people are leaving Edinburgh, and heading towards it. By car, by boat, by train, by plane.

Leaving on a jet plane.

People leaving Edinburgh, people arriving.

I'm going out to Australia to visit Aunt Chrissie and Uncle Mike, I don't know when I'll be back, I just need to get away from here.

At least she told him she was leaving. Davie's dad had just taken off. Moved to Glasgow to stay with that lassie he was shagging. She was fucking younger than Davie. Just a wee lassie. Davie's dad couldn't bear to stay in Edinburgh either. Davie wanted to warn the poor girl just what she was dealing with. He's started an affair with you because he can't handle what's happened at home. His marriage is breaking up because he's lost a son. Don't you get that's not a healthy relationship?

It didn't matter what he said anymore though, nobody listened to him. His parents didn't listen. Couldn't listen. They were too full of grief and too distracted to notice anything, even if it was right in front of them.

I start walking again. It's a slight uphill climb towards the centre of the bridge, the dinosaur's hump back.

I look down at my feet as I walk. There are gaps in the pavement. Tiny gaps where the pavement sections are joined together. It feels like me and my folks. We're joined by a gap.

I look down as I walk, can see flashes of black water at each join. It's such a long way down. So far down.

The jump down from a kitchen chair can be enough to kill you.

There's a lot of emergency phones here, eh? One hangs from the railings every couple of metres or so.

Orange, plastic boxes, the phone caught between two words of panic.

SOS

☏

CRISIS

Yeah, I know what it's like to make an emergency phone call. You know when.

Davie ran to the landline in the living room and dialled 999. Later when he thought about it, he couldn't work out why he hadn't just used his mobile. It had been in his pocket the whole time. It hadn't felt like him though. It had been like watching himself in a dream. His thoughts were dream thoughts: they made sense when you were asleep but not when you woke up and analysed them.

I can't remember what I said to them. The usual stuff. Why do you care anyway? Okay, if you must know I said I need an ambulance. Now. She asked me questions, and I couldn't answer half of them because the phone wouldn't stretch through to the kitchen. Then I pulled so hard the wire came out of the wall and we were cut off. But by then I heard them. The sirens, I mean. I was still holding the receiver when I answered the door, I never let go of it.

Help!

You know when John Lennon first played that song to the rest of the Beatles, they all just though it was a nice wee pop tune. Didn't realise it was a cry for help. Even with the exclamation mark in the title. It's only if you listen to the words, eh, you realise it's in there, hiding behind the melody.

A cry for help.

It's easy to miss a cry for help.

I didn't hear Lewis even though he was screaming. Hiding behind a melody, but screaming all the same.

Help!

I can say his name out here. Why do you think that is? I've always found it so hard to say his name out loud. One simple word: Lewis. I couldn't say it without it clinging on to me. Out here it's easier; it just disappears off the side of the bridge, it doesn't hang around.

My stomach is churning. I definitely don't have the sea-legs, Jamesy. Let's agree never to stow away on a boat, eh? I'm going to turn around, get the hell off this bridge.

I can't keep going the other way, can I? I don't have a fucking clue where I'd go. At least I know where I am in Edinburgh.

I turn on the spot and walk back the way I've just come. The sun is setting on my right hand side, over towards Glasgow. The sky's mad; I've never seen colours like it. Peach and orange and gold and pink. The clouds run through from purple to blue to lilac to grey: the colours merge like ground-up chalk.

It doesn't look real, does it? More like a painting, aye, a watercolour. The sky is in layers, built up by sweeps of the paintbrush. The trees are drawn on in charcoal, silhouetted against the sky.

Man, I've never been able to describe beauty like that in words. Lewis was much better at that sort of thing. He could have written a poem about it.

I don't remember much of what he wrote now. His notebooks all got taken away. I don't know what happened to them. I guess they got returned at some point. Maybe Mum or Dad has them? Two lines always come back to me.

I'm not afraid to die.

I'm afraid of staying alive.

In a parallel universe, I read those lines and understand them. I don't just read them and think, wow, my brother's really deep.

Jamesy, I need to stop again. I'm starting to feel really sick. Every step feels like the bridge is bouncing me into the air. The lorries just keep on coming. Where are all these people going? There's so much traffic.

I need to sit down for a bit. Get close to the pavement, the closer I get to it the better I'll feel.

I lie down on my stomach.

Down, close to the pavement.

I felt too high up when I was standing.

Too high.

Sometimes a kitchen chair can be too high.

I finger the green pavement. Standing up it looks like solid, green slabs; down here I see it's a mosaic of green stones. Lots of small, green stones squashed together. Individually they're smooth to touch, and shine like they've been polished, but collectively they're rough. The stones don't fit together, and the grooves and dips dig into me.

He was all sharp edges and angles.

I turn over so I'm lying on my back. I open my mouth and let my jaw hang open. It chatters with the vibrations of the tyres over tarmac.

Davie found Lewis standing in front of the mirror. He had pulled his top lip up and ran his tongue across his gums.

Feeling for the gap.

What is it? You still got toothache?

No, I'm just looking at my skull, Lewis said letting go of his top lip.

Eh?

If you hold your lips up you can see the outline of your skull behind your gums. I'm looking at my own skeleton.

It's starting to get dull now, and the bridge lights have switched on. I follow a thick pair of orange suspension wires as they climb skywards. Doesn't it freak you out? Well, that those rusty wires are the only things holding us up right now. If there was no traffic you could hear the ping, ping, ping, as the millions of tiny fibres inside the wires snap.

Ping.

Ping.

Ping.

Plummet.

A step off a kitchen chair can be as fateful as a plummet off a bridge.

I sit up, and lean sideways against the silver railing so I'm looking down into the water again. My hands and face are cold, and I pull my knees towards me and squeeze my hands between my thighs.

A couple of seagulls swoop across the top of the water. The surface down there is patchy, like there's an oil slick.

Directly underneath me is that funny wee island.

What's it called again?

Inchsomething. All the islands out here are Inches.

Inch.

Inch.

Inch.

The thickness of a pyjama cord.

It's chilly here, Jamesy. Once I start to feel better we can start walking again, try and warm up.

That island is meant to be covered in giant rats; they live in those ruins. They sent men with dogs over to get them, but even the dogs were too small.

Can you imagine it? I know, it's probably another urban myth, but rats a metre long.

Metre.

Metre.

Metre.

The length of a pyjama cord.

Can you whistle, Jamesy?

They say if you whistle at the sea, you mock the devil.

Sorry, that's right. You don't have any lips.

I try to whistle and end up spitting instead. My mouth is too dry, and no matter how hard I swallow my saliva's sticky not wet.

The devil doesn't frighten me, I've seen worse.

Davie dropped the orange juice.

Man, it's cold. We need to get moving.

I stand and place my feet on the step of the railings. Lean forward. Let the wind blow my hair.

I look down and my glasses slip off. This time I'm too slow and they fall. They hit off part of the bridge as they go, and the force of it ricochets them into a spin. I watch as they spiral like a dying helicopter. They fall into the gloom, and I can't see them anymore. Too far down to see. Too far down to hear the splash. Too far down.

The step off a kitchen chair.

This is the part when the angel enters, eh? Or is that you? You're Jamesy though, the angel's name was Clarence.

I didn't stop my little brother falling. I was too late.

I could drop you too, Jamesy. What would you do then? If I dropped you.

Dropped you.

Dropped you.

Dropped.

Dropped.

Davie dropped the orange juice.

Davie dropped the orange juice.

Davie dropped.

Davie dropped.

Davie.

Davie.

Me.

Me.

I dropped it. I dropped it. I dropped it. I dropped it.

The orange juice.

I dropped the orange juice.

Because.

Because of what I saw.

Because of what I saw when I shut the fridge door.

You'd think the light from the fridge would have illuminated him, but it was only when I shut the door and the light went out. That I saw.

I saw.

Him.

Lewey.

I heard the creak of the washing pulley as the weight of it strained against the ceiling.

The shadow swaying on the wall.

The kicked-over kitchen chair lying on its side.

I dropped the orange juice, the carton split and the juice poured out over the tiled floor.

The smell of squeezed oranges was sickly sweet.

I wanted to move but I was stuck. My eyelid started to twitch, the only part of me that could move. The whole fight or flight thing ran through my head. I wasn't doing either. I wasn't jumping into action or getting the hell out of there. I was just stuck.

I thought I was strong, but I was all fright.

I had to lean down, and lift my right leg and shuffle it forward.

Then my left leg. Like I was paralysed.

All the while a voice was screaming at me in my head.

Hurry up, hurry the fuck up, for fuck sake, quickly, you have to move faster.

I slipped on the orange juice and fell to the floor. I hit my head, but it woke me up. It knocked life into me. I could move again.

Lewis, Lewis, no, no, Lewis, no, fuck, no.

My hands shook, and I couldn't undo the pulley rope

from where it was attached to the wall. The figure of eight was wound too tight around the hook. The weight of him was pulling it too tight. I fumbled with it for what felt like ages. Then the voice began screaming again.

Knife, knife, knife, cut it, cut the cord, knife.

I grabbed a bread knife and began sawing through the cord. Lewis started swaying faster and faster from side to side. Then there was a thud as he hit the ground. We were both hit by t-shirts and towels and socks, hanging up to dry and he hadn't taken them down. They fluttered down around us.

It was only when he lay there, the orange juice soaking into his white socks and the bottom of his pyjamas, that I looked properly at his face.

It was puffy, like when he had the mumps. His skin was navy blue and his eyes were open and bloodshot.

My eyes ran down his body. His cock was stiff underneath his pyjama trousers, and there was a wet patch spread across his crotch where he'd pissed himself.

He was Lewey, but he wasn't Lewey. It was like those shitey waxworks at Madame Tussauds; it resembled Lewey but there was something wrong about it.

The voice was shouting again.

First aid, kiss of life, CPR, one and two and three and four.

I leant in towards his face, but I couldn't bear to be so close to him. His face was cold and his lips were blue, like he'd been out playing in the snow. I listened to see if I could hear him breathing, hear his heartbeat, but all I could hear was my own heart and the voice still screaming in my head.

Come on, Davie, move, for fuck sake, Lewis, 999.

999.

999.

I ran to the landline and dialled 999. Now I understand why they make it such an easy number to remember. Such an easy number to thump down the buttons for, when your hands are shaking so much you can't control them.

Help.

Ambulance.

My brother.

My little brother.

Lewis.

Lewey.

Deep down inside of me I knew it was too late. I was too late. But I kept pushing that voice aside. No, I won't believe you.

If I'd only come home from work when my shift ended. Straight home, no pub, no Martha.

It was all my fault.

I could have saved him.

In a parallel universe, I come straight home; in a parallel universe, he doesn't die; in a parallel universe, my parents stay together; in a parallel universe, I don't destroy my own family.

It was my fault, Jamesy. I know it, my parents know it.

It's always there, inside me. What if it was a cry for help? He hadn't meant to go through with it, expected me to walk in the front door and catch him, stop him. But I was too late.

I know what they told me: that it wouldn't have mattered. Even if I had come home after work, there was nothing I could have done. The police, the folk at the hospital, Dr Richmond, Susan. I didn't believe any of them, just telling me that to make me feel better.

I look out towards the rail bridge, it's so dark out there. Behind me the sun is setting and everything is glowing, but in front of me it's darkness. The cars have all got their headlights on now, they flash by so quickly; each set of lights merging into the glare of the next set. Without my glasses on it's all just lights and shapes and flashes.

Another lorry goes past and the vibrations get bigger, stronger, louder. The emergency phone shakes.

Good vibrations.

That's how we first started, remember?

With a vibration.

Look at us now, eh?

Out here amongst the flashing lights and the exhaust fumes inside my mouth and the tyres on tarmac and the rattling and the up and down, up and down, up and down.

There's another train, leaving Edinburgh, getting the hell out of there.

Good Bye.

Escaping.

Like Mum and Dad.

Even though they left me, I don't blame them for leaving. That city. It's full of him. Everywhere you go the memories of him grab you. Places we went, things he said. I wanted to stay and remind myself. Punish myself. Mum and Dad got away. I don't hate them for it. They're my folks, I love them. I didn't think I did until now. We abandoned each other when we should have been looking after each other.

They're still your folks, Davie, no matter what's happened. You only get one mum and dad.

Wow, this is so weird, Jamesy. Out here my mind is starting to make sense. I was trapped in Edinburgh; Lewis was always there, just behind me, standing next to me all the time. I never left because I didn't want him to leave me. I didn't want him to go.

You need to let him go.

I'm not ready.

I think I'm ready now.

I just wish I could say sorry to him. Let him know I didn't mean it.

If...

Do you think he'd forgive me? I want him to forgive me.

This traffic is hurting my head, it's just so loud. Fucking hell, I never realised how loud it was out here. Good idea, Jamesy boy.

I take the headphones out from my pocket, pull the hinges down and put them over my head. Feel the foam padding suck against my ears. Pure silence, crisp and sweet; like that advert for vodka, where all the shite flies out of the sea leaving the water clear and pure.

The sound of silence.

It's like that for a few seconds, and then I hear Jamesy. His voice moves between my ears, left to right like the breeze.

`your fault not your fault not your fault not your`
I close my eyes and let it swoosh through my head.

Left to right.

Left ear through head to right ear.

Left ear, right ear.

Not your fault.

Not your fault.

Left to right.

Then from behind the whisper I hear laughter. It gets louder and louder until I can't hear Jamesy anymore. I hear the laughter in both ears at the same time.

'Hello, and welcome to Radio Watts. I'm Davie.'

'And I'm Lewey.'

What the fuck? How are you doing this, Jamesy?

`Shhhh, just listen. Keep listening.`

'Today we have the top ten for you, so, Lewey, over to you.'

I can hear Mum hoovering in the background.

'In at number ten is... Everyday by Buddy Holly.'

'We love that song, but it's fallen to number ten. Tell us what...'

The tape clicks as someone hits Stop, then the background noise changes. The hoover disappears.

'Hello, to whoever's listening, Mum, Dad, Davie, I hope.'

I don't understand. It's Lewis. Lewis. He's taped over our radio show. What is this?

Sshhhh, don't think, just listen.

'I was going to write all this down, but I couldn't get the words right. I didn't even know how to start, so then I thought I'd just record it instead, so you can hear what I'm trying to say. Sorry, I think.   It's just too much.'

What is this, Jamesy? Why have I never heard this before?

You almost did, remember when you pressed Play? It got lost after that. Shhhh, though, you only get to hear it once remember.

'I don't even know what I want to say really. It's too hard to think at the moment.'

Lewis is crying. His voice. I never thought I'd hear his voice again and he's crying. I can't listen to this, Jamesy. Please, stop, turn it off.

It will help, trust me.

'I guess all I want to say is I'm sorry and   and I love you. It's nobody's fault   I just   I can't explain it, if you were me you'd understand. It's nobody's fault but mine, I'm just like this. I'm not afraid to die. I'm afraid of staying alive.   And, Davie, I'm extra sorry to you because I think you'll find me, and I know you won't like it, but I want someone I trust to find me, not a stranger, so I chose you. I hope that's okay and you can forgive me someday.   Nothing I say here is right, but I can't go without I have to say something, don't I? And it's just, it's me, okay, just me, nobody else.'

There's a click as Lewis presses Stop.

Why have I never heard that before?

'... was number two, so, Lewis, what's number one this week?'

The radio show kicks back in.

'Well, I can tell you that it's... Hushabye Mountain from the

344

excellent film *Chitty Chitty Bang Bang*.'

'No it's not, Lewis, we agreed it wasn't going to be that.'

'But I like this one the best.'

'But it's rubbish, Me Ol' Bamboo is better.'

'No, Hushabye Mountain, I've got it all set up to play now, it'll take ages to find Me Ol' Bamboo on the tape.'

I laugh. It feels weird to be laughing at a memory of Lewis, especially one where we're fighting. Memories of Lewis usually cause pain and guilt. I can't help it though. I listen to us arguing over which song to play, and I can't stop laughing. They're both rubbish songs, but we're arguing like it's so important. I laugh as I hear myself kick the tape player over, storm out of the room and slam the door.

'Sorry about that, listeners. Back to our number one. Dedicated to my brother, Davie Watts, iiiiitttt'ssss Hushabye Mountain.'

The tape clicks again as he presses Play on the other tape deck. Then the song begins.

Hushabye Mountain Hushabye Mountain Hushabye Mount

I can see Lewis in front of me. I remember that day now. I remember making that tape. I sat outside the bedroom in a huff and peered at him through the crack in the door.

Hushabye Mountain Hushabye Mountain Hushabye Mount

It's like I'm back there. I can see him so clearly. He mouths the words to the song, sways from side to side. I can taste the Coke floats we were drinking, hear mum's hoover whirring in the background, feel the carpet underneath me. I reach out my hand. I feel like I could touch him.

Hushabye Mountain Hushabye Mountain Hushabye Mount

I always hated that stupid song, thought it was so babyish, but it's making me cry now. Not because I'm sad, but because I'm back there with him.

Hushabye Mountain Hushabye Mountain Hushabye Mount

The song ends. Lewis opens his eyes, spots me at the door and smiles.

Then he's gone. Everything stops. I'm back on the bridge again. The carpet disappears from underneath and the green stones press into me.

I know the rules, one song played once.

I get it now. One song is all I need. One song to remember him, to hear his voice again. My final memory of him is not going to be lying on the kitchen floor, the orange juice seeping into his white socks. It's going to be in that bedroom, swaying from side to side to the music.

Something's gone from inside me.

A darkness.

The tip of the tongue feeling that always nagged at me. Told me I'd forgotten something. Something was missing. Something important I'd meant to do but hadn't.

It's gone.

You're right, Jamesy, it wasn't my fault. It was never my fault.

Jamesy? Jamesy, what's the matter?

He's silent. Like he was when I first got him off the One Dread Guy. He's lost his sheen, is all scratched again, with that crack running up one side.

It was just a few weeks ago now, but it feels like ages ago.

Jamesy?

He doesn't answer me: lies still in my hands. I take the headphones off; the noise of traffic hits me like radio static. The headphones are covered in rust again and creak as I fold them up.

Jamesy's gone. He's left me. But I don't think I need him anymore.

I'm not afraid to die, I'm afraid of staying alive.

I'm doing the hard thing. I'm living. And even though it sucks sometimes, I'm managing it. I'm living.

And so are Mum and Dad, we're all living. We shouldn't be doing it on our own.

You only get one mum and dad.

I sit cross-legged on the pavement. The headlights flash by in both directions. Even though the sea is underneath me, all I can smell is exhaust fumes. The suspension bridge slowly rocks me up and down, up and down, up and down. I'm smiling. I can't stop smiling. I taste salt in my mouth and wipe the gritty dampness away from my eyes. I'm smiling and laughing and crying.

Falling and laughing.

A single light comes towards me on the footpath. As it gets closer I see it's someone on a bike. She's almost on me before my eyes make out it's a lassie. She's wearing a cycle helmet and a reflective waistcoat.

There's a flash of blue from Jamesy.

on pass me on pass me on pass me on pass me on pass

The girl on the bike stops because I'm blocking the whole pavement.

'Excuse me.'

'Sorry,' I reply and stand up.

'Cheers.'

I nod as she puts her foot down on the pedal, propels herself forward, away from me. As she passes I drop Jamesy into the basket attached to the back of her bike. She doesn't even notice me do it.

The beat goes on.

The Wicker Tree
Robin Hardy
ISBN 978 1 906817 61 9 PBK £7.99

A black comedy of religious sexuality and pagan murder, which inhabits the same territory as *The Wicker Man*.

If I am a Rabbi, Jehova is my God. If I am a Mullah, Allah the merciful is He. If a Christian, Jesus is my Lord. Millions of people worldwide worship the sun. Here in Tressock I believe the old religion of the Celts fits our needs at this time. Isn't that all you can ask of a religion?

Gospel singer Beth and her cowboy boyfriend Steve, two virgins promised to each other through 'the Silver Ring Thing', set off from Texas to enlighten the Scottish heathens in the ways of Christ. When, after initial hostility, they are welcomed with joy and elation to the village of Tressock, they assume their hosts simply want to hear more about Jesus.

How innocent and wrong they are.

Archie and the North Wind
Angus Peter Campbell
ISBN 978 1906817 38 1 PBK £8.99

The old story has it that Archie, tired of the north wind, sought to extinguish it.

Archie genuinely believes the old legends he was told as a child. Growing up on a small island off the Scottish coast and sheltered from the rest of the world, despite all the knowledge he gains as an adult, he still believes in the underlying truth of these stories. To escape his mundane life, Archie leaves home to find the hole where the North Wind originates, to stop it blowing so harshly in winter.

Funny, original and very moving, *Archie and the North Wind* demonstrates the raw power of storytelling.

The tale is complex, but told in confident style. Although every page is marked with some unquiet reflection, these are off-set by amusing observations which give the novel a sparkle.
SCOTTISH REVIEW OF BOOKS

Da Happie Laand
Robert Alan Jamieson
ISBN 978 1906817 86 2 PBK £9.99

In the summer of the year of the Millennium, a barefoot stranger comes to the door of the manse for help. But three days later he disappears without trace, leaving a bundle of papers behind.

Da Happie Laand weaves the old minister's attempt to make sense of the mysteries left behind by his 'lost sheep' – the strange tale of a search for his missing father at midsummer – with an older story relating the fate of a Zetlandic community across the centuries, the tales of those people who emigrated to New Zetland in the South Pacific, and those who stayed behind.

Jamieson's strange masterpiece Da Happie Laand *haunts dreams and waking hours, as it takes my adopted home of Shetland, twisting it and the archipelago's history into the most disturbing, amazing, slyly funny shapes.*
TOM MORTON, THE SUNDAY HERALD

A Snail's Broken Shell
Ann Kelley
ISBN 978 1906817 40 4 PBK £8.99

What if I had been born with a normal heart and normal everything else? Would I be the same person or has my heart condition made me who I am?

For the first time in years Gussie can run, climb and jump. Every breath she takes is easier now, and every step more confident, but Gussie can't help wondering about her donor. Was she young? Had she been very sick or was there an accident?

And with her new life comes a whole new set of problems. She is going back to school at last – but she doesn't know anyone her own age. With school not meeting up to her expectations, Gussie turns to her old pastimes of birdwatching and photography, but troubling news awaits her there too...

A Snail's Broken Shell is the fourth book in the the Gussie series. The first in the series, *The Bower Bird*, won the Costa Children's Award and the UK Literacy Association Book Award.

An Experiment in Compassion
Des Dillon
ISBN 978 1906817 73 2 PBK £8.99

Stevie's just out of jail. Newly sober and building a relationship with his son, he's taking control of his own life. But what about his younger brother, Danny?

In this touching and darkly funny story of retribution and forgiveness, Stevie battles against the influences that broke him before, while Danny and his girlfriend spiral further into self-destruction. Can the bond between the two brothers be enough to give them both a fresh start?

Cycles of alcohol abuse affect individuals, families and communities. For each person who tries to break away, there are innumerable pressures forcing them back into familiar patterns. And for those that can't escape, that are fated to make the same choices again and again – can we still feel compassion?

...amongst the violence and paranoia, lies hope, love and a great deal of wit. And it is this that Dillon captures so truthfully: the backstory behind the Buckfast.
THE LIST

My Epileptic Lurcher
Des Dillon
ISBN 978 1906307 74 5 HBK £12.99

The incredible story of Bailey, the dog who walked on the ceiling; and Manny, the guy who got kicked out of Alcoholics Anonymous for swearing.

Manny is newly married, with a puppy, a flat by the sea, and the BBC on the verge of greenlighting one of his projects. Everything sounds perfect. But Manny has always been an anger management casualty, and the idyllic village life is turning out to be more *League of Gentlemen* than *The Good Life*. As his marriage suffers under the strain of his constant rages, a strange connection begins to emerge between Manny's temper and the health of his beloved Lurcher.

...it's one of the most effortlessly charming books I've read in a long time.
SCOTTISH REVIEW OF BOOKS

This Road is Red
Alison Irvine
ISBN 978 1906817 81 7 PBK £7.99

It is 1964. Red Road is rising out of the fields. To the families who move in, it is a dream and a shining future.

It is 2010. The Red Road Flats are scheduled for demolition. Inhabited only by intrepid asylum seekers and a few stubborn locals, the once vibrant scheme is tired and out of time.

Between these dates are the people who filled the flats with laughter, life and drama. Their stories are linked by the buildings; the sway and buffet of the tower blocks in the wind, the creaky lifts, the views and the vertigo. *This Road is Red* is a riveting and subtle novel of Glasgow.

...one of the most important books about Glasgow and urban life I've read in a very long time. It offers an insight into city life that few Scottish novels can emulate.
PROFESSOR WILLY MALEY

Remember Remember
Hazel McHaffie
ISBN 978 1906817 78 7 PBK £7.99

The secret has been safely kept for 60 years, but now it's on the edge of exposure.

Doris Mannering once made a choice that changed the course of her family's life. The secret was safely buried, but now with the onset of Alzheimer's her mind is wandering. She is haunted by the feeling that she must find the papers before it's too late, but she just can't remember...

Jessica is driven to despair by her mother's endless searching. But it's not until lives are in jeopardy that she consents to Doris going into a residential home. As Jessica begins clearing the family home, bittersweet memories and unexpected discoveries await her.

But these pale into insignificance against the bombshell her lawyer lover, Aaron, hands her.

It provides an amazing insight into the thought process of someone with dementia, as well as being a gripping and heartfelt narrative.
JOURNAL OF DEMENTIA CARE

Luath Press Limited

committed to publishing well written books worth reading

LUATH PRESS takes its name from Robert Burns, whose little collie Luath (*Gael.*, swift or nimble) tripped up Jean Armour at a wedding and gave him the chance to speak to the woman who was to be his wife and the abiding love of his life. Burns called one of the 'Twa Dogs' Luath after Cuchullin's hunting dog in Ossian's *Fingal*. Luath Press was established in 1981 in the heart of Burns country, and is now based a few steps up the road from Burns' first lodgings on Edinburgh's Royal Mile. Luath offers you distinctive writing with a hint of unexpected pleasures.

Most bookshops in the UK, the US, Canada, Australia, New Zealand and parts of Europe, either carry our books in stock or can order them for you. To order direct from us, please send a £sterling cheque, postal order, international money order or your credit card details (number, address of cardholder and expiry date) to us at the address below. Please add post and packing as follows: UK – £1.00 per delivery address; overseas surface mail – £2.50 per delivery address; overseas airmail – £3.50 for the first book to each delivery address, plus £1.00 for each additional book by airmail to the same address. If your order is a gift, we will happily enclose your card or message at no extra charge.

Luath Press Limited
543/2 Castlehill
The Royal Mile
Edinburgh EH1 2ND
Scotland
Telephone: +44 (0)131 225 4326 (24 hours)
Fax: +44 (0)131 225 4324
email: sales@luath. co.uk
Website: www. luath.co.uk